Also by Ann Cleeves

Ann Cleeves

THE SEAGULL

Minotaur Books

A Thomas Dunne Book
New York

This is a work of fiction. All of the characters, organizations, and events portrayed in this novel are either products of the author's imagination or are used fictitiously.

A THOMAS DUNNE BOOK FOR MINOTAUR BOOKS.
An imprint of St. Martin's Press.

THE SEAGULL. Copyright © 2017 by Ann Cleeves.
All rights reserved. Printed in the United States of America.
For information, address St. Martin's Press, 175 Fifth Avenue,
New York, N.Y. 10010.

www.thomasdunnebooks.com
www.minotaurbooks.com

Library of Congress Cataloging-in-Publication Data

Names: Cleeves, Ann, author.
Title: The seagull : a Vera Stanhope mystery / Ann Cleeves.
Description: First U.S. edition. | New York : Minotaur Books,
     2017. | "A Thomas Dunne book."
Identifiers: LCCN 2017018842 | ISBN 9781250124869
     (hardcover) | ISBN 9781250124876 (ebook)
Subjects: LCSH: Women detectives—England—Fiction. |
     Murder—Investigation—Fiction. | GSAFD: Mystery fiction.
Classification: LCC PR6053.L45 S43 2017 | DDC 823/.914 dc23
LC record available at https://lccn.loc.gov/2017018842

Our books may be purchased in bulk for promotional,
educational, or business use. Please contact your local
bookseller or the Macmillan Corporate and Premium Sales
Department at 1-800-221-7945, extension 5442, or by email
at MacmillanSpecialMarkets@macmillan.com.

First published in Great Britain by Macmillan,
an imprint of Pan Macmillan

First U.S. Edition: September 2017

10   9   8   7   6   5   4   3   2   1

For the regulars of The Rockcliffe Arms
in Whitley Bay with thanks for their company
and for the stories that inspired the book.

Acknowledgements

A novel is a more collaborative effort than we usually admit. Thanks to everyone who helped bring this one to readers: Sara Menguc and her co-agents, especially Moses Cardona at John Hawkins and Associates in New York City, to all at Pan Macmillan, especially my wonderful editor Catherine Richards and to the team at Minotaur, especially Marcia Markland, Sarah Melnyk and Martin Quinn. Maura Brickell is far more than a publicist and I'm not quite sure what I'd do without her.

Professor James Grieve spent much of his valuable time explaining about bones. He and Nicola have become great friends and if I have the science wrong I hope he will forgive me.

Vera is as well-known on the screen as the page now and I'm grateful to the cast and crew of the TV drama who have brought my character to a wider audience. Particular thanks are due to Brenda Blethyn, the magnificent actress who has become my Vera.

And as always to Tim, who cooks the best curries and keeps me steady.

THE SEAGULL

Prologue

June 1995

The woman could see the full sweep of the bay despite the dark and the absence of street lights where she stood. Sometimes it felt as if her whole life had been spent in the half-light; in her dreams, she was moonlit, neon-lit or she floated through the first gleam of dawn. Night was still the time when she felt most awake.

She was waiting for footsteps, for the approach of the person she'd arranged to meet. In the far distance, she caught the noise of the town: cheap music and alcohol-fuelled high-pitched laughter. It might be Sunday night but people were still partying, spilling out of the bars and clubs, lingering on the pavements because this was June and the weather was beautiful, sultry and still. The funfair at Spanish City was closed for the day, and quiet. She could see the silhouettes of the rides, marked by strings of coloured bulbs, gaudy in full sunlight, entrancing now. The full moon shone white on the Dome, on the tower of the lighthouse behind her, and on the seductive Art Deco curves of The Seagull. *If only you knew*, she thought, *you sophisticated customers in your dinner jackets and glittering*

1

dresses, sitting on the terrace drinking cocktails and champagne. If only you knew what really goes on there.

Lost in thought, she'd stopped listening out for him. She only knew he was there when she felt him behind her, the breath on her neck, the hands on her shoulders.

Chapter One

John watched the door from his wheelchair and wondered who'd be dragged in to speak to them today. An orderly carried through a mug of tea and left it on the floor beside him, though he must have realized it would be impossible for John to reach it from his chair. John considered yelling at him to show a bit of respect but decided it wasn't worth the effort. Because there was a visitor, there were chocolate biscuits on a plate in the chaplain's office, but they wouldn't be brought out until after the lecture. A treat released only if the group behaved well. They'd formed a circle in the chapel, a group of elderly men with the same grey skin and ill-fitting clothes, and John wondered how it had come to this. He had no place here. When he'd first arrived he'd been consumed by an anger that had kept him awake at night, planning revenge, dreaming of hurt. But the routine had become reassuring, and now he lived from meal to meal and he was drowsy for most of the time. He seemed to pass his days in aimless half-sleep, waiting for the stretch to be over and for life to begin again, for those small occasional moments of joy that made everything worthwhile. At one time he'd looked forward to these meetings as a break from the everyday boredom of the wing; now he resented them for reminding him of the world out-side.

Around him the men were chatting, but the sound washed over him and, despite the background noise, he still heard the visitor arriving before the rest of them. The sound of the key in the lock at the other end of the corridor, the heavy bell sound of the gate opening, then being locked again, and of the keys being returned to the belt pouch. One time *he'd* been the visitor being shown through the door, but that had been so long ago that it felt as though he was remem-bering another person. Or a character in a story. There were footsteps on the polished lino, then the keys were out again. Now the other men could hear the sound and there was a murmur of anticipation. *Poor suckers. Each week they thought there'd be someone interesting. A bonny young woman or a lawyer who might have ideas to get them out. A journalist who might want to buy their story and make them a fortune. And each week they were disappointed.*

The chaplain came through first. He was a pleaser with a nervous laugh and bad breath. John had had yes-men like the chaplain on his team and had got rid of them as soon as he could get away with it. John thought this would be a cushy number for a God-botherer. In prison, you had a captive audience and when people were desperate, you could convince them to believe in anything. Bribe them along to the services with tea in china mugs and chocolate biscuits. Listen to their stories of hardship and innocence. *Then* they'd get reli-gion. Some of them might mean it; they'd read the Bible in their cells even when the screws weren't looking, walk away from fights on the landings. But John would bet that it wouldn't last once they got out.

The chaplain stood aside to let the visitor walk through, before turning to lock the door again. John sensed the waiting men's disappointment before he looked up. There was obviously nothing to catch their interest in the new arrival. Nothing glamorous to bring a touch of colour to their grey lives. No young lass in tight jeans or flimsy top. No pretty young man for those who were that way inclined. He shifted his wheelchair so that he could see round the men who'd already shifted their attention back to their neighbours. The woman stood just inside the door and was caught in a patch of coloured light; sunshine coming through the one stained-glass window made it look as if she was standing in a pool of red water. She was big and she wore a tent-shaped dress covered in purple flowers. Her legs were bare, and on her feet were the kind of sandals that walkers and climbers might wear. He could tell just from the way she stood and stared back at them that this was the last place she wanted to be. She was impatient, and she wanted this over.

Something stirred in his memory. It was the way she stood there, legs planted apart as if it would take a bulldozer to shift her, brown button-eyes scanning the room. He was in a house in the hills drinking whisky. Sitting here, with the background smell of onions and disinfectant that permeated every space in the institution, he could taste the peat in the whisky and feel the heat from an open fire on his face. He could remember the shared obsession that had lost him his job and had ultimately landed him in this hellish place, away from one of the few people who'd ever needed him.

He'd seen this woman since then, of course, but that was the memory that stuck with him. And he sensed a wisp of hope, of an idea, the possibility of escape. The appearance of the newcomer was almost miraculous. He wasn't a religious man, but occasionally, here in the chapel, he'd prayed for divine intervention and now it seemed that his prayers had been answered. Because this was Vera Stanhope. This was Hector's daughter, a police inspector. And he had information to trade.

Chapter Two

Vera was at the prison because her new boss was a graduate fast-track, with a mind of his own and a charm that could manipulate. He had this thing about sharing the victim experience. She wasn't sure if he'd dreamed up the mantra by himself or if it had been directed from above. She didn't have a clue what it meant and she suspected he didn't, either. His name was Watkins and since his arrival she'd had the uneasy suspicion that he was out to get her. That he felt threatened by her and depended on her, all at the same time. And that he hated her just because he needed her. He'd called her into his office the day before.

'We've had a request from the chaplain at Warkworth for a speaker.' Warkworth was a Cat. B prison; it had enough security to keep in the scallies and the lifers coming towards the end of their sentence – a former army barracks with a series of accommodation blocks surrounded by a wall and barbed wire. In the winter it was all mud and the wind eddied around the site, chilling the inmates like freezing water. It was September now and it had been a dry summer, so the officers and men might be able to cross the site without overcoats and wellies. 'They want someone to talk to the men on the EDW.'

'EDW?' They changed acronyms as often as Joe Ashworth's wife gave birth.

'Elderly and Disabled Wing.'

Vera knew what that meant. It meant historical sex abuse. Old guys who'd committed rape when they had the sense of power and entitlement that went with celebrity. Vulnerable prisoners who'd be beaten up for messing with kids, if they were on the wing with the other prisoners, but who'd grown so old in prison that they needed carers to get them out of bed in the morning. And it also meant bent police officers who'd avoided prosecution for so long that they'd thought they'd got away with it; until a new generation with a different take on the job had thrown them to the wolves. Put *those* guys onto a wing with a bunch of cons, some of whom they might have put away for years, and they'd be literally torn apart.

'You can't send Ashworth.' Vera knew Joe would hate it. He had kids of his own and turned green whenever children were involved in abuse or neglect. 'He's needed here.'

She was thinking hard. She'd have to give the boss someone. Once he got an idea in his head, you could never get rid of it. No good trying to distract him and hope he'd forget all about it. There was something about him that was pitiless; he'd never give up. 'What about Clarke? She might learn something and it'd be good for her CV. We've always had her down as promotion material.' *And it might do our Holly good. Meet a few of the old lags. Make her realize where she's sending men to, when she wants to lock them up and throw away the key.* These days Vera felt better disposed towards

Holly, but she still felt her colleague lacked the human touch.

'I've told them you'd do it.' He looked over his desk, met her eyes. A challenge. Implacable. 'A senior officer sends the right message.'

She could have made an excuse, but he knew they weren't busy. And she knew he'd reorganize her whole week, to get his way. Just to prove he could. In the old days she would have dug in her heels, but she was old and canny enough to realize there was no point starting battles you could never win. Not power-struggles like this. Not with a man this cold. She told herself he must have a very small dick, if he saw her as any kind of threat, and nodded. 'Why not?' she said. 'An afternoon out of the office and a nice drive up the coast. Why not?' She gave him her best smile and walked out of the office.

The bairns had just started back to school, so the road up the coast was quiet. She stopped in at the Drift Cafe at Druridge for an early lunch. Crab sandwiches and home-made lemon-drizzle. A bite of bliss. She felt as she'd done when occasionally she'd bunked off school, and it occurred to her that she could take early retirement. Then there'd be no need for guilt if she wanted a day to herself. She was in her mid-fifties, with full service, so she could go whenever she liked. She wouldn't be forced to leave yet, but maybe the boss wanted rid of her early and forcing her to talk to elderly cons was all part of the message. *Sod him! I've dealt with harder than him in the job, and I'll leave when I'm ready.* She was tempted by the ice cream but thought she'd stop for that on the way home. There was nothing to rush back to the office for.

She locked her phone and her purse in the glove compartment of her car and strolled to the prison gate. There was a queue at the visitor centre. Young lasses who looked too young to be mams ignoring the babies in buggies, to fiddle with their phones before having to hand them over at the gate. Women, old before their time, visiting layabout sons. Vera didn't think anyone was here to see the elderly and disabled. The wives would have had a Zimmer frame, and the kids would have disowned their parents years before, just out of embarrassment. She showed her warrant card to the officer in reception, walked through one of the automatic doors and waited in no-man's-land until the next one opened.

The chaplain talked all the way from the gate to the chapel. Inane burbling that told her the man was nervous, but it didn't make her any more sympathetic. The one thing she'd inherited from Hector – besides the house in the hills and a freezer full of animal corpses – was a distrust of all things religious. She caught the word 'redemption' and that stopped her for a moment in her tracks.

'You think this place will redeem them?'

'They're old men,' he said. 'Some of them so close to death that they want to take stock.'

Vera thought that wasn't much of an answer, but she'd decided to give her talk, tell the criminally elderly and disabled a few stories about the effect they'd had on their victims, then piss off home early, via an ice cream at the Drift Cafe. The men would take no notice and she didn't care one way or another.

It was a game. No point engaging with them, with the chaplain or with any of the officers. After an hour she'd be on her way.

They'd crossed a concrete yard to a newer building. The education-and-admin block. In here the civilian workers didn't suffer the draughts and discomforts of the old barracks. It was protected by a locked gate that swung behind them with a bell-like clang, and then by a locked door. The chaplain walked ahead of Vera here, pointing out the library and the classrooms, praising the facilities. A woman with short grey hair was standing in front of four men, reading from a book. They all seemed surprisingly interested. 'That's Hope, our head of education, with the A-level English class. We have a remarkable success rate in exams.' The chaplain was a walking advertisement for the prison and its governor. Then they came to another wooden door. He unlocked it and stepped aside to let her in ahead of him, and for a moment she was blinded by the splash of sunlight that came as a shock after the dark corridor.

There were no pews, and about a dozen easy chairs had been arranged in a semicircle. Vera had been expecting old men, but not men with the variety of disabilities that were displayed here. Two of them used wheelchairs. One skeletal prisoner looked as if he should be in hospital; his face was gaunt and the hand gripping the arm of the chair was all bone. A couple of the men were already asleep. A few were rather more sprightly, hardly older than her, tidier than the others, shaved. She thought she recognized one as the headmaster of a private school who'd been convicted of abusing the young boys in his care more than thirty years previously. Another had been a reporter on the local television news – he'd been a fund-raiser for several police charities, jolly and witty, so they'd used him as MC at dinners and auctions. Until women had come forward to allege that he'd raped them while they were still teenagers. It had been hard for the chief constable to squirm out of that one.

She wondered what those victims would make of the concept of redemption.

Then she looked more closely at the men in the wheelchairs. One was asleep, his chin on his chest, so all she could see was the top of the head, his grey thinning hair flecked with dandruff. Occasionally he snored and made a spluttering noise, like a dog dreaming of rabbits or a wide beach with gulls to chase. The occupant of the other wheelchair stared back at her. Not with the kind of vaguely polite interest that the rest of her conscious audience had shown, as she walked in to the chaplain's over-enthusiastic introduction, but with a fierce intensity. He was demanding to be seen.

She recognized him at once, despite the withered legs and the bloated face. John Brace. Former Superintendent with CID, before Vera had helped to put him away. Egg-collector, obsessive and dealer in stolen birds of prey. Corruptor of lawyers and poor lads from the estates. Hector's deputy and one of his Gang of Four, his get-out-of-jail-free card, the reason why her father had died at home and not in a place like this.

She did the talk. Described the recognized aftermath of sexual assault, the guilt and the shame. She explained that even a simple burglary could make the victim feel humiliated. Her audience nodded in the right places, the ones who were mentally fit enough to understand, but she thought humiliation was what had turned many of them on. That sense of power. There were a couple of questions from the floor at the end, but only from the ones who liked the sound of their own voices. If she'd been in the mood, she'd have asked them to talk about the times when *they*'d felt powerless. She'd have bet fifty quid that most of them had been abused as kids. But she was a cop, not a social worker, and her job was to bring them to court, not worry about what had made them who they were. Besides, all she wanted was for this to be over. She wanted to be out of the prison, with its institutional smell of disinfectant and overcooked vegetables, to forget all about John Bloody Brace and to eat rum-and-raisin ice cream looking out over Druridge Bay, a clean wind in her face.

At last the chaplain called time on the Q&A. An orderly carried in more tea and there was an undignified scramble for the chocolate biscuits. She was about to make an excuse when John Brace appeared in front of her, blocking her way. His legs might not be much use, but he was still a big man. Broad shoulders and thick neck. Still a bully. 'We need to talk.'

'I'm sorry?' Because she'd never appeared in court. She'd pointed her colleagues in the right direction, helped them build their case, but the prosecutors had decided she'd be toxic. Hector might have been dead by the time Brace was charged, but her father's involvement with the detective had gone back years.

Brace called over to the chaplain, 'Any chance we

could use your office, Father? The inspector and I would like to chew over old times.'

'Sure.' A pause. 'I suppose you two must be old friends.'

'Not quite, Father.' This was Brace. Oily, confident. That confidence had persuaded his superiors that they could trust him. 'I knew the inspector's father, though. I have some information, and I'm sure she'd like to hear it.'

That had Vera hooked, as Brace had known it would. Even as a child, curiosity had been her undoing. And she still had an unhealthy interest in Hector and all his misdemeanours. Brace wheeled his chair ahead of her into the cramped office, not even looking back to check whether she was following.

She cleared a pile of hymn books and leaned against the desk, looking down at him. Outside, the men were waiting for an officer to take them back to their wing. The teacher with the short hair was there too, chatting to a couple of the men. There was a background noise of soft voices through the half-open office door. Only the chaplain was showing any interest in the two of them, and he was too far away to hear their conversation.

'What can you give me, John?'

He tilted his face to look up at her. His teeth were yellow. 'I've got MS. Did you hear?'

She shook her head. 'It's for your lawyers to use the illness, to get you out of here. Nothing I can do.'

He didn't answer for a while. It was as if he didn't think her response worth considering. 'Did you ever wonder what happened to Robbie Marshall?'

Another of the Gang of Four. A man who'd worked

in the Swan Hunter shipyard on the Tyne. A middle manager, he'd been in charge of sourcing components. That was like putting a bairn in charge of the sweetie shop, and it had made him popular. Local firms slipped him bribes and he had access to tools and material that he could sell on. He could find lads to do anything for a few quid. So rumour had it. 'I assumed he made himself scarce when you were charged,' Vera said.

'Nah, he went missing years before that.' John Brace smiled. 'The word was somebody made him scarce.'

'What do you mean?'

'I'm a con now, Vera. Cons don't give away information for free.'

'I've told you – there's nothing I can do to get you released early.'

'I don't want anything for myself, *Inspector.*' The emphasis on the title was pure, bitter sarcasm. 'But I have a daughter. Patricia Keane. Patty.' His voice softened. 'She married a maniac against my advice and he's run away. Left her with three kids and some mental-health problems. I don't want her ending up in a place like this, and the kids in care. Specially not the kids in care. You're a stubborn bitch, Vera. If anyone can get her the help she needs, it'd be you.'

'And what do I get in return?'

'I tell you where the body's buried.'

'Robbie Marshall's *dead*?' Vera hadn't realized she'd raised her voice, but the chaplain looked over at them. He frowned. Maybe he had *her* down as the bully, yelling at a poor, helpless cripple.

Brace slowly inclined his head.

'Did you have anything to do with that, John?' She spoke quietly, leaning forward so she was almost touching him. 'You do know that if I find out you were involved, there's no deal.'

'Are you calling me a killer, Vera?' His voice was mocking. 'And me an officer of the law.'

'I wouldn't put much past you,' she said.

'It was nothing to do with me. But I used to hear things, you know. I'm planning to talk to Patty at the weekend. If she tells me you've been to see her, I'll point you in the right direction. You can take all the glory, Vera. My friends on the job tell me you still like to do that. You're still a one-woman band.'

Chapter Three

Vera forgot about the ice cream until she was nearly back in Kimmerston and then it only caused a niggle of regret for a treat missed. Her mind was elsewhere. There were roadworks on the bypass again and by the time she arrived at the police station it was knocking-off time. When she met Joe Ashworth on the stairs, his car keys were already in his hand. Sometimes these days she thought he was more taxi driver than detective. There was always pressure to get home, to drive his kids to music lessons or football. She missed the after-work beers and the chat. It had been easier when his children were babies; he might be a new man, but even Sal had realized he couldn't breast-feed.

'Can't they just play out?' she'd asked once. 'Like we did.' Though there hadn't been many other children near the house in the hills where she'd lived. Her play had mostly been solitary and, when she'd been old enough, she'd been dragged along on Hector's adventures, acting as lookout or to be pushed up trees to get eggs for his collection, when he knew the branches wouldn't hold his weight.

Joe had looked at her as if she was mad. 'You can't just let kids wander these days. The world's changed. It's not safe.'

Vera thought the executive estate where he lived with his family was probably the safest, and most boring, place in the world. And anyway, she'd been born at about the time of the Moors Murders, and that hadn't caused a moral panic about children playing out. But what did she know about being a parent?

Now Joe paused, his feet on different steps, his body language making it clear he didn't have time for a long conversation, although he knew her well enough to tell she was fired up about something. 'I thought you were going straight home.'

'Aye well, something's come up.'

There was a moment of hesitation. She could sense his loyalty to the two women in his life pulling in different directions. 'If it's important, I could see if Sal can collect Jess from Youth Orchestra.'

'I wouldn't want to put her out, pet. It's only a sniff of a possibility at the moment. And if Holly's still around, she can make a start.'

That made up his mind. 'Nah, I'll just give Sal a ring. It's not bedtime for the little ones yet. She can just stick them in the car to pick up Jess. She'll understand.'

Vera doubted that, but allowed herself a little triumphant smile as she carried on up the steps to let him make the call in private, then thought how childish she was being. They weren't in the playground, fighting over the most popular kid in the school.

Charlie was still at his desk too, and that's where they gathered, the core of her team: Holly Clarke, bright, ambitious but with the social skills of a computer geek, as much of a loner as Vera herself. Vera had come to appreciate her more recently and thought they were getting along better. Charlie, who was from the same generation as Vera herself, rumpled and lonely but given a new lease of life by the return home of his daughter. And Joe, her favourite. Her boy.

'As you all know, the boss sent me out to Wark-worth today.' They all called him *the boss*, the word laden with irony. Some days Vera even forgot his name and had a struggle to remember it when she was sending him an email. 'I was speaking to men on the EDW.' She looked at them and they nodded. They'd obviously kept up with the new acronyms. 'In the audience was one John Brace.' A brief pause. 'Ex-Superintendent Brace.' Nobody interrupted but she knew she'd sparked their interest with this. Brace had been convicted eight years previously for offences carried out over the preceding twenty years. Only Charlie had worked with him, but the others knew all about the case. It had scarred the reputation of the police service in the North-East and everyone had been left dealing with the consequences. All the same, she thought she should spell out the details and make it clear what her role in the conviction had been. Some-times there were more myths than facts, and some officers saw Brace as a hero who'd broken a few petty rules but had caught a lot of villains along the way.

'Brace was a friend of my father's. They shared the same passions, the same obsessions.' She was on her feet now, in lecture mode, riding her hobby horse big-style. 'There's an assumption that there's no crime in the countryside. No real crime. Rustling a few sheep. Using red diesel on the roads. Not like major theft or murder. But my father and three of his mates man-aged to make a reasonable living out of apparently gentle pursuits. They traded in rare birds' eggs and sold raptors from the wild, for considerable sums. Apparently they love to fly British falcons in the Middle East. My father did a bit of taxidermy too. None of it legal. I knew about all that when I was growing up, but when I left home to join the force as a cadet at sixteen, I lost touch. Hector was already drinking too much and had lost power within the group. Later, it seemed the Gang of Four diversified, and by then he wasn't any sort of leader.' *They kept him on as a sort of pet. And because he was almost the real thing. Younger son of the landed gentry. Black sheep, but with the bloodline that counted. They were always into bloodline, whether it was peregrines, men or dogs.*

'The Gang of Four?' This was Holly. She was taking notes on some sort of electronic device on her knee.

'That was what they called themselves. Pathetic, really.' Vera had found the secrecy intimidating when she'd been young. Now Hector was dead and John Brace was in a wheelchair. And Robbie Marshall might be dead too.

'How did they diversify?' Joe wanted to keep the conversation on-track. Maybe Sal hadn't been so keen on taking on the role of taxi driver and he'd promised not to be too late home.

'They ran a recruitment service. Muscle for hire. If you wanted to break up a demo of hunt saboteurs, or warn off locals who didn't like the idea of gamekeepers poisoning hen harriers. Or if you wanted to swell the ranks of a march against the ban on fox-hunting. They picked up lads from the council estates in Newcastle or out towards the coast where the pits were already closing. Fit young lads, who needed ready cash and liked the idea of a scrap. All done at a distance. No way of connecting the muscle to the Gang. Not until the muscle started talking.'

'Sweet.' Holly almost sounded as if she admired the business model.

Vera looked at her sharply. 'Sweet? Not so sweet for the gamekeeper's wife who came home to find her man dying, because his spleen had burst when two thugs had beaten him up.'

'I thought you said the muscle was to support the keepers when they were shooting . . .' Holly consulted her notes, '. . . harriers.'

'Ah, pet, not all gamekeepers are on the side of the devil. Glen Fenwick was a lovely man. Gentle. And he didn't like the way things were moving, so he decided to come to us.' Vera paused, felt the old stab of guilt when she remembered the man's widow spitting accusations into her face, when Vera had approached her after the funeral to offer condolences. 'He decided to come to *me.*' Another pause. 'And even though the bastards killed him, he'd given me enough information to pass on that they could start an investigation into Brace's involvement. I should have been the one to blow the whistle. When I was younger. I should have been more aware of what was going on – and braver.'

She paused. The others knew better than to speak. 'By then I'd moved back in with my father. He'd had a stroke, and that and the booze triggered dementia right at the end. There was enough info in the house for the forensic accountants to track down a link to John Brace. He'd moved on, taken retirement as soon as it was possible and was still living in comfort in a posh house in Ponteland. It must have come as quite a shock when the police officers knocked at his door.' Vera paused for a moment to enjoy the thought of that. She hadn't been there, of course. Too close. They all said she was too close. Hector was still alive then. Just. But she'd liked to picture Brace's face.

'So Brace got put away.' Joe was getting impatient again. 'The lads he'd hired to scare Glen Fenwick got scared themselves when the gamekeeper died, and they confirmed what the gamekeeper had on Brace. There was a lengthy investigation and trial, but in 2009 he got done for planning the attack and for perverting the course of justice. He'd been on the take throughout his career, and that unravelled when the forensic accountants got started on him. So I don't understand what's new.'

'Like I said, they called themselves "The Gang of Four",' Vera said. 'There was Hector, Brace, someone I never met that they called "The Prof.", and Robbie Marshall. Robbie was the one they sent to make the deals with the lads on the estates. He'd grown up in Wallsend and worked his way up to middle management in Swan Hunter's yard. He could mix with the scallies in a way that Brace never could. But he disappeared. I'd thought he'd gone AWOL around the time of Brace's arrest, but in fact it happened before that. He was reported missing in '95. I checked on the way back. He lived with his mam, in the house where he'd grown up. All his spare cash seemed to go on foreign trips. He was the real obsessive about collecting birds' eggs and went all over the world to find something new.' She could have continued talking about Robbie, but again she could sense Joe getting restive and decided that could wait. 'Today John Brace told me that Robbie Marshall is dead.' Vera looked around at the group. 'He said he'd tell me where I could find the body.'

'So where is it?' Charlie was sceptical. She didn't blame him. He hadn't been there in the chaplain's office.

'Ah,' she said. 'Well, of course he wants something in return. He wants me to go and see his daughter and her three kids, give her a bit of support. Apparently she's going through a bad time.'

She heard a stifled giggle and looked around the group to see who'd made the noise. They stared back innocently.

'You don't think I can do that? Offer a bit of support to a single mam?'

No reply.

'He's given me her mobile number but no address, so those of you who can spare the time this evening . . .' Vera shot a look at Joe Ashworth – he might be her boy, but sometimes he needed reminding who was boss, '. . . can make a start on finding out all we can about her. Before I wade in with my size-seven wellies, playing at Mother Teresa. Brace is phoning her this weekend and he'll be asking her then if I've been able to help. Her name's Patricia Keane, also known as Patty. Apparently she was married to a chap Brace called a maniac. No name for him, but it shouldn't be hard for detectives of your calibre to put together a file for him.' Vera paused again, this time to catch her breath. 'Hol – Keane and her man are for you.'

Holly nodded. She moved away from the group to

her own desk and was hitting the computer keys before Vera had started talking again. The thing about Holly was that she always felt the need to prove herself. Vera had felt the same way as a young officer, but she'd been the only woman in the team, overweight and the butt of all their jokes. Holly was a graduate entrant, smart in every sense of the word. Sharp as a tack, and turned out for work like a PA for some global media company. She had two parents who seemed to care about her. She hadn't been dragged up by Hector Stanhope. Vera couldn't see how things could be tough for *her*.

She continued her instructions. 'Charlie, you give me all you can about Robbie Marshall.' She stopped short as an idea came to her. 'Did you ever meet him?' Charlie was a plodder, not much given to original thinking, but he had the memory of an elephant. He didn't answer immediately and she watched him plough through years of policing in his head, fancied she saw the images just as he saw them. The everyday events of a community police officer: drinks with informants in stinking pubs, pulling apart pissed newly-weds when the wedding breakfast turned into a brawl, endless chats with sullen tearaways in soulless interview rooms.

'He was never arrested,' Charlie said, 'but I came across him a couple of times in my early days. I was a beat officer in Wallsend. He was a young man then too, working in the shipyard. I caught him with stuff he shouldn't have had. Obviously nicked from work. Though, to look at him, you'd think butter wouldn't melt; he was always smartly dressed. Polite. The company never pressed charges.'

'Why not?' This was from Holly, looking up from her computer. It seemed she could multi-task, along with all her other virtues. It was supposed to be a feminine skill but Vera wasn't sure *she*'d ever mastered it.

'He had a good mate who was big in the union,' Charlie said. 'The company decided it was better to put up with occasional losses than have a total walk-out.'

'As I remember, he was always one for finding mates who could look out for him. Like our old friend Superintendent Brace. A useful skill to have.' Vera felt fitter than she had for months. It had been a quiet summer and they'd all been treading water. She'd been overtaken by a terrible lethargy and had started feeling her age. *Maybe I just need to feel useful. Perhaps that's what this is about.*

'What do you want me to do?' Joe was on his feet now. He still had on the coat that he'd been wearing when she'd met him on the stairs.

'I thought you had to be away.'

'I can come in early in the morning.' So Sal had only given him a temporary reprieve tonight.

Vera suddenly felt sorry for him. It must be hard to think your life wasn't your own. 'You dig away at our John Brace. He claims Marshall's death was nothing to do with him, and I don't think he cares so much about his daughter that he'd serve a full life-sentence for her, so I believe him. He's up for parole in less than a year. But he must know who *did* kill him, so let's go back through all the files, known associates, friends, rellies, bits on the side.'

'Brace could be making all this up,' Charlie said.

'For a bit of attention, or to get you to go soft on his daughter, or just to make mischief, have a bit of a laugh at our expense.'

'Well, there's only one way to find out, isn't there? We need to track down Robbie Marshall. Whether he's alive or dead.' They were all scattering now, but she called for their attention for one last time. 'One more thing. Let's have a bit of discretion here. No need for the boss to know we're digging around. Not until we've got something to tell him.'

They nodded. Her team. She could have sung with joy.

Chapter Four

Patty Keane woke to her six-year-old switching on the TV in the room below her. Somehow, he'd figured out how to put on Netflix and there was a cartoon he was obsessed with. There was always some obsession or other, but this one had lasted for months, and the music that went with the Super-Rabbit hero whizzed around her brain and made her want to scream. She knew she should get up, turn down the TV so the neighbours didn't complain again, make sure the kids had their uniform, fix the packed lunches. Like last night she knew she should make sure they'd had a bath before they went to bed, make sure Archie's sheets didn't still smell of piss and that Jen had brushed her teeth. She'd seen the perfect families on the telly and she watched the perfect parents in the playground, talking about swimming lessons and the price of houses. But her life wasn't like that. It was as though she lived in a different universe. She knew she'd never be able to match up. Not these days. Not without Gary.

When she woke again it was eight-thirty and Jen was standing by the bed, already dressed in her school uniform. The shirt collar was grey at the neck, but you wouldn't notice unless you got very close. Jen was twelve and in the comp now, though, and she was sensitive about things like that.

'I've made their lunches but I've got to go. I've had one late mark already this week. You'll have to shift your arse and get them to school.'

'Okay.' If she'd been well, Patty would have said something about the language. She'd been properly brought up. But today even that was too much effort. She rolled out of bed, pulled on a sweatshirt over the vest she wore as a pyjama top, a pair of jogging bottoms. She was going to ask Jen to stick the kettle on, but she heard the front door bang as the girl went out.

Downstairs another episode of the cartoon was just starting. The children had scavenged something for breakfast. Patty had been feeling a bit better yesterday and had managed to get to the shop. Jonnie was almost dressed, but was plugged into his tablet. She knew without checking that it would be a YouTube video and that young American men would be swearing. Jonnie had been named after his grandfather, who'd bought them this house on the new private estate on the outskirts of Kimmerston. Patty had been a couple of months pregnant with the boy, and she and Gary had thought all their dreams had come true. The purchase had gone through just before the old man had been sent to prison, but he still managed to send them enough to keep them going.

Archie was sitting in his underpants fixated on the television, his lips moving silently to the words of the theme song.

She switched off the TV and cajoled them into school clothes, only losing it with Jonnie at the last minute when he was trying to pull his jersey over his head while the earplugs were still in. Got them out of the house with minutes to spare and felt a moment of triumph because they arrived in the playground just before the bell went. Moments like that could buoy her up for half a day. Often she went back to bed when she'd got them to school, but today she thought she'd have a bath and tidy up a bit. Maybe put a load of washing in the machine. The weather was nice and it would dry on the line. It was only when Patty got back to the house that she found the boys' packed lunches on the bench and it was suddenly as if the world was crumbling around her again. There was a minute when she thought she was strong enough to go back to the school. She could drop the lunches in the office. The receptionist was kind enough. But they looked so meagre, so pathetic. Not in proper lunch boxes but in supermarket carrier bags. And she'd get the lecture about applying for free school meals, and she'd smile and nod, knowing she'd never get round to filling in the forms; and anyway, wouldn't they find out about the money that appeared like magic in her account every month? She knew it was from her father and he was in prison, wasn't he? So it was probably dirty money and she might end up in court just for accepting it. Patty stood in the kitchen, with its sticky floor and dishes piled in the sink, and she began to cry. Sometimes she felt that these days all she did was cry.

When the tears stopped, she remembered she hadn't taken her pill yet and went upstairs. Pushed it out of the bubble pack and swilled it down with water from the sink in the bathroom. Then took another because she was feeling so rotten. The doctor had said only to take two at night, but sometimes she couldn't face a whole day without the slightly dreamy feeling that two pills gave her. Tonight she'd just take the one and then she might wake up a bit brighter. She put the kettle on for tea, wiped down the surface of the bench, thought she still had time to remake the lunches and get them to school in time. But not yet.

She'd made it through to the front room with the tea, had fallen onto the sofa and just wondered if there was an episode of *The Real Housewives* she could watch, when the doorbell rang. She ignored it. Most likely it would be the neighbours moaning about the kids again. She could understand that it must be hard for them. Patty wouldn't want to live next door to a family like hers. But the bell rang again and she looked through the net curtains that the previous occupants had left behind. Sometimes she had fantasies of Gary turning up, clutching a bunch of flowers or a bottle of champagne, saying it had been a dreadful mistake leaving her and the kids and asking if they could start again.

But it wasn't Gary. It was a big woman with a dreadful frock and a green fleece. She could be collecting for charity. Or she could have escaped from the local loony bin. A couple of extra stone and twenty years or so, and Patty might look like her, if she didn't pull herself together. It was a sudden, sobering thought. Then the woman took her phone out of the fleece pocket and dialled a number. Patty's phone, a cheap pay-as-you-go, was sitting on the mantelpiece. It began to ring, and that freaked Patty out altogether. She answered it. 'Hello.'

'Is that Patricia Keane?' It was a local voice and she didn't sound mad.

Patty had a sudden thought. 'Are you from the social?' Sometimes the social workers made unannounced visits. Usually it was Freya, a nice enough kid, but sometimes they were strangers.

'Good God, no.' The woman sounded horrified. She moved towards the window. She must have known Patty was looking out. 'Do I look like a social worker?'

'No.' Patty didn't like to say she looked more like someone in need of social-work help.

'I'm an old colleague of your father's. Your birth father's. Are you going to let me in? I feel a bit daft, standing out here on the doorstep when you're on the other side of the wall. Besides, I could murder a cuppa.' Then she turned to the window and gave a little wave in Patty's direction.

So Patty went to open the door. She'd always found it was easier to do as she was told. Or to pretend to. And the fact that the fat woman was so scruffy made her less intimidating. She was the right age to be one of the playground grandmas, but she wouldn't have fitted in there any more than Patty did.

Patty took her through to the kitchen, partly because it was a bit tidier in there – she hadn't managed the washing up yet, but she had wiped down the bench – and partly because the woman had asked for tea. There wasn't anywhere to sit. It wasn't like the kitchen in her adoptive parents' house, with its scrubbed pine table and sofa against one wall. They both stood, waiting for the kettle to boil. The woman had very round, brown eyes.

'Your dad asked me to look in on you,' the woman

said. Then she gave an apologetic smile. 'But you don't know who I am! You must think I'm daft, turning up on your doorstep without any warning. My name's Vera – Vera Stanhope.'

Patty was none the wiser. The pills had really kicked in now and this whole encounter seemed unreal. The kettle boiled and she made tea, pleased that the kids had left a bit of milk in the fridge. They stood leaning against the bench and Vera sipped at the drink. Usually the social workers refused, as if they might catch germs just from being in the house. Or they pretended to drink, tipping the liquid down the sink when they thought Patty wasn't looking. That was even worse.

'He's worried about you and the kids,' Vera said. 'He wants to know if you're coping all right.' Not really expecting any answer. 'Look, I don't know about you, but I haven't had any breakfast and I bet you've not had time for much, with three bairns to get ready for school. I saw there was a caff in that row of shops on the way into the estate. Why don't we wander over there? It'd give us a bit of fresh air too. My treat.'

Patty found herself pulling on her trainers and walking over the patch of green where the kids played after school, listening to Vera talk about what a lovely summer it had been. The cafe was quiet, the breakfasts over and the lunchtime rush not yet started. It seemed out of place on the edge of the new estate, old-fashioned, a place for workers, not for the yummy mummies or the ladies who lunched. Vera asked Patty what she fancied. 'I'm going for a bacon sandwich. My doctor would have a fit, but what does he know?'

'I'm veggie,' Patty said. Her adoptive parents had

been veggie and she still couldn't bring herself to eat meat.

'Scrambled eggs on toast then?' Vera passed on the orders to the guy in the grubby apron behind the counter. 'And a pot of tea for two.' She seemed to realize Patty was in no state to make her own decisions.

They had the place to themselves and sat by the window. Patty wasn't worried about being seen from outside. None of the playground parents would come to this side of the green, which was all still social housing. The kids from here went to another school.

'So why don't you tell me a bit about yourself?' The tea had arrived and Vera sat with her hands clasped around the thick china mug. 'I never knew your dad had a daughter.'

'I don't think he knew. Not for sure. Not until I tracked him down after I got married.' Somehow Patty found herself telling the story about being adopted when she was a baby and taken to the big house on the coast, but never really feeling she be-longed there. 'They were kind, you know, my mother and father, but I always felt somehow that I disappointed them. They were both teachers and they wanted me to do well at school, but I was never a top-of-the-class kind of kid.'

'Do they keep in touch?'

Patty waited to reply because the food arrived and suddenly, with the plate of eggs in front of her, she was hungry. Vera was squirting tomato ketchup on her bacon roll and seemed in no rush, either.

'When I said I wanted to track down my birth parents, I could tell they were a bit hurt, but they were okay about it. They've tried to keep in touch,

33

honestly, but Gary never got on with them and we kind of drifted apart. They retired not long ago and moved south – they both came from Surrey and never really settled up here.' *And they wanted to move away from me and the kids. They wouldn't have thought that was what it was about, but they wanted an excuse to let go.* That had never occurred to Patty before, but now she thought it, it was true. 'They phone and they send presents for the kids. Birthdays and Christmas.' Patty still thought she had a lot to be grateful for and she wasn't going to slag them off. They'd adopted her, hadn't they? Helped her escape from care.

'How did you find your dad, John?'

'It took a bit of work, and sometimes I didn't bother for a few months. I couldn't find my birth mother and, though there was nothing official, the social worker thought she'd died.' A pause. 'A heroin overdose. She was an addict. That was why she couldn't look after me and put me into care. But my father was named on my birth certificate, and in the end the social worker put us in touch. I wasn't sure he'd want to see me. They'd told me he was a police officer. I was married by then. Jen was in nursery and Jonnie was on the way. Gary had set up his own business, and work came in fits and starts. My dad bought us that house. A lovely semi on a nice estate. We couldn't believe it.' *But perhaps moving to Hastings Gardens was where it had all started to go wrong. There was that sense of not belonging, all over again.*

The woman seemed embarrassed to ask the next question. 'Did your dad explain how he and your mam got together? A cop and an addict. It seems a bit weird.'

Patty couldn't help smiling. 'He said she was beautiful and he'd fallen for her the moment he saw her. He was married, though, and he knew it was never going to work out. But he'd never had kids and he was pleased when she fell pregnant. He was even more pleased when I got back in touch with him.'

'A real fairy story.'

Patty wondered if the woman was being sarcastic but, when she looked up, Vera only smiled back at her.

'I should get back to the house,' Patty said. 'I need to drop the boys' packed lunches into the school.' Knowing she'd probably not get round to it, but feeling a bit jittery now, needing the sofa and something mindless on TV.

'Tell you what, pet. Why don't we buy a couple of sandwiches and some buns to take out from here? We can drop them at the school on the way back to your place. Save you coming out again, if you're not feeling too good.'

So Patty sat in the cafe window while Vera made all the arrangements, and she wondered what it would have been like to have an adoptive mother like this woman. Scruffy and big, fumbling in her bag for her change. Instead of sleek and well-groomed and competent at everything.

Chapter Five

Vera could remember when this part of Kimmerston had been mostly allotments; to the east of the allotments there'd been a couple of rows of pitmen's cottages, with the 1930s council houses beyond. The cottages and the gardens had gone, the site developed for housing, but the council estate was still there, most of the better homes in private ownership now. Patty's place in Hastings Gardens still looked very new in comparison, with its raw red brick, but the garden was a mess with its pile of rusting toys, and the front door already needed repainting. The neighbouring houses were immaculate. Vera didn't go back in after they'd dropped the sandwiches at the school. She stood by the car and waved to Patty until she'd gone inside, then drove slowly away.

She was trying to work out what she felt about Patty. Usually Vera was no sucker for a hard-luck story; her own childhood had been lonely, and Hector had seemed incapable of giving affection or praise. Her mother had died when she was a very young child. But Patty seemed lost. She must be in her mid-thirties but seemed hardly more than a child herself, skinny and frail. Bonny enough, if you looked beyond the lank hair and the greasy skin. Perhaps she took after her birth mother, the beautiful addict who had captured the heart of John Brace. If you believed the fairy story that the detective had peddled to his daughter. Vera wondered if Hector would have cared enough about *her* to bribe an old enemy to keep an eye out for her, and she arrived back at the police station without having reached any conclusion.

She pushed open the door to the office shared by her team and found everyone working. All summer it had felt like a student common room. There'd been aimless banter, sporadic periods of concentration, the occasional food fight. Now there was an air of purpose. It was the equivalent of exam time. They looked up as she came in, but turned back to their computers without more than a nod of greeting. They knew she'd tell them what she'd got from Patricia Keane when she was ready.

She let herself into her own box-like office and shut the door. This was her space. The window looked onto the blank wall of the Magistrates' Court next door and then down to the street. No view, freezing in winter and roasting in summer, but in an era of open-plan and hot-desking, she clung onto it, and had threatened that if they took it away she'd resign. She hung her fleece over the back of her chair and switched on the kettle in the corner of the room, made instant coffee. Black, because she couldn't be bothered to fetch milk from the fridge in the staffroom. She switched on her computer, saw the endless list of unread emails and ignored them. Instead she looked for the number of the social-services office that covered Hastings Gardens and eventually tracked down a social worker who'd had dealings with Patty and her kids.

'Freya Samson, safeguarding team.'

'Inspector Vera Stanhope, Northumbria Police. It's about the Keane family.' Vera drank the coffee and thought she should get her filter machine repaired. Or buy a new one.

'Is there a problem?' The young woman sounded stressed. Maybe *her* summer hadn't been so quiet and the last thing she needed was one of her cases to blow up.

'I was hoping you'd be able to tell me that. What's your involvement with the Keane family?'

'I'll need to phone you back,' Freya said. 'Check out who you are.'

'Tell you what: I can come over and see you. I'll have my warrant card and we can have a proper chat. It's always better to talk face-to-face.' Vera paused, in an effort to come up with a phrase that might persuade. 'We're all supposed to be working with our partners these days, aren't we?' She wondered if she could use 'stakeholders' in another sentence, but Freya already seemed suitably convinced.

'I'm in a child-protection meeting at twelve. It would have to be before that. Or later this afternoon.'

'I'll come straight over.' Vera replaced the phone and wondered what she was doing. Chasing ghosts. Or finding a project to keep her team motivated after a sleepy summer.

The social-services area office was based in a concrete-and-glass tower block on the edge of town, not very far from the Hastings Gardens estate where Patty lived. Vera had once been allocated a social worker. The woman had turned up after Vera's mam had died; she'd been intimidated by Hector, or impressed by him, and never returned. Perhaps that had coloured Vera's attitude to the profession. Perhaps that was why she felt this ache of sympathy for Patty. As she waited at reception for Freya to appear, she thought you'd have to be a brave soul to stray into here. Everything was shiny, especially the women behind the desk in the lobby. It could have been one of a chain of smart American hotels.

Freya seemed in a hurry and almost ran out of the lift. She was young, blonde-haired, dressed in a little floral print dress and ballet pumps. She reminded Vera of Alice in Wonderland, chasing the White Rabbit. She led Vera into a meeting room with a big, pale-wood table. They sat at one end, and Vera slid her warrant card across to the social worker. Freya took it and wrote Vera's name in her notebook. Her tongue was trapped between her teeth for a moment, and now she looked like a kid concentrating on her home-work.

'What's your involvement with the Keane family, Inspector?' Freya looked up from her notebook and frowned. 'Has Patty been in trouble with the law? I haven't been notified.'

'Nothing like that.' Vera tucked the card back into her purse. She'd lost it once and it had been a nightmare. 'She might be a witness in an ongoing investigation. I called round this morning and she didn't seem very well, and I just wanted to check that someone was keeping an eye out.'

'Were the kids in school?'

'Aye.' Vera paused. 'Is school attendance a problem?'

'It has been in the past. The kids turning up late, not very well turned out.'

'How long have you known the family?'

'Me personally, about a year. The department, nearer five. Patty was married to a man called Gary Keane. Older than her.' The words came quickly. Freya was still in a hurry. 'He had his own business selling and repairing computers, but he liked spending the money he made from it better than he liked earning it. Apparently, even when he married Patty there were debts.'

Vera thought of the woman she'd talked to that morning. There'd been a big TV in the house, gadgets for the kids to play on. But perhaps Patty had added to the pile of debt, or perhaps John Brace was still funding the family from inside prison. 'Patty can't have been much of a catch, though. If he was looking for a meal ticket.'

'She had a job,' Freya said. 'She was still living with her family when he met her, and they had a nice house out on the coast.'

'What work did she do?'

'She was a nurse. Newly qualified, working on the geriatric ward in the city. She had a regular income. I guess Gary would have liked that.'

'How did social services first get involved?' Vera struggled to imagine the woman she'd met that morning coping with the responsibility of being a nurse.

'Patty was admitted to A&E with an overdose of prescription medication.'

'A suicide attempt?'

Freya nodded. 'Keane had left her a few months earlier. Archie, her youngest boy, was still a baby. She'd gone to her GP and he'd prescribed antidepressants.'

'But she was still desperate.' Vera could understand that. Being left alone on a soulless street, with three young kids. In the same place, *she*'d want an escape.

'She'd phoned 999, so I'm not sure how serious she was about killing herself.' The woman's voice sounded hard. 'We arranged for her mother to go in and look after the kids while she was in hospital.'

The adoptive mother, who cared so much about her daughter that she'd since run back to Surrey.

'And then what did you do?'

'We called a "children in need" meeting of all the people involved with the family. Teachers, health visitor, GP. Though the GP never came. Too busy, he said. Gary wasn't around – he'd disappeared for a while, without leaving Patty any contact details. Patty's parents. Patty herself, of course.'

'But what did you do practically to help Patty out?'

There was a brief moment of silence. 'What do you mean?'

'She was depressed enough to take an overdose, had no friends on the street, and you sent her back to that house with three small children.' Vera tried to keep her voice even. 'Then expected her to go through the stress of a meeting with a bunch of professionals, all judging her.'

'There was no evidence that the children had been harmed or neglected. And Patty's mother lived locally and seemed extremely competent. She was a teacher.'

She was Patty's adoptive mother and they'd never

been very close. Vera felt like crying. She was ten years old again, back in the house in the hills, watching the social worker's car disappear down the track, feeling totally alone.

'Couldn't you have put someone in? Given Patty a bit of a hand?'

Freya seemed astonished. 'That's not our role.'

'There must be someone! A charity, maybe.'

'We did refer her for a parenting class,' Freya said. 'But there was a long waiting list and, when her name did come up, she didn't attend.'

Well, there's a surprise! Send her along to something else she'd think she'd fail at. Of course she wasn't going to be keen.

'But you're still involved with the family?'

'I visit once a month. Keep a watching brief.' Freya obviously sensed Vera's disapproval because she added, 'Look, Patty loves those kids. She's a bit chaotic but she cares for them, feeds them and gets them to school on time most days. There are lots of families with much worse problems taking up our time.'

'And what would happen if you had any real concerns?' Vera paused a beat. 'No, let me answer that, pet. I know. You'd call a meeting!'

For the first time in the conversation, Freya gave a wry little smile.

Back in the station, Vera called her own meeting. She'd bought iced buns from the bakery on the corner on her way in and sent Holly to get tea. Then she sat on Charlie's desk, with her feet on a spare chair. Happy.

'So what have we got so far? Hol, let's start with you. I've been to see Patty this morning and I've had a chat with the social worker with responsibility for the family, but it'd be good to get the background.'

Holly could have been presenting an academic paper. 'Patty's not known to us, though her kids are subject to a "children in need" plan with social services. That seems to be down to her mental-health problems.'

Vera nodded. 'According to her, John Brace fell madly in love with her heroin-addict mother, but was too honourable to leave his wife, so Patty was taken into care. Hmm. And those are little piggies I see flying over Front Street. The adoptive parents were high-achievers and Patty felt a bit lost. Though she did manage to go to Northumbria Uni and get a nursing degree, so she was hardly a failure.' Vera stopped short. 'Sorry, Hol. This is your shout, not mine. Back to you.'

Holly gave a little nod, forgiving Vera for the interruption. *Cheeky madam.* But Vera was secretly pleased that Hol seemed more confident these days.

Holly went on, 'Her ex-husband Gary Keane *is* known to us. He's been done for fraud and receiving stolen goods, but has avoided prison so far.' A pause. 'There's some intelligence that he's worked for serious criminals, hacking into computers, disabling alarm systems, but he's never been caught. There's a file on him, and Organized Crime kept an eye. Recently he seems to have gone quiet.'

So Brace would have known him. Known of him, at least. 'Do we know where he's based now? Is he still local?'

'Yes, he's got a little shop in Bebington, selling reconditioned computers and mending laptops. He lives in the flat above the business. Nice-enough place in a part of the town that's on the up. You'd think it was beyond his means, but he seems to have cleared all his debts, so perhaps he's still helping out the big boys. Here's a photo.' She handed round printouts, and Vera looked at a man with film-star good looks and an easy smile. It was clear why Patty had been attracted. And she must have been bonny then. They'd have seemed a well-matched pair.

'John Brace described him as a maniac,' Vera said. 'Does he have his own mental-health issues?'

Holly shook her head. 'Never been diagnosed. But he's famous for his temper. There've been fights with bouncers, and he put one guy in hospital after a road-rage incident. When it came to court, though, the victims always decided to withdraw their complaints.'

'So he's being protected. Or he scared the victims himself.'

'Looks like it.'

Vera thought about that. A young woman who already saw herself as a failure, taking up with an older man with anger-management issues, sounded like a recipe for domestic abuse to her. 'Any suspicion that he hit Patty or her kids?'

'No record that we were ever called to that address.'

'Maybe we could check out A&E? See if she turned up with unexplained injuries. Social services weren't involved with the family until after Gary Keane left.'

Vera was aware of Joe Ashworth fidgeting. 'Got something to say, Joe?'

'I'm just not sure how relevant all this is. Aren't

we interested in what happened to Robbie Marshall all those years ago? Murder. Not some lass with domestic problems now.'

'Oh, I'm interested in everything, Joe. That's why I'm a bloody brilliant detective.' She gave him her widest smile. 'That's why I'm in charge and you're sitting there, doing as you're told.'

Chapter Six

John Brace lay in his cell and dreamed. He wasn't quite asleep but he dreamed all the same. In his head he was thirty years old, fit and at the height of his powers. A good detective. Even the officers who hated him had to admit he was great at catching criminals. He spent his off-days walking in the hills, all that space and clean air washing away the stink of foul interview rooms and filthy council flats. Giving him an excuse to escape from his respectable wife and her golf-club friends. Often Hector Stanhope was at his side, pointing out nests and finding eggs, lifting them carefully and putting them into the egg boxes he always carried in his rucksack. Making a bit of extra money for them both, though it had been the collecting that had been the motivation, not the profit. John Brace admired Hector for his knowledge of country ways, the confidence that came from being the son of landed gentry, even though his family had disowned him years ago.

That had been thirty-five years ago – 1982, two years before the miners' strike. There were still pits in Northumberland and still men working at the Swan Hunter shipyard on the Tyne. Heroin no longer the drug of rock stars, but of the unemployed kids who ranged the streets of the already decaying colliery villages. Dealers stood outside school gates to tempt the teenagers as they drifted out of the playground. And John Brace had arrested Mary-Frances Lascuola for possession and for soliciting.

When she gave him her name he didn't believe her at first. What kind of a name was that, for a working girl in tight black jeans and a white goth face? But he didn't sneer or yell or call her a liar, because something about her appealed to him. He'd traded sex before with women he'd arrested, reckoning that for them it would be just another deal. He'd be just another punter. Letting them off with a caution instead of charging them. So instead of taking her to the station and locking her up, he took her to an all-night cafe on the A1. There was something fragile about Mary-Frances. He thought she was worth taking time over. He bought her coffee and sausage, egg and chips and watched her eat it tidily. She wiped her mouth with her paper napkin, took another cup of coffee, though she said it was very bad coffee. Only then did he ask her about the name.

'My grandfather was Italian.' She looked at him over the thick china mug. Her eyes were huge and brown. 'A prisoner of war. He married a local woman.'

John liked the story. It made Mary-Frances exotic, more than just another girl selling sex on the street. He found out that she'd gone to a convent school and he found that exciting too. 'So how did you end up like this?'

She shrugged. Through the flimsy material of her lacy top he saw shoulders that were painfully thin, sharp bone poking through pale skin. 'I'm an addict,' she said. 'It's an illness, but there's no cure. Nobody to help.'

He wanted to say that *he*'d help. But he was a cop, not a doctor, and anyway she was probably playing him for a fool, telling him what he wanted to hear. He took her back to his car, which was parked in a dark corner, hidden from the road by rows of trucks, and he fucked her on the back seat. It was what she'd been expecting, but he sensed her disappointment. She'd hoped for more from him. Afterwards he felt disappointed too and came close to apologizing. He dropped her where she wanted to be taken. A flat in Whitley Bay, not far from the Dome and the Spanish City. He helped her out of the car carefully and kissed her lightly on the cheek. There'd been a smell of seaweed and candyfloss, as well as piss and squalor. 'I'd like to see you again.'

'Next time,' she said flatly, 'you pay.'

He drove back to the house in Ponteland. It was in darkness. Judith didn't wait up for him these days. Judith, his wife, daughter of a magistrate, churchwarden and Sunday School teacher. Mother to his stillborn child, and heartbroken. Cold now as the statues of the saints in the church where she knelt to pray. Judith had been his passport to respectability and he owed her. He'd sat for a while in the car on the drive, listening to a barn owl call, wondering where the nest was and if Hector would like the eggs.

In the cell in Warkworth Prison John Brace shook his head to clear the memory of the emptiness he'd felt that night. He listened for the late-night prison sounds on the ED Wing. One man with early dementia was shouting for help – he was always confused at night; during the day he seemed almost normal. And always the jangle of keys that mirrored the jangling of Brace's nerves. He longed to be out on the fells with Hector, or in the untidy house in the hills, with its view of the valley, with Hector and Robbie Marshall, the men who had become his only real friends. He'd had a deeper bond with them than with any of his colleagues at work.

Sometimes they'd waited for another visitor, for the last member of the Gang of Four. When the Prof. came, it was with tales of a very different world. *He* mixed with people John Brace saw in the smart Sunday newspapers. Sitting in Hector's cluttered living room in front of an open fire, John could relax and be himself. Sometimes a surly teenage girl made tea for them, before stamping away to her room. Vera Stanhope. He knew she was the person who'd put him in here. But now she was his hope of salvation.

Chapter Seven

Joe Ashworth had spent the morning researching John Brace and felt dirty just by association. Joe's dad had been a Methodist lay preacher, a moral man, and Joe had joined the police service because he had a sense of duty. He thought it was an honourable profession, though it hadn't been easy to convince his father of that. Things had been different during the 1980s. Joe had heard the stories of the miners' strike, the busloads of southern cops sent up to fight back the pickets, waving their overtime slips to goad the strikers to violence. Not, Joe thought, that some of them had needed much goading. His father liked simple tales of goodies and baddies, and the events of that time had been turned into myths and folk songs. In the eyes of his father and his friends, the police had always been baddies.

Even by the standards of the eighties, Brace had been a bad police officer. A bully, a corrupter of younger officers, a liar. But it had been decades before he'd been brought to justice. Joe had arrived at the station early that morning and had trawled the reports on Brace's charge and conviction in connection with the death of Glen Fenwick, the gamekeeper on the Standrigg Estate. He'd found a video clip of Brace swaggering into court in 2009 as if he couldn't believe that he could possibly be found guilty. There had been earlier disciplinary procedures: complaints from members of the public about extreme rudeness; from a solicitor whose client had been beaten up in the cells; from the leader of a women's refuge who claimed Brace had abused one of the women in her care. It seemed that Brace had always managed to slide away from the charges unscathed, and that he'd been promoted despite the suspicion of corruption and dishonour. Joe wasn't sure if that had been the culture of the service at the time or if Brace had friends in very high places.

Now, sitting in the open-plan office, Joe listened to Holly and Vera talking about Patty Keane and found himself growing impatient. He was sorry if the lass was going through hard times, but he thought the times couldn't be *that* hard if she was living rent- and mortgage-free in a house provided by a bent detective father. Vera had fulfilled her commitment to Brace; she'd done a visit and checked that there was no danger of his grand-bairns being taken into care. But Brace had said a man had been murdered, and that should be the focus of their discussion. Vera should take herself back to Warkworth and demand more information.

When she had asked him what he'd thought, Joe had told her and got one of Vera's snide comments for his trouble. He should be used to her sarky remarks by now, but still it stung, especially when it was in front of the rest of the team. So he sat quietly and listened to Charlie telling them all he knew about Robbie Marshall. The sun was slanting through the windows. It was the weather they always seemed to get in early

September, just after the kids went back to school; and, listening to Charlie's voice, Joe felt as if he was a child again, sitting on the carpet in front of the teacher, listening to stories of long ago.

'John Brace and Robbie Marshall were at school together,' Charlie said. 'They both got to Bebington Grammar, so they were bright boys. John's dad was a deputy at the pit and Robbie's father ran his own butcher's shop. Neither of the families posh, but respectable. They were friends together then, joined the school natural-history society, went out onto the hills for field trips. There was a master who sparked the interest in lots of the boys. Neither of them went to university. John joined the police when he was eighteen, and Robbie started as an apprentice at Swan Hunter's, turned out to be better with figures than with his hands and worked in requisitions. He ended up taking some exams and, when he disappeared, he was procurement officer.'

'The fourth man in the gang.' Vera couldn't help interrupting. 'The one I never met, the one they called "the Prof." Do we think he was at Bebington Grammar too? Hector was older, and at a private school just outside Alnwick, so *he* must have met Brace and Marshall later.'

Charlie shook his head. 'I don't know anything about the Prof. Brace married Judith Waterson when he was twenty-five. A marriage of convenience, according to rumours. Her dad was a magistrate and friends with the chief constable. They seemed happy enough, at the beginning at least. According to lads who knew him at the time.' He paused. 'Robbie never married and always lived with his mam. His father died soon after he left school and he was an only child. She had one of the houses looking over the park in Wallsend. Considered quite a smart address at the time.'

'Do we know why he never married?' Vera asked. 'Was he gay, do we think?'

Charlie shook his head to show he had no opinion about that and stuck a couple of photos of Robbie Marshall on the whiteboard. 'These are the pictures we used when he went missing and we were asking the public for information.' Joe looked at a thin-faced man, ratty, with specs stuck on a long nose. One photo had been taken at a works do. He was sitting with others at a dinner table cleared of food, a coffee cup and a brandy glass remaining. He grinned back at the camera and his nose was red. The other picture had been taken outside. Marshall was dressed in country-gent clothes, a sweater and a tweed jacket, leaning over a stone bridge that crossed a river. In the background and out of focus stood a tall figure wearing leather boots and a long oiled coat.

Joe wondered if the man might be Hector, but Vera jabbed a stubby finger at him. 'Could that be the Prof.?'

'No data.' Charlie glanced down at his notes, but Joe could tell he didn't really need them. Since Charlie's daughter had moved back home, the man had come back to life. After coasting towards retirement, sliding gently into depression because his wife had found herself another man, he'd become one of the most effective members of the team. 'Marshall was reported missing by his mother on 26th June 1995. The shipyard had been taken into receivership in '93, after it had failed to win an order from the government to build a new ship for the Royal Navy, but Robbie was still employed there. He was kept on by the receivers to do an audit of the equipment. He was in his early forties and he had the skills to get other work, but he would have been useful to them and I assume they paid him well. According to his mother, he'd enjoyed his new role; it suited him better than the work he'd been doing before. It was all about the figures, and he'd always liked figures.'

Charlie paused to take a breath. Joe was thinking about the great shipyard on the Tyne and all the men who had worked there, of the huge ships that had dwarfed the terraced houses when they slid into the river on launch day. One of his uncles had been a riveter and another a joiner. 'Would Marshall have been seen as a scab, working for the receivers?'

'Nah, I think they'd just have thought he was a lucky bugger, coming out of it with a job.'

'So, did the man simply disappear into thin air?' Vera was getting impatient now.

'Almost.' Charlie was looking at the statement given by Marshall's mother. 'It was a Sunday. Robbie Marshall drove north to spend a day walking and bird-watching with his friends John Brace and Hector Stanhope.' A nod towards Vera.

'I wasn't living at home then,' Vera said. 'I'd already joined up.'

'His mother expected him home for dinner. She always cooked the main meal in the evening at weekends, because he'd be out all day. When he didn't turn up at the expected time she phoned Hector's house. Hector said that John and Robbie had left half an hour before, and Robbie should be back soon. He apologized if they'd inconvenienced her. They'd been chatting and hadn't noticed the time passing. An hour later she called John Brace. He wasn't at home and she spoke to Judith, who told her she wasn't expecting John back until much later. Mrs Marshall thought perhaps they'd decided to go out together, stuck his dinner in the fridge and took herself to bed. When he wasn't there in the morning, she reported him officially missing. She told the officer taking the statement that her son had never once been absent from work.'

'What did John Brace have to say? He must have been the last person to see Robbie Marshall before he vanished.' Vera had jumped down from the desk and was walking backwards and forwards in front of the whiteboard.

'In his statement at the time, Brace says they drove in separate cars from Hector's cottage. They chatted briefly outside the house before they set off down the valley. Robbie gave the impression that he was going straight home. Certainly that was the usual pattern on a Sunday and he didn't mention doing anything different. Brace said he'd arranged to meet up with an informant in a bar out on the coast in Whitley Bay. That was why he'd told his wife that he wouldn't be back until late. Judith was already asleep when he got home, so she didn't pass on the message from Robbie's mam. Brace said he didn't know Robbie hadn't got home until the next morning, when Mrs Marshall contacted him in a panic; he told her to make an official statement that her son was missing.'

There was a silence in the room, broken only by the slapping of Vera's horrible sandals against the lino floor. She stopped suddenly. 'How much effort did they put into looking for Marshall? He was an old pal of John Brace, superhero and thief-taker at the time. You'd have thought they'd move heaven and earth.'

Charlie shrugged. 'They found Marshall's car three days later in the long-stay car park at Newcastle Airport. The assumption was that he'd done a bunk. Off to one of the sunny places where he liked to holiday. His name wasn't on any of the passenger lists, but the thought was that he knew lots of bad lads in Tyneside and he'd have access to forged papers. One theory was that he'd been creaming cash and equipment from the yard while he was doing the audit for the receivers and he knew he was about to get caught.'

Joe thought all that made sense. He imagined an elderly Robbie Marshall sitting in the sun on the balcony of a Spanish apartment, using a different name, his long nose even redder.

'Did Hector or John Brace ever hear from him again?' Vera hoisted herself up onto a desk. It took some effort.

'I'm not sure anyone asked them. Marshall was an adult. There were more important things to lose sleep about.'

'His mam would have lost sleep, though,' Vera said. 'I don't suppose she's still alive.'

'Aye.' Charlie didn't need to check his notes to answer that one. 'She's in her nineties but still in the same house.'

'That gives us somewhere to start then. If she gets flown out to Malaga every summer for her holidays, we'll know Brace is telling us porkies just to wind us up.'

'Or to make sure someone's looking after his daughter.' Joe hated to admit that Brace might have noble motives for spreading the tale of Marshall's death, but he knew how he'd feel if Jess was in trouble and he couldn't get to help her.

'Aye, maybe.' Vera sounded as if she didn't believe a word of it. But then Vera had never had any children.

Chapter Eight

Joe was better at taking centre-stage these days. When he'd first worked for Vera he could tell he irritated her with his reluctance to speak for himself. She'd given him that: a kind of confidence. A belief in his own ability. Today, though, she interrupted before he'd hardly started.

'Did you find out anything about Patty's mother? That'd be a good way in.'

'She could be any number of women. Brace was known for consorting with working girls. Most of them addicts. He saw it as his due.'

'Do you have names for these women Brace *consorted* with?'

Holly interrupted before Joe could answer. 'Patty will be able to tell you the mother's name. If she got access to her own birth certificate.'

'So she will. I should have asked Patty for her birth mother's name while I was there.' This was Vera admitting a mistake. A rarity. 'And the woman must have been special to Brace, mustn't she? If he acknowledged that he was the father of her child.' Again she moved on, before the others could reply, and was doing sums in her head. 'Patty's thirty-four now, so she'd have been born in '83. What was going on with Brace at around that time?'

'He was in his early thirties, one of the youngest detective sergeants. Married but no kids. His wife worked as an estate agent in her father's business.'

'The fragrant Judith,' Vera said. 'Is she still with us?'

'Very much so. Pillar of the community. Tory councillor, school governor, living comfortably in the same house in Ponteland. Her dad sold the business at the height of the property boom and must have invested wisely.'

'Is she still married to Brace?'

'Nah, a discreet divorce by consent, soon after he got sent away.'

'She paid him off then,' Vera said.

'Maybe. Maybe he had enough squirrelled away for it not to matter. It'll see him through to the end of his life, once he gets out.'

'But perhaps you were right and he wants more than that.' Vera was on her feet again. Pacing. 'He wants to look after his family too. It's a matter of pride for him. Patty's his only daughter, and they're his grandkids.' She stopped suddenly and seemed to have come to a decision. 'Joe, you're with me. Let's talk to Robbie Marshall's mother. You're good with old ladies.' A pause. 'Holly, go and see Patty. Get the name of her birth mother. But be gentle with her. She's clinically depressed and, if you upset her, John Brace might use that as an excuse not to cooperate.'

Before Holly could say anything, Vera was heading off to her office to get her bag and jacket.

*

The Marshall house in Wallsend was classic 1930s: red-brick, bay windows and what looked like the original stained glass above the door. Most of the street was made up of semis, but this was detached and stood on a larger plot on a corner. The garden was neat and there were still a few late roses in bloom, a fuchsia to give some colour. Joe supposed Robbie Marshall's mother had sufficient funds to employ someone to keep on top of the garden. He wondered whether she'd been left money by her butcher husband, or if Robbie was keeping the show on the road from a swanky apartment in Malaga. He thought Vera had set out on this wild-goose chase because she was bored. She had so little going on in her world outside work that she needed the drama of a complicated murder investigation to give purpose to her life. Even though, as yet, there was no body.

Vera rang the bell and Joe heard it chime, very loud, in the house. He supposed that Robbie's mother was a little deaf. After several minutes he was aware of a sound on the other side of the door. It opened to a small, bird-like woman with tight white curls. She was walking with the aid of a Zimmer and stood side-on to them, so that she could still hold onto the frame.

'I have my own church.' The voice was precise. 'I have no need to be converted.' She stared at Vera and reassessed her first opinion, thinking perhaps that a Mormon or Jehovah's Witness would be better dressed. 'And I have my own charities too. I never give at the door.'

'We're police officers.' Vera hadn't taken offence. 'We're here to talk about Robbie.'

There was a moment of silence. 'Say again!' The

woman clearly thought she'd misheard and seemed used to barking orders.

'We're here to talk about Robbie.' This time Vera raised her voice.

'Have you found him?'

Vera shook her head. 'Can we come in, pet? You don't want the neighbours listening in, and I bet they're a nebby lot round here.'

The woman gave a little smile to acknowledge the justice of the remark and stood aside. They sat in the front room. Joe thought it probably hadn't changed much since Robbie was living in the place. There were starched net curtains and an elderly television. A stuffed bird in a glass case on a shelf in the corner. It occurred to Joe that Hector might well have prepared it.

'I'm Vera. Detective Inspector. What should we call you?' Vera was sitting on a small sofa and the woman had lowered herself into a high-backed chair in the window. Joe didn't want to squeeze in next to his boss, so he remained standing.

'I suppose you could call me Eleanor. It's my given name and there seems to be a culture of informality these days.' A pause. 'Now why are you here, Inspector?'

'We've received some new information about your son. A witness claims to know that he died soon after he disappeared.'

Eleanor Marshall blinked, but otherwise there was no response. Joe wondered if she'd heard.

'You don't seem surprised,' Vera said.

'Of course I'm not surprised. If Robert had been alive, he would have remained in touch with me. The police at the time said he'd gone abroad, but he wouldn't have disappeared without seeing me first. He was a good son. Devoted. For a while I wondered if he'd been taken ill. Or there'd been a road accident. But I checked the hospitals at the time and there was nobody who matched his description. I've been mourning him since he disappeared. But it's not easy. No body to bury. No grave to visit.' A pause. 'The police said he was an adult and that people go missing every day.'

'There's a suggestion that he was murdered,' Vera said. 'Would *that* surprise you?'

This time the silenced stretched. 'There have been times when it was the only explanation I could come up with for his disappearance.' Eleanor leaned back in her chair and shut her eyes for a moment. 'If he'd been alive, he would have contacted me. He was an only child and, especially after his father died, we were very close.'

'Tell me about him.' Vera settled herself on the sofa, which hardly seemed strong enough to carry her weight. It was as if she had all the time in the world.

'He was never a sturdy boy. Not one for playing out in the street. He suffered badly from asthma as a child. Allergies. He was a reader. I taught him to read before he went to school.' A pause. 'I was a teacher before I married, but Bernard didn't like the idea of having a wife who worked, when he could support us both.'

'How come Robbie went to Bebington Grammar, when you lived down here in Wallsend?'

'We were living in Bebington when Robert started senior school. That's where Bernard had his first shop.

He opened a second here in Wallsend and we moved. But Robert had settled in Bebington; it was a good school. Bernard drove him up in the mornings and Robert got the bus back in the evening.'

'He met John Brace in school. What did you make of him?'

Joe thought Eleanor was considering before she answered. 'John was a bright boy.'

'A good friend for Robbie?'

Another pause. 'I was grateful that Robert had made a friend. He'd struggled in junior school. He was absent a lot because of illness and he couldn't share in the rough-and-tumble games.'

'But?' Vera gave a little smile to show she understood that Eleanor hadn't been entirely happy about her son's relationship with Brace.

'John was a strong character. Forceful. Another only child, but spoilt at home, I think. He was used to getting his own way. It wasn't a friendship of equals.'

'They shared an interest, though, didn't they?' Vera leaned forward, her elbows on her fat knees. 'The Natural History Society.'

'Yes, and that was another reason for keeping Robert at Bebington when we moved. The society meant so much to him. It got him out into the countryside, and I thought the fresh air was good for his asthma. He'd been passionate about wildlife since he was very young.' Eleanor looked up suddenly. 'I should have offered you something to drink. It was rather a shock to find you on my doorstep. Would you like tea or coffee?'

'Coffee would be lovely, but my sergeant here will make it, won't you, Joe?'

ANN CLEEVES

Joe thought he had a very unequal relationship with Vera, but he played the polite subordinate and asked Eleanor if she'd like one too. He left the doors open when he made his way to the kitchen and could still hear the conversation. Eleanor seemed to become more confiding when the two women were left alone in the room.

'Bernard could never understand Robert's interest in the countryside. He was more of a man's man. Football. A few pints with his pals in the club. You know.'

As he filled the kettle, Joe wondered how the teacher and the butcher had got together. They must have been an ill-matched pair. He couldn't imagine Eleanor going with her husband to St James' Park.

'Robbie never considered university?' Vera asked. 'Something like zoology or ecology? I'd have thought that would suit him down to the ground.'

'He was bright enough!' Eleanor was fighting her son's corner even after all those years.

'I'm sure. He just didn't fancy it?'

'I think it was more to do with confidence,' Eleanor said.

'Not John Brace pulling Robert's strings then? Worried that your Robert might find other friends with a similar interest if he started on a degree?'

The coffee was made but Joe stayed in the kitchen. He didn't want to break the spell that Vera seemed to have over the woman.

'I think there might have been some of that going on.' Eleanor paused. 'I tried to persuade Robert to consider university, but he wouldn't have it. And he wouldn't hear anything against Brace. I gave up in the end; he always had a stubborn streak. Besides, when

64

he joined the shipyard we all thought he'd have a job for life.'

'And he enjoyed it, did he?' Vera's voice was bright with interest.

'He seemed to. He got promoted and seemed well enough liked.' But Eleanor sounded dismissive. She would have preferred a son who was a university graduate. His choice of career path still disappointed. Joe thought Sal would be just the same, if Jess decided not to go down the uni route. She had her heart set on somewhere fancy, if not Oxford or Cambridge, then Durham. There was a lull in the conversation and he took the chance to carry in the coffee tray. He set it on a low table next to Eleanor and handed her a cup, gave the second to Vera, who took it with a sly wink.

'Robbie was out on the hills with John Brace the day that he disappeared?' Vera sipped her drink like a lady.

'With Brace and another man. Hector-something. He was a bit older. Robert had given me his phone number because he spent so much time there, and I called him that night when Robert didn't come home.'

Joe realized Vera hadn't given her surname when she introduced herself. He wondered if he'd have been that clever.

'And that was his normal Sunday routine? Going out into the hills with Hector and John.'

'But he was always home for his dinner,' Eleanor said quickly. 'He never missed Sunday evening with me. It was our special time together.'

'Did you notice anything different about your son in the days before he disappeared?' Vera sounded apologetic. 'I know it's a long time ago to remember.'

'He was scared.' The little woman seemed close to losing control, for the first time in the encounter.

'You're sure? That's not just you looking back in hindsight?'

'I knew something was wrong at the time. I asked him what it was. I wondered if there was something at work. By then Swan's had shut, but he was working for the administrators.'

'And what did he say?' Although Vera spoke loud enough for the woman to hear, her voice was gentle, persuasive.

'That there was just something he needed to sort out.'

'No details?'

Eleanor shook her head. 'He wouldn't talk to me, said it was nothing for me to worry about. But I *was* worried. I could hear him walking backwards and forwards in his bedroom all night. He didn't seem to sleep at all that last couple of days. I thought a day in the hills would relax him.'

'Did anyone call at the house in the days leading up to his disappearance?' Vera kept her voice chatty now. 'John Brace maybe?'

'Somebody came. A man I didn't recognize.'

'Can you describe him?' Vera paused. 'Again, I know it was a long time ago.'

'But I remembered him when Robert disappeared, and I fixed him in my mind then in case it might be useful. Tall. Well spoken. Not a local accent. A bit younger than Robert, I thought, but confident. A gentleman. Robert seemed pleased to see him.'

Joe sensed a release of tension in Vera, a feeling of

relief. Perhaps she'd been expecting a description of Hector and this didn't match.

'No name, I suppose.'

Eleanor shook her head.

'Did Robert tell you why he'd come to visit?'

'No. In those last weeks before his disappearance he didn't talk to me much at all.' She sounded suddenly very frail and sad.

Vera got to her feet. 'I'm sorry to have dragged this all back, after so much time.'

'No!' Eleanor reached out and her claw-like hand gripped Vera's wrist. 'I'm glad you came. It's what I've been hoping for. It's not as if I'd forgotten him. Sometimes I think the Lord's only keeping me alive so I can give him a decent burial.' She pulled herself to her feet with the aid of the Zimmer. 'Find him,' she demanded. 'Find my boy.'

Chapter Nine

Vera sat in the car, looked back at the tidy house and saw Eleanor Marshall peering through the net curtains; the woman gave a little wave.

'Poor soul. She thinks we'll get her son back for her.'

'And will we?' Joe Ashworth put the car into gear and drove off.

'Aye, I think we will. Enough of him for her to bury, at least. And we'll get his killer too.'

'If he's still alive.'

Vera thought for a moment. She turned towards her sergeant, who was focused on the road ahead. 'You think it might have been Hector?'

'Isn't that what you've been thinking?'

Vera didn't answer. She tried to remember Hector as he'd been in the mid-nineties. A big man, strong, already drinking too much, given to outbursts of temper. But sentimental too. He'd spent a fortune at the vet on a dog that he'd loved, and the only time she'd seen him cry was when it had to be put down. She thought he'd probably cried when his wife had died but he'd done that in secret, his companion a bottle of whisky, not his young daughter. It occurred to her that Brace and Marshall might have met her mother. They'd have been lads then, but she'd never found out when the relationship between Hector and them had begun. Perhaps it had been when the boys were still at school. Maybe she'd ask Brace when she next visited him. Or maybe not.

'Nah,' she said. 'I don't think Hector had it in him to be a killer.'

'Where are we going?' The car was idling at traffic lights. 'Back to the station?'

She thought for a moment. 'Let's remind ourselves of how the other half live, shall we? We'll see if the lovely Judith Brace is at home.'

'Ponteland's a bit of a way to go, if she's out. Should we call ahead and make an appointment?' That was Joe all over, never wanting to take a risk, even about something small like this.

'Let's chance it,' Vera said. 'I'd like to surprise her.'

'Did you know her? When Brace was still on the job?' Joe had already followed orders and was taking the coast road west towards Newcastle. Vera could see cranes on the river and the buildings that had once housed Swan Hunter's offices.

'I met her a few times. Charity dinners. The Christmas bash. Spouses weren't encouraged to social-ize much in those days.' *They felt more like boys' nights out. Husbands let off the leash for the evening, any female officer fair game. Though they'd have to be pretty pissed to make a pass at me. And anyway they wouldn't have dared.*

'Wives are still not encouraged much to that sort of do,' Joe said. Vera thought Sal had nagged him about that and asked why she couldn't be included in work-nights out. 'What did you make of Judith?'

'She seemed like a trophy wife before they became fashionable,' Vera said. 'Bonny. If you like them blonde and skinny. Confident. She'd been to one of those private girls' schools in Jesmond, and it showed. She knew she'd never have to worry about her future and there'd always be a job for her in Daddy's business.' Vera remembered the last time she'd seen Judith. Vera had gone with a member of the investigating team to tell the woman that her husband had been arrested. It had been early morning and Judith had still been in her dressing gown. No make-up, and middle-aged by then, but she'd still been lovely. And gracious. She'd made them real coffee and thanked them for coming to let her know before the press got hold of the story.

'This must have come as a shock,' Vera had said when Judith had let them in.

'No. Not really.' The woman had seemed frozen inside.

Now Vera remembered a story that had spread around the station long before Brace's arrest. After years of trying for a child, Judith had given birth to a stillborn baby. Perhaps nothing would shock you after that.

John and Judith had probably moved into the house when it was new. It was surrounded by a brick wall topped with an ornate wrought-iron fence and the garden was landscaped with trees and shrubs. It would be much grander than anything a cop could normally afford. A classy 4x4 stood on the gravel drive.

'It looks as if she's in.' The house was quite a way

out of the town and Vera thought it would be too far to walk to the shops for a carton of milk.

Joe drove the pool car through the gates and pulled up next to Judith's Toyota. He seemed intimidated. He was often intimidated by wealth and the educated middle classes. When Vera knocked at the door he stood behind her.

Perhaps Judith had heard the car, because she opened the door immediately. This time she *was* wearing make-up. Subtle and expensive. Trousers that fitted like a glove and showed a body that had spent too much time in the gym. A sweater that was probably cashmere. Little pearl earrings and a string of pearls at the neck.

'Yes?' But the question wasn't aggressive and Vera thought she caught a spark of recognition.

'You probably don't remember me, pet.' Laying on the accent. 'Vera Stanhope. Inspector, these days. This is my sergeant, Joe Ashworth.'

'Of course, Vera.' Still gracious. 'Come in.' She was nervous, though. She twisted the left earring.

They sat in the kitchen with a view over the garden to the back. It was as big as an allotment, with a veg patch and a fruit cage. A couple of apple trees beyond. A lawn, where once they'd have thought kids might play.

'How can I help you? You do know that John and I are no longer married? And I thought that investigation was over years ago.' She was fiddling with a coffee machine and had her back to them. 'John must be eligible for parole soon.'

'I spoke to John earlier this week,' Vera said. 'He's not a well man these days.'

'MS. I know. Such a pity.' Judith could have been talking about a stranger.

'We've had some new information about Robert Marshall. Robbie. And we're looking into his disappearance again.'

'After all this time?' Judith paused. 'Is that why you went into Warkworth to see John?'

Vera gave a little smile. 'You were married to the job long enough to know that I can't give away information about an ongoing investigation.' She paused. 'How well did you know Robbie?'

The woman shrugged, dismissive. 'Not very well at all. He was an old school pal of John's. *We* had very little in common.'

'He shared your husband's interest in natural history.'

'They still had the enthusiasms of schoolboys. Collecting birds' eggs, chasing after butterflies.' She smiled. 'But perhaps all men struggle to grow up.' Joe Ashworth might not have been in the room.

'You had met Robbie Marshall, though?'

'Once or twice. He came here occasionally when he and John were planning expeditions to the wild. To the Scottish islands.' *To steal seabird eggs.* 'Or further afield. Of course I'd always ask him to stay for supper, but usually he said he had to get home. His mother would be expecting him. That was the only social contact we ever had.'

'What did you make of him?'

'I don't think I made anything of him.' The words were sharper now. 'He was an acquaintance of my husband, that was all. I lived my own life, had my own friends.'

'We think he might have been murdered.'

Judith took a breath. 'Well, he lived in Wallsend, didn't he? I suspect he mixed with a few unsavoury characters. Daddy was a magistrate until he was forced to retire. I know drugs are a terrible problem in parts of North Tyneside.'

'Robbie was an accountant at Swan Hunter's.' A slight exaggeration of his role at the yard, but Vera felt an irrational need to stand up for Eleanor Marshall's son. 'I don't think he counted heroin-dealers among his friends.'

Judith knew she'd been rebuked and smiled. 'Of course, I don't mean to stereotype, Inspector.'

Ah, so it's Inspector now, not Vera. Putting me in my place. Even her scally husband made superintendent.

Vera's phone pinged. A text from Holly, who was back from her visit to Patty Keane. The name of Patty's birth mother. Vera glanced at the message, then turned her attention back to Judith Brace.

'Robbie's mam called you, the night he went missing,' she said.

'Yes, the police asked about it at the time. I gave a statement. There'll be a record somewhere. You can't expect me to remember the details after more than twenty years.'

'Of course not, pet.' But Robbie's mother was still mourning and she remembered everything. She remembered making that phone call. 'You told Mrs Marshall that John was out on the coast talking to an informant.'

'Did I?' As if it was no longer of any interest to her at all. 'Then I suppose it was true.'

There was a silence. Outside, a long way off, a

neighbour was cutting the grass and the mower hummed like an angry insect. 'John must have been upset,' Vera said. 'His best friend going missing.'

'I'm not sure Robbie was his best friend. They shared an interest and John always liked an audience. He always needed someone to show off to. Admirers.' Judith collected the coffee mugs and put them in the sink. A not-so-subtle hint that she'd had enough. 'Actually I don't think he had much in common with Marshall, outside the birding.'

'So he didn't seem worried when Robbie disappeared?'

Judith wasn't sure how to answer that. She needed to think about it. 'As I said, Inspector, it was a long time ago. I'm sure John did what he could to track Robbie down.' A pause, and then, as if the idea had just come to her, 'Wasn't there some thought that he'd been stealing from his employer and had run away to Europe?'

'I think that was one of the theories,' Vera said, 'but no theft came to light.'

'You're best talking to John then.' Judith had regained her composure. 'If there's nothing else, Inspector, I have to go. A council meeting.'

'Of course.' Vera could feel Joe Ashworth thinking this was all a waste of time. They'd have done better to go straight back to the police station in Kimmerston. She glanced down at her phone again. 'One last thing, Mrs Brace. Does the name Mary-Frances Lascuola mean anything to you?'

It was the last thing the woman had been expecting and the colour drained from her face. Vera almost felt sorry for her. Almost.

'I see you do recognize that name, even after all these years. It's not one you'd forget, is it? Something so exotic.'

'I believe she was an addict,' Judith said. 'One of my husband's informants. In the early days, when he worked more in the field.'

'Is that what he called her? His informant? Perhaps she was the person John was meeting, the night Robbie Marshall went missing. But according to her daughter, Mary-Frances was much more than that. Apparently she was the love of your husband's life.'

The woman collapsed back onto the high stool where she'd been sitting, all thought of a council meeting forgotten. 'She had a daughter?'

Vera didn't answer. She didn't want Judith Brace poking around in Patty's life. She should never have allowed herself to be provoked into mentioning her. 'Do you know what happened to Mary-Frances?'

Judith straightened her back, pulled her handbag from her knee and took out a lipstick and compact mirror. She replied only once she'd applied the lipstick, pressed her lips together to make sure it was even. 'Of course not! My husband mixed with lots of women of that kind.'

'What kind would that be?'

'Criminals,' Judith spat back. 'Low-lifes. He spent so much of his time with criminals that eventually he became one himself. That's why he's in prison, Inspector. That's why I'm no longer married to him. Now, if you'll excuse me, I have that meeting to attend.' She almost pushed them out of the door.

As Joe drove back, Vera was lost in thought and only noticed their surroundings when they hit the dual carriageway out of the town. 'That's the airport. Less than ten minutes from Brace's house.'

'What are you thinking?'

'If Robbie Marshall was visiting John Brace the night he vanished into thin air, it wouldn't take long to dump his car.' She knew it couldn't prove anything, but she hugged the information to her as another interesting link.

'Why would Judith lie? After all this time she'd have nothing to lose.' Vera could tell that Joe Ashworth was impressed by Judith. He was easily taken in by classy women.

'Only a charge of perjury,' Vera said. 'If she'd lied at the time.' She thought of Judith serving time in prison and gave a little smile. Classy women didn't impress her at all.

Chapter Ten

Saturday morning. Patty could never work out whether she found the weekends harder than school days or less hassle. There was always the dreadful rush to get out of the house on weekdays, but then at least she had a few hours to herself before she had to fetch Archie from school. Jonnie and Jen pretty much looked after themselves at weekends but Archie was a nightmare. Hyperactive and impossible to control. He might listen to his father more, but Gary never made any effort to see the kids and he'd never paid a penny in maintenance. It would be great to have a break from them at the weekends, and the kids would love to spend a bit of time with their father, to kick a football around in the park or go on a trip to the pictures. Wasn't that what other divorced dads did?

Patty knew that Gary was living in Bebington. He had a little shop where he did up computers and sold them on. He'd always been a bit of a geek where technology was concerned, and she missed him now whenever there was a glitch with the kids' tablets or phones. There was a flat over the shop and Gary lived there. She knew what it looked like because he'd had the shop when they were still married. He'd rented out the flat then, for a bit of extra cash, and she'd been in once to clean it before there was a new tenant. It was small – only one bedroom – but cosy enough. Sometimes, in her head, she went to see him. She'd given up the car when she was first ill, but she knew there was a bus from Kimmerston Front Street. She'd looked up the times. She knew this obsession about Gary was doing her no good. Thoughts of him clogged her brain and stopped her thinking of anything else. Made her self-absorbed and kept her from focusing on the children. In her heart she knew she'd never get him back. But it was better to have a fantasy of a future with him than the reality of a future without him. Patty had never been much good at facing reality.

Jen was still in bed. At weekends, she seldom emerged much before midday. Patty thought her daughter already behaved like a teenager without the rest of the family noticing. The boys were playing a computer game. Patty went upstairs and had a shower, got dressed and gathered up the boys' clothes, which seemed to have taken up the whole of their bedroom floor space, to put in the wash. She felt better when the place didn't look such a mess.

Walking downstairs with the bundle of clothes, she thought of the smart woman who'd come to visit the day before. At first Patty had thought she was from the school, that maybe Jonnie had done a runner or Archie had started biting again. She had the look of a teacher. About the same age as Patty but straight-backed, well dressed in a boring, professional way. A bit scary. Even when she'd had a proper job, Patty had never dressed like that. The woman had stood just inside the front door and introduced herself as Holly

Clarke. 'I'm a colleague of Inspector Stanhope's.' Anyone less like Vera it was hard to imagine.

Patty had offered her tea, but Holly had refused. 'I don't want to take up much of your time.' Meaning: *I wouldn't drink anything in this house if you paid me.*

Then she'd asked for the name of Patty's mother.

'Why do you want to know that?'

'Vera asked me to find out.' Holly had shrugged. 'You've met her. You know what she's like. She wants something, and she goes for it. No explanation. Perhaps she's just nosy.'

Patty had thought Vera *would* be nosy, but at least it showed she was interested. Patty couldn't remember the last time anyone had been truly interested in her life. 'She was called Mary-Frances Lascuola.' She always liked saying the name. It made her feel special.

'Fascinating name.' And Holly had seemed genuinely intrigued.

'Her father was an Italian prisoner of war. According to my father.' Then Patty had told the story as she knew it, as it had been told to her by John Brace. How Mary-Frances had been a heroin addict, how he'd met her through his work while she was desperately trying to get clean, and how he'd fallen in love. 'It was love at first sight. Like in the soppy movies.'

Holly had smiled then, but it looked as if it was a bit of an effort.

'She knew she couldn't take care of me properly, so she gave me up for adoption. But that broke her heart and she started taking drugs again, and in the end they killed her.'

'Do you know when she died? Exactly?'

They'd been sitting on the sofa in the sitting room at that point. Patty had swept the felt-tipped pens and the pieces of Lego onto the floor to make room, so it felt as if they were sitting on a boat in a sea of crap. The question had been asked gently. Patty could tell the woman was trying as hard as she could not to sound like a police officer. But there was something about the way it was posed that got Patty thinking. 'Are you saying she's not dead?'

'Not at all. I didn't even know her name until you told me just now.' Holly had paused. 'Have you seen the death certificate?'

'There was no need. My father told me she was dead. Why would he lie? And the social workers couldn't find any trace of her.'

But now, staggering down the stairs with an armful of dirty washing, Patty wondered just how much she could trust John Brace. He was in prison after all, partly for lying to the court about his involvement in the killing of a gamekeeper. He'd given Patty his version of events when she'd first gone to visit him and she'd believed him. Of course she had, because he was her dad and he obviously cared for her, and now it felt as if she didn't have anyone else. He *must* care for them all, otherwise he wouldn't have bought her this house and he wouldn't still be putting money into her account every month, so she didn't have to go cap in hand to the social, or force herself back to work when she wasn't ready.

He'd sent her a visiting order, just as he did every month. Usually she ignored it because she couldn't face the trek up the coast with the kids in tow. Instead he had to make do with a phone call. He phoned every Saturday night, regular as clockwork, and that must mean he cared about them all too. But now she didn't think she could talk about personal stuff over the phone. She always heard the noise in the background while they were speaking, men shouting and laughing. Even if they couldn't hear what she was saying, she'd be distracted. So perhaps she could make visiting time at the prison this afternoon. Jen would be out anyway at her mate's house – they'd planned a sleepover – and there were volunteers to look after the boys in the family centre, once she got to Warkworth. Since Vera Stanhope had turned up on her doorstep she'd felt better about herself. A bit braver.

The bus seemed to take hours, driving past newly ploughed fields, out towards the coast. The boys were good as gold, though, just staring out of the window, enjoying the day out, chewing on the sweets she'd bought to keep them quiet. When she got there she was intimidated by the other relatives, who seemed to know what they were doing, and there was a moment when she thought she'd just get the bus home. But in the end the boys pulled her on towards the building they used as a crèche. She'd phoned the prison to let them know she was coming and, when she'd dropped off the boys, she saw her father waiting for her at one of the tables in the big, echoing hall they used as the visitors' room. He'd pulled his wheelchair up to the table. The last time she'd seen him he'd still been able to walk with a stick. He tried to stand up to greet her, but couldn't quite make it and she bent down to kiss him instead. His cheek was smooth as if he'd just shaved, and he smelled clean, of soap or aftershave. Patty wished she'd made more of an effort with her own appearance. One of the prison officers came up to them. She supposed he wanted to check that she wasn't handing anything over, but he seemed satisfied and wandered away.

'This is a lovely surprise.' John Brace seemed genuinely pleased to see her. 'What's brought you all this way?'

'I was feeling a bit brighter.' A pause. 'Vera Stanhope came to visit.'

'Did she now? And what did you make of our Vera?'

'She was great.' Patty wasn't sure what else to say. 'She took me out for breakfast.'

'Ah well, she always did like her food.'

Patty was going to mention the fact that Holly Clarke had turned up at her house too, but then she thought better of it. She didn't want to get Vera into bother, and her dad always said he hated people prying into his affairs. 'Vera got me thinking about my mother.'

'Why was that?' He kept his voice cheerful but he looked more guarded. Something about his eyes.

'I dunno. I thought Vera might make a lovely mam.'

It had been the right sort of response. Brace threw back his head and laughed. 'I'd be surprised if that woman has a single maternal bone in her body.'

'When did she die? Mary-Frances Lascuola, I mean.' Again, Patty thought it was a beautiful name. Perhaps they should have called Jen 'Mary-Frances'.

But Gary had chosen the name because he had a thing about Jennifer Aniston at the time.

'I don't know the exact date.' Brace was looking serious again now. 'I lost touch with her when she went back to heroin.'

'How did you know she died, then?'

'A colleague told me. He knew she'd been my informant at one time.' A pause. 'When she cleaned up her act, she passed on information about dealers. That wasn't why we kept seeing each other, though. I told you, I fell for her the moment I met her. But she was useful too. You know how important I think it is to keep drugs off the street.'

Patty thought he was talking too much – it sounded as if he was making up the story as he went along – but she didn't make any comment. A prisoner wearing the same kind of striped shirt as her father came up and offered her a cup of tea. She shook her head and waited until he walked away.

'Did you see her body?'

'No!' The idea shocked him. 'I wouldn't have had any excuse to do that. Besides, I didn't know until weeks after that she was dead.'

'Is there a grave? I'd like to visit a grave.'

'I don't know.' Now he sounded genuinely sad. 'I would have liked a grave to visit too.'

They sat for a moment in silence. 'Why did you ask Vera to visit?' Patty had been thinking about that on the bus through the countryside. Her father wasn't the sort of person to ask favours. He wouldn't want to owe anyone.

'Because I was worried about you and the bairns. The last few times I phoned, you sounded a bit lost.

Not quite with it. I wouldn't want you ending up like your mother.'

'I don't take drugs!' Now it was Patty's turn to be shocked.

'Don't you? What about that medicine you get from the doctor? That's addictive too.' He paused. 'I'm a control freak. I can't look after you while I'm in here. Vera can keep an eye.'

'Why would she, though?'

'Because I can offer her something in return.' He'd turned away to look out of the window. It was very sunny outside; it could have been midsummer. Patty thought he was talking to himself and not to her. Then he turned back to the room to explain. 'I hear things in here. Things that might be useful to her. And I was in the job for a long time. I know where the bodies are buried.'

'So she'll visit me again?'

'Do you want her to?'

Patty thought about that only for a moment. She thought of the big woman with the crumpled clothes and the brown button-eyes. 'Yes,' she said. 'I'd like it very much.'

'Then I'll have to see what I can arrange.' He winked at her. Gary had winked like that at the kids when he'd done something he knew Patty wouldn't like, something to get them on his side.

'I should go,' she said. 'The ladies in the crèche seem nice enough, but you know what the boys are like. Specially Archie. They always play up when they start getting bored.' She stood up and looked down at him. She couldn't bring herself to kiss him again, because she couldn't quite believe what he'd told her about her mother. Perhaps Mary-Frances was still alive. And if she was, Patty thought, then Vera Stanhope would be the person to find her.

Chapter Eleven

It was Sunday and Vera had given her team the day off. They couldn't do much more until after she'd talked to John Brace; she'd already booked an official visit for Monday morning. She'd be in one of the interview rooms then, queuing up with lawyers and probation officers. She wouldn't be overheard there and she was already preparing her script. She wouldn't come away until Brace had told her where they could find Robbie Marshall. Vera thought Holly would still be working, even though it was the weekend. She didn't have much of a life away from the job, if the rumours were to be believed, and Hol had this bee in her bonnet about Patty Keane's mother. Mary-Frances Lascuola. What sort of name was that? She imagined Holly in her smart apartment in Newcastle, googling frantically.

Vera got up late. She'd had a bit of a session the night before with Jack and Joanna, her hippy neighbours. They'd been celebrating the publication of Joanna's second novel. Vera had read the first book and it had seemed very gloomy to her. She had enough of that sort of material at work. But she was happy to join in the celebration. The couple worked like mad things on the smallholding, and Vera knew there was never money to spare. Farming in the hills was never going to turn anyone into a millionaire. Any cash Joanna could bring to the venture would help. Vera had a horror of them going under or finding it too tough to stay; she hated the idea of strangers moving in next door. Jack and Joanna were good people. They dug her out when she got stuck in the snow, chopped logs for her fire and filled her freezer. And they threw a very good party.

Vera had just made coffee when her phone rang. It was her mobile and that was a shock, because usually reception was so bad here in the hills that people who knew her used the landline. She almost ignored it, but curiosity made her answer. You didn't usually get cold-selling or chuggers on a Sunday. She saw it was Patty Keane.

'Patty, let me call you back from my other phone. I haven't got much battery left.' That was easier than explaining that she lived at the top of a hill miles from anywhere, in the house where her father had once stuffed dead animals for a living.

Patty answered almost immediately. Vera could hear bairns kicking off in the background.

'Are you okay, pet?' Vera couldn't think why Patty would contact her unless there was some sort of emergency.

'It's not important.' Vera could tell the woman was already feeling foolish, regretting having made the call. 'I shouldn't have disturbed you on a Sunday.'

'No problem at all. Can I help in any way?'

'I just had some questions. About my mother. I saw my dad yesterday.'

'Listen.' Vera had already forgotten the hangover.

'Why don't I come to you? Easier than talking on the phone. I'll be there in an hour.'

She decided she'd take them all to the beach. Kids liked the beach, didn't they? And if they were running about, they wouldn't be earwigging the conversation between her and Patty. She was driving Hector's ancient Land Rover and the kids loved piling into the back of that, sitting sideways as if it was some sort of fairground ride. Patty seemed a bit brighter, more on top of things. She'd brought a towel because she said Archie never went to the beach without getting wet, and a couple of buckets and spades.

'This is very kind.' She kept saying that, as if she couldn't believe that Vera would choose to give them such a treat.

Vera took them to Druridge Bay, with its wide sweep of sand backed by dunes. Inland from the dunes there was the nature reserve, developed from subsidence ponds, with patches of scrubby woodland and hides for watching birds. They walked in a line through the dunes until they reached the highest one. Then they stopped and looked down at the beach, with the old Alcan works at one end and Coquet Island and its lighthouse at the other. The tide was out and the water formed shallow pools, glittering so brightly that Vera had to squint to look at them. Even though it was Sunday and the sun was shining, there weren't too many people. A few families and some dog-walkers, looking very tiny in the distance.

The kids shot off like racing pigeons released from a cage, even the girl, who'd been a bit moody when

Vera had arrived at the house. Patty and Vera sat on the towel at the base of the dunes, keeping out of the breeze.

'I used to come here when I was little,' Patty said. 'My parents lived just up the coast.' A pause. 'My adoptive parents.'

'That must be a bit confusing. Two sets of parents. I only had a father, and that was enough for me.'

'I don't really think of the people in Surrey as parents any more. Not really. They're Neil and Anna, and they looked after me for a bit.' Patty watched Archie jumping in the pools but did nothing to stop him. Vera thought that made sense. He'd take no notice anyway and he'd soon learn not to be so daft, if he had to shiver all the way home. 'I went to see my dad yesterday.'

'You said. I hope he hasn't upset you.'

'No. It wasn't anything like that.' Patty paused again and waved to Archie. The other two kids were jumping from the dunes. 'I asked him about my mam. Why did you send that woman to get her name?'

'Just nosy,' Vera said. 'I wanted to know a bit about you. Find out what I was letting myself in for.'

'Dad said you were nosy. He said he had information that would be useful to you.'

'Did he now?' Vera wondered what exactly Brace had said.

'I want to find out if my mother's still alive. My real mother. Social services couldn't trace her. I'm not sure how hard they tried. They assumed she must have died, because she disappeared from all the records, and I only thought she was dead because my father told me.' She hugged her skinny knees and looked at Vera. 'Can you help me?'

Vera thought she was getting in deeper than she'd bargained for here. Brace had asked her to keep an eye on the family, not dig back into the past to find the love of his life. The mother of his child.

'I don't see why not, pet, and perhaps you can do me a bit of a favour in return. Did your dad ever mention someone called Robbie Marshall? They were chums back in the day.'

Patty shut her eyes for a moment. Vera thought it was partly the glare of the low sun on the water and partly because she was taking herself back ten years, to the conversations she'd had with John Brace.

'Maybe Robbie knew your mam, Mary-Frances?' Because Vera could tell it was really only her mother that Patty was interested in.

Patty shook her head. 'Sorry. For a moment something about the name was a bit familiar, but I can't remember if Dad talked about him or if I heard it somewhere else.'

'Never mind. If it comes to you, give me a shout.' Vera thought this was like tickling trout in murky water. They were looking for two people who'd been close to John Brace and they had no idea yet if they were alive or dead. 'Now how about heading to the ice-cream shop in Cresswell, before that boy of yours catches his death. You can't come to the beach without ice creams.'

Back at home, Vera was restless. She couldn't sit still and she'd never seen the point of walking around outside just for the sake of it; she watched the hikers with their boots and walking poles who strode past her cottage and thought they must be mad. Besides, it wouldn't be long before it got dark. On impulse she phoned Holly. With any luck, she'd be as much at a loose end as Vera was.

'Ma'am?' Nobody else in the team called Vera that these days.

'Are you busy?'

No immediate answer. Holly would want to know what she was committing herself to.

'Only I've been to see Patty Keane and we had an interesting conversation.'

'Oh?' That had got Holly's attention.

'If you're not too busy, I wondered if we could get together to chat about it.' Vera was about to ask Holly to come to her house, but then had another idea. She wouldn't want to be drinking this evening. Not after the skinful she'd had last night. And she'd always been curious about Holly's private life. 'I tell you what, why don't I come to you?'

The apartment looked out over a cemetery and it was silent. Perhaps because it was Sunday, there was no distant traffic noise. When Vera arrived it was dusk, but the blinds hadn't been drawn and wrought-iron lamp posts lit up the lines of graves. Inside, the flat was just as Vera had imagined it would be. Perfectly tidy. No chipped paintwork. Clinically clean. A couple of black-and-white photographs on the wall. Holly offered her a glass of wine. 'I'm afraid I don't have any beer.'

'Don't suppose you could run to a cup of tea? I'm having a night off the booze.'

They sat on white leather sofas. The tea had a floral taste that wasn't unpleasant. No biscuits. Vera could have eaten a few biscuits. It was a while now since the Cresswell ice cream.

'Why did you go to see Patty?' Holly sounded disapproving. She thought Vera got too emotionally involved in her cases.

'Because she phoned me, asked if we could meet up. I wondered what she was after. *And* I wanted to keep her sweet until we've got some useful information out of John Brace.'

'And what was she after?' Holly was dressed for time off – jeans and a sweatshirt with a university sports logo, something she might actually have worn as a student. Vera could imagine her as one of the clean-living types. Jogging before lectures, and nights in the gym. No partying all night and throwing up in the toilet for *her*.

'She wants me to track down her mother. Mary-Frances Lascuola.'

'She told me her mother was dead.'

'Aye well, maybe she's having second thoughts about that. Maybe she thinks John Brace has been telling her porkie pies.' Vera paused. 'I wondered if you'd been poking around on that computer of yours. Doing what you do best.' She nodded towards the laptop that stood on a pale-wood desk under the window.

Holly walked towards the computer. On the way she stopped to pull down the blinds and shut out the dead. 'I did think it was a bit odd . . .'

'What was odd?'

'You'd think there'd be some record of the woman's death. Somewhere. Local newspaper, if she died in Kimmerston. Coroner's court. It's not as if it was a common name. But I can't find any record of her alive, either.'

'Not at all?'

'Well, not after the mid-eighties, a few years after her daughter was born. Patty's birth certificate is in the name of Patricia Mariella Lascuola. When she was adopted she became Patricia Smith, and when she married she took her husband's name of Keane. On the certificate, Mary-Frances is named as the mother and John Brace as the father.' Holly had been making notes on a big A4 pad and looked at them now. 'Before that, Mary-Frances was very obviously in the system. There are records of court appearances and she even spent three months in prison for shoplifting as a juvenile.'

'Feeding her habit.' Vera thought such a short prison term would have been a complete waste of time. 'Do we have an address for her at that time?'

'She had a flat in Whitley Bay. St Anne's Terrace. I've checked and it's one of those little streets between Whitley Road and the metro line. It also looks as if she spent a bit of time in rehab. A place in Bebington run by the NHS, but the assumption is that she was back on the heroin as soon as she came out.'

Vera leaned back on the leather sofa, which was surprisingly comfortable, and took herself back to the Whitley Bay of the mid-eighties. Now the town was faded and a bit depressed. The guest houses had been turned into hostels for ex-offenders and asylum-seekers. There were plans for regeneration along the sea front and on recent visits she'd felt a new spirit of optimism, but in the evenings the town was often quiet, almost ghostly. In the mid-eighties it had been buzzing, though. Nightclubs and pubs full to bursting at the weekends, noise and people spilling out onto the streets. All a bit tacky: strippers, barmaids and barmen wearing practically nothing; offers on booze that fuelled brawls at the end of the night. There'd been nothing sophisticated about most of Whitley Bay in those days, but it had been alive and thriving. It was where people from Newcastle and Northumberland came for a good night out. She opened her eyes.

'Whitley Bay would be handy,' she said. 'For a working girl needing easy access to heroin.'

'I can keep digging.' Holly looked up from her notes. 'But as far as I can tell, there's never been a death certificate in the name of Mary-Frances Lascuola.'

'Nah,' Vera said. 'Don't bother. If there was anything there, you'd have found it by now. Take a break. Let's see what John Brace has to say for himself tomorrow. I've got an appointment with him first thing. I bought all his grand-bairns ice creams at Cresswell this afternoon and they cost me a fortune. He owes me.'

Chapter Twelve

Vera drove straight to the prison. No stop at the Drift Cafe for treats today; her focus was all on John Brace and unpicking the complicated strands of his history. She thought she'd get Holly to make a chart of some kind, with dates in different-coloured felt tips. It would be a task the woman would enjoy – no need to engage with real human beings – and it might help Vera keep things straight in her mind.

It was the same officer on the gate as when she'd come to give her talk and he gave her a nod of recognition. It was early and she was there before the other professionals who would make the trek up the county to interview their clients. She was on her own in the waiting room when an officer came to give her a shout that Brace was ready for her. The room was tiny, taller than it was long. A table fixed to the floor, with a plastic chair on each side. The officer had moved the seat nearest the door, to allow room for the wheelchair. Vera hauled the canvas shopping bag that she was using at the moment as a briefcase onto the table and pulled out a notebook. She'd have liked to record the interview but had known her phone wouldn't be allowed through; besides, she never understood how those things worked. It took her a moment to find something to write with and she came out at last with the stump of a pencil. Brace's face showed no expression throughout the pantomime. No impatience. No amusement.

'Right then,' she said. 'Your turn.'

'What do you mean?'

'Time to tell me where the bones are buried. I went to see Patty. You know that, because she visited on Saturday. And I took her and the kids out yesterday too. A jaunt to the beach. I've more than fulfilled my part of the deal. Now it's your turn.' A pause. 'And don't piss me about, John Brace. You've got a cushy number in here. It doesn't have to be like that. And I don't ever have to see Patty and the kids again. You know fine well that social services won't do much. Except maybe call a meeting, to pile on the pressure.' She must have raised her voice because there was a face at the small glass window in the door. An officer peering in to check that she was okay. She gave a little wave of her hand and the face disappeared.

'She seems to have taken to you. God knows why.' Brace leaned forward.

'So. Robbie Marshall. Where can we find him?'

'I don't know who killed him.'

'Tell me the story, John. You can save the excuses for later.'

'It was June '95, a Sunday, and we'd been out for a day in the hills. Nothing unusual. Me, Robbie and Hector—'

'What about the Prof.? Wasn't he there?' Vera knew it was a mistake to interrupt but she couldn't help herself. The Prof. seemed a shady figure on the edge of the action, keeping just out of view. A mysterious fourth member of the Gang of Four.

But Brace refused to be drawn. He shook his head. 'The Prof. doesn't come into this. He never went out in the field much. Not with us. Not with the common people. He only mixed with the gentry.'

Hector always thought of himself as grander than gentry, but Vera knew better than to pursue that. She could chase it up later. She just nodded for Brace to continue.

'We ended up in Hector's place for a beer. It was a hot day and we'd done a lot of walking.' A pause. 'Robbie had been quiet all day. A bit withdrawn. I don't think Hector noticed. Not the most sensitive chap in the world, Hector. Well, you know that.'

Vera nodded but didn't speak.

'We'd come in separate cars, and outside the house I asked Robbie what was wrong and if there was anything I could help with. Robbie was a bit of a wheeler-dealer in those days. Sailed a bit close to the law. Mixed with the bad boys, the men with power.'

'His mam won't hear a word against him.'

Brace gave a little smile. 'Ah well, my mam wouldn't hear a word against me. He was a pleaser, Robbie. Weak. He liked mixing it with the bad lads, but sometimes he got in out of his depth.'

'What did Robbie say?'

'That he'd got himself into a bit of bother, but needed to sort it out himself. He'd fixed up a meeting that evening, and it would be fine.' Brace stopped for a moment. 'I should have asked for more details but I had my own plans for that night.'

'You were meeting an informant in Whitley Bay.'

'How do you know that?'

Vera tapped the side of her nose and tried to look mysterious.

'Ah,' he said. 'You've been to see Judith. Of course you have. You were always thorough, weren't you, Vera? That was your reputation. What you lacked in charm, you made up for with hard work.' In the corridor outside a door banged and there was the inevitable sound of keys. An interview would soon start in the next room. 'But yes, I was catching up with an informant in Whitley Bay. We'd arranged to meet at the entrance to Spanish City. It was busy enough on a fine Sunday night for us not to be noticed.'

'Ah, the Spanish City. That takes me back.' The funfair next to the big white Dome that had been built to rival Blackpool's Pleasure Beach. Each morning it opened to Dire Straits' 'Tunnel of Love', the song that had given it a mention and turned it into legend. In 1995 it had already passed its best, but it was still there, gaudy and loud, pulling in the trippers. On a hot night in June there'd be the smell of candyfloss and frying onions and the diesel that powered the rides. Now the site of the funfair had been flattened and there was talk of turning the Dome into some sort of retail park. The thought made Vera shudder.

'Of course we didn't all have mobile phones in those days.' Brace was almost apologetic. 'And when we did, they weren't reliable. I couldn't contact Robbie, couldn't tell him to ring me if he got into trouble. I should have done more at the time.'

'Who were you meeting, John? Let's have the name of your informant.' She paused. 'Your alibi.'

'You know I can't tell you that.' He sounded tired,

as if he hadn't slept well for months, and dipped his head as if it was too heavy for him to hold.

'It wouldn't be Mary-Frances Lascuola?'

He lifted his head and gave a little laugh. 'I don't commune with the dead, Vera. She'd already been long gone by then. And maybe I was responsible for her passing too. She's someone else I should have looked after better.'

Vera wanted to ask more about Mary-Frances, but Patty's mother wasn't the main focus of this visit. 'So you meet this mysterious informant outside Spanish City.'

'It was noisy. A couple of stag- and hen-parties finishing their weekends in style. You know how Whitley was, back then.'

She nodded.

'I'd parked my car at The Links. We went there first and then drove to St Mary's Lighthouse. It was dark by that time – it was around ten o'clock – but there was a full moon. We didn't walk out to the island because the tide was in, but we sat on a bench and chatted there. I hadn't expected anyone else to be around. During the day you can't move around the place for dog-walkers and cyclists, but at that time of night I thought we'd have the place to ourselves. Too early for the doggers and too late for anyone else.'

He stopped, but this time Vera knew better than to interrupt.

He took a breath. 'There was another car in the car park. Robbie's car. I recognized it as soon as we arrived. I thought maybe he'd had the same thought as me – that it would be a quiet place for a meeting, to sort out whatever had been bothering him – but there was no sign of anyone about. By the time I finished my business it was nearly eleven. I drove my contact back into Whitley, so he could get the metro back into the city, but I couldn't get Robbie Marshall out of my mind.'

Another pause. The meeting in the adjacent room must have been routine or the lawyer unbothered, because the door banged again and the prisoner was led out. Vera jotted a note on her pad: *Brace's informant came from Newcastle*. It wasn't much but it might narrow things down a bit.

In the end she lost patience. 'So I'm assuming you went back to St Mary's to check. You'd been friends since school. He was your best mate. You'd want to know what was going on.'

Brace nodded and shifted in his chair. 'It was Sunday night, so things were quiet by then. Spanish City had closed and there were just a few people walking back along the sea front. Robbie's car was still where I'd first seen it, right at the north end of the bay. I thought maybe he'd driven off with the guy he was meeting, but that seemed unlikely. Robbie had work the next day too and he never missed work. It was what made him respectable.'

'And it gave him his cover. Just like you, John. Wasn't that what you always claimed? You'd never had a day on the sick. Never took all your holidays. The perfect employee.'

Brace ignored her. She could see that, in his head, he was back there. There was a road, just wide enough for two cars to pass, that led along the point towards St Mary's Island and the lighthouse. The sea on one side, on the other a patch of scrubby land, with soggy areas that turned into muddy pools in wet weather. It was a nature reserve now, but she couldn't remember what it had been like all those years ago. Rough grazing maybe? The island was tidal, and the lighthouse and its cottages were run by the council these days as a visitor centre and a place for bairns to come and learn about wildlife. It occurred to Vera that Patty's kids might enjoy it, and *she* wouldn't mind paddling in the rock pools with a net and a bucket, either.

Brace continued. 'I almost just left it and went straight home, but like you say, he was a school pal, my marra.'

'So what did you do?' Now Vera was worried that some officer would come banging on the door and calling time before she had any useful information. She was desperate for Brace to finish his story.

'I got out of the car and went looking for him. I had a torch, but I didn't need it at first. Like I said, there was a full moon and your eyes soon get accustomed. *You* know that, living out in the wild, away from the street lights. I walked along the shoreline north towards Hartley Point and Seaton Sluice. Quiet. Not shouting his name. I didn't know what I might be interrupting, and a cop turning up might be the worst thing possible, if he'd got himself into bother with some of his dodgy mates.'

'You must have seen something,' Vera said, 'or we wouldn't be here now.'

'I *found* something.' He paused. 'I found Robbie's body. Thrown up by the side of the footpath, like a bit of rubbish. His head beaten in.' He looked up and stared into her eyes. 'If there'd been any chance that he might still have been alive, I'd have called it in.

Honest. But I reckon he was dead when I first got there with my contact.'

'And why didn't you call it in? Like any law-abiding citizen would?' Her voice deceptively gentle. Inside seething with fury, because Brace had been a cop. One of *them*.

'Because I had too much to lose. Once the murder team started digging around in his past, they'd find Robbie was linked to me and to his powerful friends on the other side. I'd got into enough bother already by then and I was on a final warning.'

'So why tell me all this now? Haunted by the ghost of Robbie Marshall, are you? It never seemed to trouble you before.'

'Because I love my daughter!' Brace was almost screaming. 'Because I want a better life for her.'

After the raised voices, the following silence came as a shock.

'John Brace, you soppy git, I almost believe you.' Vera shook her head. 'So you didn't call it in. What did you do?'

'There was a culvert that ran up from the shore; it cut through the rock and formed a tunnel a little way under the headland. I don't know what it was for. I think at the landward end it was a field drain, allowing rainwater to seep into the sea. I wedged the body up the culvert and stuffed some boulders behind it, so the tide wouldn't wash it out. I'd already found Robbie's keys in his jacket pocket. I took his car to the long-stay park at the airport and got a taxi back to Whitley, walked the last couple of miles to St Mary's because I didn't want anyone to remember dropping me there, if by any chance the body came to light. I chucked his keys into the sea. Then I picked up my own car and drove home. It was almost light before I got there.'

'And Judith thought you were out all night with an . . . informant.'

'It happened,' Brace said. 'It wasn't unusual.'

'And you let Robbie's mam hope that he might turn up one day.'

'How could I tell her?' He sat for a moment with his head in his hands. 'Look, I'm not proud of what I did. If I'd had more time, I might have thought of something better, staged a car accident maybe. I've gone over it in my head a thousand times. But I lost it. I couldn't have a murder investigation linked to me.'

'Especially when you were there, eh, John? You were on the spot when Robbie was killed. Some coincidence!'

'I didn't kill him. Do you think I'd risk my chance of getting out of here alive by telling you about the body, if I had? I don't love my daughter that much. Robbie was my mate. What reason would I have?'

'You didn't see anyone at all around, while you were having a cosy chat with your informant by the seaside? No cars? No late-night walkers or joggers?' For a moment Vera was distracted. Did they have joggers in 1995? Surely they did, just not quite as many.

He shook his head. 'I've had more than twenty years to think about it. I don't remember seeing anyone at all.'

There were heavy footsteps on the floor outside and the door was opened. An officer. 'Time to go, mate.' Sympathetic. Perhaps he considered Brace some sort of hero, let down by the system. Vera would have liked to put him straight, but this wasn't the time.

'We'll look into what you've told me.' Her voice was formal and bland as she packed her notebook into her bag. 'I'll probably get back to you next week.'

Brace didn't say anything as the officer wheeled him away.

Chapter Thirteen

Back at the station, the team was waiting for her. Vera sailed in, her mind buzzing, and wondered for a moment if this was what kids felt like when they'd just taken drugs. If it was, she could understand how they got addicted. There was no feeling like it: the adrenaline and the sense that anything was possible, that this might be another moment of glory. But she didn't let her excitement show until they'd gathered together around Charlie's desk. She had to play this carefully; she still wasn't entirely sure that John Brace wasn't playing games of his own, and the last thing she wanted was a public search of a popular spot on the Tyneside coast, only to find nothing. Or, even worse, a few dog or sheep bones. Brace had always delighted in making her look ridiculous.

'We'll take this quietly.' She'd hoisted herself onto the desk. Queen bee and mistress of all she surveyed. 'I've had a chat with an old pal who works with the specialist search team. They can be there at first light tomorrow. No fuss, and just a few colleagues doing a favour for a mate.' A pause and a nod towards the stairs that led to the smart offices where the senior officers worked. 'No need for them to know anything about it, until we get a result.'

'We're waiting until tomorrow?' Holly sounded horrified. Vera suspected she was uncomfortable with the break with established procedure, rather than the wait itself.

'If Robbie Marshall is in that culvert, he's been there for more than twenty years and another day won't make any difference.' But Vera was impatient too, restless, and she wasn't sure how she'd manage to spend the day. 'Holly, Brace says he met an informant in Whitley that night. He let slip that they lived in Newcastle, but he wasn't going to give me a name. Can you go back through the records? Check Brace's known associates at the time. It's a long shot, but we could do with finding someone who can confirm his story and it's the sort of thing you're brilliant at.' She'd come to realize that Holly needed a pat on the back every now and again. 'And if you get a chance, pull together some sort of timeline. Brace said that Mary-Frances had long been dead by the time Robbie Marshall went missing, but I can't help feeling that somehow they're all tied together.'

Holly nodded, and Vera could tell the woman was back on-side.

'Charlie, can you use that memory of yours to give Hol a steer? Anyone Brace might have gone to see late at night in Whitley Bay? He must have been a player, to make Brace give up his Sunday night.'

Charlie shook his head. 'You know how it is with informants, Vera. Especially then. A matter of honour to keep their identities secret.'

'But you might know what Brace would be focusing on then. What his priorities would have been and what made him get up in the morning.'

'I'll think about it.'

'You do that, Charlie, and give me a shout if anything comes of it.' She slid off the desk. Restlessness had got the better of her. 'Joe, you come with me.'

She got Joe to drive to Whitley Bay. The sun was still shining and she wondered what the weather would have been like that night in June when Robbie Marshall disappeared. It must have been clear then too, because Brace had talked about moonlight and being able to see without a torch.

They parked in the lay-by next to the cemetery that stood just inland from the bay, and that left a little walk down to St Mary's. Vera tried to walk more these days, scared – despite herself – by her doctor's dire warnings about obesity and high blood pressure. A group of mourners stood by the entrance to the graveyard, smoking, stubbing out their cigarettes quickly when the hearse arrived, frightened of missing the burial.

'What's this about?' Joe walked easily beside her. He'd always kept fit, and Sal kept an eye on his diet.

'I just want to get a lie of the land. It's a while since I've been here.'

They crossed the dual carriageway from the cemetery and got the full view of the bay, the sweep of sand that had once attracted holidaymakers from Scotland and day-trippers from urban Newcastle. Once the guest houses and hotels had been full of people; now the hotels were being knocked down or converted to apartments for commuters to the city, and the guest houses were used for people who wouldn't consider their move to the coast a holiday. But the sea was the same and the sound of the gulls; there was the sense of space and the reflected light. They could see the impressive white globe of the Dome in the distance. Vera was lost in thought, conjuring up the noise and colour of Spanish City as it had been in the nineties, thinking there'd been another building on the skyline then, a sleek white nightclub called The Seagull, which had been burned down in a fire. Built in the thirties, it had seemed to sum up the town's glory days. And when it went, the resulting gap on the sea front had seemed to represent its decline. She was trying to picture the place when she was nearly knocked over by a cyclist in Lycra.

'Bloody menace. Why can't they ride in the road?'

'You're standing in the middle of the cycle path.'

She thought there probably hadn't been cycle paths here in the nineties, either. On the other side of the road there was a caravan site; from the path they could see the kiddies' play park. Vera decided that the site had been there for as long as she could remember, but she knew it would be hard to track down any possible witnesses after so many years. They walked slowly towards the lighthouse, Joe matching Vera's pace, keeping quiet. He'd know she wouldn't want to be disturbed. The nature reserve had been newly fenced – though the fences would never have kept Hector away from the nesting waders – and there were hides for photographers and birders. The tide had just gone out and a scattering of people walked across the short, narrow causeway to St Mary's Island. Vera did a rough calculation in her head and thought it should be low water first thing in the morning. Just what they needed. In the car park at the point, one van was selling doughnuts and another ice creams. They'd be making the most of the late summer.

Next to the vans there was a big sign – wood covered in Perspex – containing a brightly coloured map and explaining plans for the regeneration of the area. They seemed to centre around a new cafe and restaurant, to be built just where they were standing. There was an architect's drawing of the proposal that was all glass and pale wood. It looked bonny enough, but Vera guessed there'd be no room then for the ice-cream and doughnut-sellers, and the vans had been there for as long as she could remember. The idea of change disturbed her. Surely there were already plenty of cafes in Whitley fighting for business. She walked on and down to the rocky shore, looking for Brace's culvert. If it wasn't there, she wasn't sure what she'd do.

The shore here was quiet. The children were back at school, so there were no families and the joggers and cyclists mostly kept to the tracks. An elderly couple sat on a bench looking towards her, but they had their eyes shut and their faces turned to the sun. Joe was nimbler on his feet and had scrambled ahead of her. Vera was struggling to keep her balance and was having second thoughts about rock pools and Patty's bairns.

'Is this it, do you think?' Joe was pointing at a cleft in the rock. It was man-made and might once have held a drainage pipe, but that had disintegrated decades ago, probably long before Brace had met his informant at the top of the bank. Vera thought the pipe might once have extended right out to the North

Sea, carrying Edwardian sewage into the salt water. There were still rusty bolts in some of the rocks, showing where the frame to hold the outlet pipe had been fixed.

'I don't think that's a field drain, but it fits the description.' And at night, panicking a bit, looking for somewhere to dispose of a body – the body of his friend since childhood – she thought Brace wouldn't have noticed the difference. 'That's where the team can start looking tomorrow, at least.' She felt an urge to start pulling out the boulders and rocks that clogged the entrance to the culvert. 'We'd best go back,' she said. 'The last thing we need is to draw attention to ourselves.'

Joe started to climb back to the footpath, but she stayed where she was for a while, staring at the gash in the shallow cliff.

When she reached Joe, he was standing by the ice-cream van with a cornet in each hand, a chocolate flake sticking out of the top. 'I thought, if we were playing the part of day-trippers, we should do it properly.'

She thought he was as excited as she was. 'Oh aye, and what part am I playing? Your mam?'

He grinned. 'Nah,' he said. 'My nan.'

'Cheeky monkey.' But, licking her ice cream, Vera thought she hadn't felt this happy for months.

They met at the St Mary's car park early the next morning before it was light. Holly and Charlie were in Holly's car, and Vera had picked up Joe in the battered Land Rover on her way from the hills. The search team spilled out of an anonymous transit van and there were lots of mock complaints about the lack of coffee and the early hour.

'You find what we're looking for,' Vera said, 'and there'll be a full English breakfast on me.' She'd slept briefly but deeply and felt very awake and alert. There was a grey light on the horizon now and she led them over the rocks to where Joe had found the culvert, without the need for a torch. They were all steadier on their feet than her, but they let her go first. It was her call and she was in charge. She was dressed in corduroy trousers and walking boots; Holly sported a pair of designer wellies covered in flowers and butterflies. They reached the culvert just as the light over the sea turned pink. Vera nodded to the slit in the shallow cliff. 'This is the place he described. We'll just let you get on with it, shall we?'

The team leader nodded and grinned. 'Aye, we don't want you amateurs getting in the way.'

So Vera and the other detectives found a flat rock to sit on and watched from a distance. Vera thought any early-morning jogger would have the men down as a team from a water company or the council, maybe doing a first survey before the planned development. She wasn't sure what they'd make of the four people gathered on the rock, watching: Charlie in his ancient overcoat, smoking a tab and turning away from the others to blow away the smoke; Holly managing to look smart and sophisticated, despite her obvious discomfort; Joe intent and anxious, staring at the men carefully lifting boulders from the mouth of the culvert; and Vera – Vera, so big that she dwarfed the rest of them. Sometimes she worried that she swamped them with her personality and her prejudices too, and that she didn't give them the space or the confidence to make their own decisions. But, she told herself now, she was usually right, and she wouldn't be doing them any favours if she let them make their own mistakes. The cold from the rock seeped through her coat and into her bones.

It was properly light now. The sunrise made an orange path over the water towards them. In the distance three merchant vessels made their way out of the Tyne, dark silhouettes against the sun. A couple of vehicles pulled into the car park above them. A birder wearing an oiled jacket and carrying an expensive pair of binoculars walked along the footpath at the top of the bank, but seemed more interested in looking inland towards the reserve than down at them. The search team had cleared the entrance to the culvert and one of the skinnier men had disappeared inside with a torch in his hand. Vera was growing impatient. They should have found what they were looking for by now. She started planning her revenge on John Brace for pissing her about.

'Guv.' The skinny man's overall was covered in sand and muck and there was a bit of seaweed on his hood. Vera thought he looked a bit like one of the characters she'd seen when the morris men performed outside the pub in Monkseaton on New Year's Day. The Green Man. He stood at the culvert entrance and looked out at her. 'There's something a bit weird in here.'

'What sort of weird? Have we got a body or not?' She was tense, couldn't believe that she might have been duped. John Brace had convinced her with his story of friendship, his love for his daughter.

'There's certainly a complete human skeleton, stuffed at the back of the culvert, but there are too many bones.'

There was a moment of relief when she heard the first words. She'd been right all along. She hadn't pulled these men out on a wild-goose chase. She could cope with most things but she hated ridicule and, if she'd got this seriously wrong, word would get out all over the service. *Vera's gone dangerously loopy this time. She dragged a whole search team out because she dreamed up some fantasy about a dead villain.* Then the last phrase registered in her brain. 'What do you mean: too many bones?'

There was a moment's silence. The officer shielded his eyes against the low sun with one hand, so that Vera could only see the lower part of his face. 'I'd say there were two bodies hidden away in here. Not one.'

Chapter Fourteen

Joe waited to supervise at the scene while Vera went back to the station to brief Watkins. The wheels of a murder inquiry would be set in motion; word would get out, and the media would soon be hounding the press office. It was better that she got her side of the story in with the boss first. She needed a plausible explanation for not keeping him in the loop from the start. She phoned him from the St Mary's Island car park, her back turned to the sea and the breeze that had picked up since they'd first arrived. The last thing she needed was some other officious officer to get to the boss before her.

'Something you should know about, sir.' She described the discovery of the body as if she'd been following a purely tentative lead. 'I didn't want the hoopla of a formal investigation until we'd checked out the possibility that it might be true. The last thing I expected was two sets of bones.'

'They're sure? It's not just one skeleton and the bones have been scattered by animals?'

She'd asked that too, but she'd not gone in to check herself. Even though the bodies had been there for at least twenty years, the scene should be relatively uncontaminated. By humans at least. It hadn't looked to her as if the boulders blocking the entrance had been moved since Brace had put them there. She imagined that rats had been in – there'd been gaps in the rocks to let water drain away. Sea creatures might have seeped through at a very high tide. The last thing the investigation needed was more cops trampling all over the place. Joe Ashworth and the CSIs were deciding now how best to keep the area secure and what to do next. It might be possible to construct a tent around the entrance to the culvert, until the bones had been photographed and checked in detail, but when the tide came in, the officers would be paddling in several inches of water. Vera thought it would be best to get the bones out as quickly as possible. They'd already cordoned off the footpath to the island and the north end of the car park, to keep gawpers away.

'We'll need the pathologist on that one,' she said. 'Maybe a forensic anthropologist. I'm assuming the bodies were placed there at the same time, but maybe they'll be able to pin it down more accurately.'

Now she was in the office where she'd sat the week before; she'd been resentful then at being sent to a prison to talk about victims. Today they were still talking about the same subject: victims of violent crime. Watkins wasn't Welsh, as far as she knew, despite the name. He didn't seem to have any sort of accent; there was no way of placing him, except that she knew he was a university graduate in his early forties. One of the smart-talking, media-savvy new breed, and he always made her defensive. Today he was wearing a grey suit that was as bland as he was.

'So you have ID for one of the victims?'

'According to John Brace. No confirmation yet.'

He raised his eyebrows. He'd heard of John Brace, even though he'd been appointed after the man had been convicted and sent to prison.

'He was one of the group, when you sent me to Warkworth to talk to the . . .' she tried to remember the acronym, '. . . EDW.'

'And Brace casually passed on the information that a body was buried in a culvert near St Mary's Island.' Watkins obviously hadn't heard that sarcasm was the lowest form of wit.

'Not then,' Vera said. 'He wanted me to check that his daughter was doing okay. He has a daughter in her thirties, three grandkids.'

'But I understand that his ex-wife's very much alive and engaged in political activity. Wouldn't she be looking out for the family?'

Vera could sense that he was losing patience, but she didn't care. 'Judith wasn't the woman's mother.' A pause. 'I went to see the woman and her family and then, as a kind of trade-off, Brace gave me the information about Robbie Marshall.'

'Who we assume to be one of the victims at St Mary's?'

Whom. She was tempted to correct him. She'd had an English teacher who'd been a stickler for grammar. But she restrained herself. Maybe Watkins wasn't as well educated as he liked to make out. The thought cheered her.

'He was an associate of Brace's.' Vera paused again. 'And of my father's.' Better to get that into the open now, because some bugger would tell him.

'Your father knew Brace?' Watkins looked up, surprised.

'They went birdwatching together occasionally,' Vera said. 'Not much more than that. Besides, Hector's been dead for years. There's no conflict of interest.'

There was a moment's silence, the background hum of something electrical in the office next door. Watkins seemed inclined to let the connection between Hector and Brace go. Perhaps he knew Vera was the detective with the best clear-up rate on the force and this was going to be complicated. Also, he'd be happy for her to carry the can if the investigation went tits up.

'Who do the other bones belong to?' Watkins looked up from the notes he was making. There was a bottle of ink on the table and he was using a fountain pen. Vera was distracted for a moment. She hadn't seen a real pen for years. It seemed an odd pretension for such a young man.

'I've no idea,' she said. 'But I'll be back at Warkworth first thing, asking John Brace why he never mentioned a second body.'

'What's Brace's story?' Watkins was poised with his pen in his hand. 'How does he say Marshall's body got into that culvert?'

Vera told him, almost word-for-word, replaying the interview with Brace in her head. The story came easily; she could almost believe she was in the box-like interview room in Warkworth with Brace again. She'd been repeating it to herself since she'd left the prison. She left nothing out, except her questions about Mary-Frances Lascuola. Later she couldn't have explained why she'd kept that information to herself.

Perhaps she truly believed the identity of Brace's lover was irrelevant. More likely, she decided, she knew that information was power, and she wanted to hold on to that particular gem, knowing that it might come in useful later.

She sent out for pizza for the team in the office; she was starving and she knew they wouldn't have eaten properly since getting back to Kimmerston. Even Holly, who usually seemed to survive on a few lettuce leaves and a tub of low-calorie hummus, took a couple of slices. Charlie ate as if he hadn't seen food for a month.

'How's Joe getting on at the site?'

'The pathologist had already arrived before we left.' Holly wiped her mouth with the napkin that had come with the meal. Very ladylike. 'They reckon they should have the skeletons away before the tide comes in, and any objects found in the drain bagged. They *could* still work onsite if the water comes up – it's not a particularly high tide apparently, and the culvert slopes up away from the shore – but it would be much more difficult.'

'What have they found so far?'

'The CSIs were in there just as I left. According to them, some scraps of clothing were still attached to the bones. Not much, but it should help with ID. There was a belt, I think. They were working on the debris on the floor of the culvert when I came away. They'll be here for this evening's briefing. I called it for seven to give us a bit of time.'

Vera nodded her approval. 'Any idea of the gender

of the second body?' She wished she could be there with the team of CSIs, asking them these questions, getting the information as soon as they had it, out in the fresh air, the salt wind and the sunshine. But she knew that wasn't her role, and really she'd just be getting in the way.

Holly shook her head. 'Dr Keating wasn't giving anything away.'

Vera started clearing the pizza boxes and sticking them into a bin. At the same time she was clearing her mind of the recent detail and trying to pull together a coherent picture of the background to the case. 'Hol, did you get anywhere with that timeline? This is going to be a bugger to work, if we don't have a framework to keep us straight.'

Holly slid off the desk where she'd been sitting and took centre-stage. It occurred to Vera that Holly was the sort of officer who'd do well under Watkins' regime. She'd make it to Vera's rank while she was still a young woman. And she'd do it brilliantly, Vera thought. She'd be terrific at all the things that were important now in policing: organizing material, supervising the team, presenting her case for more resources. Vera would always struggle in those areas, no matter how many management courses she was sent on. But she knew Holly would never be a better cop. She couldn't mix comfortably with people of different ages and backgrounds, listening, probing, understanding. She didn't find them fascinating.

Holly was fiddling with her laptop and a projector, and soon an image appeared on the whiteboard at the front of the room. 'I think this is right, but give me a shout if I've got anything wrong.' Despite her competence at all things technological, she sounded a little nervous about the facts themselves.

She'd set it out almost as a simple family tree, with John Brace at the top of the chart in the middle, running in a straight line to the bottom. Decades were marked at the side of the spreadsheet, and Brace's contacts and specific events of significance were written around the central line.

'John Arthur Brace was born in October 1950 and he was an only child. His father was a deputy in Bebington's Isabella coalmine. Brace went to Bebington Grammar School, where he met Robert Paul Marshall in 1961.' That point of first contact had been captured on Holly's plan. 'Marshall was also an only child; his father was a butcher and his mother, Eleanor, a teacher before she married. When Robbie was twelve the family moved to Wallsend but he remained at Bebington school. Eleanor still lives in Wallsend.' She paused for breath. There was silence in the room. Even Charlie was taking notes.

Holly continued: 'Brace left school in 1969 and joined the police force as a cadet. Marshall left at the same time and became an apprentice in the Swan Hunter shipyard.' Again, these facts were written clearly on the sheet. 'They both did well in their respective careers – Brace ended up as superintendent and Marshall as procurement manager.' Another pause. 'By the late seventies and early eighties the force was already receiving complaints about Brace's behaviour, but none of these seem to have been taken too seriously. In January 1983 Patricia Mariella Lascuola was born. It seems generally accepted that Brace was her father, so we can assume that he knew Mary-Frances at least by the previous year.' Holly turned to her audience. 'Is all that making sense?'

'It's brilliant, Hol.' Vera meant it. 'Dead clear.'

'Patty married Gary Keane in 2003 and their first child, Jennifer, was born in 2005. In 2007 Glen Fenwick, a gamekeeper on the Standrigg Estate, was murdered, and nearly two years later John Brace was charged in connection with the crime. Just before he was imprisoned he purchased a house for Patty and her family. Jonnie Keane was born soon after, and Patty's third child, Archie, two years after that. You can see the births here on the plan. I've updated the timeline with Vera visiting the prison last week and the discovery of the bodies today. I'll maintain it as a document online and add to it as we go along. I can make printouts for the briefing tonight and every time there's any new information about past events.' She switched off her computer.

There was a moment of silence before Vera led the applause. Holly looked uncertain for a moment, as if she thought they might be mocking her, then she grinned and pretended to bow.

'That, ladies and gentleman,' Vera said, 'is why every team needs an officer like Holly. That's how we're going to get an ID for the second body and how we're going to find our killer.'

Chapter Fifteen

Joe Ashworth got back to the station just in time for the seven o'clock briefing. In the corridor outside the operations room he phoned Sal to explain that he'd be late home.

'It'll be a big one. You'll see it all over the late news. Could be an all-nighter, but certainly don't wait up.'

Her response was one of dull resignation. After the birth of their youngest child, they'd talked about the possibility of his leaving the police service, finding something with more regular hours, but she'd always been more enthusiastic about the plan than he was. She'd investigated the possibility that he might retrain, had it in her head that he'd make a great teacher. When she'd gone into the details, though, even Sal had admitted that it wouldn't be practical. She might not like the demands that the job and Vera made on his time, but she loved the salary and the flexibility. Although he'd never let on, Joe had been overjoyed when the idea had been dropped. He'd never have given up policing, not even for Sal and the family, and had been dreading a confrontation. Sal already accused him of always putting Vera first.

'I *have* been around for most of the summer,' he

said now. He wished she understood how much he loved his work. He shouldn't have to make excuses about it.

And perhaps she did understand. 'I know, pet, and it'll be fine. *We'll* be fine. Just take care and don't take any crap from Vera. You know how bossy she can be and, when she's in the middle of an investigation, she seems not to realize that other people have a life away from the job.'

Joe thought Vera wasn't the only bossy woman in his life but he didn't say anything. He pushed open the door to the operations room and felt himself relax. He loved his wife and kids. Of course he did. But this was where he really felt at home.

They were just about to start. Holly was handing out a kind of spreadsheet that gave the details of John Brace and Robbie Marshall's contacts, and another sheet of A4, which was a biography of Marshall's life, containing everything they'd learned about him so far. In the room were officers drafted in from other teams and the senior CSI, who'd been supervising the scene at St Mary's for most of the day. Vera was on her feet, about to speak. She'd been giving it the max since before first light, but she looked as fresh as if she'd just woken up.

'Let's get going then, shall we? Now DS Ashworth has graced us with his presence.'

There were a few sniggers at the dig. Joe wondered if Vera had known that he'd been delayed in the corridor outside because he was phoning Sal, or if she'd guessed. Sometimes he thought she was a kind of witch and knew what he was thinking before he did.

'Obviously no positive ID on either body yet.' Vera looked round the room. 'But until we hear otherwise, I think we can safely say that one of them belongs to Robbie Marshall, who went missing on 25th June 1995. The only reason we were digging around in the culvert was because our old friend ex-Superintendent John Brace told us we'd find Marshall there.' She paused. 'But there was no mention of a second body and I really want to find out why. If Brace knew about it, why didn't he tell me? He'd realize we'd find it, once we started digging. And if he didn't know about it, that's even more bizarre. Brace claims Marshall was already dead when he found him, and that he stuck the body in the culvert because he didn't want anyone here to make any connection between the two of them. I can just about buy that. Brace was already under investigation and late at night, coming across the body of his best friend, he might have panicked. But that there just happened to be another dead person already stashed in the same place? Nah, that's just not possible. That's the stuff of fairy stories.'

Her eyes swept the room again, checking that they were all still with her. 'So the first priority is to ID both bodies. We take nothing for granted. We assume that Brace has been lying to us, big-style.' Her attention landed on the CSI. 'Have you got anything that can help us?'

'One of the victims is certainly male, according to Dr Keating. And the clothes would indicate that too. There are big walking boots, still pretty well intact.'

Vera nodded. 'That ties in with what we know about Marshall's activity on the day he disappeared. He must be our most likely first victim.'

'The other body was smaller, but it's not so well preserved.'

'Could it be a woman?'

The CSI shrugged 'Hey! I'll leave that one to the experts.' Not wanting to stick his neck out in front of the team.

'Did you find anything that might indicate gender?'

Joe could sense Vera's impatience. She was missing senior CSI Billy Cartwright, with whom she was more used to working. Cartwright was away on holiday with his latest woman, and the couple weren't due back until the weekend. Vera claimed to disapprove of Cartwright, but at least he was usually forthcoming in his opinions. She pressed the point. 'I'm thinking jewellery, a wedding or engagement ring.'

'Sorry, nothing so far that would suggest either gender,' the CSI said. 'No handbag or wallet, no watch.'

Joe wondered about the implication of that. Had anything that might identify the victims been removed by the killer or had it just disintegrated over time, or been washed away through gaps in the boulders at high tide?

Vera had obviously decided that the CSI had nothing useful to add and had moved on. 'Robbie Marshall was working at Swan Hunter's when he died. The shipyard had already gone into administration then, but he was still there helping tie up loose ends for the administrators. He was always good with figures, Robbie, and buying and selling was in his blood. Quite often the stuff he sold belonged to other people. His mam thinks he was a saint. We know he was far from that, but I need a picture of what was really going on in his life. According to Brace, he was anxious about a meeting he was having that night in June. We suspect he was mixed up with some of the major players, dabbling on the fringes of organized crime. Was the choice of Whitley Bay as the meeting place random, or was that where his contact was based? Can we come up with a few ideas about whom he might have been meeting there? Charlie, you can make a start on that one. It'd have been your era.'

Charlie grinned and gave a wave of acknowledgement, but Vera continued in full flow. 'Let's look at the dealers and the men who were running the working girls. Brace had a daughter with a woman called Mary-Frances Lascuola, heroin addict and likely sex worker, according to her records. Also according to her records, Mary-Frances seems to have disappeared without trace. Now I'm making a bit of a leap here, but at the moment I'd give a case of my favourite malt to know if Mary-Frances is our second body. Brace claims that she died long before Robbie Marshall went missing, but we know he's a lying bastard. So let's get everything we can find on Mary-Frances. Hol, you've made a good start on this one. Can you track down any women who might have been working with her in Whitley at that time? See if anyone knows what's happened to her. And check out the rehab centre in Bebington. If it's still there, they should still have some records.'

Joe allowed himself a brief grin. He wondered how Holly would get on with a bunch of ageing prostitutes and druggies. But Vera had directed her attention to him now.

'I want you to go and see Gary Keane.' She turned to her wider audience to explain. 'Gary was married to

Brace's daughter. He now runs a computer-repair business in Bedlington and lives over the premises. There are suspicions that he doesn't only work for the law-abiding citizens of south-east Northumberland, but that he also sorts out the technical problems for members of organized crime in the region. He'd have been young when Robbie Marshall went missing, but there's a possibility that he was already involved in criminality then. He would have known some of the players, heard the rumours. Just have a little chat. Find out what sort of man he is.' Vera leaned back on the edge of a desk and closed her eyes for a moment, showing her age and her exhaustion for the first time. She opened them again and gave a wide grin. 'And I'm going back in prison, to ask our old pal John Brace why he's been playing games with us.'

Joe arrived at Gary Keane's place early the next morning. He wanted time to talk properly, before the man felt obliged to open up his shop. The Indian summer was stretching well into September, but this early there was a chill in the air, the smell of dying leaves. Bebington was a former pit-town and had been down on its luck since the colliery closed, but Anchor Lane, a couple of streets away from the centre, had a slightly more prosperous air; there was an independent coffee shop, already open and selling cappuccinos to a steady stream of commuters waiting for the bus into Newcastle, and a bit of wasteland opposite had been turned into a community garden. Keane's business was on a corner site close to the cafe, at the end of a terrace of small independent shops. His flat would have a view of the newly tended flowerbeds.

The shop window was covered by metal shutters. The area hadn't been so gentrified that it would be safe not to take security seriously. Next to the door into the shop there was another entrance, with a bell. Joe rang that and waited. Nothing. He rang again, this time leaning all his weight on it and letting it ring. Eventually he heard heavy footsteps on bare wooden stairs. The door opened to Gary Keane, bleary-eyed, bigger than Joe had been expecting from the photograph, older but still good-looking in a haggard, well-worn way. He was wearing a dark-green dressing gown and leather slippers that flapped as he walked. Nothing else.

'What the fuck do you want?'

'Police.' Joe pulled out his warrant card, but Keane waved it away.

'No need for that. I can smell you lot a mile off.'

'Are you going to let me in?'

'Only if you bring coffee with you.' Keane nodded to the shop two doors down. 'Flat white. And an almond croissant. I'll leave the door open.' He disappeared.

Joe pondered what Vera would have made of that kind of demand and decided she'd already be halfway up the stairs after Keane, telling him to get his own bloody coffee. But it smelled good, and Joe thought that one thing he'd learned from Vera was that there was more than one way to get a result. When he got back to the flat, carrying coffee and pastries in a cardboard tray, Keane was dressed. The place was small but pleasant enough. Tidy for a bachelor pad. Arty, with a couple of posters on the walls. The posters advertised Whitley Bay as a seaside town, the design resembling 1930s railway art. There was a bookshelf stuffed with paperbacks. It seemed that, like this part of Bebington, Keane had become more sophisticated. Maybe he even volunteered in the community garden.

'What's this about?'

Joe hesitated for a moment. What *was* this about? All they had to link Keane with Robbie Marshall was the fact that John Brace had once been Gary's father-in-law. All the same, Gary didn't need to know that.

'Just a few questions. You'll have seen in the news about the bodies found in the drain at Whitley.'

Keane didn't reply for a moment. He stared at Joe across the top of his coffee. 'What would that have to do with me?'

'We suspect one of the victims was known to you.'

'I know lots of people.' No outright denial. No question about the name of the man. Joe found that interesting.

'A guy named Robbie Marshall. He went missing in the mid-nineties.'

'I heard the name when I was growing up.'

'Of course you did.' Joe felt like punching the air. He hadn't realized it would be so easy to get even this much of an admission of contact between the men. 'Everyone who lived in Wallsend knew the name. Not a real player himself, but a kind of fixer.'

'You went to Robbie Marshall if you were looking for work. When I was a kid he could get you into the shipyard.' Gary crumbled the croissant between his fingers. 'Even later, when it was taken over by the administrators, there were bits and pieces on contract.'

'And he could find people other kinds of work. Out in the country.'

'If you were that way inclined,' Keane conceded. 'I never was myself.'

'Did you ever work for him then?' Now Joe really was interested.

'Are you saying that was him? The body in the drain?'

'No confirmation yet, but it looks like it.'

Outside in the street other shops were starting to open. A young lad and lass, maybe on their way to college, stopped in the garden to kiss. Joe felt a moment of envy. They had no responsibilities. Just time to walk hand-in-hand and kiss in the sun.

Joe repeated his question.

'I was always good at electronics,' Keane said. 'I was the only kid in my school to take computer science. It wasn't cool then. Not really. There were a few basic games. Not many people even had email. Occasionally Robbie asked me to do a bit for him. Nothing organized. Cash in hand. I set up a few PCs for him and his mates, showed them how to get started.'

'And you'd have been how old?'

'I dunno. Sixteen, seventeen. It was before Robbie went missing.' Keane licked his finger and gathered up the remaining crumbs on his plate, put them in his mouth.

'Do you remember the names of any of Robbie's mates?'

'There was a guy called John Brace.' Keane grinned and looked up. 'A detective. Bent. Like most of them then.'

'And your ex-father-in-law.'

'I should have known better than to get involved, shouldn't I?'

'Is that how you met Patty? Through Robbie Marshall and John Brace.'

Keane shook his head. 'Nah, she wasn't knocking around the scene when I knew Robbie. She'd have been too young. I'm ten years older than her. Anyway, she didn't track down her father until after we were married. So I didn't know what I was letting myself in for.'

'What *were* you letting yourself in for?'

'A free house, at first. Then a load of hassle.' Keane screwed up the cardboard coffee cup and lobbed it into a blue metal waste bin.

'What do you mean?'

'John Brace was an influential man. Still is, even in prison. First of all, he didn't like the way I treated Patty when we were married, and then he didn't like it when I left.'

'How did he make his displeasure known?'

'He sent a few of his associates round to pass on a warning. That was when I got out of the relationship. Patty had pretty well lost it by then, and I thought I'd be doing both of us a favour by calling it a day.' Keane looked out of the window. Joe wondered if he'd seen the young lovers too.

'Do you still see the kids?'

'Nah. Brace made it clear when I left that I should stay out of Patty's life.' There was a pause. 'A pity. Archie wasn't much more than a baby when I went, but he was bright, sparky. But like I say, Brace still has influence. It doesn't do to cross him.'

Joe wondered if Patty knew that John Brace had warned Keane off from seeing his children.

'Can you remember anyone else Robbie Marshall knocked around with?'

'They talked about someone they called "the Prof."' Keane paused for a moment, then added: 'I never met him, though. Then there was another chap called "Sinclair". Scottish. He ran a smart club down in Whitley. The Seagull. I set up a security system on the place for him, and Robbie was often hanging around there.'

Joe cheered again in his head. At least he had one name to give Vera – Sinclair. That was one offering to make her proud.

'What was Marshall doing at the club? Did he work there?'

Keane shook his head. 'He was waiting,' he said. 'Watching. Looking out for opportunities. That was Robbie's style.'

Joe wasn't sure what Keane meant by that, so he moved on. 'I understand you were a bit wild, back in the day.'

'Aye well, when you're young, sometimes you don't know how to hold your drink. I got into a bit of bother. We all have to grow up in the end.'

'Brace said you were a maniac.'

There was a pause. 'Maybe – it takes one to know one.'

Joe walked across the garden to get to his car. The young couple was still there, sitting on a bench, school bags at their feet. They didn't notice him when he passed.

Chapter Sixteen

The Elderly and Disabled Wing had its own dining room. There was a television fixed high on the wall and it seemed to be on all day, more as background noise for the prisoners who worked in the kitchen than as a focus of attention for anyone else in the room. John Brace didn't have to queue at the counter with the more able-bodied offenders. Each morning he wheeled himself to his usual table and an orderly brought his food to him. By now they knew what he liked and what he hated and they made every effort to please him. He had a reputation; he still had power on the outside and many of them had families who'd benefited from his generosity. Now an orderly in the regulation striped shirt and ill-fitting blue jeans approached with a tray. On it a bowl of cornflakes mixed with bran flakes, milk in a separate jug. Two slices of toast. Crisp, not soggy. The toast for the other men was made in a batch at the beginning of service and lay, growing soft and cold, until everyone arrived. John Brace's toast was made when the boys in the kitchen heard his wheelchair approaching down the corridor.

He thanked the orderly and looked up at the television for the local news headlines. He was expecting the discovery of Robbie Marshall's body to be at the top of the programme. Vera was a good officer, but even she wouldn't manage to keep that secret. Besides, Brace couldn't see why she'd want to. She'd be after all the information she could get, asking people to dig back into their memories more than twenty years to a warm June night by the seaside.

As he anticipated, the local news began with a long shot of St Mary's Island lighthouse, then a close-up of the tent built over the entrance of the culvert, the white-suited CSIs emerging, looking serious. The cliché of the crime scene. Brace thought he recognized one of them. Then the reporter started to speak. She was blonde and bonny. The breeze from the sea was catching her hair and on occasion she had to use the hand that was not holding the microphone to push it away from her face.

'The police have not yet released any information about the bodies found in the culvert near St Mary's Island early yesterday, though it appears that these were not recent deaths, and officers have said that local people should not consider themselves to be in danger. A press conference will be held later today.'

Brace stared at the television. *Bodies. The woman had said 'bodies'. Plural.* His mind was racing but he continued to eat slowly, methodically. He couldn't show any signs of emotion or anxiety, couldn't let on in any way that the news item had a special meaning for him. He tried to slow his pulse and to think about what had to be done next. It was the lack of control that was infuriating, the lack of immediate access to information. There were people he needed to speak to, but that wouldn't be possible until later. It would help if he knew what the police were thinking, but over the years he'd lost his influence within the force. It came to him again that perhaps he should just let it go. Let the police carry on the investigation in their own way. Perhaps it had been a mistake to involve Vera in the first place. He didn't have such a bad life in here. Vera Stanhope had been right about that.

Then he thought that he didn't have only himself to think about and, anyway, he'd never been one for taking the easy way out. He'd always taken risks and this might turn out to be the biggest gamble of his life. He remembered what he was missing on the outside and knew that he wanted to spend his last years away from this place. It was why he'd put up with the boredom for so long. He had plans and the possibility of a new life. He finished the last slice of toast and put his dishes tidily on the tray. The orderly appeared, apparently out of nowhere, to take it away. Brace felt a little calmer. He was working his way towards a strategy when an officer approached. Brace realized that he'd spoken to Vera on impulse, but now he needed to be ordered and rational. He needed a plan of campaign.

'You've got another visit today, John. Your former colleague again.'

Brace looked up and nodded. It was what he'd been expecting since seeing the news. 'Give me ten minutes to clean my teeth?'

'Sure, why not?' The officer stretched and yawned. 'Let's make *them* wait for a change.'

Brace smiled easily and wheeled himself towards his cell. Although he waved to fellow inmates on the way and it would have been impossible for them to recognize any change of mood, he knew that he was becoming someone quite different. He had to be a kind of detective again, wily and untrusting. Making things happen. Vera might be determined to discover what had happened that summer night more than twenty years before, but he had to follow his own agenda. He couldn't let her take control of the situation. There were people he needed to speak to. He needed to gather his friends around him again.

Chapter Seventeen

At the gate Vera felt as if she was being treated as a regular. The officers nodded her a greeting, asked her if she thought the weather would break any time soon. She was early, and staff members passed through the waiting room on the other side of the automatic door. Vera nodded to the chaplain who'd set up her original visit. He was with the woman from education who'd been running the A-level English group. They were laughing and chatting, and Vera wondered what the chaplain would make of the fact that his request for a senior officer to speak to the men on the EDW had led to the discovery of two bodies. Then the flow of staff stopped. It seemed to Vera that she'd been waiting for a long time and she was just about to shout through to ask what was going on, when an officer came to take her to the interview suite. Brace was already there. They were in the same room as before and he was settled in his wheelchair on the side of the table nearest to the door. She had to squeeze past him to take her seat.

'You'll have seen the news!' She spoke before she even sat down. Before she'd arrived, she'd been determined to be angry, and the wait had made the fury real; it had fuelled her sense of righteous indignation.

'I hope you've got a bloody good explanation, John Brace.' She collapsed on the plastic chair and made herself shut up; this wasn't a time for self-indulgence. She stared across the table at him as the silence lengthened.

'I didn't know,' he said. 'Honestly, Vera, I didn't know. I was as shocked as you must have been to know that someone else was buried down there.'

'So what are you telling me? That you didn't notice the body already stuffed into the exact spot where you'd decided to hide Robbie Marshall? Come on, Brace, you can dream up a better excuse than that.' But her anger was already starting to dissipate. Something about the way he was sitting, looking unexpectedly old and ill, made her pause for a moment and wait for his response. Then she reminded herself that he'd always been a con man, and age wouldn't change him.

'Really, I didn't see anything. It was dark and I wasn't hanging around.'

'So it's pure coincidence that you and some other bastard chose the same place to hide a body?' Allowing her voice to rise into a shout.

'I know it sounds crazy, but I can't think of any explanation. The first body could have been there for years, before I turned up with Robbie. We both know it's hard to age a corpse when it's been in the ground that long.'

Vera stared at him. 'You do realize you're still our prime suspect for both murders? Any forensic evidence and you're bound to be charged.'

'There might be forensic evidence. I admitted I was there. But I gave you the information about Robbie in the first place. Why would I do that?'

Vera wasn't sure she had an answer. She stood up, frustrated. She'd come to Warkworth hoping for *answers*. All she'd ended up with were more questions.

At the door she stopped and looked back at him. 'The second body couldn't belong to Mary-Frances Lascuola?'

There was a moment of silence before he spoke. 'How the hell would I know? We had a fling. I thought she was a bit special. She was the mother of my child. But she was an addict and she couldn't give up, and I couldn't handle that. We'd lost touch years before Robbie Marshall disappeared. I guess it's possible she ended up in a grave in Whitley Bay. Probable even. But if she did, that had nothing to do with me.'

In the car park Vera got her phone from the glove compartment and checked her messages. The first was from Dr Keating, the pathologist. 'I've made a start on the bones. Come along to the mortuary early this afternoon and I might have some news for you. Valerie Malcolm, the forensic anthropologist, will be joining us.' The next was a voicemail from Brace's ex-wife. Peremptory and unemotional. 'I saw the news this morning, Inspector. I need to speak to you. I'll wait in until you arrive.'

Vera drove straight to Ponteland and the grand and rather ugly house where Brace had once lived with his wife. Judith opened the door immediately. 'I've just made some coffee, come through.' Despite the apparent welcome, the words sounded graceless and awkward. Once again they sat in the kitchen. Vera found it hard to imagine John Brace in this space, with its granite worktops and fancy gadgets. Had he made himself a bacon sandwich here, eaten pizza out of a box at the end of a long shift?

'Have you got any information for me?' Vera looked at the woman.

'Information? No! Why?'

'You phoned me and asked me to call on you. I'm in the middle of a murder investigation. You were married to a detective long enough to know I'll be a bit busy for social visits.' Vera nodded to the blue glazed mug on the table in front of her. 'I'd go a long way for a decent cup of coffee, but not this far.'

'You've found Robbie Marshall.'

'No confirmation of that yet. We've found a body.' A pause. 'Two bodies.' Vera looked up. 'Any idea who the second might belong to?'

'That's why I wanted to speak to you.'

'You have an idea who might be buried in there?'

Judith shook her head. 'Nothing like that. I wanted to tell you that if you think John is a double murderer, you're making a mistake.'

'He's in prison because he was involved in the death of a gamekeeper called Glen Fenwick.' Vera thought it was too easy to forget that. Brace wasn't only a corrupt cop who'd used his office to rake in the cash; he'd set up his own business selling muscle to country landowners, and a lovely woman was a widow as a result.

'No! He hired those men to frighten Fenwick off, not to kill him. They were wild, off their heads with drink and drugs. John was devastated when he found out what they'd done.' Judith paused for a moment.

'John wouldn't kill anyone. He certainly wouldn't have killed Robbie Marshall, whatever the provocation or circumstance. The one thing you need to know about John is that he's a sentimental man. I know everyone thought he married me for my money, but it wasn't like that. We loved each other for a while, until it all went sour. And for John, friendship is more important than a marriage. He might have given his life for Robbie Marshall, but he wouldn't have killed him.'

Vera remembered Brace's passion as he'd spoken about his daughter and thought Judith was probably right. He was a very sentimental man. 'Everything points to the first body being Marshall's,' she said. 'Do you have any idea who else might have been buried with him?'

Judith thought for a moment. 'I'm sorry, I was telling the truth when I said I didn't really know Robbie. I made an effort to get on with John's friends when we were first married. Some of it, I even enjoyed. The walks in the hills. All that exercise and fresh air. Then ending up for the night in some pub miles from anywhere.'

'You'll have met Hector, then?'

'Big man? Rather jolly.'

Was he jolly? Perhaps if he was trying to impress a bonny lass like you. A rich bonny lass. And he was big then, before the drink addled his mind and his brain stopped reminding him to eat.

Judith was still talking. 'But all the stuff that went along with it. Trading in birds' eggs. Skinning and stuffing dead animals. The sense that the rest of the world didn't understand that *they* were actually the custodians of the countryside. All that seemed rather ridiculous. I disliked it even before I understood that it was illegal and dangerous.'

'So there were three friends: John, Robbie and Hector.' Vera found herself warming to the woman, liking her even. 'But they called themselves the Gang of Four, so there was someone else. The Prof. Did you ever meet him?'

Judith shook her head. 'I don't think he was local. They talked about him in hushed terms: "The Prof. might be coming down next weekend." As if he was almost a legendary figure. He was certainly the leader, the organizer.'

'They talked about him coming *down*, not up?'

'I think so, yes.' She frowned. 'It was a long time ago.'

Which meant that he might be Scottish, but that didn't help a lot to identify him. Vera thought Judith was right and the group had been ridiculous. Grown men playing at Enid Blyton, with their adventures on the hills, their picnics and their elaborate ruses to escape capture. Their strange sense of honour. But the result of their antics had been deadly serious: two bodies left rotting for twenty years in an ancient drain.

'The second body was smaller. Probably a woman. Do you have any idea who that might have been? Did Robbie Marshall have a girlfriend?' It occurred to Vera that Robbie might have combined business with pleasure that night.

There was a moment of silence. Judith seemed to be making a genuine effort to remember. 'He certainly didn't bring anyone along when he was out in the hills with John. I had the impression that I should feel honoured to be a part of those expeditions, and that I was the only woman who'd ever been invited to join them. But there was one night when we all went out for a meal in Whitley. It would have been the early eighties. A little family-run Italian restaurant in one of the streets that runs off the sea front. I can't remember the name. I think we were the only people there. Perhaps it had even been booked by John for our own private dinner. He liked making those sorts of gestures. Robbie had a woman with him then.'

'Did she have a name?'

'Well, of course she had a name. Whether I can remember it is another matter altogether.' The old spikiness had returned.

Vera waited.

'She was rather glamorous,' Judith said. 'Big hair and big boobs. Not exactly tarty, but left nothing to the imagination. I was surprised. Robbie always came across as quiet. Not shy, but socially awkward. Cold even. He never made any effort at all to get on with me. I was prepared to be snooty about the woman, but in fact I really liked her. She made us all laugh. I wasn't drinking because I'd just found out I was pregnant. That was the first time, and it all seemed very exciting and special. I'd only told John. The others were drinking a lot.' She paused and Vera saw she was back in that little restaurant, savouring the secret of her pregnancy. 'She was called Elaine. I don't think I was ever told a second name. She worked in one of the clubs in Whitley.'

'Is that how John and Robbie knew her? Through her work?'

'Perhaps,' Judith said. 'But Elaine didn't work front-of-house. She was a kind of PA for the owner. She had some brilliant stories about the things that went on there.'

'Elaine. You're sure you can't remember a second name?'

'Quite sure. As I said, I don't think I ever knew it. And that was the only time I met her. John mentioned her a couple of times after that, in relation to Robbie, but I doubt if they were still an item when Robbie disappeared.'

'Any idea of the club where she worked?' Vera was starting to think that it might have been worth making the trek to Ponteland after all.

There was another moment of silence. 'It was called "The Seagull",' Judith said at last. 'It doesn't exist any more. It was knocked down a long time ago. There'd been a fire. It didn't burn to the ground, but it was never rebuilt. It ended up just an eyesore.'

Vera remembered The Seagull so well, partly because Hector had scoffed at the name. *Seagull? What's a seagull? There are herring gulls, black-headed gulls, common gulls. But there's no such species as a seagull.* And yet Vera thought he'd been in there, despite deriding its name. Not as a regular, but on special occasions with the Gang of Four. She pictured him at home, dressing up for a rare night out, and coming back the next day, probably still too pissed to be driving legally. On one occasion smelling of a woman's perfume, with lipstick stains on his only good white shirt.

Judith was still talking. 'I think there's a plan to build luxury apartments there now. It was right on the sea front, so there'd be a terrific view.' Another silence, and again she seemed to have travelled back in time to the first years of her marriage, the time when she still believed in John Brace and anything appeared possible. 'But it was brilliant then. A bit more sophisticated than some of the places in the town. It didn't attract the underage drinkers or the folk just wanting a wild night out. It did classy cocktails and real food. There was live music – jazz mostly – and a terrace where you could sit to watch the tide come in.'

'I remember it.' And Vera could picture the building, gleaming white, with its 1930s curved lines and a blue neon gull on the side. More California than Tyneside. But she'd never been inside. Unlike Hector, she'd never had anybody to go with.

Chapter Eighteen

Holly found Laura Webb through a friend of Charlie's who'd once worked in Vice and had the woman's address. She was still living in Whitley Bay, but when Holly knocked at the door of the little terraced house there was no answer. There were small front gardens facing out to a narrow street, and next door a woman sat on the grass watching her toddler play.

'She'll be at work at this time.' The woman seemed friendly enough.

'Oh?' Holly wasn't quite sure what else to say. Laura had a record for soliciting as long as her arm, though there'd been nothing for years. Surely she'd be too old to be working the streets these days. Besides, this seemed a very respectable neighbourhood.

'Yeah, she runs the yoga centre at the metro station. You should catch her there, though she might be teaching a class. You can always grab a coffee next door if you have to wait.'

Holly drove back to the sea front, left her car there and walked inland along the wide avenue that led towards the station. Even she remembered when this street had been heaving with people, especially on bank holidays. People had started drinking first thing in the morning and carried on all day, staggering from one bar to another. There'd been lunchtime strippers, and bar staff wearing so little that they could have been stripping themselves. Whitley had attracted hen- and stag-parties then, women in halos and wings, and men in corsets and fishnets; they'd come in minibuses and stayed in the cheap B&Bs. Some of her male colleagues had called South Parade 'Fanny Alley', had made detours so they could drive along it to eye up the teenage girls who were out partying for the first time, in skirts that left nothing to the imagination and tottering on heels, so that they looked like kids dressing up in their mothers' clothes.

Now most of the bars and clubs were closed, the windows shuttered or covered with hardboard. The street had lost its brash energy and postcard humour as well as its sleaze. There were more estate agents' 'For Sale' notices than neon. A plastic palm tree lay on its side outside the Blue Lagoon, and all the guest houses showed that they had vacancies and that contractors would be welcome. Holly supposed that soon the developers would come along, turn the empty bars and hotels into desirable flats. Gentrification was already happening on other streets. Already at the seaward end of South Parade there was a smart new Italian restaurant and something that called itself a gastropub.

The metro station had a glass roof that must once have been very grand, spanning the lines and both platforms, but now many of the panes had been removed and there were spikes on all the metal struts to keep the pigeons off. The ticketing was by machine these days, but the buildings that had once housed the station staff and waiting room remained. There was a clock tower and an arch to the town, photos of pre-war crowds streaming away from the platforms towards the sea. Now a couple of elderly women waited for the train towards Newcastle and chatted about last night's television.

Part of the redundant ticket office had been turned into a cafe, with tables and chairs outside. A big woman was drinking a latte while a dog by her side drank water from a bowl. The yoga centre was next door and, as Holly approached, the door opened and a group of people in leggings and T-shirts began to spill out onto the platform. The woman Holly assumed to be Laura stood in the doorway and waved them good-bye, then turned to greet Holly.

'Do you want to sign up? Our beginners' group starts in half an hour. We're pretty busy, but I'm sure we can squeeze you in.' Efficient and friendly. She was in late middle age now, but still striking: cheek-bones to die for, a face like a sculpture, very short hair. When Holly didn't answer immediately she contin-ued, 'It's all very gentle, at least to start with. Nothing to be nervous about.'

'Laura Webb?'

'Yes.'

'I wondered if I could ask a few questions.' Holly showed her warrant card, attempting discretion. They were still in the doorway between the centre and the platform, and the woman with the dog could hear every word. 'I'm hoping you can help.'

'What's this about?'

Holly hesitated, but the woman in the cafe seemed oblivious to the conversation. 'The bodies we found near St Mary's. You'll have heard?'

Laura nodded. 'It's all the groups have been talk-ing about since the news got out.' She led Holly into the building, which seemed suddenly shadowy and cool after the bright sunlight captured under the glass station roof. There was a polished wood floor, and bubbled windows high in the two facing walls. Laura unrolled a couple of yoga mats and sat on one, legs curled to her side. She nodded to the other and Holly took it, wondering for a moment what Vera would have made of that and whether she'd have been able to get on her feet again after the interview. A train rattled past, then came to a stop.

'I'm trying to track down a woman called Mary-Frances Lascuola. She seemed to disappear around the mid-eighties.'

'You think one of the bodies could be her?' Laura had her head turned to one side, so she wasn't looking directly at Holly. She sat very still; with her head turned in one direction and her legs in the other, she could have been holding a yoga pose.

'It's possible. We don't know anything for certain yet.'

'I knew Mary-Frances,' Laura said. 'You must be aware of my past or you wouldn't be here. Mary and I lived and worked together for a while. You know how sometimes you drift in and out of people's lives. We met up in a bail hostel in Shields and then rented a flat not very far from here. Both of us determined to stay clean.' She paused. 'We even got proper jobs for a while, waitressing in a club on the front. The Seagull.'

'Well, *you* stayed clean, at least.' Holly was finding it hard to imagine this strong and competent woman as an addict, picking up men on the streets to pay for her next fix.

'Not then. Not for long. Mary was the one who'd started pulling her life together, when we were living in the flat in Whitley. I couldn't stop.' There was no emotion in the woman's voice. She could have been talking about a stranger. 'I lost the job in The Seagull very quickly – I was far too unreliable. Mary stuck with it for a bit, then had a massive relapse and she got the sack too. The last time we were together we were attending a rehab place in Bebington. It was a day-centre, not residential, and we were still living together in the flat. The project worked for me. Not for Mary, though. She dropped out and I never saw her again.'

'When was that?'

Laura shrugged as if the dates didn't matter. Holly thought she was remembering the friend who'd disappeared from her life.

'Did you check at the club where she'd been working previously?' Holly tried to picture this chaotic seaside existence of loose connections: seasonal workers, drifters, ex-offenders. No wonder Mary-Frances had found it easy to disappear.

'No. I didn't try very hard to find her. Addicts are selfish creatures and I was focused on keeping myself straight.'

'What was the name of the rehab place?'

'Shaftoe House. It's a big Victorian pile in the middle of the town. It used to belong to a pit-owner, then it became part of a mental-health hospital. It's still there, still helping people with their recovery, but it's run by a charity now.' Laura paused. 'I go in for an afternoon a week to run a yoga and meditation class.'

'We were told that Mary-Frances had died,' Holly said, 'but we can't find confirmation. Did she use any other names?'

Laura shook her head. 'Not when I knew her. She was very proud of being part-Italian. It seemed very exotic to the rest of us.'

'She had a baby in 1983. Did you know Mary-Frances when she was pregnant?'

'No, by the time I knew her, the baby was already in care. She talked about her sometimes. You know, those sentimental conversations you have late at night. She'd imagine what the bairn would look like, if she'd started nursery. Sometimes she made out she felt guilty, but really she knew it had been the right thing to give her up for adoption.'

'Did she tell you about the father?'

Laura turned her head slowly, so she was looking at Holly for the first time.

'The bent cop, you mean.'

Holly knew it was ridiculous, but she felt herself blushing. It was as if she was being accused, along with her whole profession. 'Did you know him?'

'He came to the flat a couple of times, flashing his money around, sweeping Mary off to some smart hotel.' A train pulled to a stop and outside there were passengers' voices: teenage lads swearing. 'Always showing off, always making out that he was in control and better than the rest of us. He was famous for promising to drop the charges against us, in return for sex. All the girls knew him.'

'How did he treat Mary-Frances? Was he ever violent?'

The answer was immediate. 'No! John Brace was a

bastard to the rest of the world but, you know, I really think he cared for *her*.'

'Despite wanting sex with other women?'

'Oh, he wouldn't have seen any contradiction in that.' Laura seemed to be searching for the right words. 'He had that sense of entitlement. Because he was a bloke and a cop. It was a kind of weird power-trip. And it was a different time then, you know?'

Holly thought she didn't really know at all. 'So the last time you saw Mary-Frances was when she disappeared from Shaftoe House?'

'That's right. Occasionally I imagined I caught glimpses of her after that. Once I was walking down Northumberland Street in Newcastle and I thought I recognized her in the distance. But it was just before Christmas and the street was packed so tight you could hardly move. I couldn't catch up with her. Another time I was on the metro. Someone got off at Cullercoats and that could have been her, but I only caught a glimpse of her back. I think more likely I was daydreaming. Letting the ghosts of my past come back to haunt me.' Laura smiled. 'They bother me less than they used to.'

'Did you ever meet a guy called Robbie Marshall? He was a friend of John Brace, worked at Swan Hunter's?'

Laura seemed to consider for a moment before speaking. 'Maybe. The name's familiar. It was a long time ago. And I knew lots of men back then.'

'Is there anyone else I can speak to? Any other women who might have more information about Mary-Frances? Family?'

'Her parents both died when she was in her early

twenties. I don't think there was any other family.' She looked at her watch. 'The next class will be in soon. I should open the door for them.'

'Friends, then? People she worked with at The Seagull perhaps?'

Laura was distracted now. 'I was never in with that crowd. Like I said, I was sacked after a couple of months. Besides, I didn't really fit in.' She paused. 'Even pissed or drugged, I didn't like some of the things that went on there. Flash guys acting like film stars, thinking money could buy them whatever they wanted.' Another pause. 'You could ask the bloke who used to own the place if Mary got close to any of the staff. He's a Scot called Sinclair. Whitley's Mr Big, if you believed his own hype. He's a reformed character now, a community leader, member of every committee going.' A pause. 'I always thought he was a bit of a creep.' She got to her feet with one supple movement. 'I doubt he'd remember after all this time, but it's worth asking.

Holly scrambled to stand too. 'Any idea where I can find him?'

'Maybe at the office at the Dome. He's a consultant with the sea-front regeneration project. Trying to recapture the town's past.' The words were dismissive. 'Or his own.'

Chapter Nineteen

Vera stood in the mortuary next to Paul Keating and took in that special scent of disinfectant and decay. She'd never been squeamish and these bones, spread out over two tables, were so distanced from a living, breathing human that she found it hard to feel emotional about them. Scraps of clothing were still attached in places, but so degraded that Vera thought they'd be unlikely to tell them much. Keating hadn't been alone in the room when Vera had arrived. He'd been talking to a woman who was as tall as he was, a little stooped, as if she'd grown up apologizing for her height. She wore thick-rimmed glasses that gave her an air of academic austerity.

'This is Valerie Malcolm, the forensic anthropologist from the university.'

Vera had heard of her and knew she had a good reputation. Bodies didn't usually stay in the ground for very long in the UK, so forensic anthropologists had little experience unless they worked abroad. Malcolm had been based in the US for years. There, because of the vast spaces between communities and the unexplored areas of wilderness, it was easier to make people disappear and bodies stayed hidden for longer.

The door opened again and Billy Cartwright, her favourite crime-scene manager, scuttled in.

'I thought you were on holiday for another couple of days.' But Vera was delighted to see him; her team was complete.

'The plane got in this morning and I knew you'd never manage without my expertise.'

'You and your young lass had enough of each other, have you?' Vera let the innuendo stretch. Billy shrugged and grinned and knew better than to respond. Malcolm was already looking at the bones on the first table and seemed not to be aware of the exchange.

'The first individual is clearly adult male,' Keating said.

'Not a young man.' Valerie Malcolm looked up from the table. 'You get a feel for younger bones. They're suppler and more moist.' It seemed an odd description for bone, but Vera said nothing and the anthropologist continued, 'And there's no athleticism here. But no sign of arthritis or other major damage, either. A little wear on the spine. This was a man in middle age, I'd say. Healthy enough but not super-fit.'

'How do you know it's a man?' Vera wasn't questioning the woman's judgement; she was curious. 'You get big women.' *Like me. And you.*

'The size of the bones. Of course there's always some gender overlap, but in this case I'd say it was conclusive. Look at the skull and those pronounced orbital ridges. The facial features are all larger than you'd expect to find in a female.' The woman was leaning right over the table, so her face was very close to the bones. It was almost as if she was smelling them, then Vera realized that, even wearing glasses, she was short-sighted. She was simply examining them very closely. 'There's a little irregularity here. This man broke his arm at some point. If you have a putative identification, we should be able to confirm it. That's if we can track down the X-rays that would have been taken at the time.'

Vera thought that Eleanor, Robbie's doting mother, would certainly be able to help with that. She'd remember the name of Marshall's GP, the hospital where the broken arm was fixed. It seemed a sort of magic: all this information from a heap of bones. Alchemy, like turning straw into gold. Valerie had taken an instrument from her bag and was measuring one of the larger bones. 'I should be able to give you an estimate of how tall he was. The length of the femur is usually about twenty-seven per cent of the full height.' There was a pause as she seemed to be doing the sums in her head. Vera admired the mental arithmetic almost more than the way the woman was creating an accurate physical picture of the victim out of so little. *She* struggled to do any kind of maths, even with a pen and paper.

'I'd say he was just over six foot.' Valerie looked up. 'Does that tally?'

'I don't know, but I can check with a relative. We already have contact with the mother.'

'And there's some dental work. That should be definitive, if the dental records still exist.'

'His mother should be able to help with that too.' Vera paused. 'Any chance you could give us a cause of death? Or would that be pushing my luck?'

'Ah.' For a moment the anthropologist took her

attention away from the skeleton. 'Well, of course we have to be careful about that. Even if we find signs of an injury, there's no absolute guarantee that it caused the fatality. For instance, a nick to the rib might mean that a knife caught the bone on its way to the heart. But it might have been a relatively superficial wound, with a soft-tissue injury being the real cause of death. And sometimes substantial damage has been caused post-mortem.'

'But in this case . . .' Vera was starting to like this woman, her enthusiasm and passion for her work. Her rigour. And the fact that she didn't talk to Vera as if she were a six-year-old or a moron.

'In this case, I think we can be pretty certain that death was caused by blunt-force trauma to the back of the skull.'

'The guy was hit over the head with a heavy instrument.' Vera wasn't sure that fitted in with their theories about what might have happened on the night in June more than twenty years before. She'd been coming to the conclusion that if John Brace hadn't been involved, this was some kind of gangland murder: serious criminals settling old scores. But Robbie wouldn't have turned his back on those people, and they'd have been more likely to use a gun or a knife. Something more clinical and more certain. She pushed those ideas to the back of her mind and turned to the CSI.

'So what have you got for us, Billy? Give us the benefit of your wisdom.'

'There's very little clothing left on this one. I'm guessing he was mostly wearing natural fibres, cotton and wool that would have degraded quickly. But we do have his boots. Leather, size ten. Good-quality, but I think they'd have been quite old even when he was killed. You can see the wear on the sole. And there's a belt. It has a buckle shaped like a ship. Distinctive. Again I'd have thought a relative would recognize it.'

Vera nodded. She was thinking she'd go to see Eleanor immediately after finishing here, and that would get them all the confirmation they needed. There'd be enough to work on while they were waiting for X-rays and dental records. She thought Eleanor would be pleased to know that her son hadn't run away and left her. She'd be glad to have even these bones to bury. Perhaps that would allow her some peace in her remaining years.

Billy was turning his attention to the second body. 'This person was wearing mostly man-made fibre and there's much less degradation. All that time ago the industry didn't have the same anxieties about material hanging around in landfill sites for generations, and some of it will last forever, even in situations like our crime scene. A lot of the fabric has disappeared, of course. Nothing rats like better than a bit of nylon to build their nests. But there's enough left to give us a bit of an idea about what she was wearing.'

'She? You're saying this is definitely a woman?' Vera looked towards Valerie Malcolm for support.

The anthropologist nodded. 'Oh yes, I'd say so. I had a look earlier. The pelvic bone is reasonably intact and the features on the skull are smaller. This is a much more delicate body altogether.'

'Besides,' Billy said, 'unless we're looking at a cross-dresser, I can't see a bloke going out for the evening in lacy black underwear. There are only a few fragments left, but they're quite obvious when you look for them.'

So perhaps this is Mary-Frances Lascuola. But we haven't got any record of her since the mid-eighties, not very long after she gave up her daughter for adoption. No record of her offending, of her working. So where had she been hiding in the years before she ended up in a drain near St Mary's? Or had she been placed there at the time she dropped out of sight, and was she still lying there when Brace pushed Robbie Marshall's body in after her?

'Can we tell if she died at the same time as the man?'

Malcolm and Keating shook their heads almost in unison. 'You know pin-pointing time of death is tricky, even when the body's much more recent.' Keating sounded disapproving, as if Vera had failed to learn an obvious lesson.

'So she could have been in the culvert for ten years before the second body was put in?'

'Absolutely no reason at all why not.'

Vera wished the anthropologist didn't sound quite so cheerful. 'I thought you could narrow stuff down with the entomology.' Now she was clutching at straws.

'You could talk to a forensic entomologist, but I'd say it was unlikely to get anything helpful after all this time.'

'There are no shoes for the woman,' Billy said, 'and that seems a bit odd. She'd either be wearing leather or plastic and you'd think they'd still be intact.'

'Perhaps she didn't die on the coast that night. If they brought her in the boot of a car, for example, her shoes might have been left behind.'

'And put her in the same culvert as the first body, but later?' This was Valerie Malcolm. 'Because they thought it was a decent hiding place?'

'Perhaps. John Brace admits to putting Marshall there, but claims to know nothing about the second body. If he's telling the truth, and that's a bloody big "if", then perhaps he was seen.'

'And someone with a dead woman to dispose of thought it'd be a great place to get rid of her. I suppose there is a weird kind of logic to it. If Brace was implicated in the first murder, we'd assume he'd done the second too.' Billy looked up and grinned. 'What is it about you and complex crime scenes, Vera Stanhope? What do you do to attract them?'

Vera ignored that. 'Any idea of age on this one?'

'Younger than the man,' Valerie Malcolm said, 'and considerably shorter. Five foot five. Something like that.' She looked up. 'No dental work.'

'What does that tell us?' Vera had been expecting the same wealth of information as with the male and was starting to feel impatient, disappointed that they didn't seem able to bring the woman to life in the same way.

'Maybe just that she had better teeth. Fluoride toothpaste has done a lot to curb tooth decay. Or that she didn't have access to dental care.'

'Cause of death?'

'I don't think I can help with that, either. There are just fewer bones for this one. I assume they've been scattered by predators and the smaller ones could have been washed through gaps in the boulders at a high tide.' Valerie looked up. 'Sorry I can't be more help.'

'Not your fault, pet. And you've worked a marvel on the first one.' Vera looked across to Billy. 'Did your guys come across anything at the scene that might help with ID? A bit of jewellery maybe?'

'You know we'd have told you as soon as we found it, if we'd come across anything useful.' Billy pretended to look hurt.

'Aye well, *you* might, but I'm not sure about that chap who was in charge while you were away gallivanting.'

'The team is still there,' Billy said. 'They've expanded the search back up the drain and out towards the shore. I'm heading up there now. We find anything at all and you'll be the first to know.'

Vera found herself beaming.

Afterwards she and Billy stood together outside the mortuary. 'I could do with some help here, Billy.' She was leaning back against her car, enjoying the sun on her face. 'Anything at all to identify that woman. Tell your team to pull out all the stops.'

'No need to tell them that. Not my guys.' He walked away without saying goodbye and she realized she'd offended him and could have kicked herself for being so tactless.

Chapter Twenty

Eleanor Marshall was waiting for Vera. Vera thought she'd been waiting in her tidy house in Wallsend since news of the bodies at St Mary's had hit the headlines. She'd taken her seat in the living room, next to the window with its starched net curtains, and all day she'd looked down the street until she'd seen Vera's car pulling up outside. There was even a tray prepared in the kitchen: two cups on matching saucers, a jar of instant coffee and a bowl with teabags, chocolate digestives still in their packet on a plate, an empty milk jug waiting to be filled. No doubt the kettle just needed to be switched on. She'd had too much pride to telephone the police station – she'd been rebuffed too many times in the past – but she'd trusted Vera enough to know she'd be there as soon as there was anything to say.

Vera made the tea before they started speaking. It seemed part of a necessary ritual. After all this time there was no rush and Eleanor hadn't clamoured for information as soon as the door was opened.

'You've found him,' the old lady said. The tray was on the small round table with its embroidered cloth. Vera poured tea and milk.

'Nothing definite yet.' Vera took a biscuit. During

an investigation you ate when you could. 'I'm hoping you'll be able to help with that.'

'Of course.' She sounded grateful. At last she was being involved. At last there was something she could do.

'Did Robbie ever break his arm?'

'Yes. It was one winter, not many years before he went missing. He slipped on the ice, just walking out of the house, and fell awkwardly, said he felt like a clumsy fool. He was in a cast for weeks, but he still went into work and did as much as he could in the yard.'

Vera nodded to show she knew he'd been a conscientious man. 'We'll need the name of his GP. Where did he go to get it fixed?'

'Rake Lane Hospital. His GP was called Dr King. I think he retired years ago. The surgery's still there, though, just the other side of the park.'

Vera nodded again.

'And where did he go to the dentist?' A pause. 'You do understand all this will help identify him?'

'I know.' The woman gave a little grin. 'I watch all those detective shows on the TV. I'm addicted to them. Daft really, when I knew something violent must have happened to him, but they help me escape somehow. And the police on television always do get the killer in the end. His dentist was Moira Armstrong in Howden. She's getting on now but she's still practising.'

'We found a belt,' Vera said.

The woman's face lit up. 'I know the one. He always wore it. He bought it when he was away in Texas on one of his birdwatching trips with John Brace.

It had a ship on the buckle, and it seemed right for him. Because he worked in the shipyard. You know.'

'That's the belt we found.' Vera waited a moment so that the information had time to sink in, but Eleanor had known since she'd seen the local news that they'd found her son. 'We'll check with the X-rays at the hospital and the dental records, but I think we've found Robbie.' Another pause. 'He was murdered, Eleanor, but I'm sure you've worked that out already. He didn't put himself in that hole in the ground. Can you think of anyone who might have wanted to kill him?'

The woman shook her head. 'I think he must have had a life that I knew nothing about. At home he was a loving son, and nobody would have wanted to hurt him.'

'You'll have seen from the news that they found two bodies where he was buried. It seems certain that the other belonged to a woman. Do you know who that might have been? I know I asked you before about girlfriends, but perhaps you've had time to think about it. Even if he didn't bring her home, maybe he said something.'

'I *have* been thinking,' Eleanor said. She stared out of the window. 'I would have liked it if he'd married and had children. I told you I was a teacher before I married. I joked to him about it, told him to find someone quickly before it was too late and I got too old to play with my grand-bairns. He said I was the only girl for him. I didn't believe that. Not really. Perhaps he thought I wouldn't approve of the women he was seeing. I wondered if maybe he'd found someone on his travels abroad; I wouldn't have minded a foreign lass, as long as she made him happy. But he didn't bring anyone home. There were nights he stayed out. He told me he was with John and Hector, but he could have been with girls then.'

'A woman went missing sometime before Robbie. It's possible that hers is the second body. She was called Mary-Frances Lascuola. Does the name mean anything to you?' Vera watched Eleanor for some reaction but she only looked puzzled.

'So he *was* seeing a foreigner? No, Robbie never mentioned seeing a woman with that name. I'd have remembered it.'

'Mary was British,' Vera said. 'You wouldn't have known about her background if you'd met her.'

But the woman only shook her head again. She seemed more distressed about the secrets that her son had been keeping from her than by the confirmation of his death.

Back in the police station, the team came together over tea and buns to compare notes. The official briefing would be later in the day, but this was the core group: Vera, Joe, Holly and Charlie. According to Vera, the people who mattered.

'So you've both come up with the same name.' She nodded towards Joe and Holly, and crumbs from an iced finger spilled across the desk. 'A Scot called Sinclair. Mean anything to you, Charlie?'

He nodded. 'He ran a club called The Seagull. It had a classy reputation. Drinks you'd need a mortgage to pay for, and the place to go if you wanted to meet famous footballers and their women, rock stars, actors.

The Newcastle business mafia took it over at week-ends.'

'Judith Brace mentioned The Seagull to me.' Vera pictured the club again in its heyday. The height of glamour. When she was a kid it had been her dream to get taken there, to drink cocktails on the terrace facing the sea. She imagined Hector there with John Brace and his cronies. She found it hard to believe that her father would have enjoyed the experience – like her, he'd never been much good in civilized com-pany – but she felt an irrational stab of resentment all the same.

Holly broke into her thoughts. 'According to the woman I spoke to, Mary-Frances worked there for a while.'

Vera raised an eyebrow.

'She was a waitress, apparently,' Holly said. 'Not turning tricks. She was clean while she was there. It was supposed to be a fresh start. A new life.'

'Do we believe that? She wasn't just moving upmarket in the same profession?'

'She'd only have been doing that if it was with Sin-clair's permission,' Charlie said. 'He wouldn't have had freelancers working on his premises. He ran a very tight ship, did Gus Sinclair. He could be a charmer if he wanted to be – that was what his customers saw – but he was ruthless.'

'Mary-Frances was only there for a short time,' Holly said. 'Something sent her back on the drugs big-style and she ended up going to a rehab day-centre in Bebington called Shaftoe House. It's still going appar-ently, and I'm heading out there after we've finished here.'

'Apparently Gary Keane installed a security system in the club,' Joe said.

'What do we know about Sinclair now? The Seagull's been gone for years.'

'It was burned down,' Charlie said. 'Everyone assumed it was insurance fraud. Whitley was changing, and the kids from Newcastle, the stags and the hens from Glasgow weren't interested in champagne cocktails or fine dining. Word was Sinclair had it torched while it was still making him money, because he saw the way things were going.'

'It must have been investigated.' Vera wondered why she couldn't remember the fire. Her dreams of sophistication literally going up in smoke. She'd probably been caught up with something at the other end of the county.

But of course Charlie had the details. 'Sinclair had an alibi. Well, naturally he would. No way he would have done it himself, anyway.'

'And the alibi?'

Charlie gave a slow smile. 'He was at a police fund-raiser with half the force as witnesses.'

'Oh, a sense of humour,' Vera said. 'I do like a sense of humour in a villain.' A pause while she took the last Danish pastry before someone else could snaffle it. 'And what happened to Mr Sinclair after the demise of The Seagull?'

'He got a good payout.' Charlie frowned as if he was trying to remember the exact details and was disappointed that he couldn't come up with an accurate figure. 'After all, it was a going concern and the last set of books showed a good profit. Then he disappeared for a while. Maybe he thought it would be tactful to keep out of the way.'

'Do we have a date for the fire?' Vera thought this was like groping through the thickest of sea-frets. They needed something to make a connection with the killings.

'I'd need to check.' But she could tell Charlie was teasing. He knew what she wanted to hear.

'Not you!' Because sometimes he needed to be flattered. 'Not the man with a memory better than an elephant's.'

'It was 1995.' Charlie grinned. 'Midsummer. Early July. The start of the season, which was another reason why the investigators thought arson was unlikely. Why would you set fire to the club when it was just coming up to the most profitable time of the year?'

'To stop people being suspicious?' Holly sometimes didn't know when to keep quiet. It had been a rhetorical question. They all knew the way Charlie's mind was working, and now it was just time to let him run with the explanation.

He seemed not to mind the interruption, though. 'And because a poor summer season would give a stronger motive for the fire. It was better that Sinclair cut his losses while things were still looking good and got the insurance handout without too much fuss.' He drank the last of his tea.

'Any word on the street about who Sinclair might have got to commit the arson?'

Charlie shook his head. 'Lots of suggestions. Nothing definite.'

'So we have Robbie Marshall, who was known as

an informal recruitment officer of scallies from the estates. He found them as muscle for gamekeepers and landowners, but no reason at all why he might not have provided lads willing to set a fire. And we have Mary-Frances, who worked at one time as a waitress for Sinclair and who would have known her way around the club. She might have been useful for the arsonists too. And less than a month before the fire Marshall disappears, and now we have two bodies. Nobody's going to tell me that's a coincidence.' Vera was on her feet, drawing a plan on the whiteboard. Names and dates, and wavy lines making connections.

'And we have Gary Keane.' Joe had been quiet throughout the conversation, but now he sounded excited too. He was seeing the links, following her logic. 'If he fitted the security systems, he'd have known how to disable them so there'd be no record of the arsonists. He might even have known enough to trigger an electrical fault and cause a fire.'

'Would he talk to us, do you think?'

'Two people who might have been involved in the arson are dead,' Joe said. 'He might take some persuading.'

There was a moment of silence. They could hear the traffic in the street outside and the kids in the nearby schoolyard as they came out for their lunchtime play.

'Well, I can be very persuasive,' Vera said. 'I'd rather have a bit more information before I chat to him, though.'

'Sinclair's back in Whitley Bay now.' Holly had been making notes of her own but looked up from her computer. 'According to Laura Webb, who used to know Mary-Frances, he's the Mr Big of the seaside regeneration there.'

'I'd heard the name in connection with the re-development, but I didn't connect it with the Sinclair who owned The Seagull,' said Charlie. 'I thought he'd disappeared north permanently after the fire and, besides, he didn't strike me as a type who'd be into fund-raising and community activism.' There was a pause. 'People speak very highly of Sinclair these days. He's got an office near the Dome, not so far from where The Seagull used to be, and he lets all sorts of local groups use it. I should have made the link.'

'According to Judith Brace, they're building luxury apartments on the site of The Seagull,' Vera said. 'It'd be interesting to know if Sinclair still owns the land.'

'You think he's more bothered about turning a large profit than regenerating the town?' Charlie gave a little grin. 'That sounds more like the Gus Sinclair that I knew.'

'Maybe he's a reformed character.' Vera kept her voice light, so she might even have been serious. 'I'm told it does happen.' Another pause. 'Even John Brace claims to be reformed these days. He's turned into a compassionate family man.'

Chapter Twenty-One

Shaftoe House was on a quiet street surrounded by modern terraced houses and looked out of place, rather down-at-heel. Like a shabby, elderly woman surrounded by brash young teenagers. A little sign on the door gave its name and said it was run by the New Lives Project. There was a buzzer and Holly pressed it. A disembodied male voice asked for her name.

'Holly Clarke, Northumbria Police.'

'Just come on up.'

She pushed the door and it swung open. Inside, the place had the same air of abandonment as any institution after closing time. It held evidence of the day's activity – in some of the rooms there were whiteboards with scribbled notes, scraps of paper in the bins, a tray of dirty mugs – but now it was quiet. Without purpose. A man was coming down the wooden stairs to greet her. He was tall and gangly, in jeans and a loose striped cotton shirt. He held out his hand and, as the shirt slid back from his wrist, she saw a tattoo of a snake on his lower arm. It looked strangely incongruous. 'I'm Ian. Come up to the office. Would you like some coffee?' His voice was educated local. He led Holly up a wide staircase, which might once have been grand, into a room with a desk cluttered by paper.

ANN CLEEVES

'No, thanks.' Holly sat on a leather chair and looked out of the long sash window.

His office overlooked a wilderness of a garden. Some attempt had been made to clear a space close to the house, and a table and half a dozen chairs stood on an uneven patio. He followed her gaze. 'That's where the smokers hang out. Some addictions are hard to give up.'

'How long have you been here?'

'As a worker, for five years, but I was first here as a client when I was in my late teens.' He must have sensed her surprise. 'Most of the workers here are addicts in recovery. We understand what the clients are going through.'

'You can offer the sympathy that people need.'

'Often sympathy's the last thing on offer, though of course we can give support. More importantly, we can be tough. Recovery isn't just about stopping drinking or giving up drugs; it's about taking responsibility. Not easy, if you've been running away from it all your life. Perhaps we can be more honest than the professionals.'

'I'm here to ask about a former client,' Holly said. There was something about the man that she found compelling. His long fingers and intense face. The complete control. The smile. In another era he might have been a priest.

'Of course we might have issues with confidentiality.' He leaned forward towards her and frowned.

'We think the woman is dead,' Holly said. Ian was very close to her now and she found that she was looking at his hands, which were clasped together almost as if he was praying. 'Murdered. We need to

172

confirm her identity and then find the person who killed her.'

There was a silence. The man was still frowning, thinking.

It was Holly who spoke first. 'She was a friend of Laura Webb, the woman who runs yoga classes here.'

He looked up slowly. All his movements were deliberate. 'What's the name of the woman you're interested in?'

'Mary-Frances Lascuola.'

Another silence. 'When was she a client here?'

'Mid-eighties or early nineties.' Holly realized she hadn't pinned down Laura for an exact date. A big mistake. But perhaps Laura's life had been so chaotic then that she might not have remembered anyway.

'Shaftoe House was very different thirty years ago,' Ian said. 'It was in the grounds of a large psychiatric hospital. Although it was still a day-centre for people suffering from addiction, the model was medical and the staff were doctors, psychologists and mental-health nurses. The hospital was closed and demolished in 2006 and the rest of the grounds were sold for housing, but a charity, New Lives, took over this building. It was recognized that Bebington was an area where substance abuse was common and the facility was still needed. If the woman you're concerned about was a patient in Shaftoe before 2006, then any records will be with the health authority. We would have access to them only if she was referred here again.'

'Could you check if that happened?' Though Holly thought that was a waste of time. She was convinced that Mary-Frances had already been buried in the culvert for ten years when the charity had taken over

Shaftoe House. And if the woman had still been alive in 2006, she'd been using a different name.

Ian switched on the computer on his desk. Holly stared out of the window while the computer loaded. At last the man spoke. 'Nobody of that name has ever been a client of New Lives. Not here or at our residential centre in Kimmerston.'

Holly supposed there was nothing else she could learn from Ian. She could go back to Vera and tell her that she'd followed up the lead. But she didn't move.

'What exactly do you do here? Besides the yoga?'

'We follow the twelve-step programme. That's about fellowship, fellow addicts supporting one another. There are workshops too. One-to-one counselling. For some clients we provide basic skills education. It's about helping people to be more confident and self-reliant, and it's hard to feel confident if you can't read or write.' He smiled. 'You should come in when our folks are here. Chat to them when they're on a break. Addicts make up a large proportion of the prison population. In one sense we're in the same business. Crime prevention.'

Now Holly did stand up. In her head she was doing mental arithmetic. Ian looked as if he was in his late forties. If he'd been treated here as an addict when he was a teenager, he could have been at Shaftoe House at the same time as Mary-Frances and Laura. 'Did you meet Mary-Frances when you were here as a young man? You might remember the unusual name. And she was very beautiful, everyone says.'

Ian followed her to the door. She paused for a moment to look at him as he answered, wondering again what it was about him that she found so attractive.

'It was a long time ago, and I really don't remember.' But his eyes slid away from hers as he was speaking, and Holly wasn't sure that she quite believed him.

Chapter Twenty-Two

In Warkworth Prison John Brace woke suddenly and realized he'd been dreaming of Mary-Frances Lascuola. The dream had been so vivid that he believed he could still smell her, still feel her skin and the strong limbs under his fingers. In the dream he'd been strong again too, approaching middle age maybe, but fit after all those long walks in the hills. Not old and impotent and trapped in a wheelchair. In the moment of waking, the dream and a real memory became confused in his mind, the memory corrupted like the body of the woman Vera Stanhope had discovered in a culvert at St Mary's Island. He thought everything was shifting now, and nothing was certain. He'd lost all belief in his own judgement.

It had been late spring and one of the good times. The times when Mary-Frances had been clean and healthy, grateful to him for her sanity and willing to give him anything. She'd been working in The Seagull and, when he picked her up at her flat at the end of her shift, she hadn't had time for a shower. She was wearing the jeans and the sweatshirt she'd walked home in – she never wore her uniform away from the club. No need for Sinclair to get her a taxi, as he did for the other girls. She only lived two minutes away.

That night she still smelled of work, of cigarette smoke and perfume. It was the early hours of the morning. Not quite light, but still warm.

He'd driven her to a place he'd come across with Hector. A piece of woodland next to a shallow river; Hector and the gang had found flycatcher, dipper and treecreeper nests there. Brace had raided them for his own private collection. A group of ringers must have operated from the place because they'd found mist-net poles, the fine nets curled and tied so that the birds wouldn't get caught unless the ringers were onsite. The wood belonged to a big feudal estate, but the grand house had left it to grow wild and shored up their environmental credentials by letting the naturalists in. Once a driveway had led through the trees to the stables at the back of the house, but the track was overgrown and all that remained of the entrance was a pair of crumbling pillars. Nobody approached the house this way any more.

Brace had left his car on the verge by one of the pillars, taken Mary-Frances's hand and led her through the trees. Some were covered in white blossom, luminous in the shadow. In the milky light of dawn, he'd made love to her with a chorus of birdsong in the background. He'd felt caught by her and thought he knew how the small birds held by the soft pockets of the nets must feel. At that moment he hadn't been able to imagine life without her. Soon afterwards, Mary-Frances Lascuola had disappeared.

Chapter Twenty-Three

Vera arrived in the office early and settled herself at her desk to read through all the calls and emails that had come in overnight. She'd bought a coffee on her way in and chatted to the people manning the phone lines. There'd been no breakthrough. No member of the public who could remember anything unusual happening at St Mary's wetland on a hot summer night in June more than twenty years before. Everything seemed relatively calm. It felt like the lull before the storm.

Her personal mobile phone rang. It was Patty, her voice panicky and breathless. 'You have to come. There's been a break-in. I don't know what to do. What if there's still someone in the house?'

Vera looked at her phone. It was twenty past nine. 'When did they break in? Last night? Have you only just noticed?'

But Patty wasn't listening. 'Please, Vera! I need you.'

Vera hesitated. She had important things to do this morning, and it was one thing giving Patty a bit of support, another being her go-to person every time there was a domestic upset. But who else did the woman have to turn to? Besides, after the discovery of two bodies linked to John Brace, this seemed too much of a coincidence to ignore. 'I'll be there in twenty minutes.'

She found Patty standing outside the house. She was wearing what might have been pyjama bottoms and a tracksuit top. Although it wasn't a cold day, the woman had her arms wrapped around her body and she was shivering. When Patty saw Vera, she ran towards the older woman and held onto her. Patty was still shaking and felt fragile, as if her bones might snap with the contact. Vera found the physical contact disturbing. She couldn't remember the last time anyone had taken her into their arms. Gently, she released herself from Patty's grip. 'Why don't you tell me what happened?'

'They must have broken in when I was walking Archie to school. I got back and found that the kitchen window was smashed in. Someone reached in and undid the catch, because it's wide open.'

'Let's have a look then, shall we?' Vera walked round to the back of the house. It was just as Patty had described. There was glass all over the kitchen bench, the clasp had been unlocked and the window was fully open. It would have been big enough for a grown man to climb through. 'Not just a bairn hoying a ball then,' she said. 'They wouldn't have bothered opening the window.' A pause. 'Why don't you unlock the door and let me in? I'll just check there's no one inside.'

The place was chaotic, but no more so than the last time Vera had visited. There was no sign of an intruder. She called Patty inside. 'What have they taken?'

'Nothing, that I can see.' Patty's words still came in a rush. 'The telly's still here and the kids' tablets.'

'Maybe you interrupted them.' Vera couldn't see how this break-in could have anything to do with two bodies that had been lying in a hole at St Mary's wetland for years. 'I'll get a local officer to call round and look at the damage. And make sure we get that window fixed before it gets dark this evening.' She didn't want Patty to think she'd drop everything, any time there was a problem. That wouldn't help the woman.

'Okay.' Patty sounded disappointed and Vera felt a moment of guilt, almost as if Patty were *her* daughter, not Brace's. As if she was deserting the woman all over again. 'Yeah, okay. Thanks.'

By the time she and Charlie got to the coast, it was afternoon. Gus Sinclair was holding court in his office near the Dome. They saw him as they walked past, doing a reccie before making their first move. The office had a big glass window, like a shop front, and he sat behind a large pale-wood desk that had been placed sideways-on to the window, so that he could see outside and further into the room. Two women sat opposite him, hanging on every word. It was clear to Vera, even from that one quick look from the pavement, that Sinclair was doing all the speaking. He was one of those men who needed an audience. She thought he must have been young when he ran The Seagull, because he didn't look very old now. He had a tan that spoke of a sailor or a golfer. Or someone with property in the south of Spain. She hurried after Charlie, who seemed not even to have glanced in through the window; he walked with purpose, his hands thrust in the pockets of his navy anorak, and she had to run for a few steps to catch up.

It was approaching the spring tide and the water was right up to the Esplanade, no sand to be seen. The dog-walkers had to make do with concrete. School had finished and the kids were out on the skateboard park, focused, very serious when they made their moves, only relaxing and joking afterwards when they sat on the grass to drink cans of fizzy pop. Vera wondered what it must be like – that sudden thrill of speed and then the control of the turns and the jumps. She stood and watched for a moment, truly admiring the skill. Behind them was the sweep of the bay and the point of St Mary's Island, the lighthouse very white against the blue sky.

She'd brought Charlie with her because she thought the younger members of the team should know there were times when experience counted. He'd spent two hours over lunchtime building up a history for Sinclair. While everyone else was eating their sandwiches, he'd sat hunched over his desk, muttering into the phone, talking to his mates in Glasgow – retired officers, friends who'd transferred to other forces. He'd made notes with a blunt pencil on the sort of A4 pad that students used. He'd disappeared for half an hour and come back to tell Vera he'd been talking to a journo on BBC's *Look North* who had aspirations to do *Panorama*.

'He's been doing his own investigation into our

friend Sinclair, but the BBC won't touch it. Not enough evidence, apparently. He thinks they've been scared off.'

Then he'd refused to discuss Sinclair in any further detail with Vera until they were out of the office.

'Getting a bit paranoid in your old age, Charlie?' She'd made a joke out of it, because Charlie was the least paranoid person she knew. He didn't have the imagination for it.

He'd flashed a look in her direction and mumbled cryptically about playing it safe.

Out by the coast and in the fresh air, Vera had suddenly felt starving and she'd dragged him into Pantrini's fish restaurant next to the games arcade for sit-down haddock and chips. They'd both been too busy eating to speak in the restaurant, and anyway Charlie had still seemed nervous about being overheard. Vera had caught him staring at the other customers. It wasn't until they'd walked north, away from the Dome and Sinclair's office, and stood watching the skinny, geeky lads with their skateboards, that Charlie began talking and then he didn't need his notes. It was as if he couldn't stop.

'Gus Sinclair appeared in North-East England in the early eighties. It seemed as if he'd come out of nowhere, but he must have had contacts, because soon he was seen knocking around with local politicians, businessmen and union leaders. The shady ones. The ones open to persuasion, when it came to planning and licensing matters. And he started making friends with police officers too. Our own Mr John Brace, for one.' Charlie looked out to sea. The waves were even and relentless and broke on the sea wall.

'I thought someone must have been backing him, big-style. He was too young to have had that sort of influence in his own right and he'd no power-base at all: not long out of university, a few years working in hospitality in a big hotel in Glasgow, helping to organize events and conferences. Why would the most important men in the North-East bother with him?'

'What did he do at university?' Vera wondered if a degree would be enough to give Sinclair the nickname 'the Prof.'

'Business studies. Does it matter?'

'Probably not. Go on. Tell me why the Tyneside movers and shakers took any notice of a young Scottish lad.'

Charlie watched a moody girl perform magic on her skateboard and continued speaking. 'I found out who his father was, and it all made sense.'

Now impatience got the better of her. 'So who was the father? Come on, Charlie, we want to speak to the man and there's a briefing at seven. I'd rather not be here all day.'

'Alexander Sinclair, known as Alec. Grew up in Aberdeen and made enough money on the rigs to settle in Glasgow and set up his own business. Builder and property developer, before he moved into bars and clubs. Intelligence links him to gangs there – smuggling drugs and girls – but he was too clever ever to have been charged.'

'And he wanted to extend his empire, so he sent his son down to North-East England. There have always been ties between Glasgow and Tyneside.' Vera could see where this was going, but she was starting to feel out of her depth. Her professional world was different from this. She understood family dramas and small people fighting against the odds. The murderers she'd caught hadn't been gangland monsters, but rather pathetic little men, lacking control or the intelligence to sort out their problems without resorting to violence. She'd had no experience of organized crime until she'd worked to get John Brace put away, and even then his villainy had been local. He'd been a big fish in a very small pool. For her, gangland killings carried out to exert power or settle scores were the stuff of bad television, not real life. 'What's happening to old man Sinclair now?'

'He's dead,' Charlie said. 'A heart attack. He always drank too much and smoked like a chimney.' He looked at her. 'Overweight.'

'So what's the story, Charlie? I can understand why Gus Sinclair pissed off up north when The Seagull was torched, but what brought him back here?'

'Word is: things were getting a bit hot, up north. Nobody dared touch Alec, even when he was dying. He had a reputation that scared people off. It was almost like a superstition . . .' Charlie was struggling to find the right words, '. . . or a religious belief. If you shafted Alec Sinclair, you'd be dead. It was inevitable. But once he was gone, it was a different story. There was a gap in the market and all sorts piling in to fill it. Gus isn't like his father. He doesn't have the stomach for a fight. Running away to Scotland when The Seagull started to lose money and disappeared in flames was an admission of failure, and he was never really part of his father's business after that. When Alec died, Gus decided to retire gracefully and leave the warring factions in Glasgow to it. Maybe Whitley

Bay held fond memories. He's living in one of those big apartments on the sea front at Tynemouth; bought it with cash, according to my sources.'

Vera wondered for a moment about Charlie's sources – the army of cleaners, secretaries, estate agents and accountants who seemed to supply him with information. How had he acquired them? 'Gus inherited from his father then? Even though he wasn't at the centre of his business?'

'Alec still had a considerable legitimate property portfolio when he died. Gus is the only surviving relative, as far as I know.'

And you would know, Vera thought.

'Why isn't he just keeping his head down? Why not quietly make a heap of money by developing The Seagull site? Why set himself up as a hero of Whitley regeneration?'

Charlie shrugged. 'Maybe he likes the admiration. Rumour has it that he has political ambitions, that he'd fancy being the North-East's elected mayor, if that ever happens. Maybe he's truly fond of the place. He's got a wife who comes from here. She used to work with him in The Seagull.'

Vera remembered the last conversation she'd had with Judith Brace. 'Not a woman called Elaine, by any chance?'

'That's right.' Charlie seemed surprised that Vera had the same access to information as him.

'Apparently she was friendly with Robbie Marshall at one time. Brace's wife remembers a dinner where the four of them were together. Maybe that's another possible motive for his murder. Robbie had a fling with Sinclair's woman, and Sinclair couldn't just let it go.' *Except that didn't explain the second body at St Mary's and, according to Charlie, Gus Sinclair was squeamish when it came to a fight. But perhaps he'd hired someone else to do his dirty work, just as he'd hired someone else to set fire to his club.*

The tide was starting to go out now and a spaniel was chasing a ball in the shallow water, the spray a diamanté burst of reflected light. Vera had been leaning against the wall with her back to the sea and pushed herself upright. She thought it was time to see Gus Sinclair for themselves.

Sinclair was alone in the office when they arrived and he opened the door to them. Inside was a display board with a plan of the proposed regeneration, computer-generated images showing happy people walking through a plaza where a clown on stilts was performing. The restaurant on the headland at St Mary's a marvel of glass and pale timber.

'Just have a look,' Sinclair said, 'and come back to me if you have any questions.' His voice had a slight Scottish accent, but it was rather gentle and refined. Could this man be the Prof., the missing member of Hector's Gang of Four? Sinclair would have been the only graduate among the group, and the term could have been slightly ironic. He'd have been younger than the rest of them. But, in her memory, Hector hadn't viewed the Prof. as a figure of fun, but of respect. Someone to be a little scared of. This amiable man, with his tan and his casual open-necked shirt, didn't come across as particularly frightening.

'You designed the plans?' Vera said.

'Well, not personally!' A little laugh. 'I'm part of the consortium that's raising funding for the new development.'

'You're Angus Sinclair? I saw your picture in the *Chronicle* the other day.'

'That's right.' He smiled, pleased with the recognition.

'Could I ask you a few questions?'

'Of course, that's why I'm here. To answer any queries. We're all determined that the community should have as much of a say in the future of the town as possible.'

She sat across the desk from Sinclair. Charlie stayed where he was, staring at the plans, his hands still in the pockets of his anorak, poised to send away any members of the public who might wander in. He'd been wearing the same jacket, or a clone of it, since she'd first known him. He'd be listening, though, and he'd be picking up the significance of any information she might miss.

Vera introduced herself formally. Sinclair looked at first unbelieving, as if he couldn't accept that this woman could be a senior detective, then wary. 'Do I need a solicitor?' Making it sound like a joke, but wanting a serious answer.

'No!' She stretched out the 'o' for emphasis, to show the idea was ludicrous. 'This is just a chat, because I understand you're an influential man in the town. And because our enquiries are taking us back to the past, to the eighties and nineties. You were living here then?'

He nodded. 'Ah, great times.'

'You'll have heard about the two bodies we found out at St Mary's?'

He nodded again, interested but unsurprised.

'We believe that one of them was Robbie Marshall. You used to knock around with him in the day. Wallsend lad. Useful.'

'I remember Robbie.' Sinclair was too intelligent to deny a connection they'd be able to prove. 'He used to come into The Seagull, did a lot of his business in there.'

'Do you remember the names of the people he met?'

Sinclair shook his head and replied too quickly. 'Sorry, it was a long time ago.'

'The second victim was a woman. Any idea who that might have been?'

There was a moment of silence. Vera couldn't tell if this information was new to Sinclair or not. If someone on the force was leaking to him, as Charlie had implied, he was probably aware of it, even if he wasn't involved in the crime.

'I understand that Robbie was friendly with your wife at one time,' Vera said.

Sinclair gave a tight smile. 'My wife's a very friendly woman. And she's at home in my apartment in Tynemouth, not on a mortuary table.'

'Does the name Mary-Frances Lascuola mean anything to you?'

There was a moment of silence. 'I remember the lassie. I took her on as a favour. She served food in the bar for a while. It was a mistake. Maybe it's always a mistake to do that sort of favour for friends. You end up resenting them.' Sinclair leaned forward across the desk. 'Where's this going, Inspector? I usually pack up at about this time.'

Vera ignored the question. 'What was the name of the friend?'

'One of your lot. John Brace.'

'And Mary-Frances let you down?'

'She started using again, plying her trade. I couldn't have that. The Gull was a respectable establishment. I let her go.'

'That was a while before it burned down?' Vera was still trying to get the timing straight in her own mind. She thought this would have been much tidier if Mary-Frances had disappeared at the same time as Robbie Marshall.

'Yeah, quite a few years before that. She was only with me for a matter of months.' Outside the window, the traffic was heavier. The shops were shutting and people were making their way home.

'I remember The Seagull,' Vera said. 'It was a part of the history of this place. It was built in the thirties, wasn't it? And still full of bright young things fifty years on.'

'I loved it.' He seemed genuinely moved, reached into his desk drawer and pulled out a photograph of the club. The sun was coming up over the sea, reflecting on the glass and the curved white walls, the neon image of the bird. The picture must have been taken from the beach, and Vera had never seen it from that angle. 'I'm having this framed for the office here. A reminder of Whitley Bay's former glory.'

'Perhaps you should rebuild it.'

'Ah,' he said, 'don't think I haven't considered it.'

He left the photograph out on his desk and continued to stare at it.

'But, these days, luxury apartments make more commercial sense.'

It wasn't a question and he didn't answer.

Vera went on. 'Would your wife be able to help us identify the woman who was buried with Robbie?'

'Maybe.' He sounded uncertain. 'She was like a mother hen to the women who worked for me. Someone might have confided in her. I'll ask, shall I?'

'You do that.' Vera smiled. 'But I'd like to chat to her myself, so I'll call in and see her sometime. I've always wondered what those smart flats in Tynemouth look like on the inside. Give me her number and I'll phone to check she's in before I turn up.'

She thought for a moment that he was going to refuse, but he shrugged and scribbled a mobile number on a piece of paper. Vera got to her feet and reached across the desk to take it. She was almost at the door when she stopped and turned. There was a sense of urgency now in identifying the Prof.; besides Brace, he was the only living member of the Gang of Four.

'What do you do in your spare time, Mr Sinclair?'

'I'm a bit of a workaholic,' he said. 'There isn't much spare time.'

'You're not a birdwatcher then, like your friend John Brace?' She held her breath while she waited for his reply. 'Not into country pursuits?'

'Nah, the only bird I was ever interested in was The Seagull.' He gave a little laugh and looked up at the photograph of the club. The Seagull still glowed in the early-morning light.

Chapter Twenty-Four

Vera had stuck a picture of The Seagull on the white-board before the evening briefing, and Joe Ashworth looked at it and remembered his youth. He'd never gone to the Gull – that was for real adults, people with money and style – but for a few years he'd spent most Friday nights in Whitley Bay, getting the bus with a gang of his mates from the pit-village further north where he'd still lived with his parents, sharing taxis back in the early hours of the morning. Heading 'down Whitley' was a rite of passage when he was a teenager. Most young people got very drunk there for the first time, had their first sexual experiences in the alleys that led along the back of shops and houses. They wandered between bars and clubs, meeting people they knew from school or work, the groups shifting and melting as the night progressed, like an elaborate country dance. He tried to remember the name of the club on South Parade where the bar staff wore bathing trunks and bikinis, and the congas would shimmy out into the street and back again until they collapsed into a laughing heap, high on alcohol and hormones. He supposed drugs were sold in Whit-ley then, but he hadn't come across any dealing. Though probably he'd been too naive to recognize it.

As the rest of the team gathered for the evening brief-ing, he remembered the name of the club: Idols. That was what it was called. He said the word out loud.

Vera was talking about a Whitley Bay Joe didn't quite recognize. The Whitley Bay of The Seagull. Gangs and celebrities. Famous sportsmen: boxers and footballers. Money-men who'd invested in the town where kids had come to let off steam.

'So we're pretty certain our male victim is Robert Marshall – his mother described the belt we found with the skeleton, before I gave her any clues. Most likely ID on the female is Mary-Frances Lascuola, mother of Patricia Keane and lover of John Brace. But she seems to have disappeared from view at least five years before Robbie. So this is a priority – what was she doing between the mid-eighties, when Brace claims to have lost touch with her, and 1995? Holly, did you check that rehab centre in Bebington?'

'Yes, I went out there and spoke to one of the pro-ject workers. It's run by a charity now, but until 2006 it was part of a big NHS hospital. I'll need to check with the health authority in the morning.' Holly sounded apologetic. 'By the time I got back from Bebington there was nobody in the records office to help.'

'Let's get onto the women's refuges and talk to social services and GPs. Hol, are you okay to do that too? Mary-Frances was a known addict, and though she got herself clean for a few months when she took up with Brace, the assumption is that she relapsed. We don't have a cause of death for this victim, so it's even possible that she died of an overdose or that she could have killed herself.'

'She didn't bury herself, though, did she?' Joe realized he was being flippant as soon as he'd spoken, but Vera took the question seriously.

'Maybe she was as much of an embarrassment dead as she was alive,' she said, 'so someone decided to dispose of her body.'

'Does that take us back to Brace?'

Vera thought about that for a moment. 'Aye, maybe. And we need to track down a friend of his, a chap they called "the Prof." He was part of the gang Robbie Marshall hung out with and he might have valuable information. But Brace isn't necessarily involved, and we should keep an open mind here. He told me he lost touch with Mary-Frances years before Marshall was killed and there's an outside chance he's telling the truth for once. For instance, we know Mary-Frances worked at this place.' Vera stopped speaking for a moment and pointed to the photo of The Seagull. 'This is the club that seems to link all the players in this case. Owned by Gus Sinclair, who's back on the scene in Whitley Bay, acting as benefactor and general nice guy, involved in some capacity still to be determined, in the development along the sea front and at St Mary's. Son of Alec Sinclair, Glasgow hard man. Gus employed Mary-Frances. If she OD'd on his premises, it wouldn't have looked good for business.'

She paused again and waved a wooden ruler she might have used as a schoolgirl towards the whiteboard, tapping it as she mentioned the names scrawled there. 'Robbie was a regular. So was John Brace. The only record of a woman seen with Robbie was a manager at The Seagull, who was called Elaine. Elaine is now Gus Sinclair's wife. Patty Keane's ex-husband,

Gary, also worked for Sinclair on occasion and he installed the security system in the club.'

Vera seemed to have a sudden thought and she turned to Joe. 'Can you go back and talk to Gary Keane? He was a youngster when he worked for Sinclair and they might have talked in front of him, not seen him as any kind of threat. He might even be the sort of lad they'd use to set the fire.'

'Sure.'

'Has anybody come up with anything useful? Billy? Anything from the crime scene?'

Billy Cartwright was defensive again. 'You know I'd have told you the moment we found something significant, Vera. Just trust my team to get on with it.'

'Aye well, you can't blame a woman for hoping. I'm getting pretty desperate here.'

But Joe didn't think Vera looked desperate. She looked younger – bright-eyed and energetic – just as she would have done in the mid-nineties when she was a new detective, fighting her corner against the men.

Joe decided to call into Gary Keane's flat on his way home. If he could come up with new information for Vera this evening, she'd be delighted. Despite himself, he'd been jealous that she'd chosen Charlie instead of him to go with her to interview Sinclair and he felt the need to prove his commitment. Besides, it was bathtime for the youngest child, homework for the big ones, and the hours before bedtime were always a bit fraught. He loved the kids to bits, but sometimes work came as a relief.

A middle-aged couple were working in the community garden when he parked in the street and he stood for a moment and watched them. They scarcely spoke, but worked together in rhythm; Joe was aware of a calm understanding between them and felt jealous all over again. Perhaps they were childless, perhaps their whole relationship had been relaxed and stress-free. He pushed the thought away because it seemed like a betrayal. The cafe was still open, staffed now by a cheery young woman with a central-European accent, who said he was lucky to catch her because she was just about to close. He picked up two cappuccinos to take away, then rang the doorbell by the side of the shop. The shutters were open this time and he saw inside, to well-ordered shelves carrying reconditioned computers, laptops and the accessories that seemed essential to a high-tech lifestyle. A notice in the window advertised coding classes for kids and a beginners' computer course for the over-sixties. It seemed that Gary Keane was branching out.

Upstairs a window was open and music spilled out into the street. An instrumental jazz number that Joe vaguely recognized but couldn't have named to save his life. He wondered if that was the kind of music that had played in The Seagull when it had been at the height of its popularity. He wished he'd been old enough to go there, even once, to appreciate the romance of the place. Sal would have loved it, would have spent all afternoon deciding what to wear. The music seemed very loud and Joe assumed Keane hadn't heard the bell. He rang again and then knocked on the door. Still no response, and the sound of the knock was hidden by a sax riff above him. He turned the handle and the door opened. He climbed the stairs, the coffees in a cardboard holder in one hand.

'Mr Keane.' He shouted because the music seemed seductive and he didn't want to be embarrassed by walking in on a sexual encounter. He was easily embarrassed, and he imagined stumbling on Gary Keane and some woman in various stages of undress.

The stairs opened to Keane's living room and, through a slightly open door, he saw the small kitchen beyond. The living room was as tidy as when Joe had last been there. No flimsy underwear. No sign of a woman at all, except that on the coffee table there was a bottle of Chablis in a cooler and two glasses. Half the bottle of wine remained, but the glasses were both empty. The music came from an old-fashioned gramophone, the records delicately stacked and ready to drop onto the turntable when needed. A slight breeze from the open window tugged at the curtains.

'Mr Keane!' His voice sounded unnaturally loud because the record had come to an end. There was a click as the needle lifted automatically and then another disc fell into place. This time it was a vocal. Ella Fitzgerald. Joe recognized it because she was a favourite of his father. He crossed the room and tapped on the door opposite. Still no answer. He pulled on latex gloves, before pushing it open. He'd look ridiculous if Keane turned up after running to the shops for a carton of milk, but the situation was starting to feel weird.

This was the only bedroom, just big enough to hold a double bed, with a pine wardrobe in the alcove on one side of the chimneybreast. The bed had been made – not just a rumpled bottom sheet covered by a duvet, but properly made, the pillows smoothed. No sign of Keane. Joe gave a little laugh and thought he'd been overreacting. Keane and his friend had shared the wine and then gone out for a meal or to the pub, leaving the door open by mistake. But now he was here, perhaps he should look around. There might still be something he could give to Vera, an offering to make him her favourite again. There was nothing of interest in the bedroom – clothes stacked in drawers and in the wardrobe. Everything neat. The clothes well-worn but of good quality. How much cash could the man make by repairing and selling second-hand PCs? Surely he must have some other form of income.

Beyond the bedroom there was a small shower room. Again, it seemed unnaturally tidy to Joe, as if the man had made a special effort to make the place look good. White towels folded on the stainless-steel rail, taps shiny, bleach still in the toilet bowl. Who had he been trying to impress?

Back in the living room there was a sideboard, with a narrow drawer and two cupboards. One of the cupboards contained glasses and the other a selection of spirits. Again nothing cheap. A large bottle of The Botanist Islay gin and a malt whisky. In the drawer, a selection of papers and photographs. Joe took them out, listening all the time for voices in the street outside, footsteps on the stairs. In the background, Ella's voice. He sat on the sofa with the papers spread over the coffee table. Keane's passport, all in order with eighteen months left to run. In the last two years he'd travelled to the USA twice. The papers mostly related to the business. His most recent tax return. The shop was turning a profit, but only just, so how had Keane managed two American holidays? Joe jotted notes and thought that all this would be of interest to Vera. He returned the papers to the drawer and turned his attention to the photographs.

The first one he looked at grabbed his attention. It had been taken on the terrace of The Seagull. Five men were gathered around a woman, who was buxom and blonde, with pink lipstick and sparkly blue eyelids. Keane was there, looking hardly more than a boy, his arms around two men who already featured on the incident-room whiteboard: Robbie Marshall and Gus Sinclair. On the other side of the woman stood two more men. One was John Brace. The other Joe had never met, but knew so well by reputation and legend that he'd become a big part of his life: Hector Stanhope, who still haunted Vera from the grave. The men were in evening dress and the woman was in a long, blue silk number that revealed more than it covered. They all had glasses in their hands and it was clearly some sort of celebration. Joe took a photo of the picture on his phone and moved on.

The other photos were family snaps, mostly taken in the park and on the beach. There was one studio shot of a timid-looking woman whom Joe supposed was Patty Keane, with a baby in her arms, Keane himself standing behind them, playing the proud father. Later the images were mostly of the children. If Patty appeared at all, it was in the background, looking either vacant or harassed. John Brace appeared in one, again more formally composed. It must have been taken just before he was arrested. This time Patty had a toddler on her knee and Gary Keane held a newborn baby wrapped in a blue blanket. Brace stood behind them, looking rather stern, a Victorian grandfather. Joe took photographs of all of the images on his phone, then returned the pictures to the drawer. He thought he was pushing his luck. Soon Keane would be back to finish the wine.

On his way to the stairs, on impulse he pushed open the kitchen door, thinking there might be more photos there, stuck to the fridge or on the noticeboard that he'd glimpsed as he came into the living room. The door jammed. There was something behind it that prevented it opening fully. Joe squeezed through the gap into a room that was so narrow he could touch both walls from where he stood. He saw that this was tidy too, compact as a yacht's galley, pots washed and everything in its place. Except that crumpled behind the door, curled almost in a foetal position, lay Gary Keane, not at all how he should be. There was a thin knife in his stomach, and blood pooled on the laminate floor beneath him.

Chapter Twenty-Five

After finding Gary's body, Joe Ashworth stayed at the crime scene. He made the necessary phone calls, then ran back down into the street. The cafe was already closed and shuttered, with a sign on the door saying it would open again at seven the next morning. He'd missed the chance to talk to the barista with the cheery smile, but the gardeners were still there, packing their tools into the back of an estate car. Joe showed them his ID and they followed him back into the garden, where he could keep an eye on the entrance to Keane's flat. There was a chill in the air, the first sign of autumn, but there was nowhere else to take them. They sat on one of the wooden benches, all in a row, so he had to lean forward to talk to the woman who was furthest away from him.

'What time did you arrive?'

They looked at each other. Their name was Miller, Philip and Becky. They were both teachers, childless, nobody to rush home to except the dog, and it wouldn't hurt her to wait a bit longer for her evening walk.

'About six.' Becky did most of the talking. Philip seemed content to nod his agreement. 'We just had a cup of tea and changed from our work stuff. There's not a lot to do in the garden this time of the year, but we come once a week, just to keep an eye on things. To keep it tidy.'

'Was Keane still in the shop then?'

Becky shook her head. 'I hoped he'd still be there, because usually the shutters are down when he's closed. I'd brought my laptop for him to take a look at. I must have downloaded some virus, and Gary said he'd be able to sort it out for me. But the door was locked.'

'You didn't try to get him in the flat?'

'No. It didn't seem fair when he'd finished for the day. We don't like it when parents buttonhole us in the street to talk about their kids. Besides, it's not urgent.' There was the same calm acceptance that Joe had sensed as he'd watched them working.

'Did you notice if he had any visitors? Anyone knocking at the door to the apartment?'

They paused for a few seconds. Joe experienced a moment of tension as he willed them to answer. They'd make good witnesses. If they had seen the person who'd visited Gary, it might break the case. But then they shook their heads in unison. 'That doesn't mean there wasn't a visitor,' Becky said. 'If we had our backs to the street, we wouldn't have seen.' Only then did she show any curiosity. 'Has he had a break-in?'

Joe thought there was no harm in telling them. They weren't the sort to get hysterical or to gossip. 'No,' he said. 'Gary Keane's dead.' He was taking their phone numbers when he saw Vera pulling up in a work car. He thanked the couple and said he had to go. They walked together after him back to the street and the car. When he turned to say goodbye to them he saw they were still there, looking back at him, apparently curious at last.

Vera was putting on a scene suit, balancing against a lamp post while she pulled it over one foot at a time. When she'd done, she threw one to Joe. 'Dr Keating's on his way, and Billy Cartwright and his team. You'd better stay here until uniform arrives to monitor access. Then come up and join me.'

When he found her she was standing in the kitchen, looking down at Gary Keane. She'd heard Joe coming up the stairs and shouted to let him know where she was. 'I don't think he was a decent man, but nobody deserves that, do they?' She turned back to Joe. 'So what do you think went on here?'

'He let someone in, someone he knew. Maybe someone he wanted to impress. The flat was tidy. It was pretty clean when I came last, but I'd say he'd made a special effort. And he'd bought a good bottle of wine.'

'A woman, do we think?'

'Could have been. Or a man he wanted to do some work for. Or make things right with.'

'This can't be a coincidence.' Vera was standing with her legs apart and her hands on her hips. There was hardly any room left for Joe in the kitchen and he was still standing in the doorway. 'Two bodies, and now this.'

'There's evidence that he knew Marshall, Brace and Sinclair. I had a chance to look round the flat before I found the body.' Joe led her back into the living room and showed her the photographs.

She spread them over the coffee table, just as he'd done when he'd been there alone, and pointed to the studio image of Gary and his family, with John Brace standing behind them. 'That must have been taken just before Brace was arrested. Interesting to see that Gary knew him earlier, though, before he married Patty.' She'd moved on to the photo taken outside The Seagull and was staring at it. Joe thought her attention was focused on Hector. 'I never saw him in a penguin suit.' She was talking to herself, wrapped up in memories of her own. 'I wonder where he kept it.'

The window was still open and they heard voices on the pavement below, the uniformed officer making a note of the newcomers' names.

'That's Paul Keating.' Vera seemed to rouse herself. 'I'll get out of everyone's way before they start. There's no room to swing a cat, as it is. I've asked Hol to come and making a start on supervising the house-to-house. I don't think we'll get much this evening, though. It's businesses in most of this street, isn't it?'

'I think the visitor probably arrived before six o'clock.' Joe had been thinking about this since talking to the Millers. 'Keane usually pulled down the shutters on the shop at the end of the working day, but they were up when I arrived. I think that suggests he was still in the business when his guest came along, and he didn't have a chance to shut up properly. I spoke to a couple who were working in the community garden from six. The shop was already locked then and they didn't see anyone arrive.'

She nodded to show she accepted his reasoning and headed towards the stairs.

'Where are you off to?' If she'd had some brainwave – some idea that would make a difference in the case – he wanted to be a part of it.

'I'm going to see Patty Keane,' she said, 'to tell her that her ex, the father of her kids, is dead.'

Chapter Twenty-Six

They'd just finished their tea when the doorbell rang and Patty found Freya on her doorstep. Usually the social worker was in a rush, calling in on her way home from work. She asked if everything was okay, called out to the kids with a few questions about school, and then disappeared in her smart little car. It was as if the visit was something she had to do every month and, as long as everyone was alive, she wasn't really interested. As if Patty was a box that had to be ticked.

Today it seemed as if she had more time, and Patty wondered if that was Vera's doing. Vera must have told her about the smashed window. 'I hear you've had a break-in,' the social worker said. 'Is everything all right.'

Patty explained that nothing had been taken and that the glazier had already been to replace the glass. 'Actually, we think it might have been kids. A bit of mindless vandalism.' The words sounded very grown-up and calm and she forgot how panicky she'd been when she'd first arrived back at the house and seen the glass all over the floor.

Then Freya actually sat down and played with Archie. Snap. He beat the young woman every time, and Patty could tell she wasn't just letting Archie win. 'That's a bright spark you've got there,' Freya said. 'He must really wear you out.' Then she said there was a club he might like to go to during the half-term break. It was for able and gifted children and Archie might be easier to handle at home if he'd been doing stuff all day. 'I had a chat with his teacher and she says he's the best reader she's got in her class.'

Patty felt a glow of pride and thought that was the most wonderful thing that had happened to her for ages. Besides anything else, Jonnie and Jen would be much easier to handle with Archie out of the way.

With Freya gone, she got the boys to bed and checked that Jen wasn't watching anything unsuitable on her tablet. It was when the house was quiet that the guilt set in again. Patty knew she should be a better mother. A good mother would always monitor her kids' viewing, play board games with them and encourage them out into the fresh air while the nights were still light. But most days it took all her energy to get them fed and their clothes clean, and she carried around the weight of guilt that she couldn't do better.

Tonight it was a relief that they were quiet. She looked at the pile of dishes in the sink and wondered if washing them could wait until tomorrow. But if she left them, there wouldn't be any bowls for tomorrow's breakfast, so she ran the water into the sink and made a start. She'd just about finished and was thinking she could have a cup of tea and a few episodes of *Come Dine with Me*, before taking herself off to bed, when there was a knock on the door. She went into the living room and looked round the grey net curtains before answering. It was Vera, the big detective, and

Patty hurried to let her in, pleased to see her because it would be good to have a bit of adult company. She couldn't wait to tell Vera the good news about Archie's progress at school.

'You're out late.' Because it was dark now and the street lights were on throughout the estate. 'The window's all sorted. There was no need to come out and check.'

'There's something I wanted to tell you.' Vera walked into the house and through to the kitchen, then put the kettle on as if she owned the place. Patty didn't mind. 'Before the press gets wind of it.'

'What?' Patty already knew about the two bodies at St Mary's Island. That had been all over the news already. 'Is it my mam buried in the culvert on the coast? Is that what you've come to tell me?'

She thought Vera looked a bit confused for a moment. 'Sorry, pet, we can't positively identify both those people. Not yet. If one of them is your mother, I'll come to tell you as soon as we know. No, this is something different. It's about Gary.'

'What's he done?' Because Patty knew Gary was always a bit tricksy, always working scams. When they'd lived together, money had suddenly appeared from nowhere and, when she'd asked, he'd just tapped his nose and said he'd done a bit of business. Nothing for her to worry about.

'He's not done anything.' Vera had made the tea, wiping up clean mugs from the draining board first. She carried them through to the living room and put them on the windowsill, waited for Patty to sit down before speaking again. 'He's dead, pet. He's been stabbed. Sometime this evening, we think.'

Patty's first thought was that there'd be no more glorious dreams of the two of them getting back together. She wouldn't be able to lie in bed while the house was still quiet, with only Archie up and pottering downstairs, watching the sun on the ceiling and imagining how it would be if she plucked up the courage to meet Gary again. To pick up the phone and speak to him. Some days it had only been those dreams that had kept her going. She'd known Gary wouldn't come back to her if she was a mess, so she'd had to get herself sorted. Now, what would be the point? She realized she was crying, and that tears and snot were running down her face. Vera fished in her bag and came out with a proper handkerchief, big and designed for a man, not too clean but dry.

Patty wiped her face. 'Sorry.'

'Don't be daft, pet, it must have come as a shock.' A pause. 'He'd be glad to know that someone was crying over him.'

Patty looked up at her. 'Who killed him? Some lad in a bar? He could wind people up, when he'd got a few drinks inside him. But most of the time he was lovely.'

Vera shook her head. 'He was killed at home.'

'Who by?' Patty wondered if it was anyone she knew but she doubted it. Gary had always kept his home and business separate, and when she'd asked where he was going when he left the house most evenings, he'd come back with the same response: 'It's business.' In the end, she'd stopped asking. Perhaps she didn't want to know.

'We don't know that, and that's why I have to ask some questions. Is that all right?'

Patty nodded. The last thing she wanted now was to be left alone. 'Let me just go and switch Jen's light off. Otherwise she'll be up all night.' At the living-room door, she paused. 'Do you think I should tell her? She's the only one who properly remembers him.'

'Maybe not tonight,' Vera said. 'Not if she's nearly asleep. First thing in the morning, and maybe keep her off school so that she has time to get used to the idea.'

Patty nodded again and went up the stairs. Jen was asleep, her tablet on the pillow beside her. Patty switched it off and straightened the cover, stroked her daughter's hair away from her face and felt like a proper mum once more. She turned off the light and went back to Vera. While she'd been out of the room, the woman had piled all Archie's Octonaut figures into the toy box in the corner, drawn the curtains and switched on the standard lamp. In the half-light you couldn't see the dust or the stains on the carpet and the room seemed peaceful.

'What do you want to know?' Patty said. 'I haven't seen him since he walked out.'

'It seems a bit of a coincidence.' Vera was drinking her tea, but her eyes were fixed on Patty's face. 'We find those bodies at the coast, and then Gary is stabbed. I'm wondering if he knew something about them. Perhaps he threatened to speak, or demanded money to keep quiet. What do you think?'

Calmer now, Patty considered the idea. 'How could he have known anything about those dead people? Weren't the bodies buried years ago?'

'We think one of the corpses was Robbie Marshall.'

Vera's voice was steady. 'And we know that Gary knocked around with him. There's a picture of them in his flat. It was taken outside The Seagull, that flash club in Whitley. That was probably before your time.' She gave a little smile. 'I don't see you as the sort of girl who went clubbing. Your father's in the same photo, and a man called Angus Sinclair.' She looked as if she was going to add another name, but seemed to think better of it. 'Did Gary ever mention Sinclair?'

Patty shook her head without trying too hard to drag back any memories. She couldn't make sense of it all.

'Or someone called "the Prof."?' Vera frowned and Patty could tell that the question was important.

Patty shook her head again. 'Gary never went to college. He didn't know that sort of person.'

'You were aware that Gary knew John Brace, your dad, before you tracked him down through the adoption people?' Vera set down her mug on the floor next to her, before looking at Patty again.

This time Patty *did* remember. They'd been in the little house they were renting in North Shields. She'd found out she was pregnant with Jonny. It seemed like ages ago. 'I came back from the social-services place and said they'd traced my dad. Gary wasn't that bothered. Not really. Not until I told him the name.'

'And then?'

'He said: "John Brace the cop?" I didn't know what job my father did then, so I couldn't answer. Then Gary said: "I bet it is, the old dog." I thought perhaps my dad had arrested him at one time. Gary had got into a bit of bother when he was younger. I hadn't realized they might have been friends.'

'Gary had a bit of a temper.' This wasn't a question. 'Did he ever take it out on you and the kids?'

'No!' The idea made Patty angry, but then she remembered Gary's moods, the way he stamped around the house, yelling at them all. 'Not physically. But he got depressed, I think, and then he wasn't great to be around.'

'Did he ever go to the doctor for the depression?'

Patty shook her head. 'I suggested it once, but he wouldn't have it. I think his mam had mental-health problems. He'd lost touch with his family, but he talked about her when we first got together. She ended up in hospital and he said that was never going to happen to him.'

'When was the last time you saw him?'

Patty could remember that without any difficulty at all. 'About a month after he left us. Archie was still a baby, so it would have been about five years ago. Gary turned up at the house.' In her head, she replayed the scene. She'd been in the kitchen and she'd just come back from taking Jen to school. It had been winter and there'd been baby clothes draped over all the radiators. Everything a mess. She'd already started to let things slide. Then the front door had opened. No warning. No knock. And Gary was standing there, looking bloody gorgeous, wearing a leather jacket she'd never seen before and a Burberry scarf. In that moment she'd thought he was coming back and everything would be okay again. They'd be a proper family, and he'd lie in her bed every night and make her feel wonderful. Instead he'd looked down his nose at her, as if she was a bit of dog shit on his shoe. *I've just come to pick up some stuff.*

She'd heard him moving around upstairs and he'd come down carrying a pile of clothes. Archie had started grizzling and she had him in her arms, trying to calm him. She'd thought at least Gary would want to see *him*. He'd always liked the kids when they were small and couldn't answer back. It was as if somehow they were still a part of Gary until they developed their own personalities. But he'd just thrown his house keys onto the kitchen bench. *I won't be needing these again*. Then he'd turned and walked out of the house, slamming the door behind him.

'You haven't seen Gary since then?' Vera's voice broke into her memory.

Patty shook her head. 'He made it quite clear then that he wouldn't be coming back.' She paused. 'It was all my fault. He was older than me and he could cope with things better. Having me around was probably like having another child. I could see why I got on his nerves.'

'Is that what you really think? Or is that what he told you?' Vera paused for a moment. 'Sounds to me as if *he* was the big kid, with his temper tantrums. Not taking any responsibility now for his own bairns.'

'I loved him,' Patty said. 'I really loved him.'

'I know, pet.'

But Patty thought Vera couldn't really know, because she couldn't imagine the big woman giving up her independence for anyone. And anyway she was strong, not needy like Patty. Not desperate to be loved back.

'I have to ask this. You do understand, don't you? We'll be talking to everyone who knew him.' Vera patted her awkwardly on the arm. 'Where were you this evening after about five o'clock? We know Gary was in his shop until then, and we think he had a visitor sometime later. Someone he knew and let into the flat.'

'I was here,' Patty said. 'Just as I always am. I gave the kids their tea, sat and watched some telly with them.'

'Did anyone see you here? A neighbour or a friend?'

Patty didn't like to say that she didn't really have any friends, that the yummy mummies in the playground scared her to death. Then she remembered. 'Freya came! Freya, the social worker. She was on her way home and we'd already had tea, so it must have been about six o'clock. She wanted to chat to the kids individually and then she played with Archie, so she was here for nearly an hour.' Patty wanted to tell Vera about Archie's reading, but it seemed a bit heartless to be boasting when Gary was dead.

Vera beamed and Patty could tell she was relieved. She supposed at least Vera could cross her off her list of suspects. 'Has anyone been here looking for Gary?' Vera said. 'Or trying to get him on the phone?'

Patty shook her head. 'Not since he left. His mates would call sometimes while he was still living here, but they didn't stay. It was just to pick him up and take him out.'

'Any names?'

'Sorry, Gary didn't talk much about his life away from the family. Sometimes I think it was about work. He went to people's homes and offices to fix their computers. He was brilliant with computers.'

Vera nodded. 'Will you be all right, pet? I know

you and Gary hadn't been together for a while, but you were obviously fond of him. Is there anyone I can get to sit with you?'

'I'll be fine!' Because there wasn't anyone Vera could call to keep her company. Anyway, it was probably true. She would be fine.

Chapter Twenty-Seven

In Keane's flat in Anchor Lane, Joe was trying to zone out the activity of the crime-scene team and work out in his head what might have happened here. He found a bunch of keys on a hook in the kitchen and, when he was sure Keating and Cartwright had everything they needed, he went back downstairs. The officer who'd arrived immediately after him was still standing there, on the edge of the cordon marked by crime-scene tape. In a more residential area, this would already have attracted a crowd of gawpers, people hoping for excitement, real-life CSI, but the road was empty apart from the PC. An elderly man was walking his dog in the garden, but he seemed not to notice the police presence and disappeared down a street on the opposite side of the square.

'How long are you here for?' Joe knew what it felt like. The boredom and the hunger, the growing realization that you needed a piss.

The officer grinned. He seemed very young. 'Someone's on their way to relieve me. I should still get to the pub before closing. Just about.'

Joe thought he was being optimistic, but didn't say anything and waved the keys. 'I'm just going to see if I can get into the shop, if you want to make a note.'

The man nodded.

It took two keys to open the shop door – a Yale and a Chubb. Keane hadn't been in so much of a rush that he hadn't locked up properly. Joe found a switch just inside the door and the space was suddenly lit from a bright neon strip. The room was all contrast: sharp glare and shadow. He walked past the shelves but wasn't sure what he was looking for. He was more comfortable with IT than Vera, but that wasn't saying much. Sal was more confident than him, always on Facebook and shopping online.

The shop was cut in two, separated by a flimsy party wall. There was the area inside the door, where the public could browse the shelves for the latest techie toys, then the counter, and then a sliding door led through to what seemed a combined office, stock and repair room. A desk held a PC and a tiered basket of paper files. A small filing cabinet stood in a corner, and along one wall there was a workbench with a box of tools, a set of tiny screwdrivers and pliers. Above the bench, a shelf held machines that seemed already to have been repaired. Each was labelled with a brown tag. Joe looked for one marked with the Millers' name, but it seemed Becky would have to find someone else to repair her laptop.

He knew better than to touch the computer. A specialist tech officer would take that away, and Billy Cartwright's team would move down here after they'd finished in the flat upstairs. He began to look at the files in the basket on the desk. It seemed as if everything was in order. Invoices from suppliers had been paid and receipts kept. Joe wondered where Gary Keane had learned all this stuff. It was much more organized than he would have expected, for a lad with a temper who'd been on the fringes of criminal activity since he was a boy. It came to Joe that perhaps Keane had needed order, to be in control, and the anger came out of chaos and situations he couldn't handle. Three young kids and a flaky wife might do that to you. For the first time, he felt some sympathy for the dead man.

He pulled open the filing cabinet. On the bottom shelf, it seemed, were the historical records. Perhaps Keane had been reluctant to throw anything away. That need for control again. Joe found invoices that went back years. They were smudged, on flimsy paper, carbon copies of the bills sent out to whoever had hired him, and stored in large brown-paper envelopes with the year written on the front. Joe found 1995, suddenly feeling excited. He'd thought he was going through the motions and there would be nothing to be found here; now he might discover evidence that Sinclair had paid Keane to torch his club. Even that Keane had been involved in Robbie Marshall's murder.

He tipped the thin sheets of paper onto the desk and looked through them. Most seemed legitimate and had been sent to individuals with names that meant nothing to Joe. *For installing a security system in The Amazon Bar. For general maintenance of electricals in The Beach Hotel.* In each case, Keane had scribbled *paid* across the bill. Then Joe came across one where the name at the top of the invoice leapt out at him. *Hector Stanhope.* The description of the work provided by Keane was unspecific. *For services rendered.* But Hector must have paid up, because the same word was scrawled across the copy of the bill. Joe returned all the pieces of paper back to the envelope. He'd have to tell Vera, but that conversation could wait until morning.

He was about to leave when on impulse he picked up the telephone receiver. He heard the beeps that indicated a message. Joe dialled 1571 and waited. The man's voice on the other end of the line was plummy, but friendly. 'Hello, Gary, this is the Prof. I rather think we should meet, don't you? I believe you have something to tell me. I'll try your mobile.'

Joe replaced the receiver. He'd almost stopped believing that the Prof. existed. Now they had a voice to put to the title, and he knew that Vera would be delighted. But that too could wait until morning.

Chapter Twenty-Eight

They met early the next day, the whole team crammed into the briefing room. Standing at the door, waiting for everyone to find seats, Vera felt a moment of claustrophobia and panic, caused not just by the over-crowded room but by the fact that she was swamped with information and stressed by how much there was left to do. Watkins had been on her back, demanding answers she couldn't give him. She had the sense that he was willing her to fail.

They were still following up Robbie Marshall's contacts, but now they had to check out Gary Keane's customers and friends too. They'd pulled in staff from all over the region; it would take a while for the newcomers to be effective, though. Everyone needed briefing. She was trying to sort out priorities in her head when Joe ran up the stairs and joined her.

'Any chance of a quick word before we start?' He seemed nervous, a little awkward.

She looked at her watch. Still five minutes to go. 'If it's very quick.'

'I wanted to let you know that Gary did some work for your dad. He's kept receipts going back years and there's a record. I had a quick look at his office last night.'

ANN CLEEVES

'What year?'

'1995, so before Robbie Marshall went missing.'

Vera tried to work out where she'd been in her life then. Early thirties and trying to make a name for herself as a detective constable. Hector had still been fit, with only a red face and a short temper as clues to the heart problems that would get to him later in life.

'Would your dad have used him for anything electronic? Security system for the house maybe? Not many people had computers at home then.'

Joe Ashworth was trying to be helpful, but she found the interruption irritating. She wanted to picture herself back there, a younger woman with almost her whole working life ahead of her. Not as she was now, almost washed up, having to answer to an unsympathetic boss. 'I didn't see much of my father around then,' she said. 'Too busy.' *And I didn't like the stuff he was getting up to.*

She thought Hector might have employed Gary to disable a security system, not install one. She'd suspected her father of stealing osprey eggs from a famous breeding site in the Highlands. The RSPB had put in a camera at the site and had wardens to keep watch, but the eggs had disappeared anyway.

'There's something else.'

'Go on.' A couple of latecomers pushed past her into the room. The people who'd got there early and had been waiting were getting restive. She knew she should make a start.

'There was a message on his answering machine from the Prof. At least someone calling himself that. Our missing member of the Gang of Four. I made a

220

recording on my phone. That's something else that ties the cases together.'

'Doesn't it just?' She thought she had her priority now. They absolutely had to trace the mysterious man who'd been part of Hector's life and had arrived back on the scene at exactly the same time as Gary Keane was stabbed.

Joe played the recording at the end of the meeting. Vera had been hoping for immediate recognition. It was possible, after all, that she had met this man, had at least taken messages from him on the telephone when Hector was out.

'I thought it sounded kind of familiar,' Joe said, 'but out of context, I can't remember where I might have heard it.'

It meant nothing to Vera; there wasn't even a vague sense of familiarity. It was an old-fashioned English voice of the sort used by elderly Tory politicians and television newsreaders of times gone by. She wasn't sure that anybody talked like that any more. Perhaps the speaker had been exaggerating the round vowels to intimidate Keane. Perhaps there was even a touch of self-parody in the way he'd spoken. But they could dismiss the idea of Sinclair as the Prof. His voice was lighter and, even if he'd managed to mimic the accent, it was nothing like this.

'Get the techies to fast-track any information from the phone,' she said. 'We should be able to find a number and that'll give us a name.' It occurred to her that, to date, much of this case was about identity. They still had no ID for the female victim buried in the culvert. There was no proof she was Mary-Frances Lascuola. Now they were trying to track a potential suspect who had no more than a nickname. She sent the wider group away with words of encouragement that sounded false, even to her ears, and only the core members of her own team remained. They sat in one corner of the room. Charlie disappeared and returned almost immediately with coffee in cardboard cups, in his jacket pocket a bar of chocolate for each of them.

'Man, that was quick.' Vera was impressed. 'Are you moonlighting as a conjuror these days?'

He looked sheepish and said he'd been seeing a supervisor in the canteen.

'She's a brave woman!' But Vera was pleased. When Charlie's wife had left him, he'd sunk into a decline; now he seemed perkier than she'd known him for ages.

As Vera had suspected, Holly hadn't had much response to the house-to-house of the night before.

'The cafe next to Keane's business will be open now,' Joe said. 'The lasses in there might have seen someone go to the flat or the business. It was open when I got to Bebington last night.'

'You go back to the street, Hol. Get a bit of fresh air, after all those hours in front of a computer. Concentrate on the shops and the cafe. The business people would all have known each other and they might have recognized a stranger, especially later, as they were closing up.' Vera paused. 'Charlie, I need a positive ID on our two mysteries – the female victim and this guy who calls himself the Prof. It's getting ridiculous now. If our friends in the press find out that we still don't have a name for the dead woman at St

Mary's, they'll make mincemeat of us. And someone must have a name for the Prof. Is he a real professor? Phone the local unis, talk to the admin staff rather than the academics, see if any of them recognize that voice.' Another pause. 'I did wonder if the Prof. might be Sinclair, but he just looked bewildered when I asked him if he was into bird-watching, and the voice on the phone is nothing like.'

'What do you want me to do?' Joe seemed resentful to be last on the list. Vera almost suggested that he come along with her – nothing she liked better than the two of them working together – but there were better ways for him to spend his time.

'Keep on top of everything technical. There'll be stuff on Keane's computer: business contacts, personal emails. I'll leave you to follow up anything that might be relevant. Set your own priorities but, like I said in the briefing, I'd guess top of the list is to track down the number the Prof. was calling from when he left that message on Keane's office phone.' Vera smiled, directing her gaze to each of the team in turn, like the circling beam of a lighthouse. 'First one to find me that name gets a very special bottle of Scotch.' She began to pack away her notes. 'Anyone wants me, I'm off to the seaside, but first I've got a phone call to make.'

She walked from the room and made her way to her office, shut the door and experienced another moment of panic. A lack of confidence that felt as if there was a pit about to open up under her feet and there'd be nothing solid beneath her; no sensation but the rush of air as she plummeted to certain disaster. She hated the confusion of this investigation and the

lack of certainty. There was no straightforward narrative, nothing to cling to. She sat at her desk and clung
to that instead, told herself that all she could do was
work on until the story became clearer.

Her phone call to the Whitley Bay Regeneration
Project office was answered immediately and she recognized Sinclair's soft Scottish voice. That meant that,
with any luck, Elaine would be alone in her smart flat
on Tynemouth's sea front. Vera replaced the receiver
without speaking and made her way outside.

The Sinclairs lived in the top flat of a Victorian crescent that curved around a private garden and faced
out to the sea. Parking was limited to residents, and
Vera left her Land Rover at the Spanish Battery and
walked down past the boat club and the priory, enjoying the exercise and the sunshine, trying to clear her
mind. Tynemouth had always been the smart town on
the coast and she wandered past stay-at-home mums
with toddlers in tow, the idle elderly taking the air.
When she pressed the buzzer at the main entrance, a
crackly voice answered very quickly.

'Who is it?' The woman sounded cheery, not at all
suspicious.

'It's Vera Stanhope.' A pause. 'Hector's daughter.
I'm here about the bodies they found out at St Mary's.'

There was a moment of silence. 'You'd better
come up. Top floor. Hope you don't mind the stairs.'
Then the click of the door as it opened automatically.

Elaine was waiting for her at the entrance to the
flat. Vera could have done without that. Now their first
meeting put Vera at a disadvantage: panting and gasp-

ing for air, sweating after the walk through the village and the climb up the stairs. In contrast, Elaine looked expensive. That was Vera's first thought. And that she'd aged well. Her hair was carefully tinted and curled and she wore a flowery dress that flattered her curves, a short pink cardigan that dragged attention away from the bulging waist and big hips. There was a lot of gold: chunky chains around her neck and bangles at her wrists. Rings on most of her fingers. Gold sandals that revealed painted toenails the same colour as the cardigan. All this made Vera think of Elaine as a different species. She wasn't sure she'd be able to reach *her* toenails to paint them and, besides, it had never occurred to her to try.

Elaine stood aside to let her into the apartment. There was a small, rather dark lobby and then the living room. Sunshine flooded in through big windows onto a polished wood floor. Elaine might still like to wear bling, but if once she'd been brash and common, it seemed she'd now developed a little taste.

'Lovely place you've got here.' Vera collapsed onto a sofa made of a green-and-blue print fabric, without waiting to be asked to sit down. 'When did you move in?'

'As soon as we got back from Glasgow. Gus's father died and left us a bit of money. I've always wanted to come back to the North-East.' Elaine was bright enough to know that Vera would have checked the background, so there was no need for a detailed explanation. She took a seat opposite Vera. No offer of tea or coffee. She'd been with Sinclair long enough to recognize the police as the enemy. 'You're still a cop, then? Hector never thought you'd stick at it.'

Vera ignored that. 'We're pretty certain that one of the bodies in the culvert is Robbie Marshall.'

For a moment Elaine seemed about to pretend not to recognize the name, then she looked at Vera and thought better of it. 'Ah, I did wonder.'

'You went out with him for a while.'

Elaine threw back her head and laughed. 'No, we were mates, that's all. If he needed a woman on his arm, sometimes I'd oblige.' A pause. 'And really I'm not even sure we were mates. It felt like more of a business relationship. One favour in return for another.'

'Was Robbie Marshall gay?'

'Perhaps he was. I don't think it's something he'd have admitted to, then. They were different times. I'm not sure he was into any kind of sex; the only person he really loved was his mother. He was besotted with her. Otherwise, he was a bit of a cold fish. Birds of the feathered variety came a close second.' She shot a look at Vera. 'Not like Hector. Birds were always first with him. I did wonder how that made you feel.'

'Was Robbie working for Swan Hunter when you got to know him?' Talk of Hector freaked Vera out; she could feel something of the panic returning. But no way would she let this woman get the better of her.

'That's right.' Elaine gave a little laugh. 'He was procurement manager. That suited him down to the ground. Robbie could procure anything for anyone. That gave him as much of a buzz as a new bird.'

Vera stored away that bit of information. 'You worked at The Seagull. Is that how you met Gus?'

'Yes.' Elaine looked at her fingernails. They were a slightly lighter shade than her toes. 'We hit it off from the start. He took me on to do the admin at first, then

I became a sort of assistant manager. I took over the day-to-day running of the club. Gus had other business interests.'

I bet he did. In Tyneside and in Glasgow. 'You did all the HR stuff?'

'That makes it sound very grand.' Elaine laughed again.

It seemed to Vera that she laughed a lot. Perhaps you would, if you had nothing to worry about except painting your nails and shopping for clothes, if you lived in a lovely apartment with a view of the sea. 'But you did all the hiring and firing of staff?'

'Yes. Once I'd been there for a while, Gus trusted my judgement.'

'Mary-Frances Lascuola . . .'

'What about her?'

'She worked at The Seagull.'

Elaine looked out to sea. 'I remember her. That was before Robbie went missing, though. At least a few years before that. We took her on as a favour to John Brace. He said she'd straightened up her act and needed a chance.' She turned her gaze back to Vera. 'You'll know John Brace. One of your lot.'

Vera gave a brief nod. 'And had Mary-Frances cleaned up her act?'

'She was fine for a while. I gave her a job working in the restaurant as a waitress. She was a grafter and the punters liked her. A bonny little thing, if you like them skinny and soulful. Then she started to slip. I couldn't rely on her. Gus was keen to keep in with Brace, so I moved her to the kitchen, got her washing up. Obviously she thought that was beneath her and she left.'

'Do you know where she went?'

Elaine shrugged. 'Back on the streets, I assume. That was where most of them ended up. Too proud for washing dishes but not too proud to sell herself.'

'What did Brace make of that?' *Because, according to Patty, Mary-Frances was the love of his life.*

'What could he make of it? It wasn't Gus's fault that John Brace fell for a junkie with a weird name.'

In the silence that followed, Vera believed she could hear the waves breaking on the beach below. 'Wasn't the Prof. part of that crowd too?'

'Was he? I can't say I remember anyone called that.' But there'd been a moment's hesitation, a wariness about the eyes, which told Vera that Elaine had definitely heard of the Prof.

'What about a young lad with the name of Gary Keane? Mean anything to you?' So far they'd managed to keep Keane's name out of the news. In the morning's local media headlines, the crime had been reported in very general terms; the press release hadn't even said that the victim had died. A stabbing in Bebington wasn't quite an everyday event, but neither was it so newsworthy the journos wouldn't wait for a statement from the police to get the victim's name.

'Yes!' It seemed that Elaine was much more relaxed talking about Keane. 'Gary was a geek before that was what we called them.' She smiled. 'But if you got him out of his comfort zone, he had a helluva temper.'

'Did Mr Sinclair employ him too? Like Mary-Frances?'

'He wasn't on the staff – self-employed, I suppose

– but Gus brought him in to do a bit of work for us occasionally. It was mostly security stuff. The Seagull had a lot of classy gear inside and it needed a decent alarm.'

'Gary went on to set up his own computer consultancy and repair business.'

'Did he?' As if she didn't really care what had happened to the man. 'All that seems so long ago.'

'Has Mr Sinclair been in touch with Keane since you moved back to Tyneside?'

'Oh, I don't think so.' Elaine managed to bring a note of surprise into her voice. 'Why would he? Gus is a gentleman of leisure these days.'

'The Whitley Bay Regeneration Project seems to take up a lot of his time.'

'That's a labour of love,' Elaine said. 'Gus longs to see Whitley prosperous again. He doesn't really have a financial interest in the project.'

'What about the development of The Seagull site?'

'Oh, there's a consortium in charge of that. Gus is a very small investor and he's leaving the details up to them. He was so fond of the place that part of him can't bear to think of anything other than the club there. He can't work up any enthusiasm for the new project.'

Vera looked north out of the long, elegant window. She could see St Mary's Island, but the Esplanade where once Sinclair's famous club had been was hidden by the curve of the bay. 'Perhaps your husband could rebuild The Seagull,' she said. 'He could call it "The Phoenix", as it would be growing out of the ashes.'

'The time for that sort of club is long past.' Elaine

spoke briskly. No sentiment with her. 'Besides, as I said, he's only a small investor. Other people make the decisions about that site now.'

Vera turned back into the room. 'You must have known what happened, that night it burned down. You'd have had a good guess, at least.'

Elaine smiled easily and shook her head. 'The fire officers weren't prepared to commit themselves. It could have been an electrical fault, but they said they couldn't rule out arson. Gus managed to make a few enemies in the town.'

'Gary Keane looked after your electrics, didn't he?'

'What is it with Gary, after all these years? What's the interest?'

Vera didn't answer that. 'Did you know he went on to marry John Brace's daughter?'

Elaine seemed to consider her words for a moment. 'I think I might have heard that.'

'It seems the girl was Mary-Frances's daughter.'

'That was the rumour I heard too.'

They sat for a moment in silence. Vera was suddenly impatient. All this playing with words was wasting time. 'Gary Keane's dead. He was stabbed in his flat in Bebington early yesterday evening.'

'No!' It seemed like an honest response, shocked and immediate.

'When did you last see him?'

Elaine shrugged. 'I haven't seen him since we moved away.'

'Since The Seagull burned down?'

'That's right.' A pause. 'I never quite knew what to make of Gary. He was a bit odd. Happier with his electrics than with people, I thought, though he could be a charmer if he wanted. He was like one of those lizards that change colour, depending on their background. All things to all people.'

'What about Angus? Has he seen Keane recently?'

'I don't know,' Elaine said. 'If he has, he hasn't mentioned it.'

'It seems an odd coincidence.' Vera hoisted herself out of the sofa and stood by the window. The light was behind her and threw her shadow onto the polished floor. 'The bones are found at St Mary's, and days later Gary Keane is murdered. And what connects all the individuals involved? The Seagull. That white, shiny palace that you and your husband used to run. And yet you claim to know nothing about any of it.' She made her way to the door. 'Tell Gus to get in touch if he has any information for us. Better that he comes of his own accord, rather than we come looking for him.'

Elaine stood up. There was a clinking of the bangles on her wrists and the chains at her neck. In her heightened state, they made Vera think of handcuffs and a noose.

Chapter Twenty-Nine

Following Vera's instructions, Holly went back to Bebington. She'd been there to work on a previous case, but that had been to the town centre, where most of the shops were boarded up and she'd been left with a sense of desperation about the place. Then there'd been the visit to Shaftoe House, Victorian Gothic stranded in the modern estate of tiny boxes. This little corner on the edge of town was different from both those places. Anchor Lane felt like a community apart, almost a village in its own right. On the far side of the square the terraced houses looked cared for – the gardens were at the front, facing into the community space. It seemed that young families had moved in: there was a wooden climbing frame in one, and a woman was pegging children's clothes to a washing line in another. Holly assumed that people had moved here from the city because the homes were cheap, and that the shops had followed. The area had a slightly bohemian feel.

The pavement outside Keane's shop was still cordoned off and a bored uniformed officer stood beside the crime-scene tape. Holly showed him her warrant card. 'I'm supervising the house-to-house.' The cafe close to Keane's computer business was busy. Inside, it was small and much of the space was taken up by two buggies with sleeping toddlers. Their mothers were talking earnestly about the best nurseries in the district and the exorbitant cost of childcare. Holly, who hadn't yet felt the urge to become a mother – hadn't even met anyone with whom she'd consider sharing parenthood – felt like an outsider in an exclusive club. She ordered a flat white and wondered, too late, if she should get something for the PC on crime-scene duty. She should have asked him what he wanted. The woman behind the counter was young, efficient. English wasn't her first language but she spoke it perfectly.

'Were you on duty last night?'

'Yeah, I was on the late shift. Did you leave something? I don't remember you.'

Holly explained as quietly as she could what she was doing there. The women with the buggies fell silent and stared. 'Can anyone take over from you for a bit, so we can talk outside?'

The barista nodded and called a young man from the back to take her place.

Outside, Holly felt a second stab of guilt and handed the coffee to the constable. 'Sorry, I didn't know how you like it.'

'Hey, it was just nice of you to think of me.' He seemed very young – a schoolboy in a grown-up's uniform – and she couldn't help grinning back.

The women walked into the community garden.

'I heard what happened there,' the barista said. 'That Gary died. Is it true someone killed him?'

'Did you know him well?'

'Not outside the shop, but he was a regular. He

came in at least once a day. He needed his hit of caffeine to get moving in the morning.' Perhaps she was a caffeine junkie too, because she seemed all activity. It was hard for her to stand still to carry on the conversation. They walked past the raised vegetable beds, cleared now for the autumn.

'Did you see him yesterday?'

'I didn't start until lunchtime. He was always in before nine, when he opened the shop. A large flat white and an almond croissant.' There were old-fashioned roses growing up a trellis, the blooms faded but still reddish-brown, the colour of dried blood. She bent to smell them.

'Did you see him later in the day?' Holly knew she was no good at this. She lacked the patience to listen to a witness's story in detail. She needed them to jump straight to the relevant information.

The woman considered. 'He didn't come into the cafe, but I saw him. I came outside into the garden to have a cigarette.' Still she jiggled, a child unable to keep still. 'Do you mind if I have one now?'

Holly shook her head. She hated people smoking close to her, but better to have the woman focused.

'What time was that?'

'Five o'clock.' She'd lit the cigarette and drew on it, narrowing her eyes.

'You're sure of the time?'

'Yeah, that's when I take my break.'

'What was Gary doing?' Holly thought this must narrow down the time of the man's death. Vera would be pleased with the information.

'He was standing at the door of his shop. Maybe

business was slow, because usually if he didn't have any customers he was working in the back.' The barista paused. 'But I think perhaps he was waiting for a visitor. That's what it seemed like. He kept looking up the street for cars.'

'Did you see anyone?'

'No, I could see the cafe was busy, so I just waved to Gary and went back to work.'

'Perhaps you noticed a car parked outside later?'

She shook her head. 'It was manic. I didn't get outside at all.' A pause. 'I think there was a couple working in the garden at some point. A guy turned up a long time later, just as I was closing. He'd parked outside Gary's and I saw him knocking on the door of the flat.'

'Can you describe him?'

'About your age. Mousy hair. A suit.' She paused. 'Could have been baby-sick on his tie.'

Joe Ashworth. 'Nobody else?'

'Not that I can remember.' She stubbed out her cigarette and threw it into a bin. 'Time to go back.'

Holly watched her cross the street to the shop and moved on. There were two more business in the same block: a deli selling local cheese, beer and meat, artisan bread and organic wines; and, on the far corner, a small bookshop. She'd never have thought she'd come across these in a town like Bebington. She thought it unlikely that either would survive for more than a year.

The woman in the deli was middle-aged and motherly. The deli was called 'Celia's' and the woman wore a name-badge with the same name. She was inside, pinning a poster about a wine-tasting on the window. Holly stopped to look at it.

'Why don't you come along?' Celia had moved from the window out onto the pavement and was standing beside her. For a plump woman, she was very light on her feet and Holly was startled for a moment. 'It's all good fun. The great thing about somewhere like Bebington is that nobody gets snobby or pompous at a tasting. They just tell you what they like.'

'How long have you been here?'

'Nearly a year.'

'It must be hard going, a place like Bebington.'

'Don't you believe it! This place is on the way up. The rent and rates are low and the people have come out to support me. There's a real community feeling.' She nodded up the pavement towards the PC and the crime-scene tape. 'Are you here because of that? Press?'

'No!' Holly wasn't sure whether to be horrified or a little bit flattered. 'I'm a detective.'

'Do you want to come in? I suppose you have questions.' She paused. 'I hope you find the killer quickly. It's bad for business, unsolved murder.' But she gave a little self-mocking smile to show that wasn't really her priority.

The shop was dark and cool and smelled of cheese, garlic and yeast. Celia leaned against the counter. 'I didn't really know Gary. He came in occasionally for a bottle of wine. I don't think he was much of a foodie. Not the kind to cook, at least.'

Holly remembered Joe's description of the interior of the flat. 'Did he buy a bottle of wine yesterday?'

The woman nodded. 'In the afternoon. Chablis.

More than he usually liked to pay. I asked if he'd found himself a woman.' Celia was a gossip. The best kind of witness.

'He didn't have a regular girlfriend, then?'

'I don't think so. Nobody living in, at least.' Celia smiled. 'I did wonder if he had a thing for Felicity.'

'Felicity?'

'She works in the bookshop. Anchor Books. Her dad's the owner. I always thought she was a bit young for Gary, but when did that ever bother middle-aged men?' She paused again for a moment, laughed. 'But then I'm a cynic. My husband ran off with my best friend's daughter, and we'd been married for nearly thirty years.'

Felicity had long red hair, wild and curly, and reminded Holly of the poster of a Pre-Raphaelite painting she'd had on her wall as a student. The shop was long and narrow and every wall was covered with shelves. Felicity sat on a tall stool, reading. She wore a long green dress made of embroidered cotton and patent-leather Doc Martens boots, and seemed posed like an artist's model.

'You'll have seen there's been an incident along the street.' Holly thought *incident* was a useful word. It gave very little away. 'Can I ask a few questions?'

'Is it true Gary was murdered?' Felicity's voice had no accent at all. Holly would have bet twenty pounds that she'd been privately educated. If Gary had designs on her, he'd certainly had plans to move up in the world. Felicity was very different from Patty Keane.

'It was a suspicious death. I'm speaking to everyone

in the street, in case they heard or saw anything. Were you here yesterday afternoon?'

'Yeah, I've been here all week. Dad's away at an indie booksellers' conference. It's easy enough, because I live over the job.' Felicity flicked her eyes towards the ceiling. 'My own tiny stab at independence. I mean, you can't live at home forever, and it's quite a decent little flat.'

'When did you last see Gary?'

'The night before last, at the reading group. We run a few here. You have to, these days, if you want to survive. It builds an audience for our events. There's one for teens and one for kids, and a couple for adults. Gary's a member of the non-fiction group.' She paused. 'Mostly blokes. We buy in beer from next door.'

Holly tried to picture Gary Keane, who'd grown up on the edges of organized crime, who'd fathered three kids and then deserted his family, sitting in a circle discussing biography and narrative history. It made her shift perspective and wonder if he was the villain they'd all thought. 'Were you friendly?'

'We're all friendly here on the street. We have to be.' Which wasn't any kind of answer, as Felicity knew.

'Only I heard he took a romantic interest in you.' Holly winced as soon as she'd spoken. She sounded like something out of a Mills & Boon novel. What would Vera have said? *I heard he was sniffing around you?*

Felicity didn't mock, though. She sat on her stool and smiled serenely. 'He was actually quite an interesting guy. Self-educated. You know.'

'So you were going out?' Holly wondered if the relationship had been another form of rebellion, a way of Felicity distancing herself from her classy parents, like her choice to live in the Bebington flat.

'I cooked him supper a few times,' Felicity said. 'We saw a couple of films.'

'You don't seem upset that he's dead.' Because, so far, the young woman had shown no grief, just a dispassionate curiosity.

Felicity thought about that. 'I was shocked when I heard, but he wasn't the love of my life or anything. I mean, if you met him, you'd know we'd never have had a future together. For one thing, he was *ancient*. We got on okay, but it was just a friendship of convenience really. Do you understand what I mean?'

Holly did understand. She too seemed incapable of finding anyone with whom she'd be willing to share her life. And in the end, she was sure, Felicity would choose someone suitable, someone from the same background and with a similar education. 'You didn't see Gary yesterday?'

'No, we had a loose arrangement to go out later in the evening after I'd finished work, but he texted to say something had turned up. Business.'

'He wasn't more specific than that?'

Felicity shook her head.

'Did you see any strangers in the street? Early evening?'

'No, but then I wouldn't. I didn't get a chance to go outside at all until it was time to pack up. I'd had a delivery of stock in the morning and I was sorting that out for most of the day. There were some regular customers and a couple of drop-ins, but that would have been at lunchtime.' She pulled her fingers through her hair. 'I had to shut early because I was selling books at a library event in Morpeth. A big-name YA author was speaking to a group of kids. It started at six and I had to get there and set up. Parking's often a nightmare.' She set down her book and came down from the tall stool. 'Would you like a coffee? I was going to make one.'

Holly was tempted, but she shook her head. She felt that this conversation wasn't leading anywhere. 'YA?'

'Young adult.' Felicity gave the impression that *everyone* knew that.

'What time did you leave here?'

'About four-thirty. There aren't many customers in the late afternoon. You get some mums and kids on their way home from school, but most of our business comes from events.'

'Were there any unfamiliar cars in the street?'

Felicity shook her head. 'Not that I noticed.' She seemed bored. There was a tray on the counter with a kettle, a mug and a jar of instant coffee and she switched on the kettle.

'Did you ever meet his friends? His old friends, I mean. Not the people he'd met through the book group.'

The question seemed to amuse her; she gave a little shrug. 'Like I said, we didn't have that sort of relationship.'

'How was Gary the last time you saw him?' Holly asked this almost as an afterthought. It was a Vera sort of question. She was always more interested in mood than in facts.

Felicity stood poised, the kettle in her hand, ready to pour out the boiling water. 'He had been a bit odd recently. Excited, but kind of jittery. When I asked him what the matter was, he gave a little laugh and said his past had come back to haunt him.'

Chapter Thirty

Vera left the grand terrace where Gus and Elaine Sinclair had made their home and walked along the sea front. It was a struggle back up the bank towards the car, but she was glad to be away from the smart apartment and the woman who'd given very little away. Except that comment about Robbie Marshall being able to procure anything anyone wanted. To Vera, that suggested sex, and her mind was racing, forging strange connections. Robbie had been a traveller. It was what he'd been famous for, according to Hector and the gang. An adventurous streak that had seemed at odds with his reluctance to move away from home and his mother. He'd travelled alone to exotic places in search of birds, returned with a list of species designed to make Hector and the others jealous. There'd been slide shows in the house in the hills and afterwards Hector had sneered at the poor quality of the photographs, at Robbie's obsession with seeing species that were new to him. 'That's not real natural history. It's birding tourism of the worst possible kind.'

But at around that time a number of single and lonely birdwatchers in the region had acquired foreign brides. Women who had seemed subservient, at least at first. It occurred to Vera that Robbie might have procured these women on his wanderings. She remembered that Thailand had been one of his favourite destinations. And if he'd provided that service, could he have been involved in the same business in the UK? The procurement of women for clients with specific tastes and needs. Charlie had said that Gus Sinclair's father, Alec, had been involved in smuggling women. Perhaps Robbie Marshall had been a partner in the business.

Vera stopped halfway up the bank to look down at the dinghies racing at the mouth of the Tyne and to catch her breath. Her mind didn't stop, though. That was still chasing wild ideas and theories. Robbie Marshall had been frightened just before his disappearance. In Whitley Bay in those days, prostitution would have been a competitive business, and if Robbie had set up in opposition to the big boys, he could have upset his rivals. And if Mary-Frances turned out to be the second body in the culvert, there might have been a rational explanation for the pair to be together. Had her regular pimp killed them both, as an example to other working women who might consider looking to Robbie to organize and protect them? That was a lot of *if*s. A big supposition. But it made a kind of sense.

When Vera got back to the police station, Holly was still in Bebington, but Joe was there and she called him into her stuffy office.

'Did anyone look at Marshall's finances when he disappeared?'

Joe shrugged. 'I assume they'd have checked he hadn't withdrawn any cash. That would have proved he was still alive and would have given some indication of where he might be.'

'I've called in the financial investigator to go through his affairs, but it'll be hard because the accounts are so old. I'd love to know if he was getting money from other sources.' Vera explained the theory she'd dreamed up as she'd walked through Tynemouth. It seemed a little less credible when she described it to Joe.

'He still lived with his mam,' Joe said. 'In Wallsend. That's not exactly the profile of a major people-trafficker.'

'Which is why we need to look at his bank accounts. If he had any unexplained money, we need to find it.' She looked at Joe. 'Have you got any further in tracking down the Prof.? Any joy on the phone number from which he called Gary Keane?'

'It was from a pay-as-you-go mobile. No name registered and, if he had anything to do with Keane's murder, I guess it will have been thrown away as soon as he finished the call.'

Vera sat for a moment and dug back into her memory, tried to get a fix on the man they'd all called the Prof. She remembered Hector talking about him, but wasn't sure that she'd actually met him. Then at last there was a glimmer of recollection. It was late one night and she'd have been sixteen. Her last year at school before she joined the police force as a cadet. Winter. She'd made Hector's supper and they'd eaten it together in front of the fire, because the rest of the house was freezing. She'd cleared up and taken herself to bed, not because she was tired, but because Hector had been drinking and that made him argumentative and she just couldn't be arsed to argue. She'd heard a car pulling up outside and had looked out of the window, still wrapped up in the sheet and blankets from the bed. Ice on the window had blurred her view, but the house was single-storey and she'd been very close to the action. There'd been a sliver of moon and just enough light to make out shadows and silhouettes. It had been a big car. The man who'd emerged had been big too, tall and vigorous. Young, it had seemed to the young Vera. Nowhere near as old as Hector. She'd been of an age to be interested in any young man.

He'd banged on the door. 'Come on, Hector, you old rogue. I know you're in there. Let me in. It's fucking freezing out here.'

Of course she'd heard the F-word in the playground, but not used by adults, and had been strangely shocked by it.

She'd been aware of her father moving in the living room with the fire. He'd stumbled as he'd reached the front door and fumbled with the bolt. They might have lived miles from anywhere, but Hector had always been conscious of security. There'd been too many secrets hidden away. She'd heard the creaking of the door.

'Prof.! I wasn't expecting you until tomorrow.'

'You know me, H. Always strike while the iron's hot. Our Arabian friends need the goods now.' Vera had taken 'the goods' to mean the peregrine eggs in the incubator in the lean-to. Falconers in the Middle East set a high store on birds from traditional sites, and rumour had it that the first Queen Elizabeth had used birds from the Borders.

Now, in the cramped and cluttered office in Kimmerston Police Station, she replayed that conversation in her head. The shouting younger man on the doorstep, and Hector, blunted by drink and sleep. Could it have been the voice she remembered, captured on Gary Keane's office answerphone? Maybe, she thought. The recent recording was older, more measured, but there was the same confidence, the same hint of arrogance.

Joe was still sitting on the other side of the desk, watching her. She wondered what he made of her lapses in concentration, the times she drifted away from reality. Perhaps he just put it down to age.

'Get Charlie in here!' Her voice sounded strange in her ears. It was the shift in time, the daydreaming. Had she half been expecting to hear her sixteen-year-old self?

Joe knew better than to question or argue and got to his feet. Vera lifted a pile of files from the only spare chair in the place and pulled it up next to Joe's.

'Any luck in tracking down the Prof.?' Vera was thinking he wouldn't have been a professor when he came banging on their door in the middle of the night. He might have been doing his Masters or his PhD, the title affectionate but a little ironic. None of the others – not Hector or Robbie Marshall or John Brace – had a degree of any kind. But he might be a professor now. Probably in one of the natural sciences.

Charlie shook his head. 'Nothing definite. I played the tape to admin staff in the local unis, just like you suggested. There were a few people who thought he might sound familiar, but you know what it's like with a murder inquiry. People want to be involved, like to think they can help. I've made a note of the names and I was just about to set up some interviews.'

Vera nodded her approval but she was impatient. 'There's one person who knows the identity of the professor. He probably knows who the female corpse is too. And he's sitting in Warkworth nick, watching us flounder and loving every minute.'

She picked up the phone and dialled the prison, demanded to see John Brace that afternoon and wouldn't take no for an answer.

The interview rooms were full, so they'd arranged for her to see the ex-detective in the room on the Elderly and Disabled Wing where she'd done her lecture. An officer escorted her past the education block. The same teacher with short grey hair was running a class for younger inmates. One was standing and reading out loud from a poetry collection. There was that same institution smell of overcooked vegetables and disinfectant. Vera thought that in prisons nothing changed and perhaps boredom was the trigger for fights and riots, for the dependence on legal highs, the simmering desperation.

She was shown again to the chapel. This time the room was arranged as a social space. Small tables held board games. Half of the people there seemed to be asleep. Once again the chaplain gave up his office so that Vera could talk to John Brace.

'You'll have heard about Gary Keane?' Because although the dead man's name hadn't been released to the news organizations, Vera thought Brace *would* know. He might look like a frail old man in his wheel-chair, but she wasn't taken in by that. He'd have had a mobile phone smuggled in, and at least one prison officer on his payroll.

Brace nodded. 'We live in terribly violent times. Sometimes I think the police just aren't up to the job these days.'

'You never liked him. Never thought he was good enough for your daughter.'

'I'm in here, Inspector. I'm hardly in a position to have killed him.'

But you have money. Contacts.

'Gary had a phone call from the Prof. just before he died,' Vera said. Her eyes were fixed on the man sitting so close to her that she could see the places the razor had missed when he'd shaved that morning. There was no reaction.

'That's a rave from the grave.' Brace gave a little smile. Cold and hard as iron. 'A blast from the past.'

'But you'll have kept in touch with the Prof. over the years. You were so close. The Gang of Four.'

'Things change. People move on.'

'I need to talk to him.' Vera struggled to keep her voice even. She couldn't show Brace how much she needed this information. 'I'm having a bit of trouble tracking him down.'

'I can't help you there. I lost touch with the Prof. years ago. Once Hector passed on, we went our separate ways. He always was a bit elusive, the Prof. He liked his privacy.'

'But he was at the funeral. At Hector's funeral.' A statement, not a question. Of course he'd have been there to pay his respects. It would have been a matter of honour. Robbie Marshall would have been absent, of course. He was buried in the culvert near the St Mary's wetland in Whitley Bay. But there'd been a romance about the idea of the Gang of Four. The loud young man who'd turned up at the house in the middle of the night, calling Hector a rogue, would have turned out to see him buried. The trouble was that Vera could remember very little of that day – she'd spent the previous night drinking Hector's favourite malt – and there'd been lots of strangers who'd crawled out of the woodwork to fill the pews in the church in the village. Members of Hector's family even, minor gentry who'd disowned him while he was alive. Perhaps they'd wanted to check they were finally shot of him for good.

Brace said nothing and his head drooped a little, as if he was struggling to hold it up.

'I need a name for him,' Vera said. 'For the Prof.'

'I'm not sure I ever knew his name. That was all we ever called him. Hector would have known, of course. Hector was a bit older than the rest of us. Something of a father figure. He recruited us all.'

As if you were spies! And of course you knew his name.

'You should help me, Brace, if you ever want to get out of here. If you want to escape the stink and the boredom.' She could see that had struck home. 'You're up for parole soon.'

There was a silence. She thought she could hear one of the old men in the chapel snoring, even though the door was shut.

'I'd help you if I could, Vera.'

'Who are you scared of?'

He shook his head, offended. 'It's not like that.' *Nobody can scare John Brace.*

'What *is* it like?'

'Sometimes you just have to stick by your people. You should understand that.'

Another silence, because she didn't have an answer except that her people weren't villains and, if they were, she wouldn't stick by them. 'I went to see Elaine Sinclair this morning,' she said. 'You'll remember Elaine. She and Gus have a very flash pad on the sea front in Tynemouth. They're too classy for Whitley these days, it seems. Gus is heavily involved in the regeneration of the area now. He has ambitions to be a politician, apparently.' Another pause. 'Elaine said something very interesting. She told me Robbie Marshall could procure anything for anyone. Any idea what she might have meant by that?'

Brace raised his head a little. 'Robbie was the first contact, when we were selling falcons to the Middle East. The Prof. was the front man, but Robbie knew the people. Sometimes he came across buyers through his work at Swan's. There was lots of trade with overseas contractors. Robbie was always doing deals. He could strike a hard bargain.'

Vera knew Brace was thinking about the parole board and was giving her as much as he could, without a name for the Prof. 'What else was he procuring, John? Women? Drugs?'

There was a tight, thin smile. 'Elaine was right. Robbie could get you anything you wanted. For a price.'

'What did he do with all his money?'

Another pause. 'You should talk to Gus about that.'

'Robbie invested in Gus Sinclair's business?' Vera thought she should have considered that before. Perhaps the murder was the result of a falling-out between business partners. Or greed on Sinclair's part, when things at The Seagull started falling apart. That great shiny edifice on Whitley Bay sea front had been a facade for all sorts of deals. What had happened to Robbie Marshall's investment when he died? Vera doubted if his mother had seen any of the cash, but then she might not have wanted it, if she'd known how her son had made all his money.

'I doubt you'll find Robbie's name as partner on the books,' Brace said, 'but yeah, he was a major shareholder.'

'And what about you, John, were you an investor too?'

He looked up and smiled slowly. 'I was just a poor cop. Where would I find that sort of money?'

Chapter Thirty-One

Vera sat in her car and thought about the Gang of Four, held together by loyalty and shared secrets, that strange kind of male friendship that seemed more important to those involved than either marriage or family. Two of the men were dead and John Brace was in prison. John wasn't talking, so she needed to find someone else who might have an idea of the identity of the Prof. She wished now she'd taken more notice of the visitors to Hector's cottage. As a teenager she'd dismissed them all as loners and weirdos: the men who turned up carrying freshly killed animals to be stuffed by her father, the ones with the lust of collecting in their eyes, parting with good money for the eggs her father had stolen. Now she'd have given anything to remember the name of anyone who might give her the Prof.'s identity.

She thought again about Hector's funeral. Had there been a tall stranger with a posh voice and the confidence to know he'd always be at the top of the pile? Always a survivor. But still her memory was blurred. It had been raining, a fine grey drizzle that dripped from the trees in the churchyard, and the mourners' faces had been hidden by umbrellas and hoods. No matter how hard she tried, she knew she wouldn't remember individual identities of the assorted group of men who gathered together afterwards. Not chatting exactly, but communicating in clipped monosyllables. She hadn't sensed a strong friendship between *them*; they were acquaintances who shared an obsession, a collective group of Hector's cronies, more business-men than friends. Vera had just wanted the event over and hadn't listened to the names being given, espe-cially when she was being introduced to strangers.

But there *had* been people she knew there, stand-ing in the rain. People who'd provided real comfort. She'd been aware of Davy and Norma, the elderly couple who'd been Hector's neighbours for as long as Vera could remember. They'd lived in the farm adjoin-ing Hector's cottage until they'd died within weeks of each other, and then Jack and Joanna had taken the place on. Norma was one of the few people Vera had ever met who'd known her mother. Hector had closed down completely whenever Vera had asked about Mary Stanhope, but Norma had stories that kept the woman alive for Vera, photos so that Vera could pic-ture her. Growing up, Vera had been too proud to complain to Norma about Hector, and she would have stood up for her father fiercely if the woman had made any comment or criticism, but Norma's kitchen had been her haven. A refuge where she could do homework in peace, get a decent meal. The couple had never had children, and now Vera wondered if she'd given them as much comfort as they'd given her, seen her even as a surrogate daughter.

Vera felt a sudden moment of guilt, the realization that as a relationship, her friendship with the couple had been entirely one-way. She'd given nothing back.

Davy and Norma had grown old, entirely without family support, and she'd ignored them, just because she couldn't face spending time with Hector. Even when she'd gone back to live with him in his last few months, she'd used the excuse of work to be away from the house as much as she could and certainly hadn't made the effort to visit the neighbours.

Then she thought she was making a drama of the situation. She always did. Vera could never be part of a story without playing a leading role; this time the role was that of the heartless friend. Davy and Norma must have had family, a niece at least, because they hadn't been alone at Hector's funeral. A younger woman had stood beside them in the church, supporting them both. Now Vera felt a mixture of resentment, guilt and jealousy towards the stranger, which was quite irrational: *That should have been me. I was the first pretend daughter. You took my place.*

Still in the vehicle, it came to her as a sudden realization that the Prof. couldn't really have been in the business of countryside crime for the money. Even selling raptors to Arab sheikhs, he wouldn't have made a huge profit. Hector had died with more debts than assets; the only things he'd owned when he died were an ancient Land Rover and a crumbling cottage with no mod cons. John Brace and Robbie Marshall had made their money from their involvement with men like Gus Sinclair. Even hiring out muscle to beleaguered country landowners would have seemed petty, compared to that. No, the Gang of Four had been in it for the game. The thrill. A sentimental attachment to the land and its bizarre traditions. So perhaps the Prof. was still playing. Perhaps he was still out in the field collecting eggs and trading them, killing hen harriers on grouse moors for profit and for sport. And while Charlie had contacts and informants in the city and the coastal towns, the uplands belonged to Vera. This was her territory. She still had contacts and she'd put out the word.

It occurred to her then that if Davy and Norma were still alive, they might point her in the right direction. Davy had worked as a beater on the estates in the district and he might have come across the Prof. He'd known all the gossip, picked it up in the Lamb, the pub in the valley at the bottom of their hill. And that gave her another idea.

She switched on the engine and headed inland from the prison, driving north-west down narrow lanes, first through farmland and then a steep climb onto open moorland. Not having to think where she was going because she was on her way home.

She found her neighbours, Jack and Joanna, drinking coffee in the big, untidy kitchen in the farmhouse next to Hector's cottage. They were an unlikely pair. Jack was from Liverpool and still had the accent, the chippiness and the warm heart. He'd been a drifter until he'd taken up with Joanna, but always a grafter. Joanna was from a grand family and had been through the whole aristo thing: public school, finishing school, marriage to an arsehole. She always said that Jack had rescued her. Vera had once rescued her too, saved her from a murder charge at least; now Joanna wrote about murder and turned it into entertainment. Vera wasn't sure what she thought about that.

Vera opened the door without knocking, but gave them a shout to let them know she was on the way in.

The cluttered kitchen was poorly lit, so it always looked as if it was dark outside. Jack's Border collie was slouched on the mat next to the Aga, and standing on top of the stove was a pot of coffee, the smell of it delicious, overwhelming the smell of dog. A need for good coffee was one of Joanna's affectations. She said she'd inherited it, along with the passion for good red wine. Before Vera was through the door, Jack had fetched a mug from a dusty shelf and nodded for her to help herself. He was in his work clothes, mucky overalls and thick woollen socks. He'd left his boots at the door. Joanna had been working too; there was a pile of printed paper on the table in front of her. She nodded towards it. 'Proofreading. Nightmare!' But Vera could tell she was proud: this was what real writers did, and it had taken Joanna a long time to realize that she was a real writer.

'How can we help you, Vee?' Jack's accent was as thick as when he'd first moved to the county.

Usually Vera *did* turn up at their house because she needed their help – the Land Rover had broken down, or the dodgy electrics in the house had blown a fuse and she couldn't stop the system tripping.

'Just a chat,' she said. 'Just a social call.'

'In the middle of the day?'

She decided they knew her too well and gave a little nod. 'Well, maybe I've just got a few questions.'

'Work, Vee? You think we can help with your work?' Jack sounded surprised. Vera never brought her work home.

'You help out with the shoots, don't you? On the Standrigg Estate and other places up the county?'

He grinned. 'Sometimes you have to mix with the

devil to make ends meet. Not that we do much mixing with the shooters. I tug my forelock and do as I'm told. Act the peasant. That's what they like in their beaters, especially the nouveaux riches.'

Joanna looked at Vera and rolled her eyes. 'He's such a snob.'

'Are there many nouveaux riches?'

'They're the ones with the money. The gentry have all their cash tied up in land.'

Vera made an imaginative leap. She could picture Gus Sinclair in tweeds and brogues, a gun under his arm. 'Have you ever come across a man called Angus Sinclair? Lives in a smart apartment in Tynemouth. He's something big in the regeneration of the coast.'

'Yeah. He's part of the consortium that shoots at Standrigg. Slimy. Not as bright as he thinks he is.' Jack paused. 'A nice enough man until something goes wrong. Or he doesn't get the respect he thinks he's due. He's a great one for holding a grudge if he's been slighted. Isn't he into property? That's what I heard. That he's buying up most of Whitley Bay and waiting until the place is all gentrified. Then he'll start selling, and he'll be set to make a killing. He's got his property out on short-term lets, so he can get rid of the tenants when he wants rid of them.' Another grin. 'But that's the free market, Vee. Nothing wrong with that. Not legally at least.'

Vera didn't bite. The only time she got into politics with Jack was late at night after too much to drink.

Jack was still talking. 'Gus enjoys the shooting, but for him it's all about business. He's got the gift of the gab and pulls in investors while he's out after birds. I've seen him in action. He almost had me persuaded that Whitley Bay was about to become the most desirable place in the North-East to live.'

'What about someone called the Prof.?' Vera asked. 'He was a friend of my father's. I have the feeling that he mixes with the county set. And he certainly knew Sinclair.'

Jack thought for a minute. 'I think I've heard him mentioned by the county set, but I'm sure I never met him.'

'Mentioned in what context, Jack?' Vera leaned forward across the table.

'Important, is it, Vee?'

'Oh yes. A matter of life and death.' Her voice light and flippant, but meaning every word. The dog snored and twitched.

Jack leaned back in his chair and shut his eyes and for a moment he could have been sleeping too. 'Like he was the Pope and Paul McCartney rolled into one. Second only to God bloody Almighty.' He spoke again, mimicking the accent of the landed gentry in a falsetto. '"Did you hear, darling? Guess who's joining us next week? Only the Prof.!"'

'Anything else you can tell me about him?' Vera wondered what it was about the Prof. that generated such reverence among a group that was usually aware only of its *own* importance.

'Sorry, Vee. I'm not part of the in-crowd. I only pick up snatches of conversation.'

Joanna had set down her manuscript. 'I heard something similar not very long ago. A quite different situation, though. Probably a different professor.'

'Might be helpful, though, pet.' Vera thought she had nothing to lose. The Prof. was like a shadow in the mist drifting ahead of her, always just out of reach. 'Where was it?'

'Two writers were chatting at a book event I was doing in the Lit and Phil Library in Newcastle. One of those overheard snatches of conversation that you pick up in a crowded room. It was after the talk and the signing, and people were milling around drinking the last of the wine. One of them mentioned the Prof. It was like Jack said. It was as if he were some kind of celebrity, and so famous that they didn't need to use his name.'

'Could you get a name for me? Chat to one of your literary pals?'

'Sure,' Joanna said. 'But there are lots of professors in the world. I can't believe we're talking about the same man.' Her attention had already drifted back to the typescript on the table in front of her.

'Was there anything left behind here, when you moved in?' Vera was still thinking of Norma and Davy Kerr. 'Any belongings, I mean.'

'Masses of stuff,' Jack said. 'We bought all the furniture along with the house and just cleared out what we didn't need. One of the reasons we got the place so cheap was that nothing had been touched since the old couple died.'

Vera nodded and thought that must be why she felt at home here. Nothing much had changed since she'd escaped to Norma's kitchen as a child.

Joanna looked up from her work. 'What were you thinking of?' Her voice gentle, realizing this was important.

'I wondered if you'd come across some photos.'

'In a wooden box?'

'Yes!' Vera was back in the kitchen with Norma, sitting at this table. When Norma opened the box, there'd been a smell. Sandalwood? And then they'd laid out the photographs, spread them like playing cards all over the table. They'd looked through all Norma's family pictures: her father in uniform, Davy in uniform. The images faded and brown now. But Vera had really only been interested in the record of her own history. There'd been snaps of her parents' wedding. Not official wedding photos, but a few taken by Davy. Her mother in white, holding a bunch of deep-red roses. Hector looking happy. Vera thought now that she'd seldom seen Hector looking happy. And there'd been a later picture of her mother, sitting outside the farm on the white wooden bench that was still there. Obviously pregnant. Her hands folded across her belly. Smiling.

Chapter Thirty-Two

Joe was doing as Vera had ordered and trying to dig into Robbie Marshall's finances. The case notes just showed that none of the man's credit or debit cards had been used after he'd been reported missing. Phone calls to Marshall's bank were unproductive. First he had a twenty-minute wait, trying to answer automated questions, then a conversation with a call handler that left both of them tense and frustrated. It was so long ago. The woman on the other end of the line wouldn't know where to start and was reluctant to pass him on to someone who might be able to help. In the end the line went dead. Joe knew there would be ways through the maze – he could pass on the task to officers specializing in fraud and financial crime – but he was impatient. He needed the sort of material he'd found in Gary Keane's office: records that he could understand and access immediately.

That made him think of Eleanor Marshall in her tidy house with its view of the Wallsend park. If she'd had no proof that Robbie had died, might she have kept his room just as he'd left it, in case he turned up out of the blue? Joe wondered if Robbie would have had a computer in 1995. *He'*d had a very basic Amstrad, just for playing games on. But perhaps Gary had bought something more sophisticated for Robbie and set it up for him. Perhaps it was still in Robbie's room, a treasure chest containing records of the man's travels and his finances, all his business dealings with the Gang of Four and Gus Sinclair. Joe grabbed his jacket and keys and drove south towards the Tyne.

When he arrived, he was surprised to see that Eleanor had a visitor. He'd imagined her leading a solitary life, keeping a lonely vigil for her son, but there was a small car parked in the street outside the house and a stranger opened the door to him. She was a little, busy woman, a member of Eleanor's church, here to provide some support at this difficult time. That was explained while he was still standing on the doorstep. When Joe introduced himself, Eleanor recognized his voice and shouted from the living room, 'Come on through, Sergeant. Doreen was just leaving.'

Leaving was clearly the last thing on Doreen's mind; she was curious and would have been delighted to stay. But Eleanor's voice had brooked no dissent, and Doreen had no choice but to gather together her things and go. Joe watched the little car drive away.

'I'm sorry to have interrupted.' He sat on the sofa that Vera had taken on their previous visit.

'Don't be.' Eleanor paused for a moment. 'Doreen is a good woman, but she hankers to be told how good she is. I don't have the patience for her at the moment. Or for any of the others who've turned up over the last couple of days. But they did bring cake, Sergeant, if you'd like some with your tea.'

'I was wondering if you still had any of Robert's belongings.'

'Of course. I haven't been into his room since he

left. Not even to clean it. That was something he was always very firm about. His privacy. If we were going to live together, we had to have our own spaces.' She hesitated. 'When the inspector told me he was dead, I was tempted to go in. After all, that agreement no longer stood and Robert would never know, but I couldn't quite face it. Not on my own.'

'Would you mind if I checked in there?' He paused. What could he say to persuade her? Not: *There might be evidence that he trafficked women and drugs.* 'There could be something to help us discover who killed him.'

'I'd be very pleased.' She paused again. 'Just to have the door opened would be helpful, I think. It's been shut for so many years.'

'Did Robert lock it?'

'Oh no! He asked me not to go in, and he trusted that I never would.'

'Would you like to come up with me? I'd ask you not to touch anything. Not yet. But if you'd just like to look inside.'

There was a moment of silence that stretched. 'I think I'd rather you went in first, Sergeant. I need a little while to prepare myself. I find the idea of seeing all his possessions rather disturbing.'

'You must have looked when Robert first disappeared,' Joe said. 'You'd have been worried that he might be lying ill inside.'

She nodded her head in agreement. 'I did open the door, but I didn't go *in*. I could see from the landing that the room was empty and the bed hadn't been slept in. But I'm afraid I've allowed my imagination rather to run away from me and I'm frightened about how I'll react to the place. *His* place. Waiting for news about him sent me a little bit mad, I think.'

'I think it would drive anyone a little bit mad,' Joe said. 'But you seem very sane to me. Are you happy for me to go up?'

'Yes, see yourself up. I'm very slow on the stairs.'

'It might take me a little while to search properly.'

'I have plenty of time, Sergeant, and when you've finished we'll have tea and some do-gooders' cake.' She gave a little smile. 'And then perhaps you'll be kind enough to come upstairs with me and see me inside. His room is at the back of the house, next to the bath-room.'

The hall and the landing were gloomy, covered in mock-Tudor wood panelling. Joe thought that little had been changed since the house had been built in the thirties. Light came through a stained-glass window on the landing. The stairs twisted, so he had no idea of the layout upstairs until he reached it. The doors were identical and must have been original. Six panels with Bakelite handles. The bathroom door was ajar and he glanced inside at the black-and-white tiles on the walls and the floor and a large enamel bath. He paused for a moment outside the room where Robbie Marshall had lived since he was a boy. Something of Eleanor's superstition about the place had made him anxious too. He pulled on the latex gloves he'd brought with him, turned the handle and looked inside.

The first impression was of light. It was a large room with a big bay window looking out over the garden and the park beyond. Sunshine flooded in. Joe took a step and shut the door behind him. Apart from the dust that lay on the flat surfaces and a stuffy, rather airless smell, Robbie Marshall could have left the place that morning. Although this had been Robbie's room since he was a teenager, there was nothing of his childhood here. Any posters or models had been removed. There was a double bed against one wall and a desk in the wide bay window. No computer. If he'd used one, it must have been at work and Joe knew that would have disappeared long ago, along with the rest of the shipyard's assets. In the alcoves on each side of the chimney breast, shelves held maps and notebooks. There were travel and field guides, but Joe could see no light reading. A small television seemed oddly old-fashioned now, square and boxy; it stood on one of the shelves and there was an easy chair positioned to watch it. Joe wondered how much company Robbie had provided for his mother and how much time he'd spent alone in his room. He wondered if she'd worshipped him as much when he was alive as she had after he'd disappeared.

The notebooks had been arranged in chronological order and started when Robbie was still a schoolboy. The first ones recorded birds seen on the Bebington Grammar School field trips. There were little sketches that Joe found strangely moving. Later books detailed Robbie's travels further afield. He'd been to countries in Africa and South America that Joe had only ever heard of on the BBC news, but seemed to return regularly to Eastern Europe and to Thailand and Indonesia. There were acronyms and symbols that meant nothing to Joe; he thought Vera might be able to decipher them. She'd grown up with a birdwatcher, after all. He wondered about the practicalities of bringing all this material into the station, then decided to take a few of the later notebooks and to leave the early ones where they were. He couldn't see that a boat trip to the Farne Islands from Seahouses in 1972 would have much significance to the inquiry.

Against the wall on each side of the bay there was a cupboard, sturdy and painted white. In one, Robbie had kept his clothes: two suits and a few smart shirts on hangers, the rest the sort of outdoor wear he'd have worn on his forays into the countryside with Hector. The second cupboard had been fitted with shelves and was filled with folders. This had been his home office and Joe felt a moment of triumph; within all this paper it should be possible to find out more about Robbie's secret business dealings. He flicked through the files, looking at the references on the front, and at once found one labelled 'Seagull'. He pulled it out and could tell that it would take time to read it properly and check the contents. There were contracts, scraps of paper that had acted as receipts, something that looked like a formal partnership agreement. He thought how delighted Vera would be with his find, how cross that *she* hadn't considered that Robbie's room would be just as he'd left it.

He lifted out each of the folders and stacked them on the bed. He'd take them all back to the station for the team to work on there, along with the most recent notebooks. The last file held Marshall's bank and building-society statements. There was fifty thousand pounds in the Northumbria Building Society. Joe thought that would have been a fortune in the mid-nineties – certainly more than a middle manager could have saved or made from trading in a few birds' eggs. Joe hoped there'd be some explanation in the mountain of paper on the bed, and then he wondered how much interest would be due. He supposed the money belonged to Eleanor now, and that at least she'd spend her remaining years in some comfort.

The bank statements were held separately in a plastic envelope within the Manila file. As in Gary Keane's office, everything was ordered, and Joe wondered if Marshall had been some sort of mentor for the boy. Sal looked after the finances in their family and she was pretty good at keeping on top of things, but their household accounts looked nothing like this. Sal kept their receipts and bills jumbled together in an old shoebox. Joe scanned through the last couple of statements. He was aware of Eleanor waiting downstairs, knew she was building up the courage to come into this room after more than twenty years of staying away, and didn't want to delay any more than was necessary.

Regular income came from the liquidators of Swan Hunter and from one large monthly payment that was marked only by a reference number. The financial investigators would check that later. Joe wondered if it had come from Gus Sinclair, and what service Marshall could possibly be giving to the man to earn that sort of reward. The only other item of note was a payment from Marshall by cheque to Hector Stanhope. That was for five hundred pounds. Looking at the previous statement, Joe saw that the same sum had been paid to the same place the month before. And the month before that. Not a direct debit but a regular payment. Why would Robbie be paying his old friend a sum that would have been substantial at the time? What service could Hector be providing? In other circumstances, Joe would have suspected blackmail. But these were friends, weren't they? Surely Hector wouldn't have stooped so low that he'd blackmail his friend.

Joe carried the files from the bed in two journeys and locked them straight into the boot of his car. He'd shut the door to the living room when he'd left Eleanor and now, if she'd heard his feet on the stairs, she made no move. He would ask her permission to remove the files, but he thought it would have upset her to see him carrying armfuls of her son's belongings out of the house. Back inside, he tapped at the living-room door.

'Have you finished, Sergeant? Did you find anything useful?' She was already getting to her feet with the aid of a walking frame.

'I've taken away some paperwork. I hope you don't mind.'

'Will you bring it back?'

'Of course, though it might take a little while. I'll make sure you get the building-society passbook as soon as possible. You'll need that to access Robbie's money.'

'Robbie had money?' She seemed surprised. 'He was always generous of course, but I doubt there's very much left. He travelled so much.' A pause. 'He said he wouldn't be able to take it with him when he died.'

'He seems to have had savings. You don't know where that might have come from?'

'Ah, he was always very careful with his money, even as a boy.'

'Your husband didn't leave him anything when he died?' Though Joe doubted that a butcher would have had fifty grand to bequeath to his son. Even in the nineties, when Robbie had disappeared, that would have been an enormous sum.

She shook her head. 'There wasn't much, and that all came to me.'

'Did you ever meet a man called Hector Stanhope?'

She had to think for a moment. 'I knew the name, of course. Robert went birdwatching with him.' A pause. 'He came here once, and that was a year or so before my son disappeared. I remember because Robert didn't bring many friends home. Not even when he was a boy. There was only John Brace. Robert never needed much company.'

'But Hector did come?'

'Just once and he didn't stay for very long. I offered to cook a meal for them, but he said he was in a hurry and Robert took him to his room. It seemed like a business meeting. When they came back down they shook hands. It looked very formal, as if they'd just agreed a deal. Not at all like pals who were having a chat.' Eleanor Marshall looked up towards the top of the stairs.

Joe climbed slowly with her one step at a time until they reached the landing, and then he took her arm and they walked to the door of Robbie's room. 'Would you like to go in on your own?'

Eleanor steadied herself. She'd have been getting on in years the last time she looked inside, but spry and fit, happy to be sharing her home with the son she adored. 'If you wouldn't mind just waiting there.'

Joe stood on the landing, with his back to the bannister, and watched her walk inside.

Chapter Thirty-Three

The team was in Vera's house, seated around the table where once Hector had stuffed his birds and animals. There'd been a formal briefing in the police station and Holly had struggled to keep up with all the new information that was coming in, resorting in the end to pen and paper to make her lines and connections and still feeling that she was missing a lot of it. Vera had been out all afternoon and had returned to the office in a strange mood. Distracted. Holly had asked tentatively if she was feeling okay, and instead of getting the usual tart reply, her boss had only smiled and said, 'Ah pet, I've been wandering down memory lane. Not always a comfortable place to be.'

In the office, they'd made a start on the files that Joe had found in Eleanor's house, but it had been frustrating, each find leading to a question rather than an answer. Joe had seemed reluctant to go into details – he'd said they should all leave that until the morning, when they'd come to it with fresh eyes – and Vera had still seemed vague and unfocused. In the end, she had invited the core team back to her house. 'I'll be able to see things more clearly out of the office, and with a couple of beers inside me.' So here they were in the house in the hills, *Vera's* gang of four, with photocopies of Robbie Marshall's bank statements scattered over the table. Vera was drinking Wylam beer from the bottle and, when the others turned down the offer to join her, she'd made them surprisingly good coffee. A packet of chocolate digestives, ripped open, sat on top of the paper.

The beer and the chocolate seemed to have given Vera a burst of energy and pulled her attention back to the case.

'So what have you got for us, Joe? You must have come to some conclusions. You read through all this stuff in the Marshall house. I'd like a concrete idea of the way that Brace, Marshall and the Prof. were linked financially to Gus Sinclair. We know they mixed socially, but there must have been more to the relationship than that. I found out today that Sinclair has been insinuating himself into the landed-gentry set, so he might have been part of Brace's scheme to hire out thugs to the minor aristocracy. No way of proving it, though.'

Joe shifted uneasily in his seat. Holly wondered what that was about. Joe was Vera's blue-eyed boy. He had nothing to fear from her.

'There was a regular payment into Marshall's account. There's only a reference number on the statement, but the financial investigator has already tracked it down. It came from the business account of The Seagull.'

'What do we think?' Vera looked round at her team. 'Were they business partners and Marshall was getting a return on his investment, a share of the profits?'

Charlie was looking at a copy of the statement. 'I

don't think The Seagull ever made *that* much of a profit.'

'What, then?' Vera's voice was excited now. Almost girlish. In this mood, Holly thought she looked at least ten years younger than her real age. 'Was this a retainer for services rendered?'

'Maybe,' Charlie said. He drank the last of his coffee. 'But we know Marshall was a fixer. There would have been costs to making the Sinclair business empire run smoothly. Cops to pay. Councillors. Perhaps that was the service Marshall provided to Sinclair, and the money was a kind of slush fund for Marshall to pass on.'

There was a moment of silence. They were all waiting for Vera's reaction. 'I can see that would work,' she said at last. 'I'm not sure how it would provide a motive for killing Robbie Marshall, though.'

'Unless he was ripping Sinclair off.' Holly wanted to show that she could make a contribution. 'Keeping all the money for himself.'

'Aye, maybe.' But Vera sounded dubious. 'I'm not sure that was the sort of man Marshall was, though. He enjoyed making things happen, keeping in with the power-players. I think that gave him more of a buzz than the cash. Like Charlie said, he was a fixer. That was his reputation.' Another silence. 'It would be good to track down some of those people Marshall was paying on Sinclair's behalf. Test the theory. Any ideas, Charlie? Some ex-police who took the cash but might have a conscience after all these years?'

He nodded. 'You'd never get them to go on the record. Brace's sentence frightened them all.'

'It's information I'm after at this point, man. Not justice.'

Charlie nodded again.

Vera went on. 'I wonder if Sinclair's working in the same way now. Using someone else to do his dirty work, to bribe the planners and the councillors to let him build his gleaming new Whitley Bay. According to my neighbour, he's buying up half the town for rental properties. And that's beside his development of the old Seagull site.'

'You think he might have been using Gary Keane?' Joe had been quiet all evening, listening but staring into the fire. Now he turned back to face them.

'It makes sense, doesn't it?' Vera's cheeks were red from the flames. 'We've assumed that the Prof. was involved in his death, because he left a message on Keane's voicemail arranging to meet. But would a killer – someone we know to be an intelligent man – really leave a message that he knew we'd find? Besides, what would his motive be? But if both Sinclair's fixers have ended up dead, that would be some coincidence.' She paused for a moment and Holly could tell that her mind was racing. 'You talked to Keane's neighbours, Hol. Any sense that he might be part of Sinclair's world? His business empire or the nouveaux-riches hunting-and-shooting crowd?'

'I didn't get anything like that,' Holly said. 'He certainly had aspirations, but they were more urban. Nice food and good wine. He'd even joined a book group. And he was dating a younger woman. Someone called Felicity, the daughter of a bookseller.' Holly thought of Patty's house, the mess and the kids. 'It was as if he was trying to reinvent himself.'

'So perhaps *he* was ripping Sinclair off. Paying for his new lifestyle. I don't see him as a natural fixer, like Marshall.' Vera absent-mindedly took another biscuit. 'That might be a motive.'

'Where does John Brace fit into the theory?' Holly looked at Vera's face and hurried on. 'I'm not saying it doesn't make sense, because it does. I just want to know if we can fit all the pieces together.'

'Eh, pet, sometimes things just aren't that tidy. But I bet John Brace was getting money from Sinclair when The Seagull was still in operation. Probably through Marshall. And I think he's still got a load stashed away somewhere. Someone's keeping Patty's bairns in computer games and fancy phones. Can we find out if he's still in business with Sinclair and his associates? He could be an investor or sleeping partner. And there might be other people involved. People who wouldn't want their relationship with Sinclair, Brace or Keane made public. We know that Brace was put inside for sourcing muscle for country landowners. No one else was implicated at the time of the court case, but he could have pulled in colleagues. That's another one for you, Charlie.'

Vera heaved herself to her feet and went to the kitchen for more beer and coffee. In the gap that followed, Holly took out her phone to check for emails. No signal. She wasn't even sure that Vera had Wi-Fi.

Vera returned, took another couple of biscuits from the packet and continued talking as if she hadn't been away.

'Is there anything else we should talk about? Or is it time for you folk to piss off and let me get some beauty sleep?'

'There is something else.' That was Joe, talking quietly. 'A regular payment by cheque to an individual.' He pulled out the copy statement and underlined one of the transactions, pushed it across the table towards Vera.

She looked up sharply. 'Why didn't you tell me as soon as you saw it?'

He shifted in his seat again. A small boy caught out in a fib. 'I didn't hide it!'

'So Marshall paid Hector five hundred quid. It could have been payment for a piece of taxidermy. His share of some raptor eggs.' Now they could both have been children, fighting in the playground, for pride, to save face. Holly felt embarrassed. This was a conversation that shouldn't be happening in front of an audience.

'It wasn't a one-off payment,' Joe said. 'I've gone back through the statements and each month there was a cheque for the same amount.'

Another silence. The fire spat, and outside there was the faint rumble of a car moving down the track to the farm next door.

'It probably means nothing,' Joe said. 'It was a long time ago.'

'I think it means Hector was a crook.' Now Vera looked every month of her age. 'I always knew he was, of course. The birds and the taxidermy. None of it legal. But this links him with Sinclair. Everything that went on at The Seagull. Sex workers like Mary-Frances.'

'I'm sorry.'

'Don't be so fucking daft. It's not your fault. Mine, for wanting to think well of him, despite everything.'

She stood up, very nimble on her feet despite her weight. 'Now it's time for you to go. I need my bed.'

Outside it was dark and clear. More stars than you ever saw in the city. Joe and Charlie were travelling back together, but Holly had her own car. She stood for a moment and watched them drive away. The lights were still on in Vera's house and the curtains hadn't been drawn. Holly watched her boss sit back down at Hector's table. She was tempted to go back, to offer Vera a chance to talk about her dad, but she knew that sort of approach wouldn't be welcome.

Vera began to sort through the papers that were lying in front of her. Then she pushed them away and got to her feet, took a wooden box from the mantelpiece and opened it. Holly watched her pull out a pile of photographs and sort through them, one at a time. She must have found what she was looking for because she stopped and stared at it. Holly was too far away to see the image and she was anxious that Vera would catch her prying, so she didn't move any closer to the window. At last Vera replaced all the pictures in the box. She reached out for a chocolate biscuit but the packet was empty, and she screwed the paper into a ball and threw it into the grate.

Chapter Thirty-Four

Vera got to the station early, feeling tired and hungover, although she'd only had a couple of bottles of beer the night before. It was the complication of this case. All the tangle and mess, which had kept her up until the early hours fighting to find a single thread, one explanation to link the three victims. She longed for simplicity and order – clean lines like the sweeping curves of The Seagull of her memory. The big open-plan office was still busy with detectives working on the inquiry, but the members of her gang were out and she felt the loss of them. Now the chaos was all in her head. If she'd been able to talk to the others, she might get rid of some of it. And at the back of the confusion there was Hector, tied up with a pile of buried bones, and she had to consider that he might be a murderer. She started working through the phone calls and messages that had come in from the public overnight and tried to push all thoughts of Hector to the back of her mind.

There was a knock on the door and Charlie poked his head round. It seemed he'd made an early start too.

'Come in, man.' She knew she sounded too enthusiastic, too desperate for distraction.

'I've been talking to some of the people who were close to Brace. There's someone I think you might want to chat to.'

'Oh? Got a name for him?'

'Not a him,' Charlie said. 'A her. Janice Gleeson.'

Vera remembered Gleeson. Older than her and a bit of a heroine. She'd pushed open the door to promotion and then held it for Vera to come through. Not all women in the force worked that way. She'd ended up as assistant chief constable in a smaller county in the south, then moved back to Northumberland on retirement. 'You're not saying Brace corrupted her too?'

'Not in that way. I think she admired him. Believed him too easily. Thought he was on the side of the angels, a bit rough around the edges but one of the good guys.'

Vera nodded. Brace had affected a lot of officers in that way. 'Will she speak to us?'

'She'll speak to you.'

Gleeson lived with her husband in a windswept house in an unfashionable part of the Northumberland coast. It had a view of the sea, but also pylons, an offshore wind-farm and the site of a redundant power-station. Vera liked that. The fact that Gleeson was keeping it real, not living in a cottage in a chocolate-box village that could have been in Surrey or Somerset. The house was made of old red brick and grey slate and backed by tall trees. The leaves had started to drop and, when Vera arrived, the woman was raking them up from an untidy lawn. She was tall, angular, striking in a Glenda Jackson sort of way.

'It was good of you to see me.' Vera struggled not to add *ma'am*.

Gleeson straightened and leaned on the rake. 'Shall we go in? Edward's gone into Morpeth for shopping. We'll have the place to ourselves.'

Vera tried to remember something about Gleeson's husband. Had he been a lawyer? An accountant? Something professional, at least. Gleeson was still talking. 'I wasn't sure he'd be much good at retirement, but he loves it. He's taken to domesticity, cooking especially. We eat very well.'

She led Vera into a kitchen that could have come out of a country-living magazine. Aga, scrubbed pine table, pots of herbs. There was even a cat on a rocking chair next to the stove. Gleeson pushed it to the floor and offered Vera the seat, then disappeared to take off the mac she'd been wearing for gardening. There was a rookery in the trees, and Vera could hear the birds calling through the open window.

'Charlie says you want to talk about John Brace.' They were drinking coffee, eating Edward Gleeson's home-made biscuits.

Vera thought this domestic bliss was all very well, but she'd go mad with boredom if this was her life. And perhaps that was why Gleeson had agreed to meet her. Because she was bored out of her tree too. 'Did Charlie give you the background? Tell you about Brace putting us on to the bones buried at St Mary's? We know one set belongs to Robbie Marshall and suspect the second is Mary-Frances Lascuola. Now another associate of Brace, Gary Keane, has been killed in his flat in Bebington.'

Gleeson nodded. 'I'm not sure how I can help, though.'

'You were around at the time. A colleague of John Brace.'

There was a silence. 'I got sucked in,' she said at last. 'Brace could do that. Make you feel special. One of the gang. He was my boss, and I was the only woman in the team. He made sure there was no disrespect.'

'The common link between Marshall and Keane was a club called The Seagull in Whitley Bay. It's not there any more. Do you remember it?'

Gleeson looked straight at Vera and seemed to come to a decision. 'I went there regularly.'

'As a punter? Not for work?' Vera was surprised. She wouldn't have had Janice Gleeson down as a clubbing type.

'Edward was Gus Sinclair's accountant.'

Silence, while Vera tried to digest the relevance of the information.

'I got caught up with the glamour of the place.' Gleeson had turned away from Vera now and was staring out of the window at the swaying trees and the rooks. 'Seduced, I suppose. By the celebrities and the music, the designer dresses. I'd never been anywhere like it. And I persuaded myself that I wasn't there as a police officer, but as Edward's wife. The free dinners and the bottles of champagne sent to our table were a gift to him and not to me. I told myself that I wasn't being compromised in any way.'

'But perhaps your husband was?' Vera kept her voice quiet. There was no condemnation implied in the question. After all, what right had she to judge? Her father had been taking money from Marshall.

'Edward's a good man. Decent.'

'But like you said, it would have been hard not to get sucked in.'

Gleeson turned back into the room. 'He was glad when Sinclair left the area and moved back to Glasgow. It gave Edward the excuse to give up the work and drop all contact.'

'What was going on there, Janice? What can you tell me?'

'There was nothing criminal. Nothing you could prove.'

'I'm not asking for proof, pet. I'm asking you to point me in the right direction. We've got three deaths here. Three victims.'

Gleeson took a while to answer. It seemed she was struggling to pull together the right words. Vera had once seen her giving evidence in a rape trial and she'd been the same then. Calm. Determined to describe clearly exactly what had taken place. 'There was more money in the company account than the Whitley Bay business could possibly have generated.'

'Where was it coming from?'

'Edward asked at the time, of course. Sinclair claimed to have a number of rental properties and that might have been true, but the sums still didn't stack up.'

'So what are we talking here?' Vera could sense a rising impatience and tried to keep it under control. 'Money from trafficking? Drugs? Prostitution?'

'That was my first thought.'

'But?' Because Vera could tell from Janice Gleeson's voice that there would be a *but*.

'Edward thought it was more likely to be money-laundering.'

'From Sinclair Senior's activities in Scotland?' Suddenly the business model of The Seagull became clear. It had never been intended to make money. How could somewhere so sophisticated, so sleek, be successful in a tacky seaside town like Whitley Bay? It was there to soak up the Scottish ganglands' profits and make them respectable. In that case, why had it been burned down?

Gleeson nodded slowly.

'Could anyone else have guessed what was going on?' Because Vera thought at last they had a motive here, for Robbie Marshall's murder at least. Perhaps Robbie had wanted part of the action. Perhaps he was tired of being Sinclair's fixer and decided to become a player.

'Gus's father, Alec, started spending more time in Tyneside. To visit his son, he said, but someone might have realized that he had more interest in the business than in his family.' Gleeson sounded tired now. Drained. 'And I assume the women would have known.'

'The women?'

'Sinclair's business partners – on paper at least. Elaine, who went on to become his wife, and Judith Brace.'

Vera sat upright, so that the rocking chair creaked and the cat slid away from its place by the stove. 'Judith Brace was Sinclair's business partner?' *Judith, who'd pointed them in the direction of Elaine as a chum of Marshall's? What was that about?*

'I'm not sure she'd actually invested any cash in the place. But she came from a respectable family and her father was a magistrate. That was more important to Sinclair than any financial consideration. It gave him a certain legitimacy.' Gleeson turned to Vera with a twisted smile. 'And of course it did no harm that she was married to a senior police officer.'

There was another pause. Vera was thinking of her next meeting with Judith Brace. Relishing the prospect of the confrontation, demanding to know why Judith hadn't passed on that little piece of information. Gleeson was still talking.

'When Edward told me that Judith was involved with Sinclair, I started to disentangle myself from John Brace, first by transferring to a different team and then, when Edward was free of them, we both moved south.'

Vera was still thinking about Judith. 'I wonder if she's an investor in Sinclair's new business.'

'I wouldn't know about that.' Gleeson got to her feet and started collecting coffee mugs. 'But I bet Elaine is still the power behind the throne.'

'What do you mean?'

'Gus Sinclair's name was over the door of The Seagull, but Elaine was the person who made it what it was. He'd done the university degree, but she was the one with the brains and the business acumen. A born entrepreneur, according to Edward.'

Vera got up too. She could tell that Janice Gleeson was getting twitchy. She obviously hadn't told her husband about her conversation with Charlie or Vera's visit. They stood for a moment together at the door, then shook hands; they weren't of the generation for whom a hug and kiss were necessary. When Vera reached her car, Janice was back on the lawn, raking dead leaves into piles.

Vera's phone rang when she was driving back to Kimmerston and she pulled into a lay-by to take the call. It was her neighbour, Joanna.

'I've tracked down your mysterious Prof. *My* Prof., at least. The one those readers in the Lit and Phil were talking about.' The woman's voice was as clear as if she were sitting next to Vera, honed on a good girls' school hockey-field.

'Oh?'

'Professor Stephen Bradford. He's a poet. Rather a famous poet. Obsessed with landscape. Not in a romantic Wordsworth kind of way. But nature red in tooth and claw. You know.'

Vera wasn't sure she did know, but when the call ended she sat for a moment and thought that might make sense.

Back at the station, Charlie was waiting for her, hovering outside her office. She thought he was wanting an action replay of the conversation with Janice Gleeson, but it seemed he had information too.

'I did what you said and chased up the universities. I'd sent all the local ones the voicemail that was left on Gary's phone. Neither of the Newcastle unis recognized the voice, but I got a hit from Durham.'

'And?' She pushed open her door and let him in first. Her thoughts were chasing and she tried to stay calm, not to build up her hopes.

'A Professor Stephen Bradford.'

'Yes!' She punched the air like a contestant in a second-rate game show. And it *was* a kind of jackpot, a ludicrous coincidence: Charlie and Joanna coming to her with the same name at almost the same moment.

'You've heard of him.' Charlie seemed impressed but wary, as if she'd worked some kind of magic. 'You think he's the guy we're looking for? Only I thought it was a long shot. He's not working in Durham now and it seemed weird that someone would remember the snippet of a recording made by a man they hadn't seen for three years.'

'I've only just been given that name, and it's nice to have the confirmation. Our professor is a poet. Famous. Into nature, but not in a romantic way.'

'Eh, I didn't get all that.' Now Charlie was even more impressed. 'Just that he retired a little while back.'

'Do we know what he's up to these days?' Vera felt lighter, as if she'd shed a couple of stone and could run up a flight of stairs without pausing for breath. The failure to put a name to the Prof. had been gnawing at her almost since the start of the investigation. With a name, they could trace him. She'd started to mistrust her memories, to wonder even if the man existed.

'The university woman didn't know. She said he'd always had fingers in a number of pies.' Charlie paused. 'Are you saying this famous poet, this ex-professor of English literature at Durham University, killed two people back in the nineties and then stabbed Gary Keane in his own home? Because I just don't see it. Why would he?'

'I don't know.' She ran through the facts in her head and couldn't make them add up to provide Bradford with a motive. 'But we've got enough to bring him in. We know he contacted Gary Keane the day before the man was killed, and wanted to meet him. We know he was a friend of Robbie Marshall's and one of the Gang of Four. Elaine definitely knew who I was talking about when I mentioned him to her, so I'm guessing he was a regular at The Seagull. He's implicated in all this, in one way or another, and I want to speak to him. Go to Durham, and take Holly with you. She went to a posh uni, so she'll know what they're talking about.'

'Are you saying I'm thick?' A wide grin to show he hadn't really taken offence.

'Nah, but it's a different world, isn't it?' Like The Seagull, she thought, with its shimmering lights, the music floating into the air above the North Sea. That had been a different world too, and now she knew it was so insubstantial that it could have been built from the sand on Whitley Bay's beach.

Chapter Thirty-Five

While Holly and Charlie set off for Durham in search of the Prof., Vera sat at her desk and let her thoughts wander backwards and forwards in time. She hadn't thought Hector capable of murder, but now doubt and suspicion crept into her head. They were like roots of ivy pushing into a wall. Insidious at first, but then everywhere and impossible to ignore or to tear away.

She picked up the phone and dialled the mobile number she'd got for Judith Brace. The woman answered immediately. There was background noise, the sounds of a busy street.

'I wonder if you'd be free to call into the Kimmerston Police Station, Mrs Brace. I have a few more questions. This morning, if you're free.'

There was a moment of silence. 'That really wouldn't be convenient. Couldn't you come to the house? This evening perhaps.'

Vera felt an exhilarating surge of anger; she wasn't some servant to be ordered about. 'If you don't want your name linked to three murders, Mrs Brace, I suggest you come into the station, to explain your business connections to at least one of the victims.'

Another silence before the woman spoke again. 'I'm actually in Kimmerston now for a meeting. I suppose I could cancel, if you really think it's so important to see me.' Her voice was frosty as she added, 'I've always believed in supporting the police.'

They talked in one of the meeting rooms. It was bare and functional, but not as unpleasant as an inter-view room close to the cells. Vera didn't want to alienate Judith Brace any more than she had done already. The woman sat, straight-backed and defen-sive.

'I'm sorry to have dragged you in, Judith.' Vera had already offered coffee and, with the apology, the woman started to soften. 'It's just that we've been given an important piece of information, and of course I want to check its accuracy before acting on it.'

'Information concerning me?' A frown.

'I understand that, along with Elaine Sinclair, you were one of the major shareholders in The Seagull. You didn't give me that impression when we first dis-cussed the club. In fact you suggested that you hardly knew Elaine, when I asked about Robbie Marshall's women friends.' Vera gave a reassuring smile. 'I'm sure there's a good explanation, but you can see why we need to talk.'

'I was a shareholder only in name,' Judith said. 'John set it all up. To distance himself from Sinclair and the business.'

'Ah, so my informants were wrong then.' Another smile.

'Quite wrong, Inspector.'

'Have you had any contact with Mr and Mrs Sin-clair since they came back to Tyneside? I assume you move in the same circles these days.'

Vera could see that Judith was tempted to lie, but

then thought better of it. 'Of course I support Mr Sinclair's attempts to regenerate the north-east coast. We meet occasionally at meetings. But no, we don't meet socially.'

Vera wondered what Sinclair, with his efforts to buy into the county set, would make of that. 'Do you have financial interests in any of his regeneration schemes?'

Again, Judith thought carefully before answering. 'I have a modest investment in one of his ventures. I believe in the concept of coastal renewal.' She seemed to be gaining in confidence. Perhaps she realized that, after all, Vera had very little to implicate her in the killings. 'Now, Inspector, if you have no more questions, I really should go.'

Back in her office, Vera thought she'd been too hasty. She should have waited until she had concrete details about Judith Brace's connection to the events surrounding The Seagull. Her phone rang and she was so tied up with her speculation about the case that the sound shocked her. She felt her muscles tense as she answered it, a sudden rush of adrenaline. 'Yes.'

It was Paul Keating, the pathologist. 'The second set of bones we found in the culvert. The woman.'

'You've got an ID?' That would be one less loose end.

'Not exactly.'

'Stop playing games, man. I'm not in the mood.' Though of course Keating would never play games. He was a solid and very religious Ulsterman and the least playful man she knew.

'Your woman isn't Mary-Frances Lascuola.'

Vera was going to ask if he was sure, but then she stopped herself. Keating wouldn't have phoned her until he was sure. 'How do you know?'

'We finally tracked down Lascuola's medical records. She was admitted to A&E not long before she disappeared, with a number of broken bones. The result, the doctor thought, of a violent attack, though she told them some story about falling downstairs.'

'She was a sex worker. One of the perks of the job, getting the occasional beating.' *Though wasn't John Brace protecting her then? Or had he lost his temper with her, because she'd found it impossible to stay clean? Had he been the attacker?*

Keating was quiet for a moment. 'There was no sign of any breaks in the dead woman's bones. And there would have been, if she was Lascuola.'

'So we have no idea who she is?'

'I'm sorry, Vera. I'm a pathologist and not a miracle-worker. I'm not sure what else we can do to help you trace her.' He waited for a moment for Vera to respond, but she didn't know what to say and the line went dead.

She sat at her desk. Joe claimed she liked things complicated. He said the more difficult the case, the more she enjoyed it. So why this return of panic, the sense that she was drowning in a pool of information? She knew she wouldn't feel any better by sitting here brooding: this was no time for self-indulgence. She pushed herself to her feet and opened the door of the ops room.

'New information from the pathologist.' She yelled to be heard above the tapping on keyboards and the muttered conversations. There was a dribble of silence as officers stopped what they were doing and directed their attention away from their screens to her. 'The female in the culvert is definitely *not* Mary-Frances. So, we have a new priority: an ID of the second victim. Let's start with 25th June '95. That was when Robbie Marshall disappeared. Go backwards through the records from that date, please. We're looking for anyone reported missing at the same time. A young woman. Let's start at the coast and move our search geographically inland from there.' She paused. 'I want a list of possible victims on my desk by lunchtime.'

There was more she wanted to say. That the young woman might have relatives who were still tormented by the possibility that she was alive. To give an apology, because she'd been so convinced that Mary-Frances was the dead woman that she'd closed down other lines of enquiry. But that would have taken time, and Vera wanted them all to focus. She needed an immediate result. She went back to her office to collect her bag and left the building.

On the Hastings Gardens estate, Patty Keane seemed pleased to see her, proud that the house was tidier than on her previous visits. 'I didn't forget their packed lunches this morning!' A quick grin. 'And I've already got a load of washing on the line.' She nodded to the back garden and the rotary dryer that stood on the scruffy lawn.

'Eh, pet, I'm not some sort of social worker here to judge you.' Then, realizing that the woman needed some positive feedback, 'Great that you're doing so well, though, and that you're feeling better. Are you going to stick the kettle on?'

They drank tea in the living room, with the enormous television blank on one wall. Vera was reminded of the one-way glass they had in a couple of the interview rooms. 'It's about your mam.'

'You're here to tell me that she's dead,' Patty said. 'Like Gary.'

'I don't know if she's dead or alive, pet. But we know she's not the body that we found at St Mary's.'

There was a brief moment of shocked silence. 'But if she's alive, why hasn't she ever got in touch with me?' The words came out as a wail.

Vera struggled to come up with an answer. What did she know about families, and decent parenting? 'Perhaps she decided you were better off without her, that the kindest thing to do was to let you get on with your life on your own.'

Now there were tears running down Patty's cheeks. 'I'm a really crap mother, but I'd never abandon my kids. Not even Archie, and sometimes I want to strangle him.'

'We still don't know for certain that she's alive. Just that she's not the woman we found in the culvert.'

They sat side by side, perched on the leatherette sofa, clutching their mugs. In the next-door garden an elderly man was tidying his already immaculate flowerbeds, clearing dying plants from the herbaceous border.

'Can you remember her at all?' Vera asked at last.

Patty shook her head. 'I remember being with the foster parents a bit. Really vague stuff. Then meeting my adoptive family. My own room in a house that seemed enormous. I was old enough then to know what was happening.'

'My mother died when I was a bairn,' Vera said. 'I'm not sure if my memories of her are real or if I made up a kind of story about her in my head.'

'I saw a photograph of mine.' Patty was still crying. She took a scruffy bit of tissue from her sleeve and wiped her eyes. 'It was in my social-services file. I still dream about her sometimes, but I know that's made up. I was too young when I went into care to remember her.'

'Do you still have the photo?'

'Yeah, it's in a box upstairs.'

'Would you let me see it? It might help us track her down.' Vera didn't like to say that the only images they had of Mary-Frances were the ones taken in the nick after she'd been arrested, and those photos made everyone look like bit-characters in a horror film.

'Sure.'

She returned with a small cardboard box that had once held fancy chocolates, a present perhaps from Gary. Patty sat it on the sofa between them and opened it up. Inside were a few trinkets. Cheap jewellery: 'My engagement ring. Lovely, isn't it?' The scans of babies still in her belly. The photograph of her mother. She held it carefully by the rim and passed it to Vera.

A woman was leaning against a five-barred gate somewhere in the country. Her bare arms seemed horribly thin; she was clasping her hands in front of her. She wore a blue dress, low-cut, but still somehow modest. Not a dress she would wear for working the streets. Her face was all skin and bone, but hauntingly beautiful. A model's face of high cheekbones and huge eyes. Long, dark hair. Vera could see how John Brace had been drawn to her. 'Wow!'

'She's gorgeous, isn't she? A pity I don't take after her.'

'But you do!' A genuine response, because Vera could see the likeness. There was no doubt in her mind that the two women were related. She continued to stare at the photograph, shifting her attention from the woman in the foreground to the countryside beyond, the wide summer sky.

Patty was still talking. 'The social worker contacted my mother to ask for something to pass on to me, just before the adoption was made official. This photo must have been taken a few years before, I think, but perhaps she liked it. I would have loved a letter. Something personal. But all that came to me was this photo and the locket.'

'What locket?'

Patty fished back in the box. 'I used to wear it all the time, but then I worried that I might lose it, so I kept it in here.' She scrabbled through the costume jewellery, the dangly earrings and bangles. 'It's not here.' Disbelief in her voice.

'Why don't you let me have a look?' Vera took the box onto her lap and carefully put every object onto the glass coffee table in front of her. There were several strands of glass beads and a gold chain, but no locket. 'Are you sure it was here, pet? One of the kids wouldn't have taken it out to play with?'

Patty shook her head. 'They know they're not allowed in my room. Besides, I keep the box on a high shelf. Even I can't reach it without standing on a stool.'

'When did you last see it?'

'I'm not sure. You know how I've been lately, not sure of anything. It could be years since I last had it out.' The tissue had dissolved into shreds now, but still she dabbed her eyes with it.

'Have you seen it since the break-in?'

Vera couldn't see how the locket could be important to anyone but Patty, but she was struggling to find another explanation for its disappearance.

Patty looked at her as if she was mad. 'Why would a thief go for that, and not for the telly or the computer? It was silver, but not old or valuable.'

'Were there photos inside?'

'No. Just a lock of my mother's hair.'

Vera put her arm around Patty and gave her a quick hug, found a cleanish tissue in her bag and handed it to her. 'I need you to think quite carefully, pet. Can you remember the last time you saw it?'

'It was ages ago! I can't remember exactly.'

She sounded like a sulky child now and Vera kept her voice reassuring. 'No, of course you can't, with all that's been going on in your life. Did Gary still have keys to this house?'

Patty shook her head. 'He threw them on the bench when he came to pick up the last of his stuff.' She looked up sharply. 'You think he broke in here just to get the locket? Why would he? It only had any meaning for me. It was part of my past. Part of my mother.'

'I don't know, and I'm probably barking up the wrong tree entirely. But we can check. We've had a search team going through Gary's flat and I'll ask if they've found it among his possessions.' She watched

Patty put her treasures back into the box and then turned her attention back to the photograph of Mary-Frances.

There were no buildings in the picture, nothing to identify where it might have been taken. It must have been late spring, because there was clover in flower and buttercups in the field behind the gate. Vera was reminded of the photograph of her own mother, now in an old frame that didn't quite fit and propped by the side of her bed. She looked again at the picture of Mary-Frances. If she hadn't been thinking of her mother, she wouldn't have noticed the swelling in the woman's belly, her hands cupped around it. It would never have occurred to her that in this photograph Mary-Frances was pregnant.

Chapter Thirty-Six

Vera left Patty's home and headed straight for the council offices where social services were housed. She parked in a space that said 'Staff only', because it was the only one left, and stood in front of the shiny reception desk. 'I want to speak to Freya Samson.'

'Do you have an appointment?' The receptionist's voice was hostile and superior. She looked Vera up and down, pricing her clothes and judging her to be a client, not a professional.

'I'm a detective. Inspector Vera Stanhope. She'll see me.'

A glare. She wasn't used to being spoken to like that. Social-services customers were usually deferential and easily cowed. 'Just take a seat and I'll check.'

Vera continued standing, well within sight of the woman and close enough to hear the ensuing telephone conversation: 'I'm sorry.' Sigh. 'She says she's a police inspector. She does seem very insistent.' The receptionist replaced the receiver. 'Miss Samson will be down shortly.'

Freya was wearing a different dress, but in an identical style. Floral print over tights and flat shoes. She was angry but making an effort to contain it. 'You should have phoned first. I'm just about to go to court.'

'This won't take long.' Vera walked away from the reception desk because she could see the woman there was earwigging. 'The woman we found in the culvert at St Mary's isn't Patty's mother. I'm assuming she's still alive and I need to trace her. There must be records, if social services placed Patty for adoption.'

'But that was ages ago.' Freya looked at her watch.

'There'll be records. People try to trace their natural parents years after they were placed with their adoptive families. Patty did.'

'You need to talk to someone in Fostering and Adoption.' Freya was already edging her way to the main door. 'Talk to Alison Mackie. She's been there for ages.' And she was gone, long hair flying. Vera tried to remember what it had been like to do everything at a run and decided she had never run anywhere, not even as a child.

Alison Mackie was about the same age as Vera, but she'd looked after herself and was almost stylish. She wore a knitted dress the colour of blackberries, and her hair had a jagged asymmetrical cut that had probably cost a fortune. It seemed she held a similar place in this organization to the one Vera did in hers, because she too had her own little office, a glass box in the corner of a huge open-plan space. On the wall, pictures drawn by kids: stick-people in family groups. She stood up when Vera was shown in and held out her hand. 'How can I help you, Inspector?' No rush or sense of urgency. No resentment that Vera had insisted on seeing her immediately.

'In the mid-eighties a woman named Mary-Frances Lascuola gave up her daughter, Patricia, for adoption. I'm trying to trace her, as part of a double murder inquiry.' Vera felt herself relax. She was talking to a fellow competent female.

'I remember Mary-Frances.' A straightforward statement without drama or curiosity. 'One of my first cases in adoption and fostering. We were mostly generic social workers in those days, based in an area office, but even then, adoption was a specialism. I loved working with children and I still do. Though I'm almost entirely office-based now.'

None of that meant very much to Vera. All she understood was that there'd been restructuring within the organization. As there had in the police service. More than once. 'Tell me about Mary-Frances.'

'She'd been referred to social services by the midwife she first saw when she was pregnant. She had been a heroin addict and sex worker, and they wanted to keep an eye on things. The baby wasn't planned, apparently, and she'd taken the decision that it should be placed for adoption. I was involved until the baby was taken into care and placed with a foster family, and then I supervised Mary-Frances throughout the adoption proceedings.'

'*Had* been an addict? Was she clean when the baby was taken into care?'

'Not when Patricia was taken into care, but throughout the pregnancy. As soon as she found out she was expecting, she stopped using. Not easy and admirable. Though she did relapse later.'

'You remember it very well, after all these years.'

Alison smiled. 'As I say, I was new to fostering and

adoption. And I do remember most of them. Very sad, perhaps. I'm a single woman and my work has always been the most important thing in my life.'

'Can you tell me about her? We have such a sketchy idea of who she is.'

Alison stood up. A shelf above her desk contained a row of files, each with a year printed in black pen on the spine. She pulled out a couple, before settling on the right one. 'These weren't official records,' she said. 'More like a personal diary. Notes that I pulled together before writing my reports for the court. But you're welcome to see, if it helps. There's a separate page for each of my clients and I added a loose-leaf page whenever I saw the individual concerned. Each one is dated.' She paused. 'Look, I can't let you take them away, but if you don't mind, there's a small conference room you could use to read them now. I'm afraid you can't stay here. I have to make phone calls, and some of the conversations will be confidential.'

She led Vera out through the main office and into a small room, with an octagonal pale-wood table and eight chairs. 'Just come back when you're ready and, if you have any questions, I can answer them then.'

Vera offered up a prayer of thanks for sensible women and started reading:

16th August
  Home visit. Mary-Frances lives in a privately rented flat in Whitley Bay. Sparsely furnished but clean. She presents as a woman who is intelligent and self-aware – she describes herself as having an addictive personality and says that in the past she led a chaotic life. 'There is no

guarantee that I could stay clean, once the baby is born. I can do it now because there's a time limit. I hope I'd be able to keep off the smack, but I couldn't promise and I wouldn't want to do anything to harm my baby. Better that she goes to a family who can love her and care for her properly.' I asked how she knew the child was a girl. Had she been told at the scan? She said no, but that was what it felt like. That was what she hoped.

I asked if she had considered abortion. She said she'd been brought up a Catholic and, though she had considered a termination, she'd felt she couldn't go through with it. I asked about the father – were they in a long-term relationship? At first she was reluctant to talk about him. Then she said he was married. He had too much to lose to acknowledge that the child was his. I asked if he was a drug-user and she laughed and said no. He'd spent his whole career putting users away. He didn't know about the pregnancy and she wasn't sure if she should tell him. Perhaps it would just be better if she moved away. London perhaps. I suggested that we should get his consent to the adoption, but she only said she would think about it.

19th August
I'd arranged an office visit, but M-F didn't turn up. I visited at home later in the day. She looked tired and pale, but claimed she still wasn't using. There'd been pressure to have an abortion, she said. Not from the father. I asked if it was a

*man she'd been working for. Not a man, she
said. A woman. They were the worst. I was
worried that she might be anaemic and arranged
for the midwife to call.*

There followed a number of entries describing
routine home visits:

*M-F attending antenatal appointments regularly.
All seems well. No more talk of her disappearing
to London. Still seems clear that adoption is her
preferred choice.*

24th November
     *Home visit. Mary-Frances big now, but seems
very healthy and positive. I arrived without
making an appointment and found a man in the
flat. He was wearing a suit, as if he'd just come
from work. She referred to him as John. At first I
thought he might be a relative, but she described
him as the father of the child. Not what I was
expecting. He appeared tender and considerate,
and I asked again whether they were determined
to go ahead with adoption. It seemed to me that,
with his support, she might make a very good
mother. He hesitated and said that there were
difficult personal circumstances that meant he
couldn't leave his wife.*

At this point Vera stopped reading. Difficult personal circumstances indeed! That was one way to
describe it. The cynic in her was convinced that Brace
would never have left Judith, because of her money

and social standing. Then the more charitable side wondered if Brace really cared for his wife, that he'd decided it would be too cruel to leave a woman who was desperate for a baby of her own, for a heroin addict who was carrying his child. Vera skipped through the rest of the notes, describing more routine meetings with Mary-Frances in her flat. It seemed that Alison hadn't met John Brace again until later, after Patty had been born.

26th January: Hospital visit

Saw Mary-Frances in the Maternity Unit at North Tyneside General Hospital. The plan had been that the baby should be taken into care immediately after the birth, but I thought that the situation might have changed. It's not unusual that a woman's attachment to the child is stronger than she was expecting. Baby is a girl and has been named Patricia. All well. The father was there when I arrived, and apparently had been present at the birth. The midwife described him as supportive and loving. Mary was feeding the baby and it was clear to me that she'd already developed a bond with her. I asked whether she wanted to continue adoption proceedings. She said she needed time to think things through. Brace followed me into the corridor and said that, although he would try to support Mary-Frances if she decided to keep the baby, he still wasn't in a position to set up home with her, and the nature of his work meant there would be times when his support would be limited. It seems he's a senior police officer.

30th January: Home visit
    M-F still undecided about adoption and took
baby home. Midwife visiting daily and health
visitor will take over next week. Brace had bought
a cot and pushchair. He seems a devoted father.
Because of my previous relationship with the
client, it was decided that she should stay on my
caseload, even if adoption does not immediately
take place.

28th February
    Routine home visit. M-F still coping well.
According to health visitor, baby thriving.

15th March
    Routine home visit. M-F had a visitor,
another woman. I checked all well and left them
to it. It seemed a good sign that she was being
supported by her friends.

For the next six months there were occasional
visits and notes from the health visitor. Vera thought
Mary-Frances had received very little professional
support. Why hadn't Alison made more effort to provide it? This was a vulnerable woman on her own
with a small child. Then Vera thought that there were
probably hundreds of vulnerable women, and that
Alison would have had more urgent demands on her
time.

20th September
    Home visit. No response.

27th September
    *Home visit. No response. Looked through
windows of flat, which seems more untidy than
previously. Piles of unwashed plates in the
kitchen. Empty cans and wine bottles in bin.
Contacted health visitor, who has also missed
M-F on a number of occasions. She said she
would call early tomorrow.*

28th September
    *Phone call from health visitor. Very anxious
about Mary-Frances, who seemed depressed and
lethargic. A suspicion that she's been using
heroin again. Baby still thriving, though, and
seems to be developing normally.
Home visit. At first M-F didn't open the door,
though I could tell she was in because I could
hear the baby. When she did let me in, I was
shocked by the change in her. Very skinny and
grey. I asked if John still visited and she said he
hadn't been around for a while. Perhaps that
triggered the relapse back to heroin use. When I
asked about drugs, she was evasive. Patricia has
changed too! Crawling and will soon be walking.
She was clean and seemed well cared for.
Checked her room. Bedding on the cot and
suitable clothes in the drawers. M-F might not be
caring for herself, but she seems to be caring for
her daughter.*

29th May
    *Phone call to GP re M-F. He's had no recent
contact.*

30th May
    *Emergency case conference with child-
protection team. Mary-Frances present, but not
John Brace, although I'd notified him of meeting.
Decision made that I should be key worker and
should do alternate daily visits with health
visitor.*

31st May
    *Home visit. No response, though M-F knew I
was planning to visit. Went back in the evening.
Door on the latch. Found M-F unconscious on
sofa in living room. Patricia asleep in her cot.
Soiled nappy but otherwise well. Called
ambulance and took baby into emergency care.*

Vera stopped reading and closed her eyes. The
bald statement of the facts moved her almost to tears.
She was sad for the mother who had tried to care for
her child and failed. Vera imagined the self-loathing
and disgust the woman must have felt when she
found herself in a hospital bed the following day. And
she was sad for Patty Keane, who'd grown up feeling
unloved and unworthy of love. *But your mam did love
you; even when she couldn't care for herself, she made
sure you were looked after.*
    The remaining notes described the process of care
proceedings. Mary-Frances hadn't contested the decision. Patricia had been placed with experienced foster
parents and had thrived. Later Mary-Frances had
agreed to adoption, but Patricia was three and a half
before she was placed with her adoptive family. During

that time there had been no access to her natural mother. Alison had made one comment about that.

Mary-Frances said she thought it would be better for her and for Patricia if there were no contact.

Vera closed the file and walked back through the busy office and knocked on Alison's door. The social worker had just finished a phone call and waved her in.

Vera took a seat. 'Eh, we police officers think we have it tough, but I wouldn't swap jobs with you for all the world.'

'It has its compensations.' Alison nodded towards the children's drawings on her office wall. 'Do you have any questions?'

'Was Mary-Frances working when you knew her?'

'Not when she had the baby at home. At the time when the adoption was going through the family court, she was trying to get clean again. She had a job waitressing in a nightclub on the sea front.'

'The Seagull.'

'That's right!' The woman smiled. 'That takes me back.'

'You were a regular?' Vera felt a stab of jealousy.

'Not really a regular. I wasn't sufficiently glamorous to be part of the in-crowd. But on special occasions, you know.'

'Did you keep in touch with Mary-Frances after the adoption went through?'

'That wasn't my role, but I did see her one more time, quite by chance on Whitley Bay sea front. It was a little while later. We were quite close to The Seagull and I asked her if she was on her way to work.' Alison sat with her elbows on her desk and her head in her hands, as if she was trying to re-create the meeting. 'Mary-Frances said she didn't work there any more. It wasn't a good place to be, when she was trying to get straight.' She looked up at Vera. 'She looked really well. Better than I'd ever seen her. She said she was going away, leaving the area for a while, leaving the people who'd only known her as a junkie. She might even get an education at last. "You never know, Miss. I might end up as a social worker like you."'

'Did she say *where* she was going?'

Alison shook her head. 'That was the last time I heard from her. I said she'd make a brilliant social worker and wished her all the luck in the world.'

Back in the office, Vera tried to make sense of it all. It seemed to her that if Mary-Frances wasn't dead, she was probably clean. She couldn't have survived if she'd carried on using heroin to the extent that she had been. She must have reinvented herself like her friend, the woman who taught yoga in the place in Whitley Bay metro station. And if she was alive, she must have taken on a new identity, because there was no trace of the old one since the mid-eighties. Alison Mackie was probably the last person to have seen Mary-Frances in her original incarnation.

Chapter Thirty-Seven

It was still only lunchtime, though Vera felt she'd already done a full day's work. She was missing the other members of her team. Charlie and Holly were in Durham, trying to get contact details for Stephen Bradford. Joe was in North Tyneside council offices. He'd been to school with a lad in the planning department and Vera was hoping he might dig up some gossip about the coastal regeneration project, perhaps about Judith Brace's involvement. She was even more sceptical now of Gus Sinclair as philanthropist and community activist, and though she couldn't see how the recent developments in Whitley Bay could be relevant to the murder of Robbie Marshall, she wanted more details.

Mary-Frances haunted her. Vera was wondering if she should go back to Patty and tell her how much her mother had wanted to keep her, when there was a knock on her door. A spotty young DC came in, waving a couple of sheets of paper. 'You asked for a list of missing persons for May and June 1995.' When Vera didn't answer immediately: 'An ID for the dead woman they found at St Mary's.'

'So I did.' She stretched out a hand to take the paper.

'I've been through the reports and these are the only three who were reported missing that summer and have never been traced. The others made contact with their families soon after they were reported.'

'Great. Thanks.' She wasn't even aware of the man leaving the room.

She looked at the paper half an hour later, after coffee and a bun in the canteen and the realization that she wouldn't come up with a solution to the Mary-Frances mystery through willpower and imagination alone. Patty's mother could have gone travelling, become a mature student, married and had a family. She could have died of natural causes. She'd had contacts in the shady world of John Brace and The Seagull, and it wouldn't have been too difficult to steal an identity. Without a name, she'd be almost impossible to trace. But the dead St Mary's woman might still have relatives who woke every morning wondering what had become of her. Vera had a responsibility to give her a name too.

She made more coffee and considered the list in front of her. Three women aged between seventeen and twenty-six. The first on the list was the twenty-six-year-old. She'd lived in Wallsend, which rang bells because of the link with Robbie Marshall, and had worked at Parson's engineering company as a secretary before having her first child. She'd suffered post-natal depression and had disappeared early one morning after leaving the baby with her husband. But there was an accurate description and she'd been a big woman, nearly six foot tall, and the bones they'd found couldn't have belonged to her. The baby she'd left behind would be an adult now.

The last two were teenagers, one seventeen and one nineteen, but they couldn't be more different. The younger girl was Rebecca Murray, still at school when she went missing and living at home with apparently loving parents. A lot of effort had been put into finding her. She'd even featured on the BBC programme *Crimewatch*, without any result. Sharon Timlin, the nineteen-year-old, had been in care since she was ten, dumped out of the system at sixteen to fend for herself in a council flat in North Shields. Vera felt angry on her behalf. People like Alison Mackie put so much effort into finding alternative families for babies and younger kids, but the older ones seemed to be left to flounder without any support at all. The physical profile of both young women fitted the St Mary's body.

There was no contact number for any of Sharon's relatives, and Vera couldn't face another stand-off with social services, so she tried Rebecca's parents first. They'd been in their early fifties when their daughter had disappeared, so they'd be retired now. The phone number still worked and it was answered briskly by a man. 'Alan Murray.'

Vera identified herself.

A silence on the end of the line. 'You've found Rebecca.' He sounded breathless.

'No!' she said. The last thing she wanted was to give them false hope, or to dash the last little bit of hope they might have. 'But I wanted to talk to you about her. Could I come to see you?'

No hesitation this time. 'Oh yes. Please do. Can you come now?'

'Why not?' She still thought Sharon Timlin, the girl

who'd left care, was the more likely candidate for the second St Mary's body, but the man sounded so eager to see her, so desperate, that she couldn't disappoint him.

The Murrays lived in a small private estate in the village of Holywell, just north of Whitley Bay. It was the same house where they'd lived when Rebecca was a girl, and Vera could imagine it would be a good place to bring up a family: the dene for kids to run wild in, and close enough to the beach for them to get there on their bikes down the trails and bridleways. Meeting the parents, though, Vera thought it unlikely that Rebecca had ever been allowed to run wild.

'She was an only child, you see.' The mother was trying to explain, trying to justify the restrictions she'd placed on the girl. 'It was only natural that we were anxious.'

'So it was unusual – Rebecca going out in the evening as she did?' The Murrays had taken her into the garden, their pride and joy, a replacement child perhaps, and they sat around a little wrought-iron table. There was still colour there, a heavy scent that Vera would remember as she tried to pin down the conversation later.

'When she younger she was a lovely girl.' The mother again. The woman was faded and so ordinary that Vera would struggle to recall anything about *her.* 'Easy and obedient. She changed when she left the middle school and went to the high school. We pushed to get her into Whitley Bay because that had the best results and she was bright. Really bright. Wasn't she,

Alan? They said she could get into any university she wanted.'

The father nodded.

'But she met a different crowd there. More sophisticated, I suppose. Grown up before their years. She changed. Suddenly everything was a battle. It wasn't enough to spend an evening in with us – she had to be out. Every weekend it was off to Whitley, coming back in the early hours in a taxi.' A pause. 'Drunk.'

'Ah well,' Vera said. 'That sounds like most of the teenagers I've ever met. Rebellious. Doesn't it come with the territory?'

They stared at her. They had expected a police officer to be as shocked by their daughter's behaviour as they'd been.

'Tell me about the night Rebecca went missing.'

'It was a Friday night. The 23rd June. She'd already finished school, because she'd been taking her Lower Sixth exams.' The father had taken over now. 'The week before, she told us she'd got a holiday job, waitressing. We thought that was a good sign. It showed she was growing up, taking some responsibility.' He paused. 'But it turned out she wasn't working in a cafe, but in a club on the sea front. We didn't think that was appropriate for a seventeen-year-old. I thought it might even be illegal. She said she wasn't working in the bar, but in the restaurant; that she was old enough to make her own decisions and, if we didn't like it, that was our problem, not hers.'

'So that's where she went on the Friday night?'

The mother nodded. 'She'd done two shifts the weekend before, but they'd been during the day, covering lunchtime and the early evening. That night

she didn't start work until eight o'clock. I gave her a
lift. I didn't want to fall out with her. I asked her what
time she would finish and she said midnight. I said
her father would pick her up. She told me there was
no need for that because the club would provide a
taxi. When she got out of the car she seemed very
happy. She waved at me and blew me a kiss. There
was no parking right on the sea front and there was a
van behind me, honking its horn, so I drove away
without watching her go inside.'

'And that was the last time you saw her?' Vera
thought the woman had rerun that scene in her head
hundreds of times, brooding, feeding her guilt.

'Yes. Of course we couldn't sleep. We could never
sleep until she got home. When she wasn't back by
one, Alan got up and phoned the club. They said there
must be a mistake, because Rebecca wasn't working
there that night. They never put the younger girls on
night-shift. We thought she'd been lying because she
was out at a party. Or with some boy that she knew
we'd disapprove of. We thought she might roll in the
next morning, full of excuses.'

'But she didn't and you contacted the police.'

'Yes. I'm not sure they took us seriously, but when
she still hadn't turned up by Sunday night, even they
started getting worried. By then we'd talked to all her
friends. Nobody knew where she'd been going.'

'Was she a healthy young woman? No broken
bones?' Vera hoped they'd say that Rebecca had been
clumsy, that she'd broken her ankle skiing.

'Nothing like that.'

'And her teeth? Did she look after them?'

The parents were starting to look at her as if she

was mad. In the tree above her, a collared dove was making its soft, mesmerizing call.

'She had perfect teeth,' the mother said. 'Not a single filling.'

'Just one last question, and then I'll try and explain why I'm here and what we're going to do next.' Vera could sense their panic and kept her voice very low, very calm. The sound that came out of her mouth echoed the call of the collared dove. Gentle and reassuring. 'What was the name of the club where she was supposed to have been working?'

'The Seagull,' Alan Murray said. 'It was called The Seagull.'

Chapter Thirty-Eight

Holly thought Vera had become obsessed with Professor Stephen Bradford, the mythical Prof., one of Hector's Gang of Four. Vera was convinced of his guilt because somehow he was a part of her childhood, haunting her just as Hector had done. This was a wild-goose chase. In the real world, winners of the T. S. Eliot prize for poetry didn't commit murder. She'd googled Bradford and recognized the title of his anthology – she'd studied one of his poems for GCSE English. In the car on the way south from Kimmerston she'd tried to talk to Charlie about her reservations, but he was a Vera loyalist and always had been. 'Aye, it seems canny weird, but the woman's probably right, you know. She generally is.'

Holly had always loved Durham; the dramatic skyline of the cathedral and the castle, from the train, marked the beginning of the true North for her. The start of the strange and alien territory that had become her home. Charlie seemed to know his way around the city and slid into the last parking space in a street close to the college they were heading for.

'I phoned ahead,' he said. 'Christine's waiting for us.' They were out of the car and he clicked the key to lock it. 'She's the lass who recognized the professor's voice from the tape.'

The woman was in her forties, which didn't quite fit with Holly's definition of a lass. She was willowy, straight-backed and very grand, in a twinset-and-pearls kind of way. It turned out that she was in charge of the college's administration, as well as being an academic in her own right. But it seemed that Charlie had charmed her.

'Why don't we chat in the SCR? It's usually very quiet at this time of day.' They followed her into a drawing room with a view of a garden and the river, were handed coffee from the filter machine and a plate of biscuits. That was when the gentility ended.

'You do realize it's impossible for me to hand over information about a former member of staff without good reason.' The voice was steely.

Holly was about to speak, but Charlie was there before her, his voice very quiet.

'He's been closely linked to two murders, Christine.'

Holly winced at the use of the first name. She too was probably a professor.

'But no evidence that he's implicated in any way. You don't seriously think he's a suspect.' The woman raised her coffee cup to her lips.

'He could provide useful information that would lead to the arrest of a dangerous killer.' Charlie paused for a moment. 'One of the victims was a young woman. The same age as some of your students.' Another pause. 'You wouldn't want to be seen to be obstructing our investigation.'

'I wouldn't want the name of a prominent poet,

linked very closely to this college, plastered all over the press.' Her voice had become slightly shrill. Charlie had her rattled.

'I can promise that won't happen, Christine. We'll be discreet. Unless Professor Bradford is charged, of course. Then it would be impossible to keep his name out of the press.'

The woman looked a little ill and closed her eyes. Holly imagined her making rapid calculations about damage limitation, and finally deciding she couldn't be seen to block the police investigation. 'I'll need to go to my office to find Stephen's current address.'

'That's very kind, Christine.' It was impossible not to believe in Charlie's sincerity. 'But before we do that, perhaps you could tell us about him. As a man, I mean. What sort of chap is he?' He sat back in his chair, apparently as comfortable here as in one of the rough pubs in Shields where he usually met his contacts. Holly wondered how she could have underestimated him all the years they'd worked together.

'Bradford's a great poet. He's brilliant on the northern landscape.'

'All hills and sheep, then?'

The woman looked at him, suspecting he was mocking but unsure. 'There's nothing sentimental about his work, Constable. It captures the brutality of the countryside, the contrasting ambiguity of secret hidden places and space.' She got to her feet and pulled a slim volume from a shelf. 'Please take this. It might help you to understand what I mean about Stephen's work.' She handed the book to Holly, obviously thinking that she would appreciate the poetry more.

Holly glanced at the cover, a photograph of Hadrian's Wall stretching across a ridge towards the horizon, with dark clouds behind it. The collection was called *Walls and Freedom*. She recognized it from her school-days. There was a flattering quote from the *Observer*.

Holly held the book up for Charlie to see. He gave it a quick look and then directed his attention back to the academic. 'Aye, but that's more like a review of his work, if you don't mind me saying, Christine. And anyway, I'm not quite sure what it means. It doesn't tell us much about the man. How did he fit in with his colleagues, for example? Was he liked in college?'

'He was a very charismatic lecturer,' the woman said. 'His students adored him, especially the post-grads.'

Charlie didn't speak. He was waiting for more. Holly sat very still, frightened to break the tension.

Christine drained the coffee and set her cup care-fully on the saucer that lay on the polished table. 'He could be a little arrogant. At meetings he liked the sound of his own voice. That didn't always make him popular.' Another pause. 'I don't think he had any close friends in college. He was rather a *performer*, if you know what I mean.'

'A bit showy.' Charlie's voice was diffident.

'Perhaps. And I had the sense that most of his life was away from here. For lots of our staff, college is the centre of the universe. It wasn't like that in Stephen's case. Some members thought him rather flippant, that he didn't take his role here seriously enough. He was paid a reasonable salary, but he'd think nothing of cancelling tutorials at the last moment.' Christine must have thought she was giving too much away because her tone changed. 'Of course he was in great demand in the literary world, festivals and conferences, book tours, and all that reflected well on college. Not everybody realized the importance of his work away from Durham.'

Charlie nodded to show that he, at least, understood. 'Any family?'

'Divorced, I think, many years ago. He never mentioned children to me, but, as I've explained, he didn't discuss personal matters. He could have a whole brood. He'd breeze in, perform for his adoring audience, object to a perfectly reasonable proposal at a college meeting – just, I suspect, to cause mischief – and then disappear again. I think he had a flat in Tyneside somewhere, but his main residence was in North Northumberland and it was almost impossible to reach him there.' Suddenly she smiled. 'Sorry, that's probably unfair. As you can possibly tell, I found him a difficult man.'

'You weren't sorry when he retired then?'

The smile grew wider. 'That, Detective Constable, is the understatement of the year.'

Charlie stood up. 'We've taken up a lot of your time. If we could just have those contact details for Professor Bradford.'

But now Christine seemed reluctant to let them go. She got to her feet, but stood for a moment staring out of the window. 'I love autumn in Durham. The undergraduates will be back soon. It's always a time of promise, the start of a new academic year.' She turned back to face them. 'Perhaps that's why I resented Bradford so much. He didn't care about the place. He saw it as a meal ticket. As I said before, his passions lay elsewhere. In the countryside. Or his books. His real life had nothing to do with us.'

They sat in the car. In a few weeks' time the street would be busy with students, but it was quiet now. In the distance a church clock chimed. Charlie was behind the driving wheel, and Holly held in her hand a slip of university-headed paper with Professor Stephen Bradford's address and phone number.

'What do you think?' Charlie had turned in his seat and was staring at her. 'Go back to the station and present this to Vera, or head straight up there and give her a ring afterwards?'

It seemed almost a test of loyalty. But Holly couldn't work out if it was her loyalty to Vera that was in question, or to him. She decided to hedge her bets. 'Head straight up there, but we should give Vera a ring on the way. I don't think Christine would warn him that we were looking for him – she didn't seem much of a fan – but someone else in the uni might have got wind of the fact that we were sniffing around, and it's clear he has his admirers. Best to speak to him before they do.' She hesitated, decided to be honest. 'I'd be scared to see him without telling Vera first, though.'

'Ha! So would I.' He started the engine. 'You phone her then, pet. Give her the glad tidings. Make her day.'

The house was a detached villa just south of Seahouses. Only the road separated it from the dunes and a view of the Farne Islands, and the whole street looked sand-blasted, shuttered against potential gales.

Approaching it down a street of similar properties, Holly thought it looked rather conventional, almost suburban, for what they knew of the professor, but when they pulled up outside she saw it was quite different from the rest. The first storey had been rebuilt and extended, so that there were two huge glass windows fitted at an angle, jutting out towards the sea like the prow of a boat. A telescope had been set up on a tripod in the room beyond and pointed out towards the bay.

Vera had been in a strange mood when Holly had phoned, almost subdued. 'There's news at this end too. I think we've got an ID on the second body. It's definitely not Mary-Frances. I'll fill everyone in at the briefing this evening. Bring the professor in for questioning. His voice on Gary Keane's answerphone, and the fact that he was one of the last people to see Robbie Marshall alive, gives us enough to do that.'

Charlie parked further along the road and they walked back to the professor's house. The pavement was gritty with sand underfoot, and gulls were yelling overhead. The weather was finally starting to break and heavy clouds inland filtered the sunlight, made the reflection on the water steely, metallic. There was no car parked on the drive and when they looked through the small window into the garage, that was empty too.

'He's not here.' Holly thought this had been a diversion. They should have gone straight back to the station in Kimmerston. She felt almost as if Charlie had led her astray, that she needed someone to blame for the wasted time.

'We don't know that yet. He could have a partner.

Someone else who's out in the family car.' Charlie knocked on the door.

There was no answer, and Holly looked through the ground-floor window into a room that seemed more like a library or a museum than a domestic dwelling. Each wall was covered with dark-wood shelves or display cases. Stuffed birds and animals stood next to Bradford's own collections of poetry. It was as if he felt they belonged together. On one shelf there was a row of skulls, white and bleached, some tiny, others big enough to have belonged to much larger animals, deer perhaps. Holly thought Christine had been right. There was nothing romantic or senti-mental about Bradford's vision of the countryside. She had a sudden image of the pile of bones that had been found in the culvert at St Mary's and it occurred to her that the professor would probably have welcomed a human skull for his collection. Under the window there was a desk with a laptop. Charlie knocked again. Still no answer.

He walked round the side of the house. Holly fol-lowed. Between the garage and the main building there was a gate with an old-fashioned latch, which led into a garden that was overgrown and lush and seemed to be the professor's personal nature reserve. In one corner, almost hidden by vegetation, was a large pond. The garden backed onto open farmland and was separated from it by a hedge of hawthorn and elder. Charlie stood for a moment, looking out at the wilderness, then turned his attention to the house.

If the front room was the professor's workspace, the back of the building was where he lived when he wasn't in his first-floor eyrie staring out to sea. A wall must have been knocked through to create one space, and large glass doors led into the garden. There was a kitchen that gave the impression of a foodie who enjoyed cooking – a pot of basil on the windowsill, a cookbook on the bench – and a dining space with a table that would seat ten comfortably. Holly was starting to be curious about this man.

'Looks as if he was here this morning,' Charlie said. 'There's breakfast things on the draining board.' A small coffee pot and mug, cereal bowl, side-plate and knife. 'Maybe we're too late, and someone from the university frightened him off. But at least we know who he is now and where to find him. No doubt this is the man.' He tried the door into the kitchen, but it was locked.

They walked back to the front of the house and stood for a moment staring back at it.

'Excuse me!' A woman appeared from the neighbouring garden. 'Would you mind telling me what you're doing?' Holly recognized the accent as posh Scouse.

'We were hoping to speak to the professor.' Charlie slid in before Holly. He could have been someone selling financial advice or a new kitchen. 'We had an appointment.'

'Well, he's not there. He went off quite suddenly this morning, some family crisis apparently.' She paused. 'We were supposed to be going in for drinks this evening. The whole street. A regular thing.' She sounded disappointed. Holly thought the professor must throw a good party.

'Are you expecting him back later?'

'He said he'd be away for at least a couple of days.

Left it to me to tell everyone else that he had to cancel this evening. I suppose he'll be staying in his flat in Tyneside.' A note of disapproval. It seemed that Tyneside wasn't her kind of place. But Holly thought there was an inevitability to the professor's destination. Whitley Bay was where this investigation had started and it would be where it would end.

Chapter Thirty-Nine

The Whitley Bay Regeneration Project office was locked. Vera stood outside for a moment and wondered if that was significant. She'd heard from Holly that the professor had disappeared again, and imagined him and Sinclair on a flight from Newcastle airport. They'd have met up in the posh lounge, shared a bottle of fizz to celebrate how clever they were, and now they'd be flying to somewhere warm and anonymous where nobody would find them. Then she checked the opening times and saw that the office closed for a couple of hours *every* afternoon. She told herself that she was getting paranoid, imagining conspiracy theories where she had no evidence for them.

She drove to Tynemouth and to the grand crescent where the Sinclairs lived, ignored the signs about private parking, and slipped through the barrier after another vehicle. She almost hoped someone would challenge her, because she was in the mood for a fight. She still remembered Rebecca's parents sitting in their garden in Holywell. The father, made garrulous by the shock. 'I always believed, deep down, that Rebecca had run away and that one day she'd come back to us. Of course I saw there'd been bodies found at St Mary's, but that was two people – a couple, I thought.' Shock had turned the mother to stone. She hadn't moved even to wipe the tears that were sliding down her cheeks.

Sinclair opened the door of the flat. He looked sleek and comfortable and Vera wanted to hit him.

'Vera! To what do we owe the pleasure?' The Scottish accent gentle, the voice teasing. He thought he was untouchable.

'Rebecca Murray.' She pushed past him into the light and tasteful living room and looked down at the sea. 'You remember the name?'

'That lassie who went missing? Of course I do. Her poor parents were distraught. She was rather a wild child, I seem to recall. According to the media reports. I never met her myself. The thought was that she'd run away to London to make her fortune.'

'And whose thought, exactly, was that?'

Vera had raised her voice, and Elaine appeared in the doorway to the kitchen, tea towel in hand. She saw Vera and turned back.

'Just you stay here, lady.' Vera was at her most imperious. 'You were working at The Seagull at the time, and you probably employed her. The way I heard it, you made all the decisions. I'm told you were practically running the place.'

Vera thought she detected a brief flash of satisfaction in the woman's face – pleasure that her role in The Seagull had been recognized at last. But she said nothing, and it was Sinclair who spoke.

'There was never any record that Rebecca Murray worked for us.' He'd given up being conciliatory and was losing his temper too.

'So now she was a liar, as well as a wild child.'

They were all still standing, and it was Elaine who attempted to calm them. She seemed suddenly anxious. 'Look, why don't you sit down, Vera? I was going to make some coffee. I'm sure Gus will answer any questions you might have about the girl.'

Vera took a seat. 'No coffee, thank you, pet, though that's very kind.' She could play games of her own. 'You're right, Elaine. I'm sure Gus here has a rational explanation as to why two people, both linked to The Seagull, ended up dead and buried in a culvert at St Mary's Island.'

There was a moment of silence. Sinclair stood, frozen, for a moment. 'I thought you'd identified the second body as Mary-Frances.'

'We made an assumption. You know what they say: *Assume and U make an Ass out of Me.*' A quick, tight smile. She'd been taught that once at a training course, and for some reason it had stuck.

'Maybe you're making another assumption about the missing schoolgirl.'

'It appears not. You'd be surprised what they can do with a pile of bones these days.' If she'd had any qualms about lying, she'd have crossed her fingers behind her back, but Vera had never been superstitious. And she was convinced that the body belonged to Rebecca Murray. She didn't need Doc Keating or his anthropologist pal to confirm it. 'So now I need you to tell me everything you know about Rebecca Murray.'

There was silence, then a faint sound in the distance that might have been thunder. It was the end of the summer. 'Vera!' He raised his arms, a theatrical gesture of helplessness. 'It was a long time ago.'

'The case appeared on *Crimewatch* on the BBC. The Seagull was mentioned. Not something a businessman like you would forget easily.'

'The *Crimewatch* thing wasn't on until later, on the year's anniversary of the girl's disappearance, and by then The Seagull had burned to the ground. At the time that she went missing there was a big splash in the local media, but nothing national. And, strangely, we didn't lose any business. Rather the opposite. The ghoulish and the curious turned up to check us out. It was just before the fire, and we had the best month's takings that we'd had for years.' Sinclair gave a little smile. Now that the shock of Vera's first accusation was over, he'd regained his composure.

'Convenient,' she said. 'So the insurers wouldn't question the cause of the fire. Not if takings were rising.'

'Vera, you're such a cynic.' A pause. 'Hector would be proud of you.'

She ignored the comment, thought that Hector would *never* have been proud of her, whatever she did. 'So take me through the events of that week. Rebecca told her parents she was working for you as a waitress. She worked a couple of daytime shifts in the restaurant. Are you telling me that's not true?' She turned in her seat. 'Elaine?'

'We couldn't find any record of her working there.'

'What does that mean?' Vera felt her temper rising again. 'She either worked for you or she didn't. You would have interviewed her.'

Elaine hesitated before answering. 'I interviewed her and offered her a job. We told her we'd add her to our casual rota. She was a bonny girl with a bit of spark to her. She'd either be brilliant and the punters would love her, or she'd be arsy and a nightmare to deal with. You know the sort.'

Vera nodded. Holly came to mind. Vera still wasn't sure what category Hol would fall into – brilliant or a nightmare – but thought that these days her DC was shaping up nicely.

'I said if she wanted, she could come in and shadow some of the staff. That was the weekend before she disappeared. It was purely voluntary and she wouldn't be paid, but she'd get her lunch. I thought if she decided it was too much like hard work, she wouldn't come back and I wouldn't have to set up PAYE for nothing. But at that point she wasn't on the payroll and she wasn't an official member of staff.'

'So you told the officers investigating her disappearance that she didn't work at The Seagull. That it was nothing to do with you and, if they checked your books, they wouldn't find her.'

Elaine nodded. 'The last thing we needed was to be mixed up with a missing school kid.'

'Didn't they come and chat to the other lasses working in the restaurant?'

This time Sinclair answered. 'At that point she was a runaway teenager who'd fallen out with her over-strict parents. They weren't going to make a big deal of it. They thought she'd be shacked up with some lad and would come crawling back home when she needed her laundry washing.'

'But now it's a murder inquiry, and you've got even more to lose than you did when you were running The Seagull. These days you're in charge of the coastal regeneration, and I understand you've even got your old pal Judith Brace investing. Your shareholders wouldn't like to hear that you've not cooperated fully with our investigation. So I need you to tell me everything you know about Rebecca Murray, otherwise we'll be taking you up to Kimmerston for questioning, and I'll make sure the press is there to see you on your way into the station.'

Another long silence. The clouds had moved across the sun and the strange metallic sheen on the water had dulled. Again it was Elaine who spoke next.

'Becca. That was what she called herself. There was something special about her. She was an actor. I could tell that, even while I was doing her interview. She could tell what you wanted from her, and she was willing to give it.'

'And what *did* she want?' Vera leaned forward, elbows on her knees, not caring that it made her skirt ride up.

'Danger. Excitement. That was why I wanted to keep an eye on her. She was one of those kids who are on the edge. She could have been a great asset to the business. She was stunning to look at, you know, even dressed for school; and she wasn't far off eighteen, when we could have employed her in the club, not just the restaurant. But you could tell that it might be a risk to take her on. She had that glitter about her. Needing to be the centre of attention. Desperate for celebrity. And stifled by those parents, who couldn't understand her at all, so everything was a battle. She was used to a challenge, that was the way she operated.' Elaine stopped, shrugged. 'Sorry, that all sounds a bit daft.'

'No,' Vera said. 'You're helping me to see her. I've

known kids like that. Needing extremes. Terrified by boredom.' *The ones who become addicts. Who jump across rail tracks to paint crazy graffiti, and who steal for the fun of it. Or who become decorated soldiers, famous explorers and award-winning entrepreneurs.* 'So she was in the club the weekend before she went missing?'

'Yeah.' Elaine again. Vera wasn't sure if she was protecting her husband or if Gus really had never met the girl. Certainly he seemed to have nothing to contribute to the conversation. 'She came in on the Saturday. She was just supposed to be watching, but she was bright. Eager, you know, and she ended up working. The Sunday lunchtime, she came back and did just as much as the regulars. We gave her some cash in hand and her share of the tips.'

'What happened?' Because Vera could tell that something *had* happened. It was the way Elaine could remember it all so vividly. The way she'd been so anxious when Vera had appeared, full of questions.

'Nothing then.' A pause. 'Robbie Marshall was in the restaurant that day. He'd have meetings there sometimes, when he wanted to impress his classier contacts. Occasionally he brought his boss from the administrators who were managing Swan Hunter's assets.'

'Who was he with? That Sunday before Rebecca went missing?'

'I don't know. A man. I didn't recognize him. Honestly, Vera! Robbie didn't have many friends. Just your dad, the Prof. and John Brace. But he had dozens of contacts. People he bought from and sold to. This guy looked like some sort of businessman on a jolly. Overweight. Crumpled suit. Robbie needed something from him. I could tell that. The way he was laughing too loudly at the bad jokes. The way he splashed out on a good wine. Becca served them.'

Vera started to understand. Robbie Marshall could get you anything you wanted, after all. 'And this over-weight businessman took a shine to the lass?'

'He was practically drooling. It was gross.' Elaine shot a look at her husband, but he remained impassive. 'Gus wasn't there that weekend. He was south on business. I was running the place on my own and I didn't want to piss off any of the important punters.'

'So, did Robbie set her up with the man?' The anger that Vera had felt on storming into the flat had returned with a vengeance. She felt like screaming. But the question came out quiet, matter-of-fact.

'Not then. She finished the shift. Like I said, we paid her and shared out the tips, and I told Becca there'd be a job for her if she wanted it. But Robbie was waiting for her outside. I saw him, leaning over the rails on the Esplanade, looking out at the water. As if the cargo ships leaving the Tyne were the most important things in the world. All the time keeping an eye on the staff entrance to the Gull, watching out for Becca, because I could tell he'd promised her to the fat bloke he'd bought lunch for.'

'You didn't warn her? You didn't say something?' The words still quiet, still restrained.

'What would I say, Vera? I was probably about the same age as her mother. A girl like that, do you think she'd have listened? She'd have seen it as a challenge, met up with the guy anyway, just to prove to me that she could handle him.'

And anyway, you didn't want to piss off the important punters.

But Vera nodded. Elaine was probably right, and Becca wouldn't have listened to reason. She wondered what Robbie had said. *The guy's a lonely man, new to the town. He just wants a bit of company. A pretty young woman on his arm to share a meal and a few drinks with. Nothing more than that, and there'll be a few quid for you.* And she'd probably been naive enough to believe him. 'Did they meet in The Seagull the night she went missing, Becca and the fat man?'

'They met outside. I told Robbie she was underage and I wouldn't let her in. I presume he found them somewhere else to go.'

Of course he would! Robbie Marshall, the fixer, the master procurer. How could your mother love you so much, Robbie? When all this comes out, it'll kill her.

Elaine was still talking. 'It was a mistake. I should have let them into the club. Then I could have kept an eye on her.'

'The name of the businessman?'

Elaine shook her head. 'I'm sorry, Vera, I don't know. I'd tell you if I did.'

Vera looked at her sharply, but couldn't tell whether Elaine was telling the truth or not. She'd be a good liar. One of the best.

'And you never told this to the police at the time, when there was a missing-person's inquiry looking for Rebecca, when her parents were desperate to know what had happened to her?'

The woman's silence was answer enough.

Chapter Forty

Back in the station and Vera was as tense as Joe had ever seen her. Still seething after her conversation with Sinclair and his wife, but driven, seeing an end to the case at last. Sitting at the front of the briefing, Joe was worried about her, worried that the emotion – the anger – would trigger a heart attack. A woman of her age and with her weight shouldn't get this wound up. She'd already been warned about her blood pressure, took medication for it, when she could be bothered to remember.

'So now we have an ID for the second St Mary's body. Though the lass had perfect teeth – I bet her parents were sticklers, no sugary drinks or unhealthy food for their beloved daughter – her dentist took an X-ray once, and Doc Keating has already confirmed that it checks out with the teeth in the skull.' She paused for breath and glared around the room. 'Our second victim is Rebecca Murray, aged seventeen, only child of devoted parents. A wild young woman, given to partying and staying out late and so, while she was reported missing very quickly by her anxious mam and dad, the case wasn't taken very seriously by our colleagues at the time. It didn't take *me* too much effort to find out that she met Robbie Marshall in The

Seagull the weekend before she disappeared, and it seems likely that he set her up for a date with a businessman of his acquaintance.'

Joe was thinking of his daughter, his Jess, and wondering how he'd feel if he'd reported her missing and nobody took much notice. Jess had a temper on her, a stubborn streak, and she was already fighting for her independence. Another few years and she'd want to be out partying, meeting unsuitable boys. He shut that thought down as quickly as he could and returned his attention to what Vera was saying.

'Joe's been chatting to his mates in the council. What can you tell us about Sinclair's role in the regeneration project?'

'All above board, as far as they're concerned. He's investing in it big-style and persuading other people to back it too.'

'That's not the impression Elaine gave,' Vera said. 'Anything else?'

Joe shook his head. 'No hint of corruption, no rumour of councillors getting big handouts.'

'He probably doesn't need to bribe them. Anything that smacks of regeneration ticks all their boxes. And planning regulation is much lighter than it used to be. Because Sinclair owns so much rental property in the town, he's got a vested interest in making the place a success.'

Joe saw that Vera was calmer now. Some of the anger about the way Rebecca Murray's family had been treated had gone; she loved this, standing in front of her team, passing on her wisdom.

Vera continued, 'Holly and Charlie have been on the trail of the mysterious Prof., and now we have an identity for him too. He's Professor Stephen Bradford, award-winning poet and former lecturer at Durham University.' She turned to Holly. 'You're not convinced he's involved in any way, Hol?' It sounded like a challenge.

'He must be involved,' Holly said. 'At least with Gary Keane. Otherwise, why leave a message on the man's phone? But I'm finding it hard to think of him as a killer. He's got so much to lose.'

'Could he have been the person who took a fancy to Rebecca Murray? The businessman who was drinking with Robbie Marshall?' Joe thought that might be one way of pulling all these threads together. And that's what they needed – something to give a bit of coherence to the mess.

'Nah, Elaine Sinclair knew the Prof. well. She says she didn't recognize the man who was drooling over her young waitress.' Vera stopped pacing and sat on the desk at the front of the room, bare legs swinging. At the end of the legs flapped the sandals she always wore, with the rubber soles and Velcro straps.

Joe saw that her feet were filthy and felt a moment of revulsion. 'Elaine could be protecting the professor, by claiming the lass went off with a stranger.'

Vera thought about that. 'Aye, you could be right. I wasn't entirely convinced she was telling the truth when she claimed that she'd never seen the man before.' She turned to Charlie. 'Worth checking out with your contact at the university, to see if there were any complaints from young female students.'

Charlie nodded.

'As I see it, the identity of the second body changes any idea we have about motive.' Vera's legs were quite still now, crossed at the thick ankles, tense. 'I'm not sure how John Brace fits into this. It was a different matter when we thought his lover, the mother of his child, was buried with Marshall; now he seems removed from the action.'

'Except he admits to burying Marshall's body,' Joe said. 'He must have been involved in the girl's killing too. I can't buy the theory that the bodies were put there at different times. That's fantasy stuff.'

'Perhaps he was covering up the death of Rebecca for his old friends Marshall and Sinclair.' Holly's words were tentative. 'If Rebecca was less streetwise than she liked to believe and she was taken in by Marshall, she could have fought back when our stranger started making sexual advances. He could have killed her to stop her crying rape.'

'Then why did Marshall have to die too?' Vera's words came out as a howl of frustration. There was a silence in the room. She continued, her voice more measured, 'There's no way Marshall would have threatened to go to the police. He'd have been as keen to cover the incident up as the guy who committed the assault. Joe, first thing in the morning I want you up at Warkworth to talk to Brace. I'm too close to him. I let him get under my skin. I can't find any record that he took part in the Rebecca Murray missing-person case, but then I wouldn't, even if he was involved. He was too skilled an operator to leave any trace. See if he'll talk to you. He might underestimate you and let something useful slip.'

Joe thought Vera must be desperate if she wanted to send him to talk to John Brace. So far in this inquiry she'd saved Brace for herself. Her enmity with him was personal and she'd thrived on it.

When he arrived at the prison the next morning there'd been an incident, one of the regular disturbances that disrupted routine and kept the men locked up: a suicide attempt or someone kicking off in his cell. Joe was told to wait in the little room just past reception. They'd bring Brace out for him as soon as they could. Joe sat, bored, on a hard plastic chair. Nothing to entertain him. No phone. No newspaper. A quarter of an hour passed, but nobody came to tell him what was going on and he wondered if he'd been forgotten. He paced the small room and thought this must be what it would be like to be in a cell, but here at least he had room to pace. There was a noticeboard on the wall with photos of important people within the prison. Everyone grinning, teeth bared, so that they looked unnatural, monstrous. The governor, the chaplain and the head of education. Even the head of catering. Joe stared at them for a moment, distracted, then went back to pacing and running over the tangle of crime and motive in his mind, trying to tease the threads.

When the door was opened ten minutes later it came as a shock. He'd been so preoccupied that he'd almost forgotten why he was here, and the burst of natural light as he was led through to the interview block surprised him. The officer was apologizing for keeping him waiting, but gave no explanation. Joe was shown into a tiny interview room and was surprised to see John Brace already there in his wheelchair. For a moment Joe was thrown and stuttered an introduction. He was still lost in his thoughts on the possibilities and wild speculations surrounding the three murders.

'The organ-grinder not coming today, then,' Brace said. 'She's sent the monkey instead.'

'Inspector Stanhope's busy.' Not letting the comment get to him. Partly pleased by it. Vera had told him to let Brace underestimate him. 'But we thought we should tell you we have identified the woman who was buried at St Mary's with Robbie Marshall.'

Brace's expression was the same, arrogant and amused, but he tensed a little in his chair. 'Yes?'

'Because for some time there was a possibility that it belonged to your former partner, Mary-Frances Lascuola.'

'She was never my partner.' A spark of anger. 'She was someone I had sex with.'

'And had a child with.'

'It was her choice to have the child. Nothing to do with me.'

Joe thought this was a different story from the one Brace had given to Vera and Patty. He'd told them that Mary-Frances was the love of his life. 'But you care about Patty? You asked Vera to look out for her?'

'Aye well, I might be in here, but I still have a sense of responsibility.'

'The woman in the culvert was younger than Mary-Frances,' Joe said. 'A seventeen-year-old schoolgirl who went missing just before your friend Marshall disappeared. They were never connected until now, but she'd worked at The Seagull while Marshall was there having lunch with a friend. A friend who seemed to take a fancy to her.'

There was a silence, broken by swearing and laughter from the yard on the other side of the wall. A group of younger men released from the cells at last, on their way to work or the gym.

Joe continued, 'Her name was Rebecca Murray. Does that mean anything to you?'

Another silence.

'The thing about Robbie Marshall . . .' Brace hesitated. Perhaps he was already regretting what he was starting to say. But Joe was only Vera's monkey, and Brace enjoyed showing off. He wanted to prove that he understood men, all *his* men, inside the force and outside it, and what made them tick. 'The thing about Robbie Marshall was that he liked his reputation as a fixer. It was what gave him standing. His job within the shipyard was as procurement officer and that was his boast: "Tell me what you want and I'll get it for you."'

'So if this guy fancied the girl, Robbie would have seen it as a challenge to get him what he wanted?' Joe was feeling his way.

'A challenge, aye. But he'd got in deep with some people who had expectations. Who felt that Robbie owed them, because they'd done him a few favours. He might feel some obligation to give them what they wanted. So more than a challenge. More like a payback.'

'A way of paying a debt?'

'Something like that.' Brace leaned back in his chair. 'They were people you wouldn't want to cross.' He paused. 'People I refused to have any dealings with.'

Joe didn't reply, didn't say that he thought Brace

had no scruples at all, that he'd deal with anyone who served his purpose. 'And would you have any idea who Marshall was having lunch with, that day in The Seagull?'

Brace didn't answer directly. 'I've had a date for the parole board.'

'And you're thinking Vera might pull a few strings?'

Brace shrugged. 'It would do no harm if she said I'd been helpful.'

'So this guy in The Seagull? Marshall's contact?'

Again Brace ignored the question. 'That Sunday we spent with Robbie, before I found his body at St Mary's, he was jittery. I told Vera that. He was as close to scared as I'd ever known him, and that wasn't Robbie. He didn't have the imagination to be scared.'

'So, are you scared, John?' Using the man's first name deliberately, pulling him in, but knowing that it would annoy him. John Brace had been accustomed to respect. And he wouldn't want his courage questioned. 'Even in here? Is that why you're not willing to give me a name?'

The man looked up. 'I don't have a name for you. Nothing definite.'

'But you might be prepared to speculate?'

Another pause. 'Like I said, I talked to Robbie, offered to help if I could, but he knew there were some things that even I couldn't fix. Sinclair might know the man. Robbie had made a few trips to Glasgow that spring. The spring of 1995.'

'Robbie Marshall had been working with Sinclair's father?' Joe wondered what Vera would make of that. 'Playing with the big boys?'

'Those were the rumours, and even I couldn't pull

strings that far from home.' Another pause. 'Apparently there was some deal that hadn't worked out, and Alec Sinclair felt that Robbie owed him.'

'Could you describe Alec Sinclair?' Joe was starting to feel his way towards a solution. If Alec Sinclair was the man in the restaurant, that might explain Gus Sinclair's reluctance to help the police when Rebecca Murray disappeared.

'Obese. Unfit. A heart attack waiting to happen.'

Joe thought that fitted the description of the man Elaine had given to Vera. Another image flitted into his mind: his boss. He thought it was also a description of Vera herself.

Brace looked up. 'He's dead now, you know. So even if he killed Robbie, that line of enquiry won't get you anywhere.'

Joe stood up so that he towered above the elderly man in the wheelchair, wondered if this was the power that bullies felt. 'What I don't understand is why you didn't see the girl's body when you buried Robbie Marshall. There's a scenario that makes sense: old man Sinclair killing the girl because she won't go along with what he's been promised. Rage, frustration. He'd be a man on the edge maybe. Then I can see him killing Robbie, so he couldn't talk. Or as a message, because he hadn't delivered what Sinclair had been expecting. But why were they all at St Mary's? And if they were killed elsewhere, why was Robbie's car there?' *And why was Gary Keane murdered after all this time, if Alec Sinclair was already dead?*

'You're the detective, lad. I'm not, any more.'

'Are you still sticking to your story that you didn't see the girl's body?'

'I'm not telling you anything else, Monkey. Send the organ-grinder.' Brace raised his voice. 'Officer, take me back to the wing. We're all finished here.'

Chapter Forty-One

Vera shut herself in her box of an office and wedged the door closed, then opened the narrow window to let in some air. There was a damp, gusty wind blowing from the west, a storm forecast. It was heavy, with the threat of thunder. Again she thought this was the end of a very long summer. Now they had a definite identity for the woman's body, she hoped she was approaching the end of the case too, but she was still grappling with the facts. Everyone involved, from smart Judith Brace in her grand house in Ponteland to the still-mysterious Professor Stephen Bradford, was slippery and unreliable. Everyone, apart perhaps from Patty Keane, was lying.

She found a sheet of printer paper and a pencil and started to write down the facts. The things they knew, not the things they'd been told. Three people dead. All linked in some way to The Seagull. And perhaps to St Mary's Island. Whitley Bay was at the heart of this case. She got to her feet and stood by the window, but the air was warm and humid and did nothing to clear her head. She pulled open the office door and shouted to Charlie, who was sitting at a desk beyond.

'Have we got a phone number for the Prof.?'

'A landline and a mobile. A different mobile from the one he used to phone Gary Keane. I haven't tried either, because I didn't want to warn him that we were onto him. I asked the techies to try to track him through the mobile, but it wasn't switched on.'

Vera thought they were too late to worry about giving Bradford warning. His sudden departure from the house by the coast meant that someone had tipped him off already. She phoned the landline, expecting nothing, imagined it ringing in the empty house looking out at the sea. When it clicked to the answer machine she had her message prepared. 'Stephen, this is Vera – Vera Stanhope. I'm not sure if you remember me, but you'll remember my father. We need to talk. I'll be at St Mary's Island from two p.m. for an hour. I hope to see you there.'

Then she tried the mobile, thinking it would still be switched off and that she would leave the same response, but it was answered after a couple of rings. A woman's voice, cheerful, businesslike. 'Hello. Stephen's phone.'

'Could I talk to Stephen, please?' It had taken Vera a couple of seconds to realize there was a real person on the end of the line, but she managed to keep the surprise from her voice.

'Just a minute.' A shout: 'Dad!' Then there was a muffled sound and the line went dead.

Vera tried the number again, but this time there was nothing at all. No woman's voice. No automated voice telling her to leave a message. Silence. Back at the door, she shouted to Charlie that she'd had a response from Bradford's mobile phone and that the techies should try to find a location for him, then she gathered up an old raincoat and hat from the stand in the corner and stomped out, without telling anyone where she was going.

She drove Hector's Land Rover towards Whitley Bay. She hoped the vehicle might be a kind of talisman or lucky charm, because it was a link to the Prof. Then she decided again that she wasn't superstitious. She parked on the newly cleared space next to the Dome but avoided Sinclair's office, with its shiny images of how the sea front might look one day. The smell of frying fish drew her to the chip shop, and she bought a bag of chips with batter scraps to eat as she walked. She'd just flung the polystyrene container in the bin when Joe phoned. She found a seat on the front, close to the sweep of beach and the water but out of the wind, and spoke to him there, watching the ball-chasing dogs and the fit mothers who jogged with their baby-buggies ahead of them.

'So,' she said, having to shout to make herself heard over the waves, 'you think Gus Sinclair's dad was the man who met up with Rebecca Murray the evening she disappeared?'

Thoughts and ideas chased through her brain: *Gus Sinclair was away from the area when the first encounter with Rebecca took place, but wouldn't Elaine have recognized the man? Maybe not. She only worked for Gus then; they weren't an item.* Then: *Anyway, if Elaine was the power behind the throne, like Janice Gleeson suggested, perhaps she knew Alec Sinclair very well, had her own links to the Glasgow outfit and her own reasons for protecting him.* Then: *Did Gus know that Robbie was doing deals with his father?*

'I think it's a possibility,' Joe said.

'Did Brace explain how he came to miss a dead seventeen-year-old in the culvert when he buried his mate Robbie Marshall?' Herring gulls were screeching above her head, landing to swoop on pieces of chip she'd dropped onto the concrete.

'He stopped answering my questions at that point. He said he wanted to speak to the organ-grinder and not the monkey.'

She couldn't help grinning at that. 'Aye well, he can go whistle. We've done enough chasing around after that man.'

'Where are you?'

'I'm at the seaside. A wild-goose chase. But it was driving me crazy sitting in that office. No fresh air and no space to let in new ideas.' She wondered if she should tell him about the message she'd left on Bradford's phone, but decided against it. There was no way Bradford would pick it up and she'd just look foolish when he failed to turn up for the meeting. 'Sometimes it helps to visit the scene again. It can trigger ideas. You know.'

There was no reply and Vera thought Joe probably didn't know. That wouldn't be the way he worked.

'What do you want me to do now?' he said at last.

'Same old, same old. Track down the people we still need to talk to. Stephen Bradford. Mary-Frances Lascuola. Even if she's using an assumed identity, there must be some way of finding her.' She paused for a beat. 'Go and talk to that old friend of Mary's. The one who teaches yoga. She might have an idea. And if she was waitressing in The Seagull, then she'd be a good person to talk to about Rebecca Murray.'

'Holly has already talked to her.' Joe sounded reluctant. Maybe he was hoping to slip home early, earn some brownie points from Sal.

'Aye, but you can charm her.' Vera was about to replace the receiver when something else occurred to her. 'Get an up-to-date photo of Stephen Bradford. There must be something online. Holly and Charlie didn't get anything useful when they went to Durham.' Then she snapped shut the phone and got to her feet.

There was moisture in the air, but it still wasn't raining. Three huge cargo ships hung motionless close to the mouth of the Tyne. They'd been there for weeks; they weren't just anchored, waiting for high water so they could slide up the river to dock. Vera had heard rumours that the Russian company that owned them had gone bust and they were just sitting there waiting for a new buyer, or until the money could be raised for them to get into harbour. The crew imprisoned, waiting for release. That made her think of John Brace, trapped in his wheelchair, trapped in his prison cell, and she felt a moment of sympathy until she remembered Fiona Fenwick, the gamekeeper's widow, equally trapped with her anger and her grief.

She walked north, keeping to the lower esplanade, and looked at her watch. One-fifteen. Forty-five minutes until the time she'd told the Prof. she'd be on the island. Past the Rendezvous Cafe, where there was a small queue for ice creams at the kiosk, and elderly couples inside tied their dogs' leads to chair legs while they drank tea. Vera was tempted for a few seconds – she could have murdered a mug of tea – but she was anxious about being late and sauntered on, now taking the top path, which had a better view of the bay, her raincoat over one arm.

At the wetlands nature reserve there was a group of men in the hide closest to the road, binoculars fixed on the wading birds on the pond, and on the other side of the lake one individual leaned across the fence, looking at the same group. He was too far away for her to make out his features and, besides, she thought now that she wouldn't recognize Bradford even if she saw him. She should have waited until she'd seen a recent photo, before setting up this crazy meeting. Her own rendezvous. He certainly wouldn't recognize *her*, because he hadn't seen her since she was a girl, though he'd probably have been able to track down a photo on a local news website. He'd surely have had the sense to do that. More sense than her.

In the car park closest to the island she stopped to look again at the big display that showed the proposed development of the place. A computer-generated image of a glass-and-concrete building. She realized that the new restaurant was very much in the style of the old Seagull and wondered how much say Sinclair had had in the design. And how much money he had invested in the project.

Now it would be just a short walk across the causeway to the island. She could see the cottages, with the lighthouse behind. She'd checked the tide times before phoning the Prof. and knew that it would be safe to cross until five o'clock. She expected to be back in the station long before that. This was just a ridiculous escape from duty, an excuse to leave her office for half a day.

She'd started down the slipway towards the path

that had been built across the rocks to the island, when there was a disturbance behind her. The siren from an ambulance, on its way down the narrow road from the dual carriageway, pierced the calm afternoon, scattering walkers. It was followed by a police car. Both slowed at the causeway, so that families could pull their children from the concrete path onto the rocks on either side. On the island a uniformed officer jumped out of the police car and started moving the curious onlookers back towards the mainland: 'Give us a bit of space here, folk. Let the paramedics do their job.'

Vera was pushing against the flow of the retreating families. Kids were whingeing because their exploration of the rock pools had been cut short, because they hadn't had the chance to climb the spiral staircase to the top of the lighthouse or spend their money in the visitor-centre shop. She felt a rush of adrenaline, almost of excitement, because she couldn't believe that whatever incident had attracted the emergency services was a coincidence. She'd arranged to meet the Prof., and now this was happening. They'd needed something new to help bring the inquiry to a close and this might be it.

The uniformed officer stood in her path. 'Sorry, love, there's been an accident.' His voice not quite rude, but obviously irritated, because the stupid, overweight woman hadn't realized earlier that he was turning people away.

She pulled out her warrant card, feeling a ridiculous moment of triumph because she'd found it immediately. She enjoyed his surprise and the sudden change in attitude. 'What sort of accident?'

'Nothing life-threatening. A bairn climbing around on the rocks to get a better look at the seals fell awkwardly. The first-aider in the visitor centre thought the child's wrist might be broken. I'm just here to clear a path for the ambulance.'

Vera felt the adrenaline drain away and realized how ludicrous it had been to suppose that the accident had anything to do with her presence. That was the trouble when you got obsessed with a case: you lost perspective, saw everything through the prism of the investigation. She turned away from the island and began the walk back towards the car park, avoiding the causeway and plodging through the rock pools, occasionally losing her footing and nearly falling. She came ashore close to the culvert and rinsed her sandals in the closest pool, shaking out the grit and pieces of seaweed.

When she straightened, the crowd had cleared a little, had seemed to realize that any drama was over. On the bank above her she saw a figure looking down at her. The same man who'd been birding on the opposite side of the pond on the wetland reserve, but closer now. There was a sudden jolt of recognition. She was the teenager in Hector's house in the hills on a freezing winter's night, hearing a jolly male voice. 'Hector, you old rogue. I know you're in there. Let me in. It's fucking freezing out here.' Staring out of her icy window and seeing him for a moment, when her father had opened the door and the light from the living room had spilled onto the path. This was the same man. Professor Stephen Bradford. Older, but dressed in almost identical clothes. Tweeds and boots and a waxed jacket. He might even be wearing the same cap. There was the same almost-military bearing. He looked nothing like her image of a poet. He was solid and big-boned but he'd never been overweight, and she realized that they'd been right: there was no way he'd been the fat man drooling over Rebecca Murray in The Seagull. He was too full of his own importance to drool.

She called out to him, but he was just too far away to hear. As she began to walk up the bank towards him, the police car started back across the causeway, its siren blaring. Vera supposed it was clearing a path for the ambulance, but Bradford must have thought it was coming for him. He'd probably seen Vera talking to the constable on duty, and anyway he'd be as obsessed as she was. He'd always been certain that the world revolved around *him*. He turned away, almost running. He must have had his vehicle in the car park, because by the time she pushed her way to the top of the bank there was no sign of him. As she walked back to Whitley Bay to collect her car it started raining.

Chapter Forty-Two

There was a sign on the door of the yoga centre at Whitley Bay metro station saying that it was closed for the afternoon. Joe bought himself a coffee in the cafe next door and sat at one of the outside tables while he decided what to do next. He was still running the visit to the prison through his head; he had a sense of something missed, something important. An itch that he couldn't quite reach to scratch.

Inside the cafe a group of half a dozen women sat around a table knitting. A couple of ageing hippies, one with purple hair, and three younger women who talking earnestly as the needles clicked. Joe had those down as stay-at-home mothers stealing an hour away from the kids. He couldn't blame them. As he watched, they gathered up their belongings and made their way out, shouting goodbye to the girl behind the counter. There were a few drops of rain heavy on the glass roof of the station, then a downpour, rain bouncing off the concrete in the uncovered area of platform. The group of women gathered in the archway leading out to the town, waiting for it to ease, before running for their cars. As he left the cafe he saw that one of the older women was in the road, her face turned to the sky, laughing until she was drenched. The watching women cheered and clapped.

Joe stood on the platform and phoned Holly. 'Laura's not here. And I tried her home on the way. Any idea where she might be?'

'You could try Shaftoe House, the rehab centre. She does a weekly session there.'

He decided that Shaftoe House was on his way back to Kimmerston anyway, so he didn't bother ring-ing in advance. His car was parked in a side street close to Whitley Bay metro station, and the standing water in the road was already ankle-deep. He drove to Bebington with the heating on full, in an attempt to dry his feet. In the gloomy afternoon, looking in from the road, the rehab centre looked like something out of a cheap horror film, all turrets and pointed gables. Inside it was overheated and his wet trousers started to steam.

Joe arrived at the centre just as Laura was finish-ing her class. They sat in one of the workshop rooms. Ian, the project leader, had showed them into it and he appeared outside in the corridor occasionally throughout the interview, peering through the glass door. Perhaps he'd once had a bad experience with the police and thought Laura needed protecting. Outside it was still raining and it was so dark that they needed the light on.

Laura wasn't unfriendly, but she was hardly wel-coming. Perhaps, after speaking to Holly, she'd been expecting another visit and was slightly wary.

Joe introduced himself. 'I know you spoke to my colleague, but we have more information now and a few more questions. Different questions, perhaps.'

'I'm really not sure how I can help. I told the other woman everything I know.'

The centre was closing for the day and, through the window, Joe saw a group of clients run giggling from the front door to the bus stop in the street beyond. A couple stopped under the dripping trees to roll cigarettes.

'When DC Clarke talked to you we hadn't identified both bodies at St Mary's wetland. As Mary-Frances was a friend of yours, we thought you deserved to hear. It'll be in the press tomorrow. There'll be a request for information.'

'One of the bodies was Mary's?'

It was impossible to tell what she was thinking, to know if she was upset that her old friend might have been lying in a hole in the rock for so many years. Joe thought she'd always be in control. Of her body and of her thoughts. Perhaps, if you'd been an addict, you'd need that. He wondered if she had a partner, someone with whom she could relax, let down her guard. 'No,' he said. 'We know that the man was Robert Marshall. He was a regular at The Seagull. The young woman was a schoolgirl who went missing in 1995. She'd just started working as a waitress at the club. Her name was Rebecca Murray.' He looked at the woman, but there seemed to be no reaction to the name. 'Do you remember working with her? There was a big media campaign when she disappeared.'

Laura shook her head briefly. 'Are you saying Mary-Frances might still be alive?' Again, it was impossible to judge her response to the news. Joe couldn't help feeling that she was holding back information.

The itch that had disturbed him in the prison returned. It was a sense of unease and of connections missed.

'If she is, we think she changed her name.' Joe was feeling clammy, a bit feverish. He'd never been any good in thundery weather and now he was finding it hard to focus. 'Did she ever work under a different name when you knew her?'

The woman thought for a moment. In contrast to Joe, she seemed poised and perfectly cool. 'Your colleague asked me that,' she said. 'And I told her Mary always worked under her own name. She made stuff up, but she was proud of the Italian heritage. It made her stand out.'

'What do you mean – she made stuff up?'

'She was always writing in a notebook. I thought it was a diary, but I looked once when she was out of her head, and it wasn't. It was stories. Bits of verse.' Laura glanced up. 'Made-up stuff.'

'Did she ever talk about it?'

Laura shook her head. 'She talked about what she was reading, though. She was always reading. Sometimes she was so excited by a book that she'd read it out loud to me. I didn't usually get why she thought it was so special.' A little laugh. It sounded unnatural, as if she didn't laugh very often, as if she was always serious. 'Mary was much brainier than me.' Another pause. 'Sometimes we talked about what we'd do when we got clean. It was when we were *trying* to get clean. Again. When we were in here.' She looked round the room.

'That would have been after Mary-Frances's daughter had been taken into care and adopted?'

Laura nodded. 'It's hard to believe I'm the same person as I was then. This is where my new life started. I always said I wanted to get fit, get into yoga, not just for the exercise. I was attracted by the spirituality, I think, though I didn't really understand it then. It filled a gap.'

'And Mary-Frances?' Joe asked. 'What was her dream, her ideal future?' He'd never considered that druggies and winos might have dreams beyond getting their next fix or drink.

'She wanted to get some A levels and then go to university, get a degree and a proper job. She wanted to do English.'

It occurred to Joe that Stephen Bradford might have made that happen for Mary-Frances. Had she been in Durham, along with the professor? Maybe she'd done her A levels and got *herself* into further education. But she wouldn't have called herself Mary-Frances Lascuola if she'd been studying. Holly would have found some record of her existence if she'd been using her real name. 'You told my colleague you stopped working at The Seagull because you didn't like some of the things that went on there. What sort of things?'

Laura was staring out of the window and he could just see her profile, the skin stretched over fine bones. 'I can't remember saying that.'

'Did you know Robert Marshall, the dead man?'

'He came to visit Mary-Frances a few times. We were still living in the flat then, but the last time I saw him, we were coming here to Shaftoe House every day. I remember Robbie waiting for her outside the centre one evening when we'd finished for the day. She didn't want to speak to him, but he must have said something to persuade her, because she went with him in the end. She told me to go ahead and get the bus back to Whitley and she'd be along later.'

Laura turned her head so that she was facing him. She had a tiny nose-stud and three small rings in each ear. He'd never been a fan of piercings of any sort, but somehow these looked classy.

'It was about three hours later. I was getting anxious. I wasn't sure she'd be strong enough if he offered her smack. I wasn't sure what to do, who to contact. Then I heard her key in the door.'

A long silence. Joe thought she was reliving that moment. The relief of her friend appearing. 'Was she on her own?'

'Yes.'

'And how was she?'

'She swore she hadn't taken anything, but she was in such a strange mood. It was as if she was glittering, hyper. She wouldn't tell me where she'd been or what Marshall had said to her. She insisted that we went out for supper. There was a Greek place we went to sometimes when we had cash. Not smart at all, but friendly. Run by an elderly guy and his nephew. And the food wasn't bad. She said it was her treat and, when she opened her purse, I saw there was a lot of cash there.'

'How much cash, would you say?' Joe tried to keep his voice even. He wanted the question to appear natural, for Laura to think this was an ordinary conversation, not some kind of interrogation. He didn't want to break the spell that had taken her back more than twenty years.

'I'd say about a hundred pounds.' Laura gave one of the sharp, quick grins that changed the shape of her face. 'Not a fortune, but a lot of money in those days and she certainly hadn't had it that morning.'

'You must have asked her where she'd got it.'

'She wouldn't tell me anything. She said she'd been sworn to secrecy.' Laura had turned again to look out of the window. It was cloudy with condensation. She rubbed a hole with her palm so that she could see through.

'And the next day?'

'The next day was much the same as usual. We got up, waited for the bus to come to Bebington. I asked her again about Robbie Marshall. "I don't think he's a very nice man," she said. Something like that. "I'm not sure John should trust him."'

'She meant John Brace?' Joe tried to put himself in that bus to Bebington. People would be on their way to work, and kids on their way to school. The two women talking. They must have been close. The sort of experiences they'd shared would bring them together. And yet Mary-Frances had kept secrets.

'Yes, John Brace. I thought he'd given up on her, but they must still have been in touch.' The words impassive. This too was something that Mary-Frances had kept from her friend and he could tell it still rankled. Perhaps that was why she was speaking to him so freely now.

'So you were here in the centre?' he prompted.

'It was a bit different then. More formal. There was a workshop, first thing. It might even have been in this room. I suppose a sort of group therapy. People coming together to talk about their experiences of addiction. There was a lot of that. Mary was there but she was quiet. There was a psychiatric nurse in charge and he noticed the difference. Usually Mary was happy to contribute. Mary said she was fine; she just had lots to think about. We had a break for coffee. I couldn't see her. I went to look for her in the loo, but she wasn't there, either. She'd disappeared.'

'They'd just let her walk out?'

'It wasn't a prison, Sergeant.'

'And that was the last you saw of her?' Joe wondered what Laura had made of that – had she seen Mary's disappearance as a betrayal of their friendship?

'I assumed that Robbie Marshall had tempted her back onto the streets or had some special client for her.'

'He was her pimp?' Joe knew the team had considered this previously, but he was still shocked. Vera always said it didn't take much to shock him. Robbie Marshall had come from a loving family, though; he'd got himself a good job. Why would Marshall degrade himself by hiring out vulnerable women to the highest bidder? He pictured Eleanor, with her tidy house and her memories of a kind and considerate son.

'He wouldn't have thought of himself like that,' Laura said. 'He would have called himself a trader.'

She said she had to go then. She had an evening class in Whitley. But when Ian, the centre worker and former addict, showed Joe out through the big front door, Laura stayed behind and, as the door shut behind him, Joe had a glimpse of the two of them talking together.

*

Back at the station, Joe found Charlie at his desk. He'd just put a call through to his contact at Durham University, hassling again for details of Bradford's students, hoping that she might have tracked down someone who could be Mary-Frances. Joe sat on the desk, trying to listen to Charlie's conversation when Vera phoned, the signal breaking up occasionally so that he had to ask her to repeat herself. He walked into the corridor so that he could hear her without the background noise of the shared office.

'I think I saw the Prof. in Whitley.' Then there came a long and garbled story about leaving a message on Bradford's landline and a child's accident, and Bradford scarpering when a cop-car arrived.

'Why didn't you tell us you had arranged to meet him? You shouldn't have been there on your own.'

'Aye well, it was such a long shot that I didn't want to waste anyone's time. I'm heading back home now. It pissed down when I was walking back to the town to pick up my car and I'm soaking.'

Joe thought that served her right.

When he'd finished talking to Vera, Charlie was still on the phone: 'Thank you, Christine. Yes, if you could get back to me as soon as possible that would be very helpful. While you're there, could I just ask one last thing . . . Were there any complaints of sexual harassment against Professor Bradford? Any rumours that he might have behaved inappropriately with any of the female students?' Charlie listened to an answer that Joe couldn't hear, thanked the woman again and replaced the receiver.

'Well?'

'In that department at least, the professor was as pure as the driven snow.'

Joe wasn't surprised. He was already convinced that the man whose attention had been caught by school-girl Rebecca Murray was Gus Sinclair's father, Alec.

Charlie was fidgeting with a notebook on his desk. 'Techs called, just before you got here. Bradford's mobile was activated today and they have a location for him. A street in Bebington. Anchor Lane.'

Joe wondered what that meant. 'That's Keane's address. Vera said she'd got through on his mobile but a woman answered. Do you think Bradford is at Gary Keane's place? Do we still have a man outside?'

'I doubt it. Scene-of-Crimes have finished there, so no point. Worth taking a look, do you think?'

'Nah, Vera saw him in Whitley not very long ago. Even if he was in Bebington earlier, he'll be long gone. He's probably back in his big house by the sea. We haven't got anyone watching there.'

Outside the light was going. The torrential rain had stopped, but the clouds were still low and dark and the days were drawing in. There was a text from Sal asking what time he expected to be home. She was hoping to get out to Pilates. He texted back to say he was just leaving, then remembered that Vera had asked for an up-to-date photo of Bradford and fired up his machine. Google found him a picture of the man receiving a literary prize at some do in London. He was standing in front of a microphone and he wore a bow tie and dinner jacket. The photo was only two years old. Joe hardly looked at it, his focus now on getting home to Sal before she had another of her meltdowns. He printed out half a dozen copies to leave on Vera's desk. It was only then that he stared at the photograph more carefully. He was sure he'd seen this person recently, but in a different context. A totally different context.

Chapter Forty-Three

Vera was at home. She'd shed her soaking clothes as soon as she came in through the door and now she was in the bath, water to her neck, topping it up every so often when it became tepid. She thought best in the bath. Now she was thinking about the phone conversation she'd had with Joe on her way home. She'd pulled the Land Rover into the verge as she'd been winding up the narrow roads to the house, but the signal had still been bad.

'We know Professor Bradford has been back in Bebington.' Joe's voice strangely distorted because of the poor reception.

'What's he been up to there?'

Then she'd sat in silence while he explained his theory. When he'd finished she'd ended the call, saying only that she'd see him first thing in the morning. But in her head, she'd congratulated herself on training such a fine officer. Someone who could make links and see beyond the obvious. Joe was still in the station with Charlie and Holly, and they were pulling in as much information as they could, ready for action the next day. If she hadn't been dripping wet, she'd have been tempted to go back and join them. She didn't like to think they could manage without her.

Lying in the bath and staring at the cracks in the ceiling, she wasn't at all sure what Joe's ideas might mean, except that they needed to talk to the Prof. as soon as possible. She decided it was time to get out of the water. If she stayed any longer, she'd go wrinkled and prune-like. Even worse, she might fall asleep and wake up only when it was cold. She hauled herself out of the tub, grabbed a large grey towel that had once been white, wrapped herself up in it and stuck her feet in a pair of cotton slippers that she'd nicked from a posh hotel where she'd stayed for a management course.

In the bedroom she got dressed, pulled on the pair of jogging bottoms she'd bought when her doctor had suggested she needed to get fit, and a big sweater. All the time her thoughts chasing, and her mind making connections. After the steaming bath, she felt a bit chilly and wondered about lighting a fire, but got distracted by new ideas before she'd lifted kindling and newspaper from the basket by the grate. She'd taken the photo of Mary-Frances from Patty's house and looked at it again. She was reminded of the image of her mother, also pregnant, in an earlier picture. In her head, Vera was a child, running to her neighbour's house for comfort. She felt again the direct connection with Patty. They were both women who'd been abandoned, in one way or another, by their mothers; both had fathers who bullied and blustered. She phoned Joe but got directed to the voicemail. She couldn't find the right words for a message, so she hung up. It would wait until morning.

It was already getting dark. She could see the lights of the village in the valley, hear the faint noise of the heavy rock that her neighbour was playing as he worked in his barn. She was overcome by a sudden hunger and rifled in the freezer for something to eat, found a mutton stew she'd made years ago, right at the bottom. Another small moment of triumph. In Hector's day, the freezer had only held dead birds and mammals. While the meal was whizzing around in the microwave to defrost, she collected the armful of sodden clothes from just inside the kitchen door and pushed them into the washing machine. *Eh, pet, you're a domestic goddess.* She even managed to wash up after she'd eaten and to get the fire alight. The wind had moved to the north-west and the air was fresher.

She must have slept, because she came to with a start and realized that it was quite dark now and the fire had died almost to nothing. She shook on a few lumps of coal from the bag. No need for smokeless, out here. The wind was stronger. She could hear it rattling around the chimney and the fire flared immediately. She was deciding between making a brew and pouring a whisky before bed when she heard the noise of a vehicle on the track. It was probably Joanna coming home from one of her library gigs. She was promoting her new book, and these days she was out a lot in the evenings. But the car didn't move on to the farmyard next door. It stopped outside Vera's cottage.

She hadn't pulled the curtains – she didn't usually bother unless it was blowing a hoolie from the east and she needed to shut out the draughts – so she could see outside from her chair. It was a smart car, not Joanna's old banger. Even when the car had stopped, she'd thought for a moment it *might* be Joanna, that she'd seen Vera's light on and decided to call in for a gossip and a drink. Joanna sometimes did that; she'd turn up with a bottle of red and regale Vera with stories of publishers and readers, acting out the drunk agent she'd come across at a party, the little public-school girl who saw working in publishing as a temporary inconvenience between university and marriage to a wealthy banker. Joanna could always make her laugh. She could always make Vera believe that her team were mistaken and she did have real friends after all.

Vera wasn't laughing now. She remained in her seat, looking out of the window, glad that she'd locked her door when she'd come in. She didn't always bother, but sometimes the neighbours wandered in with a present of veg from their garden and she hadn't wanted them seeing her bollock-naked as she discarded her wet clothes. The car door opened and for a moment the interior light was still on and it backlit the man climbing out. Because it was a man. Vera wondered if she'd been expecting his arrival since she'd seen him looking down at her near St Mary's Island wetland. The Prof. wasn't patient and he wasn't a person to give up. He'd be wondering what she had on him. Wondering how he'd be able to stop her passing it on.

He was dressed just as she remembered him. Tweed cap and waxed jacket. Looking more like a gamekeeper or country gent than a poet or academic. Vera thought she should read his poetry some day, though she'd never much seen the point of poetry unless it told a story. She imagined the Prof.'s would be very clever. He'd be a show-off. She slid her chair back, so it couldn't be seen through the small window.

She hated the idea of him peering in at her. He banged on the door. She didn't move. For a moment she was frozen and indecisive, a teenager wrapped in a blanket, looking out on the world ruled by loud older men. He knocked again. 'Come on, Vera, let me in. It's fucking freezing out here.'

Almost the same words, only this time they made her angry and she didn't feel intimidated. Sod it, she wasn't going to cower here in a corner, waiting for him to go away. She pulled herself to her feet, pleased that she'd fallen asleep before pouring herself a whisky. Now she needed a clear head more than ever. She turned the heavy key in the lock and opened the door.

She made him wait outside for a while before letting him in, wanting to make it clear that this was her home and she was in charge. Not succeeding. He walked inside, slowly took off his cap and jacket and hung them on the stand in the hall, then made his way through to her living room, not needing to be shown the way.

'Nothing's changed much.' He sounded amused. 'I thought you'd have done it up a bit, Vera. Introduced a few feminine touches. It's still a bit basic.' He shook more coal onto the fire and sat in the chair that stood opposite hers. The one where she'd sat when Hector was still alive.

'What are you doing here?'

'Catching up with the daughter of an old friend. No harm in that. I'm a great believer in friendship, Vera. Loyalty.' He turned towards her. 'That's what I want to talk to you about. Hector and loyalty.'

Chapter Forty-Four

In the station Holly watched Joe directing operations, and she realized how much more confident he'd become since she'd first known him. He seemed to trust his own judgement now and didn't need to keep running to Vera for reassurance. Holly wondered how long it would be before he looked for promotion, a team of his own, and whether Vera would see that as progress – a validation of her skill as a mentor – or as betrayal.

Now Joe was taking Holly back to her trip to Bebington, talking her through the interviews with Gary Keane's neighbours. The centre of their attention had moved away from Whitley Bay for now and back to the former pit-village where Keane had lived and died. Joe had begun by saying how easy it was to overlook a detail that might turn out to be vital: 'That's how it was on my visit to Brace in Warkworth nick this morning. I knew I'd missed something important. You know how it is, like when you see someone you know but you can't remember their name. Then I saw the photo of Bradford and it suddenly clicked.' He was trying to make Holly relax and feel better about herself: not beat herself up about how she'd messed up with the interviews on the ground. She thought again that he'd make a good boss.

Charlie was at another desk, on the phone prising information from contacts and strangers. They were still trying to track down Bradford's present where-abouts. There was a trace on the registration of his car, and CCTV and traffic-police vehicles would alert Charlie if it was seen. A community police officer had been sent to his home in Seahouses. If Bradford turned up there, he'd be arrested.

Holly couldn't help it, but she was feeling defen-sive. She knew she wasn't any good at the face-to-face stuff. She'd tried her best with Patty Keane, for ex-ample, but had felt the woman's awkwardness in her presence, her lack of trust. Talking to Joe Ashworth now, Holly realized she hadn't been as thorough as she should have been when she was talking to Gary Keane's neighbours. She'd gone through the motions, but hadn't taken enough time to get it right. She hadn't asked the right questions.

She tried to explain to Joe how she felt. 'I'm just no good at it. Vera goes in and people start talking to her. They tell her their secrets. How does she do it?'

'She's interested,' he said. 'Whether it has any rele-vance to the case or not, she's interested in what they have to tell her.' A pause. 'Because she's a nosy old bat, with not much else going on in her life.'

Holly thought about that. How much did she have going on with her life? Maybe it was time to get out more, meet people, make friends away from the job.

'Besides,' Joe gave her a sudden grin, before look-ing serious again, 'you're not the only person who cocked up in Anchor Lane, are you? I got it wrong, big-style.'

It was late and the rest of the building was quiet. They could hear traffic on the road outside, a gang of young people, rowdy after an evening in the pub. Now Charlie was on the phone to the prison, but it seemed that nobody was willing to take responsibility for passing on the information they needed, because there was only a skeleton out-of-hours service at night when the men were locked up.

'There must be an on-call governor,' Charlie said. He too seemed to have blossomed in the past year, to have become more assertive. Holly thought she was probably the only one of them who'd shown no development at all. 'Well, why don't you do that, and get him to give me a call back as soon as you get hold of him?' Charlie replaced the receiver and muttered something under his breath about jobsworth pricks.

Joe was still asking his questions about Bebington, getting Holly to tell him all she could remember about the people who ran the businesses in Keane's street, to re-create the conversations.

Charlie's phone rang and he answered it immediately. Perhaps he thought they'd managed to get the prison governor out of his bed, or wherever he was. But it was clear this was somebody quite different. The call didn't last for long and Charlie only asked one question. 'Where?' He replaced the receiver and they all looked at him.

'A patrol car in Morpeth picked up Bradford's vehicle half an hour ago. For some reason, it took the daft twats this long to pass on the information.'

'Did the officer follow him?' This was Joe, taking

control again. Holly didn't mind. This time she didn't want the responsibility.

'No, he didn't want to spook him. Bradford was heading out of town on the road towards Mitford and Cambo. This time of night there wouldn't be much traffic out there, so Bradford would realize he was being followed.'

There was a moment of silence. 'What was he doing there?' Charlie said. 'He'd be on the road up the coast or the A1, if he was making his way home to Seahouses. That road would take him inland.'

'That's the way to Vera's house.' Joe already had his hand on the receiver and was banging out the numbers to her landline. No answer.

'Maybe she's already in bed,' Charlie said.

'She has the phone by her bed, and I've known her drunk as a skunk, but she's still answered it.' A pause. 'Anyway, she wouldn't get that pissed in the middle of a case.' Joe was dialling again. 'I'll try her mobile.' He held out the receiver so they could hear the dialling tone and then the automated message telling them that Inspector Stanhope couldn't get to the phone now and to leave a message.

'She could be round at her neighbours' place. You know what mobile reception's like up there.' But Holly knew that Vera wasn't at the neighbours' home.

Joe turned round and looked at them. 'What should we do? I think we need an armed-response team out. We know Bradford's a killer, and he'll be desperate.'

'No!' Suddenly Holly was prepared to take responsibility for a decision. She knew that would be the last thing Vera would want, even if Bradford was at her house. Even if he was threatening her life. She'd see it as an admission of failure and she'd hate the drama. 'We have to trust her, don't we? She knows the man, and she got in touch with him and arranged to meet him in Whitley Bay this afternoon. She must think she can talk to him. She wants a confession. An explanation. After all this time, there's no proof.'

'She hasn't seen him since she was a kid, and this afternoon she arranged to meet him in a public place, not at a house in the middle of nowhere.' Joe's default position was always caution. 'I'm not prepared to take that risk.'

'Vera would take it,' Charlie said. Not his usual mumble. The words came out loud and clear. 'I think Holly's right. No panic, and keep it low-key. We'll go ourselves.'

They went in Charlie's car and he was driving. He said this had been his patch for years and he knew all the shortcuts. Holly was beside him and Joe was in the back. His choice. Nobody spoke as the car raced down the narrow country roads. They soon left the flatlands behind, and the hedges and overgrown verges were replaced by drystone walls as they climbed into the hills. The weather had changed again; it was no longer muggy and damp, but breezy with sharp, gusty showers. Holly shivered and Charlie reached down to switch on the heating. They flashed through a village, with a couple of street lights and a row of dark cottages. Then they were moving up the familiar track towards the house where Vera had lived since she was a child.

Charlie pulled into a farm gateway when they still had a couple of hundred yards to go. 'We don't want to warn him, do we?' He snapped off the headlights and switched off the engine. Everything quiet.

'So what's the plan?' Holly had turned to face Joe.

'She doesn't close her curtains. Let's see what's going on. Then we decide.'

Holly was wondering what Vera would make of this, the three of them riding to her rescue when she probably didn't need rescuing. Would she give one of those uncontrollable laughs that had her in tears, or would she have one of her cold, white rages? But better this than flashing blue lights and an armed-response team. They began walking towards the house, feeling their way, occasionally straying from the track into the cropped grass on either side. There was a bend in the road and there was more light then, because Joe had been right and light was spilling out through the windows. Bradford's smart car was parked outside. By now they all recognized the registration number. That was when they smelled the smoke and saw that the light in the house wasn't the steady glow of electricity, but that the place was on fire. There were flames licking around the front door, poking through the gap between the door and the lintel, as if they were struggling to escape.

Chapter Forty-Five

Vera had been sitting in Hector's chair closest to the fire. Bradford sat in the upright that looked comfortable enough, but knackered your back if you were in it too long. In her father's day, that one had always been hers. Classic Hector.

'Aren't you going to offer me a drink, Vera? For old times' sake.'

'Nah, pet. I only drink with my friends. Not with criminals.'

'Hector was a criminal. In purely legal terms. I'm sure you had a few drinks with him.' But Bradford was less sure of himself now. Vera thought he was feeling his way through the conversation. Bradford had only had Hector's opinion of Vera to work on, when he'd planned this encounter, and Hector had been dismissive of his daughter. Vera could tell that Bradford hadn't expected her to be so strong, so hard to intimidate, and she felt a surge of confidence.

'He wasn't a killer.'

'Are you sure about that?'

So that's how you're going to play it. You're going to blame it all on Hector. Not sodding likely. 'Absolutely,' she said. 'Because we know, you see. We know what happened. All those years ago, and again last week when Gary Keane died. We know the full story.'

Bradford tried to lean back in the chair but it forced him upright again. Vera wasn't sure why she'd kept it. Perhaps for moments like these. 'I very much doubt that, you know.' His voice oily. Too rich for her stomach. 'But why don't you talk me through it? Why don't you tell me the story as you know it?'

'We'll start with the Gang of Four, shall we? Hector, Robbie Marshall, John Brace and you. Odd friends. All misfits of a kind. Just held together by a shared interest and an old-fashioned image of the English countryside, which you believed should only belong to people like you. Hector thought he was the leader, but you were always the young pretender, the power behind the throne.'

Vera saw a smile flit over Bradford's face and she thought he liked that. It was pathetic, but he needed to be told he was important. All those awards and accolades for his poetry and he still needed a middle-aged woman's opinion to boost his self-esteem.

'We were great friends, you know,' he said. 'Real friends.'

'You all had your separate lives,' Vera went on. He might not have spoken. 'Hector got more set in his ways, drank too much, probably became a liability. It must have been a relief when he died. You followed your academic career, became a famous poet, got married. Had a child.' She glanced up at him but there was no reaction and she continued, 'Divorced. John Brace married and used his profession to further his own ends. Robbie Marshall was the strangest of the lot of you. Not really interested in fame, like you; or money, like John Brace. His interest was in doing deals. Making things happen. Pleasing the rest of you.'

'Robbie was always a little . . .' Bradford paused to choose the right word, '. . . feral.'

'Eh, pet, you can be snobby about him now, but you didn't mind him doing your dirty work for you then.' She looked up. 'And you included him when you socialized. He's there in the photos. The Gang of Four out for public viewing. Dinner at The Seagull every now and again to celebrate your successes—'

He interrupted again. 'To celebrate our friendship.'

She let that go. 'Then John Brace fell in love. Hector was out of it by then. Not really part of the team, but Brace needed your help, didn't he? Yours and Robbie's. To rescue the woman of his dreams.'

There was a silence. Perhaps Bradford had realized by now that she did know the story. Most of it, at least. She threw an apple log onto the fire and watched it flare, thought she could smell the fruit in it.

'The lovely Mary-Frances.' Bradford spoke almost in a whisper.

'So you were taken with her too,' Vera said. 'I did wonder.'

'Oh, we were all a bit in love with Mary-Frances. Even Robbie Marshall, and I'd never seen him have a sexual impulse of any sort before.' The man stared at the flames.

Vera went on with her story. 'Brace pulled a few strings and got her taken on at The Seagull, but that wasn't a good place for her to be. She was an addict and she needed more support than Sinclair was willing to give. Especially after she lost her daughter. And there were things going on at the club that even Gus

Sinclair couldn't control. So, she started the rehab course at Shaftoe House.'

'But John didn't like her being there.' Bradford took over the tale. 'He knew the sort of people she'd be mixing with. He couldn't see how she'd stay straight.'

'Besides, she'd upset someone, hadn't she? She'd been to A&E not long before, badly beaten up, broken bones. Had one of her old punters refused to take no for an answer? Someone powerful that she needed to escape from? John could protect her from the police, but he admitted to me himself that there were people even he was scared of.'

Bradford looked into the fire and said nothing.

'So you had a brainwave,' Vera said. 'You'd ship her out into the country. The magic countryside that you all believed in – the place you thought would cure all her ills.'

He stared straight at her. 'Don't sneer, Vera. You live here, don't you? How long would you last in a town?'

She didn't have an answer to that, so she went on, 'You called on your old friend Hector to help out. Did he know anyone who might take in a young lass who needed to hide for a while? To hide from her pimp, and from herself. Who could help her to stay clean. No matter that he couldn't look after his own daughter, never mind some other bugger's.'

Bradford gave a little laugh. 'I never expected him to do it.'

'No, but he knew a couple who would. Lovely pair who'd never had a child of their own. They lived right next door to him. Norma and Davy Kerr took her in and told the world she was their niece. And Hector got paid every month for setting it up and keeping an eye. The money went through Robbie Marshall, of course. Robbie the fixer, who could make anything happen. Hector might have been one of the Gang of Four, but John Brace knew he was unreliable and he wouldn't have wanted any cash traced back to him.' Vera wondered if Hector had passed any of that money on to Norma and Davy. She hoped he had, but suspected it had all gone on rare birds' eggs and cheap whisky.

'Mary-Frances did an access course while she was living there,' Bradford said. 'Took her A levels and got a place at university. She still went back to the farm at weekends and during the vacations, though.'

And Hector still got his five hundred pounds a month, right until the time Robbie Marshall disappeared.

'Did she go to your place? Durham?'

He nodded. Proud. 'She got a first. I wanted her to do an MA, but she had other plans. A social conscience.'

Aye, she told Alison Mackie she wanted to be a social worker.

'But she didn't study under her own name. What did she call herself while she was there?'

'Hope,' Bradford said. 'Hope Lethbridge.'

'Of course.' Now Vera was enjoying herself. 'I bet you dreamed that one up. Being a poet and all. Very significant, Hope. And of course I've heard that name recently too. In a very different situation.' She was tempted to explain, to show how clever her team had been, but she didn't want to get ahead of herself. This was a tale that had to be told in order. 'I met Mary-Frances, you know. Or Hope, as she was calling herself then. At Hector's funeral. She was there with Norma and Davy.'

'We were all there,' Bradford said, 'to give him a good send-off.'

There was a moment of silence, broken by the wind rattling the loose slates on the roof. Vera continued her story. 'In the meantime, Robbie Marshall could see that he wouldn't have a long-term future at the shipyard. His contract with the receivers was coming to an end. Perhaps Gus Sinclair was already planning his retreat to Glasgow. Robbie decided he should start making moves in that direction too. But he thought he'd go straight to the organ-grinder instead of dealing with the monkey.' She allowed herself a little smile at that, though she knew Bradford wouldn't understand the significance.

'Robbie always did have ambitions beyond his intelligence,' Bradford said. It was almost as if he and Vera were on the same side now. The tension between them seemed to have dissipated. 'Yes, he started to ingratiate himself with Gus's father, Alec.'

'Who was spending more and more time in The Seagull,' Vera said. 'Washing all his dirty money through the business, recognizing Elaine as a competent woman who'd make a better business partner than his son. Until a schoolgirl died. I suspect that was the reason for the fire at The Seagull. It had nothing to do with insurance fraud – who cared if it was losing money, as long as it was laundering all his cash? It was about Alec covering his traces and heading back north.'

Bradford looked across at Vera. 'You do know the old man is dead?'

She nodded, decided she'd better get a shift on, if this wasn't going to take all night. 'Alec Sinclair had a taste for very young women, and Robbie helped him to indulge his fancy by setting him up with a schoolgirl called Rebecca Murray.' Vera looked at Bradford. 'Do you know what happened that night exactly? Do you know how she died?'

'No!' He seemed horrified. 'Really, Vera, I wouldn't have had anything to do with that.'

'Perhaps you wouldn't, pet. After all, you had a daughter of your own by then, didn't you?'

There was no response. Outside the wind was getting even stronger. Vera was tempted to get up and draw the curtains to shut out the weather, but again she thought she needed to move on more quickly. There was still a lot more of the story to tell. 'I'm not entirely sure what happened next.' Her voice was brusque now. She didn't have time for games. 'Two of the people involved aren't talking and the other two are dead.' She looked at Bradford. 'Were you there that night? The 23rd June, when the poor lass died? Did they call you out when Alec Sinclair killed the girl? Did they ask your advice?'

'No,' he said. Shut his mouth tight, to show there was nothing more to say.

'Let's move on a couple of days. It was 25th June. The others were out in the hills with Hector. Robbie was nervy and jumpy. Hardly surprising, because he had a body to dispose of. Rebecca Murray, killed by old man Sinclair. But he must have realized John Brace couldn't get involved. Even our John would baulk at covering up the murder of a young schoolgirl from a respectable family. Hector was already unreliable. So Robbie had to deal with it himself. Brace told me he was meeting an informant at St Mary's that night, but I think it was Mary-Frances that he'd arranged to see. I imagine they'd planned a romantic walk in the moonlight, followed by a night in a swanky Tynemouth hotel. She wasn't a prisoner up here in the hills.'

In her mind, Vera was there on the headland with Mary-Frances, looking out over the bay and waiting for her lover. 'Brace kept as close to the truth as possible when he told me about that night. He did come across Robbie Marshall's car by chance. But Marshall wasn't dead then. He was very much alive and he was getting rid of Rebecca Murray's body.' She paused. 'Who killed Robbie, Prof.?' Her voice very soft, almost persuasive. 'Was it Brace? Did he decide that Marshall was getting too dangerous to handle? That he had to be stopped before Brace got caught up in the scandal that was bound to surround him? Or was it Mary-Frances? Did she see what had happened to that poor girl and snap? Pick up one of the boulders lying on the shore and smash it on Marshall's head as he was bending to put the body in the culvert. I think Mary-Frances realized in that moment that the dead girl could have been *her*. Because the man who'd beaten *her* up was Alec Sinclair and that was why she'd had to disappear so dramatically.'

'I wasn't there, Vera. I can't tell you.' He shifted in the uncomfortable seat again. 'But I can tell you this: if you try to charge Mary-Frances, John will confess. He'd rather spend the rest of his life in prison than see that woman in court.'

Vera was thinking about that, thinking she'd been right about John Brace being romantic to the point of soppy, when the lights snapped out.

Chapter Forty-Six

Bradford seemed more thrown by the sudden darkness than Vera was. She knew that every time there was a bit of a gale, the power would go off. There was a faulty wire up to the two houses, which the electricity board had promised to fix but had somehow never got round to. She found her way to the front door and saw that Jack and Joanna's farmhouse had been blacked out too. The problem would get sorted in the morning, and until then there were candles and the Tilley lamp. The candles were still in saucers on the mantelpiece, left over from the last time this had happened, and there were a few matches remaining in the box, from when she'd lit the fire. When she'd got the candles alight, she saw that Bradford hadn't moved. There'd been a small grunt of shock and then he'd seemed frozen. The Tilley was on the wide windowsill and she soon had that going too, lighting the wick and then pumping the brass handle until it glowed white.

Bradford leaned forward as soon as she took her seat again. His face was lit on one side by the embers of the fire, and on the other by the harsh white glare of the lantern. He'd been preparing his pitch while she'd been fannying on to bring some light to the situation. 'Don't you think we've got the right outcome here, Vera? Nothing will bring the little schoolgirl back, and the man who killed her is dead. John Brace is ill and up for parole. Let him and his love spend their last years in peace.' There was a slight sneering emphasis on the word 'love'.

Vera was distracted for a moment. 'Have you ever loved anyone?'

He gave a choking little laugh, astonished by the question, then he answered all the same. 'Not my wife, certainly. That was a disaster from the start. I loved Hector, my mentor and good friend.' He made his voice earnest. 'He'd have known what the best thing to do here is. He'd have let things rest.'

She wanted to tell him to stop playing her for a fool, that she didn't give a damn about what Hector would have done. But she had other, more important things to say. 'What about your daughter? You do care for her? You gave her the bookshop in Bebington, after all.'

'Ah, I gathered you knew about Felicity.' Another little laugh. 'Perhaps Hector did underestimate your intelligence after all.'

There was a moment of silence, then she was aware of the background hiss of the lamp and the wind still gusting outside.

'You know I can't let it rest,' she said. 'You and Hector got it wrong for all those years, thinking it was clever to break the rules. Stealing eggs. Trading in raptors.'

'They were very foolish rules.' His voice was amused. He could have been talking to one of his less bright students.

'That's not the point, is it? You might believe that. You might even be right. But the law matters. All those little people you despise so much have to abide by it, and so do you. So do I.' She looked over to him. 'Besides, there's the matter of Gary Keane. It's impossible to make that go away.'

There was no response. He sat with his elbows on his knees, staring at the rag mat on the stone floor.

'So I'll continue with my story, shall I?' she said after a while. 'Let's bring things up to date. You and Sinclair created a bit of a monster with Gary Keane, turned him from a bad lad who was good with electronics and computers into someone with pretensions. He even had the nerve to go out with your daughter, didn't he? The lovely Felicity. Did you know he had the place on the corner of Anchor Lane, when you set up the bookshop?'

'We'd kept in touch,' Bradford said. 'From the old Seagull days. There were times when he was useful. He knew I was looking for a place. Felicity had her heart set on a bookshop. Some romantic dream of bringing fiction to the masses. It never occurred to me that the two of them would become so friendly.'

'That wasn't why you killed him, though, was it, Prof.?' Using the old name, Hector's name for him, because here in the cottage that seemed more appropriate. 'You killed him as a favour to your pal John Brace. Because Gary was trying a bit of blackmail. Perhaps he thought Felicity would take him more seriously with some cash behind him. Perhaps he cared for her so much that he didn't see he was playing a dangerous game, trying to extort money from her father's best friend.'

Bradford looked up slowly. 'You do know you'll never be able to prove any of this?'

'Ah, there's that arrogance again. Thinking you're cleverer than the rest of us. That was what let you down. It was the small things. Like leaving the voice-mail on his answering machine; and hanging around afterwards, so that a reliable witness can put you at the scene of the crime.'

She was pleased that he had no reply to that.

'Let me see if I've got it right.' Vera flashed him a bright smile. 'See if I'm nearly as clever as you. Gary knew the woman's body at St Mary's wasn't Mary-Frances Lascuola – he'd helped provide a new identity for her – and he thought he could prove it. Patty had a locket with some of her mother's hair. Everyone knows about DNA these days. The magic answer to solving crime – the silver bullet. Gary broke into the house while Patty was out and took the locket, then threatened John Brace that he'd bring it to us, if the old man didn't pay up. We'd know then that Mary-Frances was probably still alive and we'd start looking. In fact we didn't need DNA to tell us that buried woman was someone different altogether. But when Gary started piling on the pressure, John contacted you and asked for your help. He was still in love, after all these years; as you said, he'd do anything to protect Mary-Frances. So he turned to his friend. And, ever the gentleman, you agreed. A matter of honour.'

Vera hoped he heard the sneer in her voice. The fire was almost out now, but she didn't throw on any more wood or coal. Her story was nearing its end. She was tired, pleased that all this would soon be over.

She turned back to Bradford. 'Gary had no idea,

had he, when you asked to meet him? He thought you were there to make a deal; was even flattered that you were coming to his home, treating him as an equal. The father of his smart new girlfriend. He bought a good bottle of wine and made sure the place was tidy. But you stabbed him with his own kitchen knife and left him there to bleed. I assume it was you? Not Mary-Frances. I assume you left her standing outside, keeping watch.' A pause. 'I must admit it was a good cover. Two middle-aged people working in the community garden. Who would ever suspect them of murder? Did it amuse you to play the part of Mary-Frances's husband? Did it give you a bit of a thrill? It must have been a shock when my sergeant turned up, asking questions. You must have thought Gary's body wouldn't be found until the following morning. And you were always anonymous, the pair of you. Mysterious, impossible to track down. Until my sergeant printed out a photo of you at some grand book award and realized he'd seen you in Anchor Lane on the evening Gary Keane died. And that triggered a memory of another picture: a bad photo of the head of education stuck up in the waiting room at Warkworth Prison. Hope Lethbridge, aka Mary-Frances Lascuola. Trying to turn more lives around. Getting as close as she could to the man she loved.'

'You'll never be able to convince a court, you know, Vera. We're respectable people, and a jury's always taken in by the articulate middle classes. There's no forensic evidence.'

'Convincing a court's not my job, pet. That's down to the lawyers. My job's getting you to court, and I think I've got enough to do that.' Her throat felt dry because she'd done so much talking and she felt her eyes begin to close. She was wondering if they might get some sleep before she took him to the station to charge him. She thought he was right, and a jury would probably acquit them both, but somehow that mattered less now than knowing the truth.

Perhaps she did doze for a moment, because she wasn't aware of him getting to his feet until the Tilley lamp was thrown across the room towards her. She must have moved instinctively, because it just missed her head and instead smashed on the floor at her feet. The mat must have caught at once because the fire licked across it. The curtains were long there; they'd needed hemming since she was a child, and in seconds they were aflame. Then she saw that the bottoms of Bradford's trousers were alight. Vera ran to the kitchen and filled a washing-up bowl with water and brought it back into the living room to throw over the man. He'd made no move to stamp on the flames or to move away from the centre of the fire. He still stood, apparently transfixed, his arms a little way from his body as the flames consumed him. He made no sound. Only his contorted face showed the pain he was in, and Vera knew that image would remain with her forever. She threw the water at him, but she realized it would do no good. She couldn't get close enough and it hardly touched him. This was a sacrifice, his last grand gesture of friendship.

There was a banging on the front door and she ran towards it.

Chapter Forty-Seven

'What I don't understand,' Holly said, 'is why Brace told you about Robbie Marshall in the first place. Why take the risk? Even if he was concerned about Patty, there were other people he could ask to keep an eye on her.'

They were in Whitley Bay, walking along the sea front. Vera had promised them a team day out, had bought them fish and chips, and now they were eating ice cream and looking down at the sea. She was feeling an unusual calm. The investigation was out of her hands now. One wrist was still bandaged because she'd burned herself getting out of the house, but it didn't stop her holding the sugar cone, cold and crisp with the ice cream inside. She bit into the chocolate flake. 'Because he knew the bodies were likely to turn up anyway and he wanted to manage the way the news came out. He was always a control freak. He hated being inside, helpless, waiting for events to unfold. Me turning up to give that talk at Warkworth must have seemed like a sign to him. He thought he'd manage to persuade us that Mary-Frances was the second body.'

Vera nodded towards the headland and St Mary's Island. 'Once they start work on the spanking new restaurant, they'll start digging drainage ditches and foundations. Brace didn't think the bodies would stay buried. This way he could make us think Mary-Frances was one of the corpses. He thought there'd be so much disintegration to the bones that we wouldn't be able to make a definitive identification. Things have moved on while he's been inside. His story about only seeing one body in the grave was a pretence; he knew we'd find the other. He hoped he could make Mary-Frances stay dead forever.'

'I'm not sure the new restaurant will be built.' Charlie had eaten his ice cream quickly, biting into it before it had a chance to melt and dribble down his chin. 'The council might have been happy cosying up to Sinclair, but they weren't all aware of his background. My pal at the BBC thinks he's got enough evidence about Sinclair's history with the Glasgow gangs to make the council a bit squeamish. If the development does go ahead, it won't be any time soon.'

'What will happen to Mary-Frances?' Joe asked.

Vera shrugged. 'She's not talking. I don't think she cares so much for herself. She understands prison. She's worked in one since she got her degree from Durham. But she wants to stay close to Brace. She wants to support him through his illness. The CPS doesn't believe they've got enough to charge her. I'm sure she was the one who killed Marshall. Judith might be involved in Sinclair's schemes up to her neck, but she was right about Brace. He wouldn't have had it in him to murder a friend. Without a confession, that'll be impossible to prove after all this time. And while Mary-Frances was implicated in Keane's death, I don't think she was the one who stabbed him.

That was Prof. Bradford, and now he's dead too.' She paused. 'Do you know she's been teaching basic literacy at Shaftoe House? Making sure she was never there at the same time as Laura Webb.'

'A good woman,' Joe said.

Vera thought about that. Could a murderer be a good woman? Maybe she could. But as she'd told Bradford, that wasn't for her to judge. All she had to do was enforce the law. They began to amble back towards their cars.

'What will you do about your house?' Today it seemed Holly was asking all the difficult questions. She was the person prodding Vera back to action.

For the time being, Vera was camping out with Jack and Joanna, living in their spare room, being spoilt with tea in bed in the morning and proper food each night.

'With the insurance money, you could knock it down and build something more comfortable.' That was Holly, persistent as ever. She'd refused an ice cream. She was walking beside them, their slow pace making her impatient, her hands in her jacket pockets. 'Or move somewhere a bit more civilized.'

Vera shook her head. Her mouth was full of chocolate and vanilla. Bradford had been right. She would never leave the hills.

'I never got round to paying the insurance,' she said. 'Jack's said he can patch up the building for me.' She thought Hector's house had always been comfortable enough for her.

Chapter Forty-Eight

John Brace sat in the chapel of Warkworth Prison. He'd been moving his wheelchair backwards and forwards, only half a turn of the wheel, a kind of fidget. He forced himself to sit still. The officer had brought him in because he'd said he needed some time to himself. His best friend was dead, killed in a house fire. He couldn't bear being on the wing with the other men. Not just now. The officer had a kid with behavioural problems, and Brace had paid for him to see a private psychologist who'd worked wonders. The officer brought him to the chapel most nights. There was always a different excuse and nobody questioned it.

He heard the keys first, could picture them being taken out of the pouch in the belt, then opening the chapel door. He thought it might be the chaplain and prepared himself for the sympathy and the bad breath. It was always best to limit your expectations. But it was her. She was still slight and upright, and he could still see the beauty that had first attracted him. She wore black trousers and a black shirt, little silver earrings shaped like birds. He looked at them and thought they were new. Shaped like terns or gulls. Her hair was almost as short as his, and streaked with grey. She had no vanity now and never bothered dyeing it.

She knelt beside him and put her arms round his shoulders. 'Oh, my poor love,' she said. 'Did you think they'd keep me in the station? Remand me in custody? No, it's all over. The police have dropped the charges. There's not enough proof. They might charge you, of course, but what would be the point?'

She'd never pretended that he wasn't ill and that he'd soon be better. He realized he was shaking. He was so relieved to see her. He'd live out his days here, but she'd be with him.

Chapter Forty-Nine

Patty Keane stood outside Warkworth Prison. It was almost dark and the wind was still gusty. Her mind flitted back to the kids. Social services had found someone to sit with them for a few hours and she hoped they weren't playing up. Vera stood beside her. Solid and comfortable. A narrow door in the big wooden gate opened and a small figure walked out. She looked about a thousand miles away, but she must have seen them standing under one of the street lamps that marked the end of the car park, because she headed straight for them. As the woman got closer, Patty she saw she was wearing earrings, silver, gleaming in the light.

When there was a short distance between them, Mary-Frances Lascuola stopped, uncertain.

'She's scared,' Vera said. 'She thinks you might not want to see her. That you hate her.' Her voice was so low it was carried away by the wind and Patty thought she might have imagined the words.

Still the woman didn't move, and it was Patty who had to walk towards *her*. They stood, just a yard apart. Vera had drifted away into the shadow. Then Mary-Frances raised her hand and stroked Patty's cheek. 'Patricia,' she said. 'My beautiful girl.'

Author's Note

This is a work of fiction and though readers in the north east of England will recognize St Mary's Island and might remember Whitley Bay in the time of Spanish City and Idols Night Club, they will know that The Seagull never existed. I'm proud to live in the town and if occasionally I describe it as a little shabby, that doesn't mean I love it any the less. Plans to regenerate the coast are to be applauded; the villainous developer Gus Sinclair is a figment of my imagination and bears no relationship to any of the people – volunteers, councillors or businessmen and women – fighting to give my town a more prosperous future. I'm fighting with you in my own way and hope that as a result of the book more people will visit us and get to know Whitley for themselves.